ALSO BY RUTH RENDELL

CHIEF INSPECTOR WEXFORD NOVELS

BY RUTH RENDELL WRITING AS BARBARA VINE

THE ROTTWEILER

RUTH RENDELL

SEAL BOOKS

Seal Books and colophon are trademarks of
Random House of Canada Limited.

THE ROTTWEILER
Seal Books/published by arrangement with Doubleday Canada
Doubleday Canada edition published 2003
Seal Books edition published December 2004

ISBN 0–7704–2948-3

Cover image: Ricky Leaver/Londonstills.com

Seal Books are published by Random House of Canada Limited.
"Seal Books" and the portrayal of a seal are the property of
Random House of Canada Limited.

Visit Random House of Canada Limited's website: www.randomhouse.ca

PRINTED AND BOUND IN THE USA

OPM 10 9 8 7 6 5 4 3 2 1

For Jeanette Winterson
with love

CHAPTER 1

The jaguar stood in a corner of the shop between a statue of some minor Greek deity and a jardinière. Inez thought it said a lot about the world we lived in that to most people when you said 'jaguar' they took it to mean a car and not an animal. This one, black and about the size of a very large dog, had once been a jungle creature someone's grandfather, a big game hunter, had shot and had stuffed. The someone had brought it into the shop the day before and offered it to Inez at first for ten pounds, then for nothing. It was an embarrassment having it in the house, he said, worse than being seen in a fur coat.

Inez only took it to get rid of him. The jaguar's yellow glass eyes had seemed to look reproachfully at her. Sentimental nonsense, she said to herself. Who would buy it? She had thought it might seem more attractive at eight forty-five in the morning but it was just the same, its fur harsh to the touch, its limbs stiff and its expression baleful. She turned her back on it and in the little kitchen behind the shop put the kettle on for the tea she always made herself and always shared these days with Jeremy Quick from the top floor.

Punctual as ever, he tapped on the inside door, and came in as she carried the tray back into the shop. 'How are you today, Inez?'

He, and he alone, pronounced her name in the Spanish way, Eeneth, and he had told her the Spanish in

Spain, but not in South America, pronounced it like that because one of their kings had had a lisp and they copied him out of deference. That sounded like an apocryphal story to her but she was too polite to say so. She handed him his teacup with a sweetener tablet in the spoon. He always walked about, carrying it.

'What on earth is that?'

She had known he would ask. 'A jaguar.'

'Will anyone buy it?'

'I expect it will join the ranks of the grey armchair and the Chelsea china clock that I'll be left with until I die.'

He patted the animal's head. 'Zeinab not in yet?'

'Please. She says she has no concept of time. In that case, I said, if you've no concept of time, why aren't you ever early?'

He laughed. Inez thought, and not for the first time, that he was rather attractive. Too young for her, of course, or was he? Not perhaps in these days when opinions about that sort of thing were changing. He seemed no more than seven or eight years her junior. 'I'd better be off. Sometimes I think I'm too aware of time.' Carefully, he replaced his cup and saucer on the tray. 'Apparently, there's been another murder.'

'Oh, no.'

'It was on the news at eight. And not far from here. I must go.'

Instead of expecting her to unlock the shop door and let him out, he went back the way he had come and out into Star Street by way of the tenants' entrance. Inez didn't know where he worked, somewhere on the northern outskirts of London, she thought, and what he did had something to do with computers. So many people did these days. He had a mother of whom he was fond and a girlfriend, his feelings for whom he never mentioned. Just once Inez had been invited up to his top-floor flat and admired the minimalist decor and his roof garden.

At nine she opened the shop door and carried the bookstand out on to the pavement. The books that went in it were ancient paperbacks by forgotten authors but occasionally one would sell for 50p. Someone had parked a very dirty white van at the kerb. Inez read a notice stuck in the van's window: *Do not wash. Vehicle undergoing scientific dirt analysis.* That made her laugh.

It was going to be a fine day. The sky was a soft pale blue and the sun coming up behind the terraces of little houses and the tall corner shops with three floors above. It would have been nicer if the air had been fresh instead of reeking of diesel and emissions and green curry and the consequences of men relieving themselves against the hoardings in the small hours, but that was modern life. She said good morning to Mr Khoury who was (rather optimistically) lowering the canopy at the front of the jeweller's next door.

'Good morning, madam.' His tone was gloomy and dour as ever.

'I've got an earring that's lost its what-d'you-call-it, its post,' she said. 'Can you get it repaired if I bring it in later?'

'I shall see.' He always said that, as if he was doing you a favour. On the other hand, he always did repair things.

Zeinab, breathless, came running down Star Street. 'Hi, Mr Khoury. Hi, Inez. Sorry I'm late. You know I've no concept of time.'

Inez sighed. 'So you always tell me.'

Zeinab kept her job because, if Inez were honest with herself and she nearly always was, her assistant was a better saleswoman than she was. She could have sold an elephant gun to a conservationist, as Jeremy once said. Some of it was due to her looks, of course. Zeinab's beauty was the reason so many men came in. Inez didn't flatter herself, she'd plenty of confidence but she knew she'd seen better days, and though she'd been as good-looking as Zeinab once upon a time, it was inevitable that at fifty-five she couldn't compete. She was far from the woman she had been when Martin first saw her twenty years before. No chap was going to cross the street to buy a ceramic egg or a Victorian candlestick from her.

Zeinab looked like the female lead in one of those Bollywood movies. Her black hair came not just to her waist but to the tops of her slender thighs. In nothing but her hair to cover her she could have ridden a horse down Star Street with perfect propriety. Her face was as if someone had taken the best feature from the faces of half a dozen currently famous film stars and put them all together. When she smiled, if you were a man, your heart melted and your legs threatened to buckle. Her hands were like pale flowers on some tropical tree and her skin the texture of a lily petal touched by the setting sun. She always wore very short skirts and very high-heeled shoes, pure white T-shirts in summer and pure white fluffy sweaters in winter and a single diamond (or sparkling stone) in one perfect nostril.

Her voice was less attractive, her accent not the endearing musical tones of upper-class Karachi but nearer Eliza Doolittle's Lisson Grove cockney, which was odd considering her parents lived in Hampstead and, according to her, she was practically a princess. Today she was wearing a black leather skirt, opaque black tights and a sweater that looked like the pelt of an angora rabbit, white as snow and downy as a swan's breast. She walked daintily about the shop, carrying her teacup in one hand and in the other a rainbow-coloured feather duster, flicking dust off silver cruets, ancient musical instruments, cigarette cases, thirties fruit brooches, Clarice Cliffe plates and the four-masted schooner in a bottle. Customers didn't realise what a task it was keeping a place like this clean. Dust soon gave it a shabby look as if the shop was seldom patronised. She paused in front of the jaguar. 'Where did that come from?'

'A customer gave it to me. After you'd gone yesterday.'

'*Gave* it to you?'

'I imagine he knew the poor thing wasn't worth anything.'

'There's been another girl murdered,' said Zeinab. 'Down Boston.' Anyone not in the know might have thought she was talking about Boston, Massachusetts, or even Boston, Lincs, but what she meant was Boston Place, NW1, which ran alongside Marylebone Station.

'How many does that make?'

'Three. I'll get us an evening paper the minute they come in.'

Inez, at the shop window, watched a car which was pulling into the kerb behind the white van. The bright turquoise Jaguar belonged to Morton Phibling who dropped in most mornings for the purpose of seeing Zeinab. No vacant meter was required as his driver sat in the car waiting for him and if a traffic warden appeared, was off circling round the block. Mr Khoury shook his head, holding on to his luxuriant beard with his right hand, and went back indoors.

Morton Phibling got out of the Jaguar, read the notice in the back of the dirty van without a smile and swept into the shop, leaving the door ajar, his open camel hair coat billowing. He had never been known to utter any sort of greeting. 'I see there's another young lady been slaughtered.'

'If you like to put it that way.'

'I came in to feast my eyes on the moon of my delight.'

'You always do,' said Inez.

Morton was something over sixty, short and squat with a head which must always have looked too big for his body, unless he had shrunk a lot. He wore glasses which were not quite shades but deeply tinted with a purple glaze. No beauty and not, as far as Inez could tell, particularly nice or amusing, he was very rich, had three homes and five more cars, all of them resprayed some bright colour, banana-yellow, orange, scarlet and Caribbean-lime. He was in love with Zeinab; there was no other word for it.

Engaged in sticking a price label to the underside of a Wedgwood jug, Zeinab looked up and gave him one of her smiles.

'How are you today, my darling?'

'I'm OK, and don't call me darling.'

'That's how I think of you. I think of you day and night, you know, Zeinab, at twilight and break of dawn.'

'Don't mind me,' said Inez.

'I'm not ashamed of my love. I trumpet it from the housetops. By night in my bed I sought her whom my soul loveth. Rise up, my love, my fair one and come away.' He always went on like this, though neither woman took any notice. 'How splendid in the morning is the lily!'

'D'you want a cup of tea?' said Inez. She felt the need for a second cup; she wouldn't have made it specially.

'I don't mind if I do. I'm taking you to dinner at Le Caprice tonight, darling. I hope you haven't forgotten.'

'Of course I haven't forgotten, and don't call me darling.'

'I'll call for you at home, shall I? Seven thirty do you?'

'No, it won't do me. How many times do I have to tell

you that if you call for me at home my dad'll go bonkers? You know what he did to my sister. D'you want him sticking a knife in me?'

'But my attentions are honourable, my sweetheart. I am no longer married, I want to marry you, I respect you deeply.'

'It don't make no—I mean, it doesn't make no difference,' said Zeinab. 'I'm not supposed to be alone with a bloke. Not ever. If my dad knew I was going to be alone with you in a restaurant he'd flip his lid.'

'I should have liked to see your lovely home,' said Morton Phibling wistfully. 'It would be such a pleasure to see you in your proper setting.' He lowered his voice, though Inez was out of earshot. 'Instead of in this dump, like a gorgeous butterfly on a dungheap.'

'Can't be helped. I'll meet you at Le whatsit.'

In the little back kitchen, pouring boiling water on three teabags, Inez shivered at the thought of Zeinab's terrible father. A year before Zeinab came to work at Star Antiques, he had nearly murdered her sister Nasreen for dishonouring his house by staying overnight in her boyfriend's flat. 'And they didn't even do anything,' said Zeinab. Nasreen hadn't died, though he'd stabbed her five times in the chest. She'd been months recovering in hospital. Inez more or less believed it was true, though no doubt exaggerated, that her assistant risked death if she got herself any suitor except one approved of, and chaperoned by, her parents. She took the tea back into the shop. Morton Phibling, said Zeinab, had gone off down the road to buy them a *Standard*.

'So we can read about the murder. Look what he's given me this time.'

Zeinab showed her a large lapel pin of two roses and a rosebud on a stem, nestling in a bed of blue satin.

'Are those real diamonds?'

'He always gives me real diamonds. Must be worth thousands. I promised to wear it tonight.'

'That won't be a hardship,' said Inez. 'But you mind how you go. Having that on show puts you in danger of being mugged. And you want to remember there's a killer at large who's well-known for stealing something off every girl he kills. Here he is, back.'

But instead of Morton Phibling it was a middle-aged woman in search of a piece of Crown Derby for a birthday present. She had picked up a paperback on her way in, a Peter Cheyney with a picture of a strangled girl on its jacket. Appropriate, thought Inez, charging her 50p for it, and wrapping up a red, blue and gold porcelain plate. Morton came back and courteously held the door open for her. Zeinab was still gloating over her diamond roses, looking like an angel contemplating some beatific vision, thought Morton.

'I'm so glad you like it, darling.'

'It still don't—doesn't—give you the right to call me darling. Let's have a look at the paper, then.'

She and Inez shared it. 'It says it happened quite early last night, about nine,' read Zeinab. 'Somebody heard her scream but he didn't do nothing, not for five minutes, when he saw this figure running away down past the station, a shadowy figure, it says, man or woman, he don't know, only it was wearing trousers. Then he found her—they haven't identified her yet— lying dead on the pavement, murdered. They don't say how it was done only that her face was all blue. It would have been another of them garrottes. Nothing about a bite.'

'That bite business is all nonsense,' said Inez. 'The first girl had a bite mark on her neck but they traced the DNA to her boyfriend. The things people do in the name of love! Of course they called him the Rottweiler and the name has stuck.'

'Did he take anything of hers this time? Let me see.' Zeinab scanned the story to its foot. 'Wouldn't know, I suppose, seeing they don't know who she was. What was it he took the other times?'

'A silver cigarette lighter with her initials in garnets from the first one,' said Morton, showing his considerable knowledge of jewellery, 'and a gold fob watch from the second.'

'Nicole Nimms and Rebecca Milsom, they was called. I wonder what it'll be off this one. Won't never be a mobile, I reckon. All the bastards on the street nick mobiles, wouldn't be like his trademark, would it?'

'Now you be careful coming down to Le Caprice tonight, darling,' said Morton, who seemed not to have noticed the jaguar. 'I've a good mind to send a limo for you.'

'If you do I won't come,' said Zeinab, 'and you've called me darling *again*.'

'Are you going to marry him?' said Inez when he had gone. 'He's a bit old for you but he's got a lot of money and he's not so bad.'

'A bit old! I'd have to run away from home, you know, and that'd be a wrench. I wouldn't like to leave my poor mum.'

The bell on the street door rang and a man came in, looking for a plant stand. Preferably wrought iron. Zeinab gave him one of her smiles. 'We've got a lovely jardinière I'd like to show you. It came over from France only yesterday.'

In fact, it had come from a junk shop having a clearance sale in Church Street. The customer gazed at Zeinab who, squatting down beside the jaguar to pull this three-legged object out from under a pile of Indian bedspreads, turned her face up to him and lifted from it the two wings of black hair like someone unveiling a beautiful picture.

'Very nice,' he mumbled. 'How much is it?' He didn't demur, though Zeinab had added twenty pounds on to the agreed price. Men seldom tried bargaining when she was selling them something. 'Don't bother to wrap it up.'

The street door was held open for him as he struggled out with his purchase. A shy man, almost bowled over, he took courage once on the pavement and said, 'Goodbye. It was very nice to meet you.'

Inez couldn't help laughing. She had to admit business had taken a turn for the better since Zeinab had worked for her. She watched him go off in the direction of Paddington Station. He wasn't going to take it on a train, was he? It was nearly as tall as he. She noticed that the sky had clouded over. Why was it you never seemed to get a fine day any more, only days that started off fine? The dirty white van had gone and another, cleaner, one was being parked in it place. Will Cobbett got out of it and then the driver got out. Inez and Zeinab watched from the window. They saw everything that went on in Star Street and one of then usually provided a running commentary.

'That one that's got out, that's the one called Keith what Will works for,' said Zeinab. 'He'll be going down the Edgware Road to the building materials place. He always comes over here on account of it's cheaper. What's Will doing home at this hour? He's coming in.'

'I expect he's forgotten his tools. He often does.'

Will Cobbett was the only tenant who hardly ever came through the shop. He went in by the tenants' door at the side. The two women heard his footsteps going up the stairs.

'What's with him?' said Zeinab. 'You know what Freddy says about him? He says he's a couple of dips short of a limbo.'

Inez was shocked. 'That's nasty. I'm surprised at Freddy. Will's what used to be called ESN, education-ally sub-normal, but now it's "learning difficulties". He's good-looking enough, I must say, learning difficul-ties or not.'

'Looks aren't everything,' said Zeinab, for whom they were. 'I like a man to be intelligent. Sophisticated and intelligent. You won't mind if I go out for an hour, will you? I'm supposed to be having lunch with Rowley Woodhouse.'

Inez looked at her watch. It was just gone half past twelve. 'You'll be back around half past two then,' she said.

'Who's being nasty now? I can't help it if I've no con-cept of time. I wonder if you can go to a class in time management? I've been thinking of an elocution course. My dad says I ought to learn to speak right, though him and mum have got accents straight out of downtown Islamabad. I'd better go or Rowley'll create.'

Inez recalled how Martin had taught elocution for a while. That was before *Forsyth* and the big-time, of course. He'd been teaching and taking bit parts when she first met him. His voice had been beautiful, too patrician for a detective inspector on the television now but not in the eighties. She listened to Will's footsteps drumming down the stairs. He ran out to the van, his toolbag in his hand, just as the traffic warden arrived. Then Keith appeared from the other direction. Inez watched the ensuing argument. Bystanders always do watch confrontations between traffic wardens and hap-less drivers, wistfully hoping for a punch-up. Inez wouldn't go as far as that. But she thought Keith ought

to pay up, he ought to know a double yellow line when
he saw one.

She waited while two blonde women with thickly
painted faces wandered round the shop, picking up
glass fruit and figures which might or might not have
been Netsuke. They were 'just looking', they said. Once
they had gone, checking that the doorbell was in working order, she went into the kitchen at the back and
switched on the television for the one o'clock news. The
newscaster had put on that expression presenters such as
he are (presumably) trained to assume when the first
item is grim or depressing, as in the case of the girl murdered in Boston Place the night before. She had been
identified as Caroline Dansk of Park Road, NW1. She
must have come down Park Road, thought Inez, crossed
over Rossmore and gone down into Boston Place on her
way to somewhere, perhaps to the station. Poor little
thing, only twenty-one.

The picture switched to the trainline out of
Marylebone and the street running alongside it, with its
high brick wall. Quite upmarket, the houses smartened
up and trees planted in the pavement. Police were about
and police vans and crime tape everywhere, the usual
small crowd gathered behind, seeking what it could
devour. No photograph of Caroline Dansk yet and no
TV appearance of her distraught parents. That would
come in due time. As no doubt would a description of
the object her killer had taken from her after he had sti-
fled her life out with that garrotte thing.

If it was the same man. They could only tell, now the
biting had proved a nonsense and therefore the sobriquet inappropriate, by the stealing of one small object.
These young people had so much, thought Inez, all of
them with computers and digital cameras and mobile
phones, unlike in her day. A sinister expression that, as

if everyone had her day and when it was over started on the long decline into night, twilight first, then dusk and finally the darkness. Her day had come quite late in life, only really begun when she met Martin, and it was after he died that the daylight began to dim. Come on, Inez, she said to herself, that won't do. Get yourself some lunch, as you've no Rowley Woodhouse or Morton Phibling to get it for you, and switch on to something more cheerful. She made herself a ham sandwich and got out the Branston pickle but she didn't want any more tea, a Diet Coke would be all right and the caffeine would wake her up for the afternoon.

I wonder what he's taken off this girl? I wonder who he is and where he lives, if he has a wife, children, friends. Why does he do it and when and where will he do it again? There was something degrading in speculating about such things but almost inescapable. She couldn't help being curious, though Martin could have helped it, risen above such relish for ugly details. Perhaps it was because he was obliged to involve himself in fictitious crime each time he acted in a *Forsyth* production, that he wanted nothing to do with the reality.

The doorbell rang. Inez wiped her lips and went back into the shop.

CHAPTER 2

Saturdays were to be treasured. Sundays weren't the same at all because Monday loomed dangerously near and hung over the day, reminding you that only one night lay ahead before the grind began again. Not that Becky Cobbett disliked her job. Far from it. Hadn't it raised her up the class ladder and given her all this? By 'all this', vaguely waving one hand, she meant the large, comfortable flat in Gloucester Avenue, the Shaker furniture, the rings on her fingers and the small Mercedes parked at the kerb. All of it achieved without the intervention of a man. Men there had been but all of them less successful than she, none of them remarkable earners and not a serious present giver among them.

Realising it was Saturday within seconds of waking was one of the high spots of her week. If she wasn't going away somewhere or her nephew wasn't coming over, the morning always followed the same course—well, and half the afternoon too because she'd have lunch out. It wasn't always the West End she went to, Knightsbridge sometimes and Covent Garden at other times. Today was an Oxford Street and Bond Street day. She might not buy anything big but she would buy something, little items, small toys really, a lipstick, a CD, a scarf, a bottle of bath oil or a bestseller from the top ten. The window shopping was extensive, and the inside-the-store-gazing shopping and the exploration of departments she had never visited before, and the slow considered purchase of some cosmetic in order to get the free gift. Her bathroom cabinet was stuffed full of toilet bags in every shape and colour because they were what had contained the free gifts. Large items of clothing were a different matter, choosing them a serious business and one to which she devoted much prior thought.

'I'm not rich,' she was in the habit of saying, 'but I think I can say I'm well-off.'

Clothes she bought rarely and when she did they were very good and very expensive, but selecting them and paying for them was not to be undertaken on these Saturday jaunts. Those were entirely frivolous and had nothing to do with finding a new black suit for the office or a clingy dress for the firm's annual dinner. Everything about Saturdays was to be enjoyed light-heartedly from the moment she left the house to get the tube from Camden Town station, to her return home five or six hours later in a taxi.

She never wasted time having coffee, but pursued her chosen itinerary until just before one. Then it was time to find a restaurant or a cafeteria or oyster bar inside a store and have her lunch. Afterwards there were a few more shops to be visited, perhaps even to turn her thoughts towards those serious clothes purchases but only in cautious anticipation. It was out of the question for her actually to buy anything or even make up her mind to buy it at some future date. Garments in that price range would also be bought on a Saturday but a Saturday set aside for that purpose, the frivolity and the enjoyment absent.

She knew all the best spots for picking up a cab. Unlike those who barked out a command to the driver, she always spoke politely.

'Would you take me to Gloucester Avenue, please?'

They didn't always know where it was but confused it with Gloucester Terrace or Gloucester Place or Gloucester Road.

'North of Regent's Park,' she usually said. 'You go towards Camden Town and turn left at the lights.'

She asked him to stop while she bought a *Standard*. At home again she made tea, spent ten minutes with the paper. That poor young girl who had been strangled in Boston Place the night before had her picture all over the front page. 'Caroline Dansk, 21', the caption said, latest victim of the Rottweiler.

'Police have no new information as to the identity of the shadowy figure seen running away from the crime scene,' Becky read. '"It is impossible to say", said a spokeperson, "whether this was a man or a woman." The garotter is distinguished by his habit of taking some small artefact from the victim's body and by a more macabre detail, a bite. This time the stolen object seems to have been a keyring, from which Ms Dansk's keys had been removed and left in her bag. However, sources close to the family say there was no sign of a bite.

'"Caroline had her keys on a gold keyring with a Scottie dog fob," said her stepfather, Mr Colin Ponti, 47. "It was a Christmas present from a friend. She never went out without it."

'Noreen Ponti, Caroline's mother, was too distraught to speak to the media . . .'

Becky shook her head, folded up the paper and examined what she had bought. If it was music she played it, leaning back in an armchair. The bag which held the free gifts had to be opened and each sachet or small bottle examined. This time it was a CD and she put it into her Walkman, resting her head against a cushion and closing her eyes. This evening she would devote to watching television or the video from the cassette she had also bought while she was out.

All in all it was continuous hedonistic pleasure, innocently luxurious and self-indulgent. But it wasn't unalloyed. There was always, as she had overheard someone say in Oxford Street, a bone in the kebab. The bone in her kebab was her outsize sense of guilt and this was particularly active on a Saturday, especially this Saturday when she knew quite well she hadn't seen Will for over a week and instead of strolling down South Molton Street she should have been on the phone inviting him to lunch. Lunch, not dinner. They had had their main meal at midday in the children's home, he had got used to it and that was what he still liked best.

Becky had managed to banish thoughts of her nephew from her mind while she was choosing the night cream and the body toner that would make her eligible for the free gift. She had kept those thoughts away while she was lunching at Selfridges, but now she was home and the CD had come to an end, they came flying back on the dark wings of guilt. Will would have been all alone. In spite of looking like a heavier and more burly David Beckham, he was too simple and naïve to make friends, too diffident to take himself alone to the cinema or some sporting event. Tonight, with luck, the man whom he called his friend, who had been one of the social workers in the home, might take him across to the Monkey Puzzle for a drink but that didn't happen every Saturday or even every other. Besides, someone else's intervention did nothing to dispel her own feelings that she had failed Will and been failing him for twenty years. Self-disgust washed over her, making her feel quite sick, when she thought how she had spent her day and how much she had enjoyed it.

Becky's sister Anne had been killed in a car crash. The car belonged to a man who was driving her to Cambridge to meet his parents, the first man Anne had been out with since Will was born. Not that she often went out with him. That was the first time for months. The car was hit head-on by a lorry on the M11. Its driver fell asleep at the wheel and crashed through the barrier on the central reservation. He died and Anne died while the man she had almost decided to marry lost both his legs.

Two policemen came to Anne's flat to tell Becky about the accident. She had been looking after Will, aged three. Of course she stayed with him, taking a fortnight off work. She and Anne had been very close, she was almost as familiar to Will as his own mother, and she had been in the habit of saying that she had all the pleasures of motherhood without its responsibilities. That remark came back to her in the days that followed Anne's death. Would she be expected to take Anne's place, stay with Will and be a mother to him? Would she be expected to *adopt* him?

Now she remembered how she had often told Anne she loved him as if he were her own. Was that true? At the time she was working for a travel agent and studying for a degree in business management in the evenings. That would go if she became a foster-mother to Will, there wouldn't be any evenings. Going to work at all would be hard enough. But, of course—what was she thinking of?—he had a father. She tracked him down and phoned him. He had never paid any child support and his visits to Will had been rare but now he said he would come.

Becky took another two weeks off and her boss wasn't very pleased. While she was at home she managed to get Will into a nursery and, bracing herself to do it, screwing up her courage, she phoned Social Services to acquaint them with the situation. Will's father came and Will, who was friendly and trusting with everyone—too friendly and trusting—sat on his knee while the man told Becky how impossible it would be for him to have the little boy living with him: his wife was only nineteen and she was pregnant, she couldn't be expected to look after a child of three as well.

Will was taken into care. Becky cried for most of the night before Social Services came to take him away, but she couldn't keep him, she *couldn't*. A little comfort was to be derived from the happy and innocent way he took the social worker's hand and smiled at her. He will be all right, she kept saying to herself, he will be all right, he will be better than he would be with me, he will go to good foster-parents or maybe someone longing for a child will adopt him. But no one did. Beautiful though he was and sweet-natured and good—too good—no one wanted a child who had 'something wrong with him'. Becky's worst torment was wondering whether he was this way because she had allowed him to be taken into care, if she had done it by her selfishness. She spent long hours trying to recall instances of his difference from other children *before* his mother's death and she did manage to recall Anne's saying he was too quiet, too well-behaved, not wild and rebellious the way a little boy should be. Remorse still haunted her.

She compensated, or tried to, by visiting him at the home, which was frowned on, and taking him out, which had limited approval. As her fortunes improved and her business prospered, she began buying him presents she had to keep in her own home lest they excite envy in the other children. When he was twelve she offered to pay the fees of a private school in New England where pupils of his sort received one-to-one attention. Social Services put a stop to that. They were very progressive, very left-wing, and they reminded Becky that she had no control over his fate or future, she was only his aunt. As for his father, he had gone off to Australia, leaving behind another woman and a child.

'The ball is in our court, Ms Cobbett,' said Will's social worker. 'The decision is down to us.'

So Will went to a special school where all the children had learning difficulties, a school without enough teachers and where the ones it had were all exhausted by the amount of paperwork they had to do. It was remarkable to Becky that he could read at all, and he could only when the words were short and simple, but he was rather good at sums. Perhaps he would have done no better at the Vermont private school. What would become of him when he was sixteen and had to leave? How would he earn a living?

Social Services found him a place on a college building course. He was nice to everyone, polite and anxious to learn, but the diagrams he was expected to look at, the technical handbooks he was expected to read, meant nothing to him. There was no simple arithmetic, only weights and measures and calculations, all of which were beyond him. He was living at the time in a house occupied by six young people who had been in care and selected to get on together, but although he never complained, Becky sensed that they teased or bullied him. What would he like to do?

'Live with you,' he said.

The ground under her feet shifted, her world turned over. Afterwards she thought it was the worst moment of her life. She had a boyfriend at the time who spent Saturday and Sunday nights with her and the occasional night in the week. When he wasn't there she needed her peace, her special Saturday mornings. But saying what she had to say was her low point.

'This flat isn't big enough for two, Will. You know there's only one bedroom. How about living on your own if you and I saw each other often? If you came over here a lot and we went out?'

He smiled his sweet smile. 'I don't mind.'

The local authority that ran the course got him his job, unskilled labouring for Keith Beatty, and after a while he did pick up basic skills. It was Becky who found the flat above Star Antiques. Convenient for his job in Lisson Grove and not too far from her, it was the right size for him to manage, just a bedsit with kitchen and shower room. And the other people in the house were nice: Inez and a very jolly Caribbean chap called Freddy something, and a pleasant man on the top floor. Ludmila she had never encountered. She worried that Will wouldn't know how to keep it clean and she prepared herself for the chore of cleaning it for him, but there he surprised her. Not only did he maintain it in spotless condition but he added all kinds of pretty things to the basics Inez provided. Some of them, a green glass vase, a china cat, a lamp whose stand was a Chinese abacus, she suspected Inez had given him, some she had provided herself, but some he had bought, the pink-and-grey cushions, the white cups and plates with rainbow-coloured spots. He had to have a phone, she would never have had a quiet moment if he were without a phone, though she doubted if he knew how to make a call properly.

He loved going to the zoo, so she took him there. They went in the canal boat to Camden Lock and on the river as far as the Thames Barrier. Once or twice they went to the cinema but these visits made her uneasy because what he saw on the screen he believed to

be real. Sex he found bewildering, while violence terrified him, he whimpered and clutched at her till she had
to take him out. Harry Potter, which had seemed innocent enough to her, so affected him that next time they
met he told her he had been to King's Cross Station
looking for platform nine and a half and couldn't
understand why it wasn't there. Mostly she invited him
to Gloucester Avenue, but she told herself it didn't happen often enough, it ought to be at least once a week
and more would be better. What did he do when he was
alone in Star Street? In doubt and trepidation because of
his reaction to the cinema, she had bought him television and he loved it. How he managed about violence
and sex she didn't know and was afraid to ask. Reading
beyond the level of the simplest children's book was
beyond him and he had no interest in listening to
music. He cleaned the flat, she supposed, and
rearranged his ornaments. And there was always that
occasional mainstay, the childcare officer who took him
round to the pub for a beer.

The really desirable thing, she thought, as she slipped
a new video into her recorder, would be for him to find
a girlfriend. A nice sensible girl, a bit old-fashioned if
such a person existed, who would mother him and care
for him. A dating agency? The worst thing in the world
for the likes of Will. Perhaps Inez would know someone. Becky made up her mind to talk to Inez and soon.
Before starting the video, she dialled Will's number and
when he answered, as he always did, with a timorous,
questioning 'Hello?' asked him over for lunch and supper the following day.

He accepted, with the excited enthusiasm another
young man might have shown responding to the offer
of a round-the-world tour.

CHAPTER 3

Will Cobbett was very likely the only occupant of the house, thought Inez, who knew nothing about the latest murder and didn't even know it had taken place. The only resident of Star Street, probably. Everybody was talking about it, but Will, whom she had encountered in the back hall when she went down to pick up her Sunday paper, said only that it was a nice sunny day, Mrs Ferry, and that he was on his way to spend it with his auntie. His mild blue eyes seemed to glaze over as he looked at the 48-point headline on the front page and he registered no interest, only lifting his head and saying how much he looked forward to the day ahead.

'I do like going to her place. She cooks me my dinner at twelve and we always have the things I like.'

He was so handsome and always so clean and neat that he looked as if he must be intelligent too. How could a man be so tall and slim, have that straight nose and firmly cut mouth, that blond hair and those eyes, and be—well, not quite like other people? Most people expected the illiterate and the simple to be ugly and squat but Will was beautiful. There was no other word for him and if she had been thirty years younger she'd have gone overboard for him.

'You say hello to your auntie from me.' She liked Becky Cobbett who was marvellous with Will. Few aunts would go to all the trouble she did. Selflessness wasn't common. 'Give her my kindest regards. Next time she comes over here you must bring her down for a drink.'

'And I could have raspberry and cranberry juice.'

'Of course you could. We must make a date.'

She wasn't going to mention Caroline Dansk or what had happened to her. Becky had told her that any sort of violence, even the idea of it, upset him a lot. There were plenty of other people in the house or, come to that, the street, more than willing to discuss the murder. Inez took the paper upstairs, made herself coffee in the little one-cup cafetière and ate a Danish pastry. Caroline Dansk's picture had been in yesterday's evening paper but this was a different one. She looked older but prettier, her lips parted, her large eyes, thought Inez, full of hope. Much good that had done her, dead at only twenty-one.

It was the age she had been when she married her first husband. If she had been a bit older she would have known better than to tie herself up to a man who couldn't keep his eyes or, as often as not, his hands, off every girl he encountered, attractive or not. Inez had been very good-looking, fair-haired and brown-eyed with regular features and long thick hair, but that hadn't been enough for Brian. She ought to have seen the signs and she saw them. It was a matter of interpreting them wrongly, a matter of the old, old story, that she thought she could change him. Really, it wasn't until Martin came along that she had a man she didn't want to change. She sighed, went back to the front page.

There it was again, a keyring the murderer had taken this time, the ring itself made of onyx and gold plate, a gold-plated chain and a scottie dog in onyx suspended from it. The police and the newspaper hadn't seen the keyring, of course, but an artist had drawn his impression of it according to the description given him by Caroline's stepfather. Inez didn't see the use of that.

The garrotter wasn't going to leave it lying about for anyone to find. The paper said Noreen Ponti, the poor girl's mother, had recorded an appeal for her killer to be found. Understandable but pointless. Everybody would like to find him, that wasn't the problem. She turned the page to a Tory scandal, a top doctor involved in a flagellation ring, and the wedding picture of an elderly politician who had got married to another elderly politician.

Inez had kept for herself the first floor of the house. She had a large living room, fair-sized kitchen, two bedrooms and a bathroom. With the money Martin left her, she had had the three floors over the shop she and Martin shared converted into flats and all the rooms fitted with cupboards, rewired, new fitments put in and the floors carpeted. No philanthropist, she knew she could get far more rent that way and she had long ago resolved, like Scarlett O'Hara, never to be poor again. On the level above her the two studio flats, basically one room with bathroom and kitchen, were occupied by Will at the back and Ludmila Gogol at the front, Ludmila's more than half the time by Freddy Perfect as well.

Ludmila's footfalls could be heard overhead now. She never got up till very late on Sundays and stayed in one of her many dressing gowns all day, even if she went up the road to get a paper or a pint of milk. Gogol, Inez thought, had been the name of a famous Russian writer. That didn't mean it couldn't be Ludmila's real name, there were people called Shakespeare and Browning, Martin had had a cousin called Dickens, but it somehow made it less likely. Her accent came and went. Sometimes it was quite strong, central European movie-speak, and at others more the way the clients spoke in the Lisson Grove Job Centre.

Inez was interested in people. It had failed to make her a judge of character, though. She knew that but didn't know how to change. How, for instance, was she to know if Freddy Perfect was what he seemed, a cheerful though unfunny clown, or a bit of a small-time crook? And Zeinab—why would she never allow anyone to visit her at home, not even let anyone drive her home? Her father, being strict as some Moslems are, might dislike the idea of boyfriends, especially non-Moslem boyfriends, but why, unless he was a raving paranoiac, would he object to her being brought home by a woman? She, Inez, had only last week offered her a lift home in the course of delivering a bronze bust of Field Marshal Montgomery to a house in Highgate, but she had become quite frightened at the prospect. Human beings were impossible to understand.

These two old people in the paper who had got married, for example, what prompted that? Their combined ages added up to a hundred and forty-six. How did they think they could learn each other's by now rigid habits and idiosyncracies at their age? And did they have the energy to make the attempt? After Martin, Inez was resolved on never marrying again, even supposing someone asked her, but she would have liked a man around. A nice man in his late fifties, who would take her about, take her out for a drink sometimes or to the pictures. And occasionally stay the night, why not? Sometimes, on warm summer nights, she would walk past a café with tables out on the pavement, soft light falling on the couples who sat there, and feel almost sick with longing to have Martin back again. Failing that—and it must always be failing that—a man with certain of Martin's traits, someone who, for the time being, would rather be with her than with anyone else. She wasn't asking for passionate love or even the kind of devotion she had had from Martin, only a nice man who attracted her and enjoyed her company.

She had done her best with her looks, kept her figure, been lucky in having that kind of dark-blonde hair that seldom goes grey, but every man who came into the shop saw Zeinab as well as her and that was it. Invariably. She wouldn't have looked twice at Morton Phibling but, as any reasonable woman would agree, someone of her age was a far more suitable choice for him than a girl of twenty. Men never saw it like that.

Sunday stretched ahead of her. Refusing to admit to loneliness the rest of the week, she was very solitary on Sundays, on her own unless friends invited her to lunch or dinner or she made the effort and invited them. Perhaps she should try to do that more often, even though it meant cooking and dressing up. The day would be spent doing the washing, the ironing, running the vacuum cleaner round the place, and if it didn't turn cold, an early-evening walk through the park or along the Bayswater Road where the couples sat in the cafés, holding hands across candlelit tables. And when she got home—even perhaps instead of going out—the videos. The twelve hour-long films that had become her most precious possession.

Like most actors, except those at the very top, Martin had had long periods without work. That was when he had taught elocution, stacked shelves in Sainsbury's and, at a very low point, cleaned flats. Some of the people he had worked for remembered him when he became a big star and went about saying, 'You won't believe this but Martin Ferry was once our cleaner.' He was near to not bothering to audition for the part of Chief Inspector Jonathan Forsyth but a friend urged him on. It was the same friend who had introduced him to Inez a week before. Martin was in the process of being divorced from his first wife and Inez had just divorced Brian. He phoned her and reminded her who he was, asked her out and told her he was auditioning for the lead in a new detective series, but not to keep her fingers crossed because he hadn't a hope in hell of getting it.

Even when he got it and rehearsals had begun, hopes for the series weren't high. The books on which it was based were hardly bestsellers and Inez, who had read some of them, thought them badly written and unconvincing. But either they were transformed by a good scriptwriter or Martin's charismatic performance as Forsyth quickly took them to the top of the polls. Within three months of the first six episodes going out he was a household name. Inez thought he would be bound to drop her, find someone nearer his own new stature, someone younger and also in show business. Instead, he asked her to marry him.

He owned nothing, had been living in a rented flat, but just before the wedding he bought the Star Street house and they moved into the top three floors, shutting up the long defunct shop area. To say it was a happy marriage, as some of those she knew did—'Oh, Inez is happily married, aren't you?'—was utterly to underrate and lower it. They were in bliss. The kind of breathless passionate love that never never lasts, that only the very young have and then briefly, endured completely for them from the wedding at Marylebone Register Office to the day Martin had a heart attack and died. Thin, tall, active, abstemious Martin who had never smoked a cigarette, had a heart attack at the age of fifty-six and died within minutes.

The house and his considerable savings became Inez's. She didn't care. She wouldn't have cared if he'd left her nothing and some thief had stolen everything she owned, putting her out on the street to lie with the dossers on the pavements. Nothing could be worse than losing Martin and there was no comfort. Or so she thought then. Finding the twelve videos of *Forsyth* among his things, made her flinch. Why she didn't put them out for the rubbish collection she never knew, but perhaps it was only because she couldn't bring herself to touch them. She always knew where they were, in a drawer she avoided opening. One glimpse, on the cassette box, of his face had been enough to make her collapse in inconsolable tears.

Then, about six months after his death, she went down into the pit, the depths of despair and hopeless longing. Just to see him for a moment, for five minutes, to have him in the room. She gasped for that. She thought that without a brief sight of his face she could no longer bear it. She'd go into the bedroom and take all the sleeping tablets the doctor prescribed for her, washing them down with gin. It was then—she never knew why—that she remembered the videos. She could have that brief sight, she could have more than that, she could see him, hear him, watch him move and walk and speak, for hours on end. And if the seeing and hearing were terrible? She could hardly feel worse than she did.

Her hands shook as she took the cassette out of its cover. It was the first one he had ever made, *Forsyth and the Minstrel Boy,* and the familiar signature tune was the first shock, a Handel air that she had never heard in any other context. But when the picture began and the camera moved on to Martin going up the stairs to his office, she had let out a cry, she couldn't help herself. It was going to be as agonising as she had feared.

It wasn't. Here, after all, was her beloved husband, her lover, her treasure, the only man she had ever really loved, and he was with her, in this room, speaking, she felt, to her. All that was missing was that she couldn't touch him, and that was a big 'all', but this film was giving her so much else. And it wasn't a one-off. He wouldn't disappear again for ever, for she could play these videos whenever she liked, as much as she wanted, and have the second-best, a printed, recorded Martin, his smile, his beautiful voice, as often as she wished. There were more videos too, that she didn't have. But she could get them, she could get everything he had ever made that had been put on tape . . .

Later on, instead of a walk, seeing in the golden evening light sights that only brought her a bitter nostalgia, she could have a long evening with Martin.

Star Street runs westwards, connecting the Edgware Road with Norfolk Square, Paddington Station and St Mary's Hospital. It is a street of terraces of once humble houses, each one three storeys high with a basement, but where the cross streets intersect, on each of the four corners is a shop in place of a ground floor, with three storeys above it, raising it to a considerably greater height than the terraces. Since this occurs at three intersections in precisely the same way, it is evidently by design, an architectural innovation thought up by whoever planned these houses in the nineteenth century.

The streets are fairly wide and there are few trees, a deficiency compensated for by the planes and limes of the Norfolk Square garden. Cars line the roadway, for, as in most parts of inner London, there are no other parking places. No one would call Star Street beautiful but it has its own Victorian attractions. A symmetry about the houses is pleasing and the shops have an old-fashioned charm: a hardware store, the inevitable estate agent, a hairdresser, a newsagent and Star Antiques, this last on the corner of Bridgnorth Street.

Once a second-hand bookshop, it had been kept closed for years. Soon after Martin's death, Inez's Aunt Violet died at the age of ninety-two, leaving her a big old house in Clapham and its contents, enough Victorian furniture to stock an antique shop. And that was what Inez did with it. She had the boarding taken off the windows, opened up the shop and began by filling it with Aunt Violet's things. The tenants for the flats came gradually, Ludmila first, then Will Cobbett, lastly Jeremy Quick. The stairs from the top to the bottom led directly down into a small hall where there was a door into the shop, another to the street and one to the garden. The door into the shop had a sign Inez had attached to it which said *Private. No Admittance,* but no one ever took any notice, not even Jeremy Quick, whom Inez would have called the ideal tenant, almost faultless as he was. For some reason, mysterious to her, they preferred a prior wandering through the shop to going straight out into Star Street.

She had been in there for no more than ten minutes on Monday morning and Star Antiques was still closed, when there came a ring at the street door and a smart rapping on the glass.

Without looking up from the two toby jugs she was dusting, she called out, 'We're not open till nine thirty.'

'Police,' said a voice. 'If we might have a word.'

Inez unlocked the door. There were two of them, both men. The elder, who introduced himself as Detective Inspector Crippen, said he was sorry to trouble her but they were making routine enquiries. Inez thought his an unfortunate name for a police officer but supposed that to younger people it would mean nothing. Both of them were very different from handsome, suave, elegant Chief Inspector Forsyth.

'What can I do for you? Is this something to do with the girl who was killed in Boston Place?'

'That's right, madam.' She would almost have preferred him to call her 'love'. 'I expect you've seen about it on your TV.'

'It happened nowhere near here. Boston Place must be a mile away.'

The younger one smiled indulgently. 'Not quite as far as that. A person, gender unknown, was seen running from the scene of the crime, and a similar figure, according to a reliable witness, observed entering Star Street from the Edgware Road ten minutes later.'

'What do you mean, "entering"? Still running or what?'

Crippen was about to speak when the door to the back hall opened about a foot, Jeremy Quick put his head round it, said, 'I'm awfully sorry, I didn't mean to interrupt,' and withdrew.

'Who was that?' said Crippen.

'The tenant of the top-floor flat.'

'We'll want to talk to him. Where will he have gone, madam?'

'Towards Edgware Road tube, I expect,' said Inez.

'You run after him, Osnabrook,' said Crippen. 'Come on now, be quick. Have you any more tenants, Mrs—er?'

'Mrs Ferry. Yes, two. You were telling me whether this person, gender unknown, was running.'

'Still running. Was there any possibility of you seeing this person? It would have been around nine fifteen on Thursday night.'

'I was upstairs in my flat. The curtains were drawn.' Inez gave a sigh of exasperation as the door was again opened.

But this time the intruder came in and closed the door behind him. Freddy Perfect was never, as Jeremy had once said, backward in coming forward. 'Good morning, all,' he said. 'Not often we have callers this early, is it, Inez?' He winked at her. 'Must be pressing business.'

'Is this gentleman another tenant, Mrs Ferry?'

Freddy answered for her. 'I am not the tenant, sir. The tenant, Madame Ludmila Gogol, is my paramour.'

If this was the first time anyone had called Freddy a gentleman, so it was also probably the first time Crippen had been called 'sir' by any but subordinates. His reaction to Freddy's word for his girlfriend or partner was a rapid blinking of the eyes. The street door opened and Osnabrook came back, preceded by Jeremy Quick.

'It mustn't take more than five minutes,' said Jeremy. 'I shall be late at the office.'

Osnabrook asked him about the running man but before Jeremy could answer, Freddy Perfect chimed in. 'Now why would he have been running, is what I ask myself,' he said conversationally. 'I ask *you*. What or who was he running from? Was someone in pursuit?'

'That we don't know.'

Crippen said it impatiently and repeated his question to Jeremy. In the corner, by the large urn with the Parthenon frieze round its circumference, Freddy stood, sagely nodding his head and palpating in his hands a pair of Victorian opera glasses as if they were worry beads.

'I did see him as a matter of fact,' said Jeremy. 'It was about ten past nine, a quarter past nine. I heard feet pounding along outside, you see, and brakes squealing. It was as if the person running had crossed a street, maybe the Edgware Road, and a car had had to brake to avoid him. I looked out of my window. Two of my windows look down on Star Street. He was running down the street towards Norfolk Square.'

'You told no one about this?'

'I didn't make the connection.'

'Of course he didn't,' said Freddy, putting the opera glasses down and picking up a silver napkin ring. 'Why would he? Every time you see a person running you don't think he's escaping from the scene of the crime, now do you?'

'Mr Quick?'

'Exactly. He's right. This chap might have been doing his evening work-out for all I know.'

Osnabrook cast up his eyes. 'It was definitely a man? You're sure of that.'

Jeremy suddenly looked nonplussed. 'Now you say that, I'm not sure. I suppose it might have been a woman. Look, I do have to get to work.'

'Just let us have a description before you go, Mr Quick.'

'Now we shall see how observant he is, Inez,' said Freddy.

At this third uncalled-for intervention, Crippen exploded. 'If you don't mind, Mr—er, whatever-your-name-is?'

'Perfect,' said Freddy. 'Perfect by name and perfect by nature, as I always say,' and with dignity, 'I intended to be helpful.'

'Yes, well, thank you. Did you get a good look at him—er, her, Mr Quick?'

'Man or woman, he, she was quite young, twenties anyway, wearing jeans of some sort, ordinary jeans and a top, long-sleeved, no jacket. The lot a darkish colour, dark-grey or blue, I couldn't tell, it was dark and colours look different by artificial light. I really do have to go now.'

'Pity I didn't see this—this hermaphrodite,' said Freddy. Pleased with the word, he repeated it. 'Hermaphrodite, yes.

I could have furnished you with a detailed description.'
He held up a Venetian glass champagne flute to the light
and peered through it. 'As luck would have it, though, me
and Ms Gogol were out having a refresher in the
Marquise Restaurant.'

'Please put that glass down, Freddy,' said Inez
sharply. 'I'm sure I don't know who said you could
walk about in here examining everything as if you
owned the place.'

Freddy looked injured. 'It's what customers do in
junk shops.'

'This is not a junk shop and as a customer you have
yet to buy anything at all. Haven't you anything better
to do?'

Osnabrook said, 'We'll be going, then, so long as
there's no one else we ought to talk to. Haven't I seen a
young Asian girl about in here?'

Inez sighed. What man could forget the sight once
seen? 'She doesn't live here. She works for me.' Or
would, she thought, looking at the grandfather clock,
one of these fine hours.

'We may want to talk to you again,' warned Crippen,
departing as Osnabrook held the door open for him.

'Are you surprised we're on the crest of a crime wave?'
asked Freddy. One thing you could say for him, he
never took offence. This, too, had its disadvantages.
'You know, if you're ever looking for a second assistant
I wouldn't mind obliging, provided, of course, the
money was right.'

He sat down in a grey velvet armchair that had been
aunt Violet's and settled himself for a cosy chat. Before
Inez could reply to his offer with a categorical 'no'
Zeinab came in.

'We've had the Old Bill in here,' said Freddy, 'asking
questions about the Rottweiler. Our mutual friend Mr

Quick was able to give them some perfunctory details. Funny, they never said a word about the bite, wasn't it?'

'He doesn't bite them,' said Zeinab. 'That was a mistake. It's too distasteful for me to explain.'

Today's miniskirt was of black leather with discreet gold studs, the angora sweater snow-white and shimmering. She had a golden bird on each of her fingernails to match the studs. Inez wondered that her strict father didn't object to the way she dressed herself but perhaps he didn't know, perhaps she sneaked out of the house in secret or even covered herself up in a *chador*.

'Time you went, Freddy,' Inez said briskly. 'Ludmila will be wondering where you are.'

That would, in fact, be the last thing Ludmila was wondering. She would know very well and had an ongoing vendetta with Zeinab whom she suspected of setting out to fascinate Freddy. He got to his feet reluctantly, spotted for the first time the jaguar and began walking clockwise round it, nodding his head as if in approval.

'Freddy!'

'I'm going.' He waved to the jaguar, said he was in need of something 'to wet his whistle' and would return upstairs.

'Now he's gone,' said Inez, 'I'll belatedly make the tea. How was your dinner with Mr Phibling?'

'Much the same as usual. Nag, nag, nag and bits of poetry, lot of stuff about wanting to be with me under a tree with a loaf of bread and a bottle of wine. God knows why. Men do go on and on, don't they?'

'Some of them do.'

'Rowley Woodhouse wants me to get engaged. He's a real nutcase, he's already bought the ring. I wish I could have the ring without the bloke.'

Inez went away to make the tea. When she came back with two mugs on a tray a woman in a fake-fur coat much the same colour as the jaguar had come in. She was standing in front of a long gilt-framed wall mirror Zeinab was doing her best to sell her, but after twenty minutes of giving it close examination she walked out without buying it.

'I'm not sorry,' said Zeinab, as if she owned shop and mirror. 'I don't know where I'd be without that. I do my make-up in it.'

The best-regulated builders start work early and finish early. Keith was a good builder in that when he told a householder he would be with her early in the week he meant Tuesday and not Thursday afternoon and when he said he'd be back tomorrow he really did go back, if only for ten minutes. He turned up more or less when he said he would in the morning, that is, around eight, and kept his radio turned low or even switched it off if the client was a stickler for silence, as some peculiar people were. The work he did was quite good too. At first he had thought having a childish guy like Will Cobbett to work for him too much of a responsibility. Could he leave him alone in someone else's place? Would he be ready on time when Keith called for him? Could he rely on him to do a simple job? No one had ever mentioned 'learning difficulties' or 'chromosomal problems' to Keith and he probably wouldn't have taken Will on if they had. All he knew was that Will had been in care and was rather 'slow'. But Will turned out to be a good worker, did what he was told, didn't smoke or even want to smoke—Keith himself was odd in that he didn't either—and seemed entirely reliable. All had been well until today, nothing to complain of, and if conversation with him was like talking to his ten-year-old nephew, better that than some of the crap previous employees had come out with. But now

something disquieting had happened. His sister had
taken a fancy to Will.

She still lived at home with their parents in
Harlesden. He'd been over there on Sunday and while
his mum was having her after-lunch nap and his dad was
doing the dishes, Kim got him alone in the sitting room
and confided in him. 'Has he got a girlfriend, Keithy?'

'I doubt it,' he'd said. 'He's never said.'

'I really fancy him. He's ever so good-looking. He's
more like a Hollywood star than those actors that get
on TV.'

'Look, Kimmie, you know he's not very bright.'

'Well, what? Don't say anything about brains, please.
Dominic had brains, he was going to university, and
look how he treated me. He'd have raped me if I hadn't
stuck a safety pin in his leg.'

'I'll tell you something,' said Keith, 'Will'll never ask
you out. You'll have to ask him if that's what you want.'

'Where are you working tomorrow? Place in Abbey
Road, isn't it?'

'Right, but you can't come there.'

'Why not? You said she's out all day. I'll pop in in my
lunch-hour.' Kim, who spoke with more courage than
she felt, worked in a hairdresser's in St John's Wood
High Street. 'I'll ask him. I don't mind. I'll tell him
there's this film I want to see.'

'You've got a cheek,' said Keith admiringly, 'asking a
bloke you don't know to take you out.'

'Well, that way I'll get to know him, won't I?'

He had laughed but still he was troubled. Will was
young and big, he could be a more efficient rapist than
that wimp Dominic. Still, his sister was a free agent and
no innocent. No doubt she could handle it with the pin
in the leg technique. Maybe they'd go out just the once
and that would be an end to it. Having brains enough

to go to a university was one thing, but a huge gap existed between that and Will's level. Weren't there plenty of men in that gap, on the scale from genius to vegetable, who would do for Kim? But Will was so very good-looking . . .

Morton Phibling had just left, having arrived in his orange Mercedes and spouted (Zeinab's word) for a long time about his love being a garden enclosed, scented with many spices. Not for the first time Inez wondered where she had seen him before. Long ago it had been and somehow she connected him with Brian, her first husband, but further than that she couldn't reach. A small mystery.

Zeinab opened a drawer in a Victorian medicine cabinet, took something out of it and flashed the diamond she had slipped on to the third finger of her left hand at Inez. 'What d'you think? I popped it into the drawer while Morton was here. Rowley told me to wear it for a trial run. I haven't made any promises.'

'Very pretty,' said Inez. 'It's reminded me about my earring. I'll just go next door and see Mr Khoury, I won't be long.'

She had a feeling they wouldn't sell any more that day. As it was they had done rather well, offloading the big urn with the Parthenon frieze, which had been hanging about for months if not years, and selling all the Venetian glass to a woman who collected it. The white van with the notice about undergoing scientific dirt analysis was back. About time they clamped it, Inez thought. She was still looking suspiciously at the van when Keith Beatty's drew up in front of it and Will got out. Ten past four. They always finished at four sharp.

She said, 'Hello, Will, how are you?' and he said, 'Fine, thanks, Mrs Ferry.' He stood there trying to

puzzle out the notice and either failing or else understanding it but not finding it funny. Inez went into
the jeweller's.

Mr Khoury seized upon her as the person he had been
awaiting all day on whom to unload his grievances.
'Policemen came,' he said in a shocked tone. 'What am
I to think? I tell you what I think. They come to arrest
me as Al Qa-eda terrorist.'

'Surely not, Mr Khoury.'

'As you say, it is surely not true. It was the latest dead
young lady. Am I seeing a running person on Thursday
evening? You think I live on these premises? I say. Here?
I say. Me, in this neck of woods?' This was not very flat-
tering to Inez but she let it pass. 'I have fine detached
home in Hampstead Garden Suburb, I tell them. Has
anyone tried to sell me fob watch or keyring, they ask.
They think I can't read media? I am no fence, I tell
them. Besides, will I touch this trash? Not with a bean-
pole. When they hear that they go away. Now, how may
I help, madam?'

'My earring,' said Inez.

It was still being repaired, having been sent off to
some mysterious workshop in Hungerford. No, he had
no idea when it would be back. Re-entering the shop,
Inez passed a satisfied-looking customer holding one of
Star Antiques' dark-blue carrier bags.

'What did she buy?' Inez asked, her guess having
proved wrong. 'It looked quite big. Not the Chelsea
china clock with the man in a turban and the harem
lady on top? I'd given up hope.'

'No, and it wasn't that animal either. It was a couple
of brass candlesticks and them dried flowers.'

'Shall I make another cup of tea?'

'Not for me,' said Zeinab. 'Can I go home now, Inez?
My dad gets funny if I'm not in by six.'

Why, then, didn't he get funny when she went out with Morton Phibling or Rowley Woodhouse? Or did he think she was always in the company of women friends? Inez was tired of asking how she was going to get home—up to the West Heath from here was an awkward journey by public transport—and even more tired of having her offers of a lift refused. A pity, because she wouldn't have minded going out, even if it meant being on her own after she had dropped Zeinab. There was a kind of melancholy pleasure in anticipating sitting in her car by the Vale of Health pond or down at South End Green, looking at all the young people going into the lighted cafés, late shoppers buying greengrocery and men bouquets of flowers. It was warm for April. The sunset had coloured the sky with long bands of coral and apricot and primrose, clouds like tails of grey fur between them. Ah, well, she wouldn't go on her own without a reason . . .

Zeinab touched up her lips, flicked back her hair and said cheers and she'd be seeing her. A possible choice of transport for her would be the 139 bus up to Swiss Cottage and then a change on to one that went up Fitzjohn's Avenue. But Zeinab turned her back on the bus stop, crossed the Edgware Road at the Sussex Gardens lights and walked up towards Broadley Terrace and Lisson Grove. Passing men turned their heads to look at her and one, whom Zeinab categorised as a lowlife, called out, 'What you doing later, darling?'

She ignored him. Entering Rossmore Road, she began to hurry for it was down there, in Boston Place, that Caroline Dansk had died. When Zeinab thought of the wire garrotte round the girl's neck and then, when it had done its work, the ugly mask of a face closing over the swollen veins and the trap of a mouth biting, her whole body began to shake until she remembered he didn't bite them after all.

But she was nearly there. She crossed the road and at the sign which said City of Westminster, Local Authority Housing, turned into the lane that ran between the blocks. At Dame Shirley Porter House the lift had broken down. Surprise, surprise. Zeinab walked up the three flights, inserted her doorkey into the lock on number 36 and called out, 'Hi, kiddos, I'm home!'

CHAPTER 4

Refusing an invitation was so unlike Will that Becky could hardly believe she had heard him correctly. But made peculiarly sensitive by her guilt, she felt unable to ask him why not. She wouldn't have asked any other potential guest so why ask him? After he had said he couldn't come on Saturday, there was silence at the other end of the phone, pleasant and companionable but silence all the same.

'Why not come over on Friday evening, then?' She was always exhausted on Friday evenings. If it were anyone else, she could take him or her to a restaurant but Will wouldn't like that. It was home he liked, familiar things about and familiar food. 'If you can find your own way over I'll take you home.'

'All right,' he said and then, in his ten-year-old way, 'I could come on Saturday if you *really* wanted, if I could go at five and get ready.'

The temptation could no longer be resisted. 'Where are you going, Will?'

'Me and a young lady are going to the cinema.'

Her astonishment at his refusal of her invitation was as nothing to the shock of this. She tried not to let amazement sound in her voice. 'That's nice.' Would he tell her who it was?

'She's Keith's sister. Her name's Kim. She came to the place where we were working and she said, "Will you come to the cinema, Will?" and I said, "Yes, please," because Keith had told me it was a good film about buried treasure.'

It sounded very much as if those two, Keith and this Kim, had cooked it up between them. And why not? There seemed no harm in it. Will was physically a normal young man with a normal young man's needs. Was he to be deprived for ever of sexual fulfilment and a nice female companion because he had what some doctor had labelled Fragile X Syndrome? She had considered it some years before, but as an intellectual concept rather than a real problem waiting round the corner. If she had given this possible girlfriend actual form it was as a young woman incapacitated as he was, someone met in a day centre. But he no longer attended day centres . . .

'I'll come on Friday,' he was saying. 'Can we have spaghetti and chocolate cheesecake?'

'Of course we can.'

She looked up the film in the *Guardian* cinema guide. *The Treasure of Sixth Avenue* must be the one Will meant. The guide gave it three stars and noted that it was classified as suitable for the over-twelves. In a few satirical lines, whoever wrote these capsule pieces said it was more suitable for the under-twelves, being a ridiculous adventure of two men and a girl burying a haul of jewels from Tiffany's in the backyard of a building in some unspecified American city. It sounded entirely harmless, which was mostly what Becky worried about.

After she had taken Will back to Star Street, said hello to Inez and refused the drink she was offered on the grounds that she was driving, after she had seen Will happily settled with Inez (who had been pressing with her invitation) in front of the television, she departed for home. Becky hoped there weren't any scenes of violence to upset Will, but as far as she could remember, apart from the inevitable car chase, the series they were watching concentrated more on country life than fast-moving action.

Perhaps this new departure of Will's, this going out with a girl, would be the best thing for him—and for her. She found herself imagining inviting the two of them to lunch or for the evening. Marriage, eventually, and the girl—Becky hoped very much she was a nice girl—discouraging Will from spending so much time with his aunt. Visits were fine, the bride might say, but not twice weekly, Becky will want a life of her own. She remembered a day some years ago now when Will had asked her if she was married. She had no idea where the idea of marriage came from. She said she wasn't and then he said, 'I'd like to marry you.'

It was another heartbeat-missing occasion. She wanted to shut her eyes and groan. 'I'm your aunt, Will,' she'd said. 'You can't marry your aunt.'

He took no notice of this. 'Then we could live in the same place. We could get a big house with room for both of us.'

'It isn't possible,' she'd said, though this last part of it was.

She thought he looked sad and that made her wonder if any other man had been sad because she wouldn't marry him. Not as far as she knew. All this might be mended if this girl was good to him, even loved him. And she, Becky, would be liberated. She relished the idea of Will-free holidays, untrammelled Saturdays, of freedom from guilt, of knowing Will was happy. As it now was, Will had no friends except Monty, who was plainly actuated by a sense of duty, and she was growing older, alone, without a partner. If Will had another woman to love, perhaps she wouldn't end up like Inez

Ferry, reduced to spending her evenings watching television with a tenant.

As soon as Becky had gone, Inez did what she had
meant to do before she impulsively asked her and Will
in, turned off the scheduled programme and put on a
Forsyth video. Will wasn't like other people, he wouldn't
find doing this odd or sentimental or embarrassing. The
story this time had been of Forsyth tracking down the
killer of a number of young girls. Not unlike the
Rottweiler murders, Inez thought, only in the film you
didn't see the murders or any violence, come to that.
Will asked her where it was, was it near here, and
seemed in chatty mood, so she put one finger to her lips
and said, 'Ssh, not now, Will. Let's watch the film.'

Will looked wary but he obeyed. 'I liked that,' he
said when it was over.

'I'm glad,' said Inez. 'That was my husband playing
Chief Inspector Forsyth.'

This was a difficult concept for Will but with
an effort which creased his forehead and pursed his lips,
he seemed to understand. 'He was pretending to be
that man?'

'That's right. His name was Martin Ferry.'

'Where is he now?'

'He died, Will.'

'Was he nice?'

'Very nice. You would have liked him.'

To Inez's astonishment, Will laid his hand over hers.
'If you liked him, I'm sorry he died.'

He couldn't have much important lacking if he could
say things like that, Inez thought. Her heart warmed so
hugely to him that she would have liked to take him in
her arms, but that of course she couldn't do. He was a
young man, not a child. She realised that this was the

first time she had ever watched a *Forsyth* film in the
company of someone else. But everything had been all
right, she had found it as comforting as ever, and she
understood that perhaps there was no one else she knew
she could as easily have had with her as Will. Except
perhaps a child as quiet and attentive as he.

He looked at her and said, 'My mother died, but I've
got Becky. I'd like to live with Becky but her flat isn't big
enough. You haven't got a Becky.'

'No. I'll be all right. Shall we watch the news now?
And then I shall send you upstairs.'

The moment she heard the lead item she was sorry
she had let him stay. A north London girl had gone
missing. She was eighteen, a student, living at home
with her parents in Hornsey. They hadn't seen her since
Wednesday evening when she went clubbing with
friends. The club was in the Tottenham Court Road and
the friends said they had all left at just before two in the
morning. Jacky Miller, the missing girl, they had last
seen inside the entrance to the club phoning for a taxi
on her mobile.

My parents would have gone mad if I'd stayed out till
two when I was eighteen, thought Inez. These parents
had apparently been frantic, her mother lying awake listening for her to come in, waiting, then getting up and
watching the street from the window. It was the thing
all frightened mothers did, a quite useless act, which
perhaps made things worse. When it got to morning
and still no sign of their daughter, they had called the
police. No one had seen or heard of Jacky Miller for two
nights and two days. The picture of her which appeared
was of a rather plump girl with a childish face and very
blonde curly hair. She looked innocent, vulnerable and,
although this may have been Inez's imagination, unable
to take good care of herself.

'What's missing?' said Will.

She was reluctant to answer him but she had to. 'A girl went out on Wednesday night and didn't come home again. She doesn't live around here.' This was irrelevant but she thought it might make him feel better. 'She lives a long way from here.'

'She'll come home,' he said in a reassuring tone. 'Don't worry.'

'All right, I won't. It's time you went home too, Will. Would you like something before you go? A hot drink?'

He said very politely, 'No, thank you, Mrs Ferry.'

Half a mile away, in Dame Shirley Porter House, Zeinab and Algy Munro had also watched the *News at Ten*. The children had gone to bed and were now asleep. Between their parents, on a black marble and gilt table, was an open box of Belgian chocolates from which they absent-mindedly helped themselves. The room in which they sat, though of the same measurements and proportions and with the same sort of windows as in every other flat in the block, its walls painted the same 'magnolia' and its woodwork the same 'snowflake' gloss, was far better furnished and appointed. The television, for instance, was the plasma kind that hangs on the wall like a picture. A music centre with man-high speakers filled one corner and a pianola another. From the central light fitment hung a large chandelier composed of at least five hundred prisms. On a workstation between the windows was a desktop computer with maximum-size screen, Internet access and every possible accessory.

'I reckon that's another one the Rottweiler's got,' said Algy, popping a white chocolate rum truffle into his mouth. 'Only he's not left her out in the street for anyone to find. Still, it's like they say, dead bodies always turn up.'

'You know something, Alge? Rowley Woodhouse told me there's something called the National Rottweiler Society and they're kicking up a stink about people calling the killer a Rottweiler, writing to the papers and whatever. They say it's got to be stopped on account of it's not fair, it's a libel on their dogs because Rottweilers are lovely friendly beasts when they're treated right.'

Algy didn't answer. 'I don't like you seeing so much of that Rowley Woodhouse, Suzanne. It's not right, you wearing his ring. It's time I spoke out.'

Zeinab helped herself to a rose cream with a crystallised rose leaf on top. 'You'll have to look at it like work. It's my work.' She started laughing. 'Inez's is like the day job and going about with Morton and Rowley is sort of overtime. It's not as if I liked it. About the ring—well, I'll have to give it back, you know that. I can't keep on having dinner with old Morton if I'm supposed to be engaged to Rowley.'

'I don't like it,' said Algy. 'I don't like any of it.'

'Yes, you do. You like the electronics and the music centre and the TV, don't you? You like us all going on holiday to Goa. You like your Armani suit and the kids having a Harry Potter castle and a Barbie and all the video games they want.'

She might have said, you're never going to give it all to them, not living on the Benefit, you're not, but she was a nice girl at heart with far tenderer feelings for Algy Munro than she ever had for Morton Phibling and Rowley Woodhouse. 'You want to know what I got for that diamond spray Morton gave me?' She told him. His face was a mixture of wonder, concupiscence and bewilderment. 'That's going to take us all to the Maldives and Hawaii too if you want, and plenty left over.'

'Where's it all going to end, Suzanne?'

'I'll tell you. You've got to think of it like I'm a model. A model's finished when she's twenty-five—well, twenty-eight at most. Not all, I grant you, but the vast majority. You think of me like that, working to make a pile of dosh, and when I start going off that's the end, curtains. We'll have enough to buy a detached house in Arkley by then. D'you want a drink? There's two bottles of champers left.'

'It worries me,' he said. 'I don't like it and it worries me.'

'You mean you don't like being stuck here with the kids and my mum half the time. What you want to do is start thinking of others. Worries! That poor woman whose daughter's gone missing, that Mrs Miller, now she's got something to worry about. Put yourself in her shoes and you'll soon see you're OK, you're laughing.'

Zeinab got up, bent over his chair and gave him a kiss. He tried to pull her down on to his knee but she eluded him and went into the kitchen to fetch two Waterford crystal glasses and the Pol Roger.

There had been no further visits from the police, though Inez had half expected them every day. Perhaps they realised that there was no more information to be got out of the occupants of the house in Star Street, in spite of all their talk of wanting to see them again. She sat in the shop, drinking the first cup of tea of the day—the first of the week—and reading her two morning papers. One had a photograph of Jacky Miller, the other of the three friends who had accompanied her to the Tottenham Court Road club. That one had an interview with the man who had answered the phone at the taxi firm Jacky had called at two a.m. on Thursday. Not that it was much of an interview. He could only tell them that he had called one of their cabs on its car phone, the driver had gone to the club but found no Miss Miller, though he had enquired inside and then driven up and down the street looking for her. The paper that didn't have the taximan interview was linking the missing girl with the two girls murdered by the Rottweiler. Anticipating the worst, one of the three clubbing friends had even told the paper Jacky had been wearing a pair of earrings she had given her for her birthday, silver circles set with brilliants, which she was sure the murderer would have taken from her. There was nothing about the running man. That lead had been abandoned.

Inez sighed and immediately told herself she must stop sighing. It was becoming a habit. When Jeremy Quick put his head round the door and said, 'Good morning, Inez,' she offered him a cup of tea and asked him if she sighed too much.

'Not that I've noticed. It's a miserable world we live in, so I don't wonder if you do. Belinda sighs a lot. Plenty to sigh about when you come to think of it. She had to go home at nine last night to relieve the next-door neighbour. She has to get the neighbour in to sit with her mother when she goes out with me.'

'How old is she? The mother, I mean.'

'Oh, very old, late eighties. There's nothing wrong with her but she's very demanding and she won't be left alone.'

Inez had never met Belinda Gildon, though she'd seen a photograph of her with Jeremy in some Mediterranean holiday resort, and once caught a glimpse of him sitting at a table in one of those summer evening restaurants she walked past. He kept looking at his watch as if he were waiting for someone. Belinda, surely. She had been tempted to go in and say hello, for she had been acutely lonely that night, just go up to his table, be introduced to Belinda when she came and maybe have a quick drink with them. But of course she didn't, it wasn't really a serious idea. She used to wonder why they didn't marry but this was obviously the answer, the answer too to why Jeremy seemed so often on his own.

'I was just thinking', she said, 'how the police said they'd come back but they never did.'

'We couldn't tell them any more. Now there's this girl missing, poor kid. I'll tell you what I was thinking. There are hundreds of thousands of people go missing every year and they're never found. Belinda says she wouldn't be surprised if this chap they call the Rottweiler had killed some of them before he ever moved down here.'

'If he always takes some ornament or whatever from them, the police would make the connection, wouldn't they?'

Jeremy said he supposed so, it had crossed his mind, and he must go. Inez poured herself another cup of tea and read the rest of one of the papers, the page of home news, the foreign news and a feature about self-tanning products. At nine she turned the sign on the inside of the glass door to 'Open' and lugged the book rack out on to the pavement. She was going back when the side door at the foot of the stairs opened and Ludmila and Freddy Perfect came out, arm in arm. Ludmila was wearing a long brown cotton skirt, a red tunic with gold frogging that looked like part of a hussar's uniform and high-heeled purple boots, Freddy a suit in dog-tooth check and what Inez was sure was an old Harrovian tie. They waved to Inez but didn't stop, perhaps because Morton Phibling's orange Mercedes had just drawn up at the kerb.

'She isn't here yet, Mr Phibling.'

'It's nearly half past nine!'

'Yes, I know.' Inez was tempted to say more about Zeinab's gross lateness, but maybe that would be spoiling the girl's chances. Phibling might be a stickler for punctuality, make a fetish of people getting to work on time and be put off. She really didn't know much about him and never had, in spite of being sure she had known him before. Now, no doubt, he would go away and return later.

To her surprise he followed her into the shop. 'I particularly want to see her.' He produced a jeweller's box from the pocket of his camel-hair overcoat. 'What do you think of this? I took her out to dinner on Friday night and she said she'd give serious thought to getting engaged.'

'Really?' Inez was almost stunned by the flashing beams from the blue and white stones nestling in blue velvet.

'A diamond and sapphire parure,' said Morton Phibling. 'It cost a packet but I can afford it. She's worth all the treasures', he said, slipping into his Arabian mode, 'of Haroun al Raschid. She should have the Topkapi Palace if I could get my hands on it.'

He sat down in Aunt Violet's armchair, leaned back and lit a cigar.

'If you don't mind, Mr Phibling,' said Inez. 'I really can't allow smoking in here.'

'Worry you not. I shall go outside and smoke it on the pavement while I await my love.'

Zeinab was even later than usual. Her delay was due to Carmel having a tantrum about going to school and Bryn backing her up by lying on the floor screaming, but this, of course, couldn't be explained to Inez. 'My dad beat mum up last night and there was things I had to do for her.'

'I'm sorry.' Inez had been going to say she thought Zeinab ought to make excuses on the rare occasions she was on time, not for being late, which was a daily occurrence. But she couldn't, not in the face of domestic violence. 'How is your mother?'

'All over bruises,' said Zeinab. 'She said she was going to tell the police but it's all talk with her, she never does.'

Morton Phibling came back into the shop, his cigar extinguished. 'My love, my fair one, is looking even more stunning than usual today. The time of the singing of birds is come and the voice of the turtle is heard in our land.'

'Turtles don't have voices,' said Zeinab and, more kindly, 'We're having dinner at Le Gavroche tonight, right?'

'Right, my star. And I want you to meet my friend Orville; he'll only pop in for five minutes to be introduced. He's dying to meet you but he's just recovering from his second divorce so his spirits are a bit low.'

'He's the one who owns all those hotels, isn't he?'

If Phibling had been more observant he would have noticed a brighter than usual gleam in Zeinab's eyes but he saw only the long, long black hair, the red softly parted lips and the white fluffy sweater. 'That's right,' he said, 'and he's got a five-star one in Bermuda that specialises in weddings. I thought we might think about . . . ?'

'Why not?' said Zeinab happily as she received the jeweller's box from Phibling's hands.

No work on Saturdays, so Will usually had a lie-in. He wasn't nervous about the evening ahead but nor was he excited, only anxious to behave properly and do what was expected of him. Long ago, when he was still living in the children's home, he had seen a television film in which a young man, going out with a girl, took her a bunch of flowers. Will himself had sometimes taken Becky flowers because he had known her take a bouquet of daffodils to a friend. Perhaps he should buy flowers for Kim.

He got up and made himself breakfast, the kind a child who knows nothing of cooking can prepare, cornflakes and a slice of brown bread with marmalade. Several slices. When Becky had asked him what he would like for Christmas he had said a toaster, but she hadn't given him one, he didn't know why not, though she had given him an electric kettle and even a microwave. He hadn't really expected a gas hob, they were too expensive. After breakfast he washed up his dishes and the mug he had had his milk in, and then he cleaned the flat, dusting the surfaces and vacuuming the floors. He cleaned the sink and the basin in the bathroom but not the shower. That could wait until after he'd been in it. He and Becky had been out shopping together and he had wanted to buy himself razors but she didn't like that and got him an electric shaver instead. Shaving wasn't something he did every day, being so fair, but he would do it before he went out with Kim.

It was going to be a fine day. It was a fine day now, the sky blue and dotted with little pure white clouds, the sun shining and flowers coming out everywhere— even in the Edgware Road. Spring was really here. More signs of it could be seen outside the immediate area, and as Will walked through Church Street to Lisson Grove and up Lisson Grove into Grove End, he saw narcissi coming out in the gardens of the big houses, though he didn't know the names of the white flowers with orange centres, and he saw others whose red buds were opening and which he knew were tulips. Hyacinths scented the

air and in front of a block of flats where Grove End
Road curved away from Abbey Road stood a pink tree
covered in blossom.

In St John's Wood High Street he went into a florist's
and bought a bunch of violets for Kim because they
smelt so lovely and were quite small. She could take
them into the cinema with her and smell them while
the film was on. Will also bought a pizza for his lunch
and a tub of chocolate chip ice cream, which the shop
assistant wrapped up in several layers of newspaper so
that it wouldn't melt on the way home.

He had a little fridge in his flat, not much bigger
than the microwave, but large enough to hold a carton
of milk, 200 grammes of butter and a chop or piece of
chicken. Will was quite good at measuring things in
grammes and millilitres and millimetres but hopeless at
pounds and ounces. Becky couldn't manage grammes
and one of the things that pleased him most was teaching her about grammes in shops, he was proud of that.
He knew he wasn't clever like some people and although
he tried, knew too that he would never be cleverer. It
brought him great satisfaction when he found that there
were things he could work out that others couldn't, like
knowing fourteen degrees was warm for March, what
five centimetres looked like and how to put things
together. When Becky had sent for a mail order cabinet
and it had come in pieces packed flat in a box, she hadn't
been able to assemble it but he had. He had followed
the plans on the papers that came with it and within an
hour all the separate pieces were a nice cabinet with
drawers and a door that opened and shut. Perhaps Will
differed in several respects from a ten-year-old who was
good with his hands but in one in particular: he didn't
boast about his accomplishment like the child would
have. He'd mention it once and then say no more.

After he had had his lunch he had a shower, cleaned up after himself and sat quietly, doing nothing, thinking about the evening ahead.

She called for him in her brother's van, which she had borrowed for the evening. *The Treasure of Sixth Avenue* was showing at the Warner Village in the Finchley Road. It had car parking so Kim was able to put the van inside, somewhere it wouldn't be towed away or clamped. Will, well-dressed in a white shirt, blue tie and his leather jacket, had given her the violets and she had seemed genuinely pleased. No boy had ever given her flowers before, she said. She was wearing a white jacket over a purple T-shirt, the same colour as the violets, and when she pinned the bunch on to her lapel Will thought they looked fine.

Inside the cinema he bought a big polystyrene beaker of Coke and an even bigger bucket of popcorn for each of them. He couldn't remember ever eating popcorn before but he was happy to try it. Will never had much to say but Kim did and he listened quite contentedly while she talked about her family, her mum and dad and brother Keith and brother Wayne, and about the hairdresser and the problems of getting to work by public transport, and the weather, and where was he going for his summer holiday? If Will had been more sophisticated or experienced or simply had more nous, he would have recognised this last as the stock enquiry all hairdressers put to their clients. But Becky always cut his hair, so he told her he would go wherever his auntie went—for which he got a wary look—and that his mother was dead but he liked the spring because all the flowers came out. On the question of his mother she was sympathetic, she couldn't imagine anything worse than her mum dying, but maybe his aunt had taken her

place. Will agreed that she had, they drank their Coke
and ate their popcorn, the commercials came to an end
and *The Treasure of Sixth Avenue* began.

Kim had already said how much she liked Russell
Crowe and Sandra Bullock, so Will identified these
actors and was pleased with himself when they soon
reappeared and he recognised them. The story wasn't
difficult to follow. The principals were a bank robber,
his girlfriend and a sidekick, played by an actor even
Kim had never heard of before, but this time, instead
of a bank, the three were planning a jewellery heist.
Where all this was taking place was unclear to a
British audience. It might have been New York but it
might also have been almost any big city in the
United States, a forest of towers, a row or two of
shopfronts and the residential streets spokes that ran
from this central hub.

Will didn't much like it when the Russell Crowe
character shot a guard in the jewellery store but no
one else in the audience seemed much affected. Kim
went on calmly eating popcorn and the man on the
other side of him continued chewing gum, so he told
himself to shut his eyes tightly next time it looked as
if people were to be hurt. The three broke into a kind
of vault where they found dazzling amounts of jewellery, diamonds mostly in necklaces and bracelets
and rings. Worth millions, said the Sandra Bullock
girl, maybe as much as a billion.

They escaped from the place without anyone finding
them and went back to where Russell Crowe lived in a
strange dark old house which would have frightened
Will even to set foot in.

'Scary,' Kim whispered to him with an exaggerated
shudder.

Pleased he wasn't alone, he nodded. 'I'm scared too.'

He was also enjoying himself but just as he was growing sure he was going to understand everything that
happened on the screen, things became complicated.
There were new people appearing who found the dead
guard, then swarms of policemen, the camera moving
into places never before seen, clubs and bars and cellars,
all full of people the officers questioned in harsh incomprehensible accents. It wasn't really for children any
more and Will had completely lost it. He tried to sit still
because he had been told by Becky on previous cinema
visits that he mustn't disturb the people around him,
but it was hard not to fidget. There was also a strong
sense of disappointment, which made him indignant. It
had been so straightforward and simple. Why couldn't
it go on the way it had begun?

And then, suddenly, it did. The three jewel thieves
were in a car, which was racing at top speed through the
streets. Will had never seen a real car go so fast. Its
brakes squealed as it sped round corners, shaking off
pursuers who were chasing it. The thieves' car turned
into a street where a sign on a lamp-post read 'Sixth
Avenue'. Will could read it without difficulty because
the letters were big, they lingered on the screen and he
recognised what they said from the title of the film.
Sixth Avenue. The car swung into a parking lot and the
three got out, Russell Crowe carrying the leather bag in
which the jewels were, the other man a spade. There
wasn't much talk. Now it was action. They were in a
backyard, a squalid place with dustbins and an old iron
dump and a ruined shed. But there were bushes too at
the end of it and areas of earth on either side of the broken and crazed concrete path, out of which straggling
grass and weeds grew. Overhead the cloudy wild sky was
stained red by city lights. The man who wasn't Russell
Crowe began digging a hole. When her boyfriend

shouted at her to help, the girl found another spade in the remains of the shed and got to work. There seemed to be a desperate urgency in what they did and again Kim shivered. She clutched Will's hand, which was unexpected, but somehow nice and comforting. He gave the hand a squeeze.

The three robbers buried the leather bag in the hole and shovelled the earth back. They stamped it down and threw a couple of bricks and a piece of board over the top so that it looked as if the ground hadn't been disturbed for years. Then they heard sirens in the distance and Will, with a shock of excitement, recognised the sounds as those he heard in Paddington every day. All this was happening here, in London! The robbers heard the sirens too, they all listened, looked at each other and within seconds were over the wall, over the next yard and the next wall, and back in the parking lot. After that complexities came back and Will had difficulty following it, but five minutes from the end Russell Crowe was shot dead by a policeman, the friend was crippled by a bullet and would never walk again, and the girl was getting into an aircraft that took off as soon as she had fastened her seat belt. Will shut his eyes during the killing and maiming, opened them to see Sandra Bullock on a beach with palm trees and bright blue sea, a new man beside her, saying, 'Why don't I go fetch us a drink, babe?' and walking away.

The girl waited till he was out of earshot, then said dreamily, 'I guess the treasure's still there. It's not for me, I can never go home again . . .'

The lights went up and Kim got to her feet. Will followed suit. He thought of asking her if she thought the treasure was still there now. But Sandra Bullock had said it was, she seemed sure. Why couldn't she go home? He worked it out carefully. Because she'd done something wrong, so wrong that the police had shot the men who'd also done it and if she went back they'd shoot her too. Was that it? It must be.

'I'm starving,' said Kim. 'That popcorn doesn't fill you up, does it? It's so light.'

Excitement had killed Will's appetite, but he might start to feel hungry when he saw food. There were cafés in the complex. They went into one, sat at a table over-looking the Finchley Road and Kim ordered a pizza and Will omelette and chips. He had already had a pizza for his lunch, a fact he imparted to Kim. Ordering food wasn't unfamiliar to him. He sometimes went out for his lunch when he and Keith were working near a restaurant. They had more Coke to drink and Kim talked about the film while Will, somehow knowing it wasn't necessary to listen or say more than yes and no and that's right, thought about it.

The treasure must be still there. Sandra Bullock had said it was and she would know. Russell Crowe couldn't go back and dig it up because he was dead and the other man couldn't because he couldn't walk and never would. It must be still there. But where? Wherever there was a Sixth Avenue.

'Do you want any more to eat?' Kim was saying.

'I wouldn't mind some ice cream.' He had had it also at lunchtime but he didn't mind how much ice cream he ate or how often.

'Let's both have it, then. Chocolate?'

'I like chocolate best,' said Will happily.

'So do I, it's my favourite. Isn't that funny, us both liking chocolate best?'

Will laughed out loud because it was funny. Not only was chocolate ice cream their favourite but they found they both hated coffee and quite liked a nice

cup of tea. So they had that too. He noticed that the
violets in her buttonhole still looked quite fresh. She
saw him looking.

'I'll put them in water the minute I get home.'

Will paid for the meal. She offered to go halves but
he said no, he'd pay, the way Becky always said she
would.

On the way out she read a headline on an evening
paper someone had. '"Fears Grow for Missing Girl.
Mother says, 'I'm Devastated.'" I'm glad I've got you
with me, Will, I'd be scared out on my own.'

This time it was he who took her hand. 'You'll be
OK,' he said, but he said it automatically. Inez had said
something like it. He was thinking about the film, wondering where Sixth Avenue might be.

Kim drove him home. 'Thank you for coming with
me,' he said politely, the way Becky had taught him.
Thank you for having me, thank you for the tea, thank
you for coming . . .

She gave him a kiss on the cheek, locked all the doors
on the van and drove off. Will went upstairs. How
could he find out where Sixth Avenue was?

CHAPTER 5

At the rear of Star Antiques was a small garden. Americans would have called it a yard and that description best fitted it. The walls which enclosed it were so thickly hung with ivy that no brickwork could be seen, while the area in the middle was mostly covered with large concrete slabs between which weeds were starting to sprout. But just inside the walls were narrow borders of earth scattered with bricks and pebbles and broken shards of pottery, where scrubby bushes struggled for life and the withered stalks of golden rod and Michaelmas daisies and fireweed still lingered. Freddy Perfect, who never looked at the garden much when those plants were in fresh bloom, now gazed with concentration on the two men who were poking under bushes, lifting up dead stems and peering into the ancient coal bunker which, squeezed into the far left-hand corner of the garden, was similarly overgrown with ivy.

'Ludo,' he said to the woman who was still in bed. 'There's a couple of guys outside searching the place for something. Come and see. They're going to start digging.'

'You can give me a running commentary. I'm not getting up yet.' Her accent today was north London with hints of Estuary English. Ludmila Gogol had long given up much pretence with Freddy. 'Is it the police?'

'They're not wearing uniform. Wait a minute, there's another one come and he is, helmet and all. Shame, though, they're not digging.'

'Why is it a shame? You don't want them finding a body, do you?'

'Is that what they're looking for? That's an idea. I wouldn't mind them finding a body, I could do with a bit of excitement. Wait a minute, though, they're finished, they've done. One of them's got mud all over his trousers. I'm going down, see if they come in the shop.'

Ludmila turned over and quickly went back to sleep. She could sleep anywhere, at any time. Like a cat, Freddy said, lie down, curl up, close her eyes and she'd be asleep in thirty seconds. He padded down the stairs. True to his hope, the two policemen not in uniform were in the shop with Inez, Crippen and a different bloke, not Osnabrook.

'Good morning, all,' said Freddy. 'How may I help you?'

Inez ignored him. Crippen and the other one, a man Freddy thought resembled his friend Anwar Ghosh, nodded in his direction. Freddy strolled through the shop, coming to rest at the place where, for the past two years, the urn with the Parthenon frieze had stood. A miniature display table had replaced it, the key to its glass lid in the keyhole. Freddy turned the key, lifted the lid and began taking out objects to be scrutinised.

'As I was saying,' said Crippen in rather a sour tone, 'before I was interrupted, in answer to your enquiry, Mrs Ferry, we are in fact searching all the backs of premises in this area today. The area we're covering extends from Paddington Station in the west to Baker Street in the east but today we're concentrating on the Edgware Road neighbourhood.'

'What are you looking for?' said Freddy, waving a Victorian lorgnette in their direction. 'A body? Or those bits and pieces the Rottweiler took off the corpses?'

'It's my job to ask questions,' said Crippen, 'not answer them.'

'Oh, dear, sorry I spoke, I'm sure. Excuse me while I apologise for existing.' Freddy wasn't really offended, as his broad smile showed.

'Please put that lorgnette down, Freddy. Of course they're searching for that poor girl's body, the one that's missing. Is there anything else, Inspector?'

'I don't think so. Except—yes, well, if anyone comes in here asking questions of the kind we've just heard from that gentleman, if anyone shows too much curiosity, we'd like a name. I mean, you're in touch with a lot of people. It might be helpful.' When Inez promised nothing, he addressed his sidekick, 'Come along, Zulueta, we've work to do.'

'Unpleasant job, they have,' said Freddy cheerfully. 'I don't suppose there's any tea going?'

'I'm sorry but I've had mine and washed up the cups.'

'Cups with an "s", is it? I think you've got a secret admirer, Inez, coming calling in the wee small hours.'

'It was Mr Quick,' said Inez distantly. 'And now if there's nothing more, Ludmila will be wondering where you are.'

With infinite slowness Freddy shambled to the door he had come in by, pausing on the way to examine an ivory fan, a ship in a bottle, a framed primitive of the Garden of Eden and a brass lion's head door knocker. Inez carried the book rack outside as a distant clock struck nine. It was cold today and grey, a fine rain spreading a film of damp on concrete surfaces. The white van whose owner boasted of its dirty condition was again outside.

Seeing her on the pavement, Mr Khoury came out of the jeweller's. He pointed to the van. 'Back again,' he said. 'The police are searching your garden also, I observe. What I ask myself is, how is the murderer getting this body into my backyard? Over the wall maybe, that is two metres high? But first over all the other walls that is two metres high. Or is he carrying it through the shop? Is he saying, "Good afternoon, please excuse me while I carry this corpse through your shop to bury in the back"? Is he maybe asking to borrow a spade? That is what I ask myself.'

'You should have asked them. Is my earring ready yet?'

'Ready and waiting for you. Twelve pounds fifty and no credit cards for repairs, please.'

'I'll come in later,' said Inez and went back indoors out of the rain.

She was thinking about Jeremy Quick. A nice man, no trouble, the ideal tenant. If he moved out she would never get anyone half so pleasant to replace him. Of course, she had no real reason to fear his moving. It was just that while he was drinking his tea half an hour before, he had talked about Belinda and more frankly about her mother than he had ever done before. Mrs Gildon had a terminal illness, it appeared, only at her age its progress was much slower than it would have been in a younger person. Even so, the doctors had told Belinda she couldn't last more than a year. They had said that before and been proved wrong by Mrs Gildon's basically strong constitution and healthy heart. Jeremy had looked so despondent when he said this that Inez had laid her hand on his arm, a comforting gesture. His rapid recoil surprised her. It was almost as if he thought she was making an advance to him. Her face grew hot. He went on talking as if nothing had happened. The house in which Belinda and her mother lived in Ealing would be hers 'one day'. When 'something happened' to her mother, he said, and he implied—or Inez thought he implied—that in that event he and Belinda would marry. Nothing was mentioned about the Star Street flat but Inez reasoned that if a couple had a three-bedroom house in Ealing (once known as the 'queen of the suburbs') at their disposal they were unlikely to prefer a top flat in Paddington.

'Is Mrs Gildon in a hospital?' Inez had asked, recovering from her discomfiture.

'For the present, yes, but that is only temporary.'

'Yes, I'm sure. Still, it must mean Belinda has a bit more freedom for the time being. Why don't you bring her in for a drink one evening? Tuesday or Wednesday?'

'I'd like that. And so will she? Could we say Tuesday?'

So at last she would meet Belinda. They probably drank wine but her spirit stock was getting low. To be on the safe side she'd go up to the corner while she was out collecting her earring and pick up gin and whisky from the wine shop. Her thoughts reverted to that touch on the arm and his flinching away. Was she so repulsive? It was useless to worry about it. He had probably already forgotten the incident. She glanced at the grandfather clock. Twenty-five past nine and not a sign of Zeinab. For the first time Inez saw her as a potential victim of the Rottweiler. There she was, a young girl, who waited for a bus to Hampstead in the gathering dusk of these not-yet-quite-spring evenings, who must brace herself for the tedious journey ahead, catching one bus, changing on to another. Would she accept a lift if offered one? Would she get into a stranger's car? If her father was as wealthy as she said, possessor of a house on the West Heath and three cars, surely he would have lent her a car for her own use or even bought her one.

Reluctantly, Inez admitted to herself that she didn't entirely believe in Zeinab's father's fabulous riches or the

house or the three cars. More likely the family home
was part of a modest terrace, there was one car and this
draconian patriarch comfortable but not mega-rich.
Still, he must be a monster in his way to lay down such
harsh rules for his daughter, yet not extending to her a
father's care by, say, meeting her when she had to pass
through the Rottweiler's hunting ground in the dark.
Half past nine. Morton Phibling would be along in a
minute, paraphrasing the Song of Songs and smoking
his cigars.

Instead of Zeinab's admirer, a woman came in with a
child who proved his unruliness by immediately homing
in on the most delicate things in the shop, a tray of
Georgian liqueur glasses. In the nick of time Inez picked
up the tray and put it on top of a bookcase well out of
reach. The child began to howl.

'Oh, shut up,' said its mother.

'Can I help you with anything?' said Inez.

'I'm looking for something for a birthday present.
Maybe jewellery.'

'We don't stock much.' Inez opened a drawer. 'This is
all we have. It's mostly Victorian, pinchbeck and tiger's
eyes and lockets with locks of hair, that sort of thing.'

The child thrust both hands into the drawer and
scattered its contents on the floor. His mother screamed
and fell on her knees just as Zeinab came in through the
street door. Inez looked pointedly at her watch and
Zeinab said, 'You know I've no concept of time.'

A pinchbeck and rose quartz ring was the customer's
choice. She had lifted the child and set him on her hip.
Most of the necklaces and bracelets still lay on the floor.
After she had gone, Zeinab knelt down to pick them up,
her black hair falling forward to envelop her face.

'On the subject of jewellery,' said Inez, 'I've never
seen you wear any of the things Mr Phibling buys you.

That diamond rose spray, for instance. He can't be very pleased; he must think you don't care for them.'

'Then he'll have to think, won't he? If I wore those diamonds, if my dad even knew I had diamonds, he'd kill me.'

'Oh, I see,' said Inez.

In the house in Abbey Road, Keith and Will were renovating the dining room. All the furniture was stacked in the hall. They had laid a new floor of mahogany woodblock, built display shelves into the two alcoves, and now they were preparing the walls for a coat of eggshell vinyl. Because the owners of the house were out at work and the woman who came in to clean had said she liked a bit of background music, the radio was on, the volume turned quite high so that she could hear it in the kitchen.

Keith would have liked to know how his sister and Will got on together on Saturday evening. He hadn't seen Kim since and, in any case, he would have hesitated before coming straight out and asking her. Will might say a word, he thought, but Will said nothing. He seemed more preoccupied than usual, in a dream. In spite of the early hour Kim had got home, information imparted on the phone by his mother, perhaps things had progressed further than anticipated. Perhaps even now Will was recalling their encounter with quiet pleasure. Kim had driven the van back yesterday morning and left it outside his place, but she had put the keys through the letter box, she hadn't come in. If they had got on really well and the back of the van had been the venue for more than a hug and a goodnight kiss, she might look in today, around lunchtime. Once he'd seen them together he'd be able to tell.

He would have been deeply chagrined had he succeeded in reading his assistant's mind, for Will wasn't

thinking about Kim, he had almost forgotten her existence. Saturday evening was another matter. That was the
most important thing that had happened to him for
years, perhaps for always. With intense enjoyment he
recalled the scene in the film where Russell Crowe,
Sandra Bullock and the other man dug the hole and
buried the treasure. Their exchange of words was perfectly contained in his memory, as if a device in his brain
had accurately recorded them.

'Did you hear a siren?'

'In this city there's always sirens. Night and day. A
siren don't prove a thing.'

'Listen, it's coming nearer.'

'For God's sake!'

'We gotta get outta here. Now. Over the wall, outta
here . . .'

And the man who had uttered the last sentence was
shot in the spine and would never walk again—Will
had forced himself to keep his eyes open at this point—
while Russell Crowe died when he advanced on the
policeman with a gun in each hand. Only the girl was
left unharmed to say, once she was safe in South
America, that the treasure had never been recovered,
that it must still be there today . . .

He could remember it but he would go and see the
film again, just to make quite sure. Would Becky come
too? He always liked being with Becky, better than with
anyone in the world, but nevertheless he admitted to
himself that going alone would be best. Tonight maybe,
or tomorrow. Recalling most of it so well, he couldn't
really remember what the house looked like where the
digging had taken place. Nor had he heard or noticed
the house number in Sixth Avenue. As yet, he didn't
even know where Sixth Avenue was, but he'd find out.
Once he'd got hold of the treasure all his problems

would be past and all Becky's too. Because he'd sell the jewels and get a lot of money and buy a house big enough for both of them. The only reason he couldn't live with her was the size of her flat and the fact that there was only one bedroom. He'd buy a big house with lots of bedrooms and plenty of room for both of them.

Kim didn't come in at lunchtime. Keith was disappointed. He knew for a fact she wasn't going anywhere this evening. It was the night her friend came round and they did each other's nails and put on face packs but the friend couldn't come today, so she'd be free and maybe they'd arranged to go out again. He wished he could ask Will but he couldn't. The noise from the radio and its steady beat, trolls hammering in the underworld, would have been deafening to the owners of the house in Abbey Road but not to Will, who scarcely heard it. It did nothing to interfere with his musings. Nor did eating the pork luncheon meat sandwiches he had made himself and brought with him, nor did wielding the paint roller as he made a start on the window wall.

How did you buy a house? People did it all the time, he knew that, he saw removal vans parked in this street and in his own, and furniture being loaded on to them. They were moving, that's what they called it, 'moving'. But making another house your own that you could move into, getting a key to open its front door, putting your own things inside it, all that was a mystery. Finding out how to do it, the very idea, made his head swim.

'How do you buy a house?' It was the first thing he had said to Keith for more than an hour.

'Pardon?' shouted Keith above the radio's racket.

'How do you buy a house?'

'What d'you mean, how?'

Explaining something was very difficult for Will. He could only say, 'How do you?' and, 'You've got to find it, how do you?'

'You read the advertisements or go to an estate agent, is that what you mean?'

Will nodded, though he wasn't much the wiser. Better wait till he had got the treasure and then maybe Becky would do the house buying. He wouldn't tell her yet, he'd tell her when the treasure was his and he could show it to her. It would be a surprise, the biggest surprise she had ever had.

Inez was watching *Forsyth and the Crown Conspiracy* when her doorbell rang. At once she stopped the video and switched off the set. It must be one of the tenants at the door, for no one else could get in, but for all that, she looked through the little spyglass at the reassuring sight of Jeremy Quick before opening it.

'I'm so sorry to disturb you, Inez.'

'Not a bit,' said Inez, sufficiently pleased to see him to invite him in.

'Only for a moment, then.'

It must be the first time he had been in her flat. She noticed him looking around the room with discreet appreciation and she couldn't help contrasting his reaction to what she imagined Freddy's might have been— 'Lovely place you've got here', wandering about nosily and handling everything, but sitting down when he liked without waiting for her to ask him as Jeremy did. He was always so well-dressed, his shoes polished to the gleam of black basalt. Did he have his hands manicured? It rather looked like it and as if the manicurist had used a white pencil under the nail tips. Inez found she didn't altogether care for the idea.

'Can I get you anything? A glass of wine? A soft drink?'

'Oh, no, thank you. I wouldn't dream of troubling you. As a matter of fact, that's why I came. To tell you I really regret this but we won't be able to come tomorrow. For drinks, you know. Mrs Gildon has taken a turn for the worse and Belinda has had to rush to the hospital.'

'I *am* sorry,' said Inez. 'Is it serious? Of course it must be at her age.'

'Well, she is eighty-eight and I'm afraid it's her heart this time. The cancer progresses very slowly in these old people but if the heart fails—well, I don't have to give you the prognosis there.'

'No, indeed. I suppose Belinda will have to stay at the hospital while her mother is so ill?'

'They have made up a bed for her in a side room. I've just come from there now. Took me ages, of course. Buses never run according to the timetable.'

'You haven't a car?'

He seemed well-off. She had concluded that, like her, he had a car somewhere on the residents' parking down the street.

'Oh, good heavens, no. Odd though it sounds, I can't actually drive.' He gave a laugh, which sounded slightly ashamed. 'Now, as to Mrs Gildon, Belinda says she wouldn't want her sufferings prolonged and there I quite agree. She has had a good innings and if her life is drawing to a close Belinda will of course be heartbroken but eventually she may see it as being all for the best.'

Inez nodded. She disliked being intrusive but he seemed to want her to take an interest in his and his girlfriend's doings. 'I suppose Belinda is young enough to want a life of her own now?'

'I don't mind telling *you*', said Jeremy confidingly, 'that she would like the chance to have a child or even children. She is only thirty-six, after all.'

'Well, as you say, poor Mrs Gildon's life can't be much prolonged, I should think.'

'You know, I will have that drink.'

Inez fetched a bottle of white wine from the fridge and poured two glasses.

'You're very kind,' said Jeremy. 'Do you mind if I ask you something? Why are you called Inez? You're not Spanish, are you?'

Inez smiled. 'My father was in the Spanish Civil War. I don't say "fought", but he was in it. He wasn't married then but my mother said he told her he had a job "on the ground staff". It does sound a bit strange, I know. There was a girl he liked, maybe more than liked, her name was Inez and she was killed.'

'Didn't your mother mind you having her name?'

'I don't think so. She liked it too.' Inez laughed. 'It's coming up to ten. Would you mind if I had the news on?'

'Of course I wouldn't.'

'Only I heard they'd found that girl. Jacky Miller, I mean,'

They hadn't. The girl's body, discovered under a stack of concrete waste and bricks on a building site in Nottingham, was that of a girl older than Jacky who had died maybe as much as two years before. So far, she was unidentified. As the investigating officer said, address-ing a press conference, so many young girls were on the missing list that it was impossible at this stage even to speculate as to who it might be. The police were unable to say how this girl had met her death. Meanwhile, the search for Jacky Miller went on.

'I've never been to Nottingham,' said Jeremy.

'One of the films my late husband made was shot there and I went up with him for a couple of weeks. That must have been in—oh, the early nineties, I suppose.'

'Don't they have parents, these girls, who worry about where they are?'

'I'm sure they do,' said Inez. 'We know that all three girls who died and Jacky Miller have parents who have been nearly mad with anxiety about them. But if a girl disappears and can't be found, what can they do? Employ private detectives? That's far too expensive for most people even to consider.'

'I suppose so. I must go. Thank you so much for the drink and for being so nice about tomorrow.'

Inez went back to her video. But *Forsyth and the Crown Conspiracy* wasn't one of her favourites, perhaps because—and she was almost ashamed to confess this to herself—there was more sex in it between Martin and the female guest star than in any other of his films, what looked like actual lovemaking in a bedroom setting. When that part was reached she switched it off and thought of substituting the Nottingham one, *Forsyth and the Miracle*, but instead of exchanging the tape, she sat in silence, finishing her wine and thinking first about the girl who was still missing and the body which had been found in such squalid and ugly circumstances. How would a parent feel, especially if he or she lived nearby, to learn that their beloved daughter—surely she was beloved—had lain for years, her body mouldering in the wet earth, under a pile of builder's waste materials to which, no doubt, loads of rubble and bricks were constantly added? In her mind's eye she saw again the picture on the screen, the pyramid of rubbish that was finally being removed for disposal and from which a fall of bricks like an avalanche had revealed—an outstretched hand.

Inez had never had a child, though she would have liked children, a desire not shared by either of her husbands, and this had somewhat lessened the bitterness of her disappointment. Martin, the one she had really cared about, already had children, by his first marriage, wanted no more but would have been pleased for her if . . . She sat up suddenly, holding the wineglass. Her mind had gone back to something Jeremy had said. How could Belinda be only thirty-six if her mother was eighty-eight?

Perhaps it was possible for a woman to give birth at fifty-two, in certain rare cases, *Guinness Book of Records* cases. But such events were very likely myths or distortions. It was possible *now* with IVF treatment. But in nineteen sixty-six, which must be the year of Belinda's birth? The answer must be that she was adopted. Of course. Any other explanation would place Jeremy Quick in a rather bad light . . .

CHAPTER 6

As the weekend approached Becky's thoughts turned to Will and the question of inviting him over for the Saturday or the Sunday. She hadn't spoken to him since she left him with Inez on the previous Friday evening and now her usual guilt was building up. But something unusual these days had happened to Becky on the previous Sunday. She had met a man.

It was at the home of someone she worked with who had asked her to dinner, and the invitation had seemed to come out of the blue. She had been caught and having just remarked that she had nothing particular to do on the day in question, had to say yes. The man was her hostess's cousin. He was about Becky's own age, good-looking, nice and newly divorced. Because it was dark when she left and her car was necessarily parked a couple of hundred yards up the street, James came out with her and escorted her to it. As he saw her into the driving seat, he asked if he could take her out to dinner the following Friday or Saturday. Becky said yes without much hesitation but her yes was to Friday, for she was already wondering which weekend day she would be obliged to invite Will.

James had phoned her and been just as charming. He only wanted to hear her voice, he said, and have five minutes' chat if she could spare the time. The five minutes were extended to twenty and by the time Becky rang off she was starting to think that if Friday evening was as successful as it promised to be he might want to spend

Saturday with her and she might want to spend Saturday with him. She hadn't been so attracted to anyone in years and she thought he felt the same about her. So should she wait and see or go ahead and invite Will for the Sunday?

And if *he* wanted Sunday with her too? If she said, yes but my nephew is coming and he said that was all right, he could meet her nephew, what then? Dreadful feelings came to the surface of Becky's mind, feelings of which she was deeply ashamed. She didn't want James encountering Will who was such a near relation but was a builder's labourer and—well, not quite, oh, God, how to put it without making herself the vilest kind of rat?

Yet weekends never went by without her inviting him. Suddenly she thought of the girl called Kim. Maybe it was possible that Will and she had been out together every evening, that because of this Will wouldn't want to spare a day for her. No one, not the God she didn't believe in, no human judge, could surely expect her to devote what free time she had to her dead sister's child, a grown man, with a job and friends and a life of his own. No one. Of course, she told herself, it wasn't quite like that. It looked that way on the face of it but because it wasn't a general condition but a case of individuals, the ordinary rules didn't apply. If her conscience, that inner voice, that old-fashioned concept, kept telling her to invite him she should obey. If James really liked her he would come back and not be put off by a reasonable refusal. That, she knew, was the advice the agony aunt she never wrote to but often thought of writing to would give her.

Why was it that these columnists' recommendations were never appealing and only persuaded one to choose the alternative instead?

While most people, without home duties or children, who go to see a film simply look up the times of showings and go, for Will careful preparation was required. How to find out when to go, for instance, to eat before or after or during and what to eat, what means of transport to use. Like a child, he seldom had to make decisions or assume responsibility. Others, Becky, the children's home and his social worker friend Monty, and Inez, and Keith, did those things for him. Even Kim had supplied a van to drive him to the cinema last time. Now he was on his own, which a psychiatrist would probably have said was good for him.

The Treasure of Sixth Avenue was still on at the Warner Village. It wouldn't have occurred to him that it might not be and he went past it on the bus going up the Finchley Road, not with the purpose of checking but to practise getting on to the bus and buying a ticket and making sure it was going in the right direction. In a newspaper cinema guide Inez found the times of showings for him. He was comfortable with figures, and he found it easier to hold two fifty, six twenty (the time he had gone with Kim) and eight thirty-five in his head than reading this information would have been. More difficult was to decide when to go. If he chose the first showing it would have to be on a Saturday or Sunday, and one of those days he was sure to be asked to Becky's. The idea of refusing Becky a second time alarmed him, for the result might be that she stopped loving him, and her love was the most important thing in his world.

Eight thirty-five was very late, and strongly present in Will's code of conduct was a rule of the children's home, enforced by Monty, that its occupants had to be in bed by ten thirty. That evening at Inez's he had stayed up until twenty to eleven because he had been enjoying himself so much but he wasn't anxious to repeat this late retirement. Then there was the question of his evening meal. He always had it at seven but if he went at the

time he had gone with Kim he would be in the cinema
at seven. At half past five he wouldn't be hungry enough
and at nine, the time he might get home if the first bus
came and the bus he had to change on to came, it would
be too late. Eight fifteen, which was the time he had
eaten with Kim, had been possible but he was nervous
about going into any of those cafés alone.

His head swam when he confronted the difficulties
and he very much wanted someone else to take this
load off his shoulders. Becky could be that someone
else but to ask her would mean phoning her; receiving calls he could manage but he had never yet made
one. Of course, she would phone him. She would
have to in order to invite him for Saturday or Sunday
and then he would ask her. He would just ask her
which showing to go to and when he should eat.
Maybe she would say, 'You come over here on Sunday
this week, Will, so you can go and see your film on
Saturday afternoon at two fifty.' Instead she might
even say, 'You come over here on Saturday and then
you can go and see your film on Sunday afternoon.'

She might want to come with him on the afternoon
he didn't go to her. That would be lovely, as being with
Becky always was, but there was a difficulty. Once she
too knew about the treasure she might want to help him
look for it and then it wouldn't be a surprise when he
told her about the money and the house. Surprising
Becky and seeing her delight was nearly as important to
Will as the treasure itself.

So many customers came into the shop on Thursday
morning and again in the afternoon that it was after
four when Zeinab had the chance to tell Inez her news.

'I didn't think that woman was ever going to make
up her mind about silver teaspoons, did you? You'd

think they were platinum the way she went on. And talking of platinum, what d'you reckon to my engagement ring? Morton gave it me at lunch. A perfect fit. He says he knows the measurements of my darling little fingers, his words not mine, like they was his own. More like a bunch of bananas, yours are, I said.'

Inez admired the ring in which a solitaire diamond the size of Zeinab's thumbnail was set. 'But aren't you already engaged to Rowley Woodhouse?'

'Sort of. But they don't know each other, don't know the other one exists, there's no risk.'

Inez could barely repress her laughter. 'Are you going to marry them both?'

'Frankly, Inez, and this is between you and I, I'm not planning on marrying no one. D'you know what Rowley said to me, he's very clever. "Sweetheart," he said, "engagement is the modern marriage."'

'Yes, and the law isn't going to punish you if you've got two fiancés. But what's your father going to say if you bring home two different men you're engaged to?'

'I'd never take them home.' Zeinab sounded quite shocked. 'My dad reckons I'm going to marry his cousin's son in Pakistan. I didn't tell you, did I, about this bloke Morton introduced me too last evening? He's called Orville Pereira, nothing to look at, ugly as sin and God knows how old but Morton told me he's making thirty grand a week. A *week*.'

Inez shook her head. Often she didn't know what to make of Zeinab.

'There's Will getting out of Keith Beatty's van. He's been very preoccupied lately, lost in a dream.'

But Zeinab wasn't interested in Will Cobbett. 'I'll wait till that Keith's taken himself off and then I'll just pop round the corner for the evening paper.'

'See if they've found Jacky Miller yet. There was nothing on the one o'clock news.'

While she was gone Inez set about tidying up the shop. Every box and case of silverware they had lay open on tables, the top of the spinet and various plant stands. She was closing the lid of the last one when Freddy Perfect and Ludmila Gogol came in by the street door. Inez hated that. In her own phrase, it made her hackles rise. There was a door at the foot of the stairs for the tenants—why couldn't they use that?

Ludmila was dressed today in an antique floor-length dress of figured pink velvet that hadn't come from Star Antiques but from some emporium in the Portobello Road, as its wearer proceeded to tell her. In the accent of the steppes, or something approximating to it, Ludmila said that though she had paid only fourteen ninety-nine, the dress was worth at least a hundred pounds. She took a cigarette from the handbag she carried and called a reticule, inserted it in a black and silver holder, lit it and blew a perfect smoke ring. Freddy was at his usual pursuit of picking up and examining small artefacts.

'Excuse me, Ludmila,' said Inez, unable to contain herself any longer and torn between the two complaints she had to make. 'I don't allow smoking in here. It's a rule, I'm afraid.'

'Oh, but I am resident. Freddy, now he is different, he is not resident but only my lover, he is not living here.'

'Really? You could have fooled me. And another thing, haven't I seen that cigarette holder somewhere before? In this shop, for instance?'

Zeinab came back but Inez didn't let her arrival stop her. 'I am quite sure I didn't sell it to you, and nor did Zeinab.'

'Definitely not.'

With a continental shrug and a half-smile, Ludmila removed the still-alight cigarette and put it in her mouth. As if by magic it adhered to her lower lip while she talked, bobbing up and down. 'Oh, I am so sorry. Freddy is culprit, Freddy is naughty boy. He is so in love with me, you know, that he want to buy me gifts all the time but he has no money. What would you? I tell you, he borrow this from your shop. Just for a day or two— that is right, Freddy?'

'Didn't hear a word,' said Freddy, who had been totally absorbed in tugging at a chain which varied the levels of light, dim, normal and very bright, obtainable from a brass table lamp. 'Tell me again.'

She did, word for word, smiling ruefully and holding out the cigarette holder to Inez. With a snort, Zeinab snatched it, cleaned the bowl on a tissue and put it on the spinet top alongside an egg which was a Fabergé copy and a pair of minute ballet shoes. 'They've identified that Nottingham girl,' she said to Inez. 'That headline's a disgrace, don't you reckon? They don't care what they put in the paper.'

"Waste Dump Girl was in Vice Trade," Inez read. 'It does seem a bit hard on the people close to her. Her name was Gaynor Ray and the place they found her was a stone's throw from where she lived with her boyfriend.'

'Depends how far you can throw a stone. Rowley was the Greater London champion of putting the shot a couple of years back. He could throw it half a mile.'

'There's a lot here about what her mother said. She doesn't seem to have had a father. And—oh, they're tying this one in with the Rottweiler's murders.'

'Absolutely.' Zeinab appeared to have read the whole story on her way back from the newsagent's. 'She was garrotted and that's not what you'd call a common sort of murder, is it? Her bag was beside her under all that muck and a carrier bag she must have been carrying with food in it. Yuck, it makes you feel like throwing up.'

'I wonder what he took. I mean, what was the small object?'

'If he was doing that then. Mind you, I reckon he was. I reckon he lived in Nottingham and probably killed a lot of girls, only they haven't found them yet. They'll all come to light. There was a man in Russia killed more than fifty people. I saw that in a book somewhere.'

'In Russia are many terrible things,' said Ludmila, accepting a star fruit from the packet Freddy held out to her, presumably in lieu of the cigarette, which Inez had stubbed out when it was left for a moment on a Wedgwood ashtray. 'All things that happen in Russia bigger and worse than all other places. Me, I know, I am born in Omsk.'

Last time Russia had been mentioned in conversation she had named Kharkov as her birthplace. Still, Inez didn't expect anything but fantasies from Ludmila. Fleetingly, she thought of Jeremy Quick, but produced one of the formulas she used to Freddy in the mornings. 'And now, if you'll excuse us, we have to get on.'

Taking at least five minutes about it, the two of them drifted to the interior door. Impatiently, Inez watched them go. 'I wonder how many other unconsidered trifles she's picked up,' she said. 'I'm sure it wasn't Freddy.'

'You want to chain everything down when she's around. It says here that poor girl has been dead at least a year. She looks nice in that picture, quite attractive, not much like that when they found her, I bet.'

'Don't,' said Inez.

Babysitting was something Mrs Sharif would never have considered doing if it hadn't been for a television set

even larger and more versatile than her own, the stack
of videos, the Marks and Spencer's Chicken Tikka in the
fridge and the Godiva chocolates on the table. All these
goodies made waddling the two hundred yards from her
home to Dame Shirley Porter House a pleasure rather
than a chore—or at any rate a bearable means to an epi-
curean end. She often dropped in during the afternoon
as well and settled down for a chat with Algy over one
of the creamy, grated-chocolate-topped cappuccinos he
made her.

Reem Sharif had never been married. The 'Mrs' was
a courtesy title she had awarded herself after the fashion
once established by unmarried cooks in the houses of
the gentry. In her own phrase, Zeinab's father had 'buggered off' as soon as she told him of her pregnancy. He
had been a very good-looking white man called Ron
Bocking but always referred to by her as 'the Rat' or 'the
scum of the earth'. Reem had also been good-looking
and now at only forty-five would have been so still but
for the mountains of fat which had engulfed her. Much
of this was due to her having made up her mind, as soon
as Zeinab went to school, that insofar as she could, she
was never again going to do anything she didn't like and
as much as possible of what she did.

So she had given up work in the bra and pants-
producing sweatshop in Brentford and psyched herself
into developing a bad back. Doctors can do little about
back pain, either in diagnosis or amelioration. They
can't prove you have it or don't have it, but they assume
you do if you stoop and groan. Reem was a good actress.
She stooped and groaned with the best of them, and
occasionally managed an artistic flinch and gasp when a
twinge grabbed her. Incapacity Benefit amounts to
much more than ordinary Social Security Benefit and
Reem, who had nothing else to do but study the forms

and concentrate her mind on the pamphlets, secured for
herself every possible extra. Her local authority paid the
rent of her flat and had agreed to supply her with a
wheelchair. At present, alone with Carmel and Bryn,
Zeinab and Algy having gone to the pictures, she was
giving this offer her serious consideration and wondering if she wouldn't prefer a car. She couldn't drive but she
could learn . . .

'Can we have a video, Nanna?' said Carmel. 'We'd
like *Basic Instinct*.'

Their father banned it along with *Reservoir Dogs* and
The Shawshank Redemption but Reem didn't care. She
always let the children do exactly as they liked so long
as they didn't bother her and they loved her for it.

'Bryn have a choc.' The little boy did his baby talk
act whenever he wanted anything. 'White choc, not
brown,' he shouted as the wrong kind was produced.

'Go on, help yourself, and shut up,' said Reem, pushing the box towards him. It was time for her curry, anyway. Many years had passed since she had cooked
anything. She lived on Indian takeaway from the
Banyan Tree, eating the previous evening's tikka or
korma leftovers for breakfast, followed by a Mars bar, a
meal she took when she got up at midday. A strict
upbringing by devout Moslem parents in Walworth—
they threw her out when she was pregnant—had left her
with only one moral principle, an antipathy to alcohol,
and she was fond of saying in a virtuous tone that she
never drank anything stronger than Coke, the non-diet
kind. There were about ten cans of it in the drinks and
ice department of Zeinab's enormous American fridge.
She took a can and lit one of her own king-size cigarettes, Zeinab and Algy having unaccountably omitted
to provide any. The Chicken Tikka heated in the
micowave, she tipped it on to a plate and carried it back

to her chair. Alternately taking a mouthful of food and a draw on her cigarette, she watched impassively Carmel's highly unsuitable video choice. Bryn, his face coated in chocolate, white and brown, climbed on to her big soft lap and laid his cheek lovingly against her neck. Giving him an absent-minded one-armed hug, Reem took a swig of her Coke.

Zeinab and Algy seated themselves in the Warner Village cinema. Thanks to Algy, as timely as Zeinab was unpunctual, they were early for the six twenty showing.

'This is a stupid time to go to a film,' grumbled Zeinab. 'I don't know why we couldn't go at eight thirty-five.'

'Because your mum wouldn't come at eight, that's why. She says she don't fancy not getting home till midnight, she needs her sleep.'

'She what? She hasn't done a bloody stroke since nineteen eighty-one.'

'The Rottweiler's at large, she says, and if you live on an estate you're a prime target. Specially at night. I'm only telling you what she says.'

Never ill-humoured for long, Zeinab started laughing. 'He won't go for her, will he? They're all young girls he gets his eye on. Or youngish. Who does she think she's kidding?'

'You know your mum.' Algy opened the drum of popcorn and passed it to her. 'You haven't seen any TV today, have you? And you never got the *Standard*? Only there's a bit about Gaynor Ray's boyfriend and what he's said.'

'That's the Nottingham one?'

'Right. I reckon the police must have told him to, because he's been right through their bedroom and he's seen what was in her bag on that rubbish heap, and he says there's something missing Gaynor always carried.

Couldn't separate her from it. he said it was her lucky mas-
cot and her guardian angel, but they can't find it now.'

'What is it?'

'A silver cross. It was supposed to go on a chain
round her neck but she never wore it for work, just carried it with her. It'd put the clients off, wouldn't it, a lap
dancer wearing a cross?'

'I reckon.'

'He gave this interview. I mean, this chap the
boyfriend did, and he said all that—well, not the bit
about putting the clients off—he said the cross would
have been in Gaynor's bag, bound to be. It wasn't no use
searching the bedroom on account of it wouldn't be
there, not unless Gaynor was.'

'Poor thing,' said Zeinab. She was looking around
her to see how the cinema was filling up. Of course, no
one in their right mind would come at this time unless
they had to, like her and Algy. She was supposed to be
having dinner with Morton Phibling in an hour's time
and then going on with him to Ronnie Scott's, but she
was going to stand him up. A good-hearted girl, she
could see what a bitch it was for poor Algy to be left
alone with the kids night after night. She owed it to
him. She'd tell Morton her dad had stopped her going
out, locked her in her room, something like that. Not
for the first time, she congratulated herself on inventing
such a harsh father. It solved every problem that came
up in the business of juggling Suzanne with Zeinab. A
stroke of genius, really. Suddenly, turning her head to
the left, she spotted someone she knew.

'Look, Alge, there's that Will I told you about, the
one that lives upstairs at Inez's. He's all on his own.
Shame really.'

Algy turned round. 'Where? That one that looks like
David Beckham?'

'Does he? I hadn't noticed.'

'You hadn't? I'd have thought any girl would fancy him.'

The lights began to dim. Zeinab took Algy's hand. 'Oh, come on, love, you know I'm a one-man woman. You're the only bloke for me.'

The only thing about the film that much interested her was the cache of jewels stolen from Tiffany's. The emeralds were especially beautiful and a lovely bluish-green, a colour that suited her. She might mention them to Morton when he was sympathising with her over her cruel father's locking her up. She wouldn't mind a change from diamonds and sapphires. Like many people, she was unable to follow much of the gangsters' machinations in the film and the purport of the talk between men who spoke with a clipped accent in noisy underground bars eluded her. Of course, she was sorry when Russell Crowe got shot, as any woman might be, and she couldn't care less about the fate of Sandra Bullock stranded on a beach in Brazil.

Leaving, they encountered Will. Zeinab made the introductions and Will muttered about being pleased to meet them and blushed dark red. Now he had been reassured about Will's place or lack of a place in Zeinab's life, she was half afraid the sociable Algy would ask him to join them for a meal, but thanks to her poking her stiletto heel into his ankle he didn't.

'We don't have to be back till ten,' he said, 'or even half-ten if I walk your mum home.'

Will waited on the opposite side of the Finchley Road for his bus. He had done what he had set out to do, seen the film again, got a good picture in his head of that backyard and proved to himself that the front of the house or shop or whatever it was, was never shown. He had studied the position of the place where the jewellery was buried and the kind of bag, a black leather briefcase, it was in, and noted once more the hanging sign on a lamp post, saying this was Sixth Avenue. But he wasn't as happy as he usually was on a Friday evening. Becky hadn't phoned.

That was why he had decided, only that morning, to go to the cinema on Friday rather than Saturday or Sunday. Becky might still phone to make an arrangement for one of those days. She might even be phoning now while he was out. It was something he dreaded. He fretted for the bus to come so that he might soon be home to take her call.

Will's nature, or his mind, was such that unlike people without his difficulties, he was unable to distract himself from worrying by concentrating on something else. The treasure and its whereabouts might have served this purpose but, for the time being, he had almost forgotten the treasure and could think only of Becky and the phone call which hadn't come. She might be ill, something might have happened to her. Without much imagination, he couldn't conceive of what, and his mind was filled only with a drifting foggy unhappiness. He felt bereft and bewildered, like a pet whose owner has gone away and left it with food and water but without companionship.

The search for Jacky Miller had disappeared from Sunday's newspapers, having been driven away by the more exciting disclosures about Gaynor Ray, her way of life, her job and the men she had known. One story in a tabloid described her as 'working in the sex industry', another, in a broadsheet, carried interviews with three men who had been intimately associated with her. She had gone missing not one but two years ago. Her boyfriend expressed himself as 'devastated' by the revelations. 'In spite of the kind of work she did,' he said, 'I had no idea I was not the only man in her life. We were going to get engaged at Easter and were already planning our wedding. Hearing about these others she was seeing has completely devastated me.' From what they had discovered, journalists implied that Gaynor was easy prey for the Rottweiler—in spite of the Rottweiler Society's protest and the absence of bites, the name was by now universally used—as she would accept any lift offered her by a man.

These stories, breaking on the Friday evening and the Saturday, had provoked Caroline Dansk's stepfather into an angry defence of her moral character. Anyone who suggested Caroline had ever picked up a man or accepted a lift from a man would be guilty of casting a slur on a girl who had never even had a boyfriend. It was well-known that when she encountered the Rottweiler in Boston Place she was on her way to visit a girlfriend and the girlfriend's parents who had 'a beautiful home' in Glentworth Street. His wife, Caroline's mother, had been prostrate ever since the discovery of her body and he really feared that aspersions of this kind might kill her. The parents of Nicole Nimms and Rebecca Milsom had confided nothing to the press.

Inez, reading all this, began to feel rather ashamed of herself for buying the tabloid and reading it in addition to the newspaper which had been delivered. She put both into the recycling bin and sat down to consider how to spend her day. The house was utterly silent, though it was by now almost noon. Ludmila and Freddy were very likely still in bed. They would get up around one and go out, as they always did, to eat the huge lunch of roast beef, Yorkshire pudding, roast potatoes and two veg provided by Crocker's Folly up in Aberdeen Place. Jeremy Quick might be up and moving about but he was always quiet as a mouse without a mouse's proclivities for scratching and burrowing. It looked like a fine morning, the sky a milky blue with tiny white clouds like yogurt curds, the sun shining mildly, yesterday's wind entirely gone. In the garden the old pear tree was coming into blossom. Jeremy was probably having coffee out in his roof garden or even an early lunch. This afternoon he would be bound to pay his twice-weekly visit to the hospital where Mrs Gildon languished and Belinda spent four nights out of the seven.

As for Will, he no doubt had gone over to Gloucester Avenue to spend the day with Becky. She hadn't heard him go out but she slept in the back from where footfalls on the stairs weren't always audible. Becky was so kind and thoughtful, she thought, far beyond the call of aunty duty. Will must think of her as his mother . . . Listening again, she heard only the silence, then a car pass along Star Street, the distant moan of a fire engine siren. Feelings she usually tried to suppress, a sense of isolation, of utter solitariness in a world where everyone else had someone, enclosed her in walls of glass. Last evening she had gone for a walk but the combination of a bitter wind and the equally bitter sight of so many couples inside lighted windows had driven her home where, as her never-failing remedy, she had put on a *Forsyth* video. It had done its job, but as sometimes happened, only up to a point. She had gone to bed longing not for the ghost on tape, the shadowy entity which looked like and spoke like Martin, but the real man with a real man's arms and lips and voice.

But she might as well play another now. How about *Forsyth and the Miracle*? It was her favourite because in it Forsyth's young wife died and he mourned her, just as she, Inez, mourned him, and in a melancholy way she reflected that if it had been she and not he who had died—something she occasionally wished had happened—he would have been as grief-stricken as was the character he played.

She kept the set turned down low so as not to disturb anyone, which was why after about twenty minutes she heard feet descending the stairs. Because they halted outside her door she stopped the tape. Whoever it was must be standing there, just waiting outside. She listened, heard silence, and because she knew it must be an occupant of the house, she opened the door. It was Will.

'Is something wrong, Will?'

He had been crying. She could tell from the puffiness of his eyes, though the red flush on his face was probably due to her having caught him when he had been hesitating about ringing her bell.

Instead of replying, he said in a faltering voice, 'I'm going out, that's all, I'm going out,' and he threw open the street door, slamming it behind him, most unusual behaviour for Will.

Inez didn't know what to make of it. But she told herself he was very likely only late in leaving for Becky's or had omitted to buy something for her—it would be that sort of thing. She went back to *Forsyth and the Miracle*, to her favourite part, the bit where Forsyth wakes in the morning and briefly thinks he has only dreamt his wife's death. How many times had she too felt that about Martin!

Running along Star Street towards the Edgware Road, Will heard the crash of the door behind him and began to worry that it would get him in trouble with Inez. He didn't want that. After Becky, he most wanted Inez's affection and, although he couldn't have articulated this, Inez's protection. Anxiety slowed his step but he didn't go back. Outside the door of her flat he had been bracing himself to ask her to phone Becky for him. He simply didn't know how to do this himself. But Inez would do it and ask Becky why she hadn't phoned him, where had she been, what was wrong. In the event, he had lost his nerve and he was going to her instead, walking to Gloucester Avenue, though it was a long way. The treasure of Sixth Avenue had disappeared from his mind as if it had never had its exciting place there.

Reaching the house where Becky's flat was on the first floor took him an hour. By now it was nearly a quarter to two, he had had very little breakfast and no lunch. His appetite, that trusty mainstay of his existence, was gone. It would come back when he found Becky and was there in her flat with her. But no one answered when he rang her bell, the second one up from the bottom of the row, marked with her name on a red tag. He rang and rang. She couldn't be out but she was. His imagination was insufficient to form ideas or pictures of where she might be, it was enough that she wasn't where she should be, the place in which he believed she always was. The prisoner of love, she must always be in those rooms thinking of him, waiting for *him*.

There was only one thing to do. Stay there till she came. Sit on the steps that led up to the front door and wait for her. If there had been a seat in the front garden of the house he would have sat on that but there were only the steps. He sat there in the spring sunshine. A woman from the bottom flat came back from her lunch date, passed him and said an uncertain 'Good afternoon'; a couple who lived on the top stepped over him because he had fallen into a doze; a visitor for tea to number three gave him a wide berth, thinking he was a rough sleeper.

By the time Becky came home, hand in hand with James, Will was fast asleep.

CHAPTER 7

For the first time in years Becky was taking a day off work. She had phoned and said she wouldn't be in. As a partner in the firm she didn't have to give a reason or make excuses. She felt genuinely ill, weak, tired and shaky, due no doubt to not sleeping at all the previous night. Or, rather, she had finally dropped off at about four and been wakened by someone's car alarm at five. She would have preferred never again to think about the previous afternooon and evening but she couldn't help herself, it had been so horrible, was horrible still.

They had had a nice time, she and James, at James's sister's buffet lunch party to which he had taken her. Rather too much wine but after all, it had been a fine day, they were mostly out in the garden and there were interesting people to talk to. The house was not far, only in a Regent's Park mews, so James had left his car in her street and they had walked there and back through the park. She had forgotten all about Will. If she had thought of him at all it was to tell herself that he was very likely out with Kim somewhere. She must break herself of the habit of inviting him over once a week and now might be the time to start.

Yesterday had begun well. Of course, she saw now how silly she had been when making weekend plans (or not making them) to have imagined James might want to spend the whole of Saturday and Sunday with her as well as Friday evening. It was much too soon for that.

But Friday had been a success and she felt gratified
when he phoned on Saturday morning, before she went
on her shopping jaunt, and asked her to come with him
to his sister's on the following day.

Walking back with him after the party she was
happy. And she came close to saying so. 'I *am* having a
nice day.'

'Good,' he said, 'so am I,' and he smiled and took
her hand. They walked along holding hands, up over
the bridge and into Princess Road. At five in the afternoon the sun was warmer and brighter than it had been
all day.

If she had seen Will sooner she might have found a
way of stopping James coming in with her or at any rate
have prepared him. But she hadn't even looked in the
direction of the front entrance until they were almost at
the steps. Even then, it was James saying, 'Do you get
much of this sort of thing?' plainly meaning, do you get
many of these rough sleepers taking a nap on your
doorstep, that made her look down at the sleeping man.
She felt the hot wash of a blush flood her face and neck.

At that moment Will woke up. He was always clean,
or he always started off clean, but he had been lying in
the sun on a dirty step and he had been crying. His face
was tear-stained, pale runnels through a dusty layer, his
hands were black and his hair stood up in spikes.

She said, 'Oh, Will . . .'

'I waited for you to come back,' he said, apparently
unaware of James. 'I waited and waited.'

But James wasn't unaware of him. 'Do you know this
man, Becky?'

Prevarication was useless now. 'He's my nephew.'

'Oh. I see.' He said it in the tone people use when
they don't see at all and don't want to. 'Look, it might
be best if I left you with him. Better not be around.'

Plainly, he thought Will was drunk or on something, very likely took him for an addict desperate for his next fix. She didn't watch him go but she heard the car start up. 'Come on in, Will,' she said.

He didn't explain why he was there. He didn't need to. She understood perfectly. She hadn't asked him over and he had pined and fretted until at last he could stand it no longer. A broad smile transformed his dirty face and he chatted away as they climbed the stair-case—wasn't it a lovely day? Had she seen all the flow-ers that were coming out? It was really spring now, wasn't it? She sent him to wash his hands and face and comb his hair while she looked in the fridge for what she could possibly have to cook for him. He had said wistfully as she let them into the flat that he had had nothing to eat all day.

There were eggs and a piece of bread. In the freezer she found frozen chips that were past their sell-by date but you couldn't come to much harm from old chips, could you? She fried two of the eggs, put the chips in the microwave, toasted the bread because it was stale, and while she was doing so poured herself a stiff gin and tonic. She had already had nearly a whole bottle of wine but she needed something to calm her down and stun her feelings. Will ate voraciously, pouring tomato ketchup over everything and buttering slice after slice of toast. He drank Coke and she made tea for them both. She couldn't have eaten to save her life. His training in the children's home stopped him turning on the televi-sion without first asking her but she anticipated the request. Over the years she had learned to read the shift-ing expression that crossed his face.

The serial for the under-twelves and then the banal game show satisfied him completely—or being in her flat and her company while he watched them satisfied him—and he laughed with glee, darting at her happy smiling glances. There were to be no recriminations, no inquests, that wasn't Will's way. That she had been absent when she should have been present, that she should have failed to invite him, that she had omitted to phone, all that was forgotten in the entirely contented *now*. He watched television, he sat with his head against the cushions, blissfully eating crystallised fruits out of a box someone had given her but which, for reasons of staying slim, she had never eaten.

All the time he was there she had stopped herself thinking. Not only about what had happened but what its consequences must be. I must not think, she told herself over and over, I must not think, not now. Television had become unsuitable for him, with only hymn singing on offer or ancient civilisations or a murder drama. The news was a slightly lesser evil than this last. She switched to it tentatively and saw the screen filled with an enlarged photograph of Gaynor Ray wearing her amulet, the silver cross lying against her soft young skin, a rather provocative smile on her lips. Then the pendant alone appeared, rather blurred because it had been so much magnified, a cross that had at first looked plain but now revealed a chasing of leaves on the surface of the silver. The photograph had been taken a few weeks before she disappeared. There was nothing about Jacky Miller. That neither she nor her body could be found was no longer news.

Becky drove Will home to Star Street. She knew she shouldn't drive, she had had far too much to drink, but at this point she was so desperate not to hurt him again that she couldn't bring herself to send him away to make the awkward journey by two buses or on foot. It was after eleven, long past his bedtime, but he was too happy to notice.

'How is Kim?' she asked him, reminded as she passed near to Abbey Road.

He looked at her, puzzled, then said, 'She's Keith's sister. She's all right.'

'Have you seen her again?'

'We went to see a film,' was all he said.

She went to the door with him and stood in the little hall while he climbed the stairs and she was so touched by the way he went on tiptoe so as not to disturb anyone, turning round once to lay his finger on his lips, that she felt the tears start in her eyes. But when he was gone and the door closed, if she had cried it would have been for herself. She didn't cry, she let those suppressed thoughts take shape.

Back in Gloucester Avenue it was useless to attempt to sleep. To be in the dark, lying in bed alone and staring at an invisible ceiling would be the worst thing. Better sit here in a soft chair with a cup of tea. It was always better to be miserable in comfort. Obviously, she had lost James. He had gone and he wouldn't come back. She couldn't blame him. Better end a possible relationship at such an early stage than go deeper into it and find oneself involved with a woman closely associated with a drug-addicted layabout. She understood, but if only he had been a little more forbearing, a little patient, willing to wait and see . . . Still, it was too late for that now. Her first thought should have been for Will and what he must have gone through. She must never never let that happen again. As a matter of course he must be invited here for one day in every weekend.

But even as she thought that, she was aware of an unfamiliar sensation rising in her, rising, it seemed, up through her body, making her convulse and shiver. It was a little while before she recognised it for what it was: panic. The meaning of what she had been thinking about hit her with full force. It wouldn't stop, this inviting of Will over once a week, this sacrifice of one day a week to someone she could no more have a real conversation with than she could with a child of ten, it would go on till he was middle-aged and she was old, till she was dead. She would never be able to ease herself out of it, slacken the frequency. Look what happened when she dared to try. Like a faithful dog, he slept on her doorstep, he broke his heart, he starved from misery.

One possible—more than possible—lover had been frightened away. Looking back, she saw that this had happened to at least one other since Will left the house he shared with the other former inmates of the home. She hadn't realised at the time why this man had unaccountably stopped seeing her, stopped phoning, but she did now. Wouldn't any successor of James's also be scared off, perhaps further on in the relationship certainly, but sooner or later, by this unwelcome presence, this spectre at the feast, dominating her, clinging to her, uttering banalities about the weather and food and spring flowers? She hated herself for thinking this but at the same time she knew it was true. In a way you could say that while Will was in it, and he would always be in it, there could never be anyone else, man or woman, friend or lover, in her life. All unknowing, he had made a cage, put her in it and thrown away the key.

So when she finally got up after her almost sleepless night she had known she couldn't face work that day. Not that there was anything she could do at home. Nothing was to be done. While she lived and Will did, the situation would endure for ever. Very obviously, he hadn't given Kim Beatty another thought, he much preferred her, Becky. And she must forget James and, come

to that, any other men, it was all pointless. Panic had
given way to a dull despair.

Will also had been subject to an exchange of mindsets.
His hopeless misery forgotten, memories of the treasure
surfaced. Now to find out where it was, or rather, where
Sixth Avenue was. He knew about America, more or less
where it appeared on a world map, that films and television shows came from there, and the people spoke differently from the way he and Becky and Inez and Keith
did. The actors in *The Treasure of Sixth Avenue* were
American, you could hear it in their voices. Did that
mean the street was in America? Those sirens had
sounded like London but he didn't know. He could ask
Becky but she would ask why and again he came back
to the question of the surprise. If Becky, who was clever,
knew there was a treasure buried in the back garden of
a house and he was looking for it, she would guess a lot
of things and there would be no surprise. In Abbey
Road, applying a coat of gloss paint in a shade called
Cultured Pearl to the dining room window frames, he
asked Keith, 'Where's Sixth Avenue?'

Although Keith had probably heard of the film, he
appeared not to make the connection. 'Don't know, mate.
I can tell you where Fifth Avenue is. It's in New York.'

'This is *Sixth* Avenue,' said Will, disappointed.

They went back to their work, Will to his painting,
Keith to french-polishing the cupboard doors. Ten
minutes went by and Keith said, 'You seen any more of
my sister, have you?'

Why did everyone keep asking him about Keith's sister? 'No, I haven't.'

What was he going to do now? The kind of simple
research most people take for granted, looking up
names in the phone book, finding out entertainment

showing times, even checking out sales outlets and prices on the Internet, all this was beyond Will.

Inez might help him, but something indefinable made him shy of asking her. Not quite indefinable; he had a vague notion that she might be cross with him. She hadn't exactly been cross that time when he'd asked her about the streets in the film her husband was in, but she'd shushed him and told him not to talk. If he did it again she might not be so nice.

Keith finished making figures of eight in french polish on the last door, put down the cotton wool and rag pad, and said, 'We can wrap this up today, mate. You nearly done?'

Nodding, Will indicated the last bit of frame to be painted. It would take no more than half an hour. 'Early home, then,' said Keith. 'Take the afternoon off, right? Tomorrow we're starting bright and early on them flats down Ladbroke Grove.'

With a sigh, Will said, 'All right.'

'I'll pick you up in Star Street eight sharp, OK?'

He couldn't ask Becky and he couldn't ask Inez. Keith didn't know. Will found Ludmila and Freddy overpowering. He never spoke to them unless they spoke to him first. As for Mr Quick, Will was afraid of him. Something about him made him think of the doctor who had once come to talk to him and take his blood to find out something, the tone of his voice perhaps, or his eyes which were a mauvish-grey, the colour, Will thought, of dying tulips. They weren't like human eyes but not like animal eyes either and when he encountered Mr Quick on the stairs, as occasionally happened, he tried not to look at him.

Monty might know where Sixth Avenue was but now it was some weeks since Monty had been in touch to ask him out for a drink. Although Will had his phone number, he wouldn't call him, he never phoned anyone. Reaching home so much earlier than usual, he plucked up his courage to go into the newsagent's in the Edgware Road and ask him. First he bought a Mars bar and then he asked, 'Where's Sixth Avenue?'

'Sixth Avenue?' The man had come to London from Turkey a few years before, married a Lebanese woman and lived in a flat on the Lilestone Estate. Apart from Antalya, the only part of the world he knew well was that which lay between here and Baker Street. 'I don't know.' He took a copy of the *London Street Atlas* from a shelf and handed it to Will. 'You look,' he said.

But Will didn't know where to look or even how to look. He turned pages hopelessly, handed the book back. By this time the Turkish man was selling *Vogue* and the *Evening Standard* to another customer. Will meant to go back to his flat by the street door at the foot of the stairs but he had to pass the window of the shop and as he did so, Inez waved to him and smiled. So, hesitantly, he went in. Zeinab was standing by the till holding an enormous bunch of flowers, wrapped in pink paper and tied with pink ribbon.

'You're finished early, Will,' said Inez.

Will nodded, saying nothing, though remarks of that sort pleased and comforted him. They were true and he could understand them.

Zeinab read aloud the card attached to the flowers. '"To the only woman in the world for me, Happy Birthday, sweetheart, with all my love for ever and ever, Rowley."'

'I didn't know it was your birthday,' said Inez.

'It's not but he thinks it is,' said Zeinab, giving another clue to character analysts like Inez that she might not always be too extravagant with the truth. 'What am I going to do with them? I mean, give me a break. I can just picture my dad's face if I take this lot home.' Without asking him, she suddenly thrust the tulips, anemones, narcissi, hyacinths and multicoloured freesias into Will's arms. 'There you are, give them to your girlfriend.'

She inhabited a world in which it was unthinkable that any young person could be without a partner. Will stammered out his thanks and hurried to the door at the back before she could change her mind. Flowers he loved but no one ever before had given him any. He spent the next hour happily arranging them in every vessel he could find that would hold water.

At five the white van with the notice about not washing reappeared in Star Street. A man got out of the cab and ran up the street before Inez could catch more than a glimpse of him. Traffic wardens were always up and down here but they never seemed to be around when that van was parked outside. A turquoise-coloured Jaguar pulled up behind it.

'Here's Morton,' said Zeinab. 'He's early. I said half past. Men!'

For the past half-hour she had been sitting on a mahogany and pink velvet stool in front of the mirror she called hers, repairing the ravages of the day, brushing her hair, remaking up her face with such sophisticated utensils as lip pencils, eyebrow gel and a lash curler, and painting her fingernails iridescent purple. She kicked off the sandals she wore for work, slipped her feet into pumps with four-inch heels, tripped out and over to the car. Seconds later, her head round the door, she said to Inez, 'Can I go? Morton's got champagne waiting on ice and he wants to talk about a date for our wedding.'

'Off with you,' said Inez, laughing. 'How you'll ever get out of this one I don't know.'

She noticed that on the hand which held the door ajar Zeinab had changed Rowley's engagement ring for Morton Phibling's fingernail-sized rock. You had to laugh. Alone, she waited till six and then she closed and locked the street door. Customers had been in and out most of the day but no one had bought anything since eleven in the morning. Just as she had turned the hanging sign to 'closed' she had the satisfaction of seeing Ludmila and Freddy cross the street, look at the sign and confer, while Freddy tried in vain to turn the door handle. They gave up, Ludmila burrowed in her red velvet shoulder bag, found her key and let them in by the tenants' street door.

The shop was looking uncared-for and frowsty, Inez thought, in spite of Zeinab's daily efforts with the feather duster. She found clean cloths and spray polish, and set to work. There must be hundreds, if not thousands, of small objects, bric-a-brac, inside these four walls, and each of them seemed to draw dust as if it were iron filings and they magnets. She worked methodically, first lifting every little vase and clock and wineglass and picture frame on to a tray before she dusted the surface where it had stood, then replacing everything and starting on the next table or plant stand or cabinet.

It was strange, as she always thought when she performed this task, how many tiny objects came to light that she couldn't recall ever having seen before. She must have seen them because nothing came into the shop without her knowing, and everything was numbered and catalogued. Sure enough, there was a number on a small label on the underside of this quite unfamiliar cut-glass scent bottle and another on this Egyptian cat with rings in its ears, but she could remember nothing of their provenance nor their previous owner.

The worst bit she always left till last. Perhaps she should think about rearranging things in this dark corner, now guarded by the jaguar, where the plaster statue of the goddess beside it excluded most of the light. On the round table behind them must be at least fifty plates and cups and silver spoons and little enamel boxes and pieces of glass fruit and brooches and Victorian hatpins. Patiently, she began lifting them one by one on to her tray.

It was then that she saw it, a silver cross on a broken chain, the cross itself chased with a tiny design of leaves. On the television news the night before she had seen that cross, hugely magnified and filling the screen. She stood back, her hand up to her mouth. It couldn't be. Not Gaynor Ray's, not this one. There must be hundreds of such crosses . . .

She turned it over, looking for the assay mark that would prove it was silver. It was there, on the underside of the cross, but the label with the catalogue number was not. Was it possible that it had found its way here quite legitimately without being entered in the catalogue? If Zeinab had bought it for the shop perhaps, but that hardly ever happened and, anyway, Zeinab was meticulous enough except in matters of punctuality. Inez had no recollection of ever having seen the cross before. She abandoned her cleaning and took the catalogues, three heavy volumes of them, out of the drawer where they were kept. Three hours later, having forgotten all about a drink or eating or watching a video, she had been through each volume with great care from start to finish.

The silver cross wasn't there. The nearest thing to it was of gold on a black velvet ribbon she remembered buying at least two years before. The silver cross which might be Gaynor Ray's, which surely was, appeared nowhere in the lists. Inez, who had been holding the cross and broken chain in her hand, dropped it when she realised this was very likely the murder weapon.

CHAPTER 8

Unable to sleep much, Inez got up early and was downstairs in the shop before eight. Now, in April, it was broad daylight. She saw Keith Beatty's van arrive and heard him give a blast on his horn. They could have heard it at Paddington Station, it was so loud. There was no need to make that noise at all as Will was always ready, and before the final reverberations had died away, was out in the street opening the passenger door. Inez sighed and once more told herself she must get out of the habit of sighing.

The night before, she had touched the silver cross once before thinking that she shouldn't touch it at all, and after that had picked it up by its chain. But if the chain had been used for the purpose she could hardly bear to think about, should she be touching it at all? When Martin (or Forsyth) found a piece of evidence of this sort he always slipped it inside a sterile bag for forensic examination. Inez had gone up to her kitchen and torn a plastic bag off a new roll. The cross inside the bag had spent the night with her, on her bedside table. Though not usually paranoid, she had had the unpleasant idea, now it had been shown on television, that whoever had put the cross there might come back to the shop in the small hours to retrieve it.

She had brought it downstairs with her. In half an hour or so she would phone the police and ask for Inspector Crippen. Should she search the rest of the place, go over the area, nearly a third of the shop space, she hadn't touched last evening? In case she found a silver cigarette lighter with Nicole Nimms's initials in garnets, a black and gilt keyring with an onyx Scottie dog suspended from it and a gold fob watch? No, let the police do that. Inez was thinking about the implications of what she had found and where she had found it, that the Rottweiler or some accomplice of his, must have been inside Star Antiques, when a tap on the interior door announced the arrival of Jeremy Quick for his cup of tea. Inez went quickly to put the kettle on.

He was wearing a new suit. His shirt was snowy white, his tie a plain deep bluish-green.

'How nice you look,' said Inez.

'Well, thank you. I actually bought this suit with my wedding in mind but it looks as if that's a long way off, so I thought I might as well wear it.'

Should she tell him? She badly needed someone to confide in about this, preferably before she called the police. Oh, how she needed Martin! But seeing that was impossible, would Jeremy do? 'How is Mrs Gildon?' she said.

'Much the same. It's very thoughtful of you to ask. Belinda is still staying at the hospital four nights a week out of the seven. I don't get her to myself much.'

He drank his tea while Inez thought again of telling him, then rejected it. There was something else she needed to clear up. 'I suppose she's very attached to her mother?'

'Very,' he said, and Inez thought his voice had grown sad. 'I sometimes think adopted children can be closer to their adoptive parents than natural children, don't you?'

Inez hardly knew why she was so relieved. Belinda's age and her mother's had been teasing at her mind ever since her conversation with Jeremy in her flat. The only explanation for her being the child of a fifty-two-year-old was of course the true one. 'Oh, is Belinda adopted?'

'Yes, didn't I say? Mrs Gildon adopted her when she was two months old. She and her husband had already adopted a boy five years before, but he can't give Belinda much support, he lives in New Zealand.'

Should she tell him? She was sitting at her desk and the bag with the cross in it was in the desk drawer. As she touched the handle Jeremy said, 'I'd better go. I want to be in bright and early, I've got a meeting of top management at nine fifteen.'

Inez went with him to the street door. She felt rather guilty because she had come close to suspecting him of lying—well, of fantasising, reinventing his past. Nothing worse than that and yet she felt she had to make it up to him. 'Which nights won't Belinda be at the hospital this week?'

'I'm not sure. Wednesday, Thursday and Sunday probably.'

'Bring her in for a drink on Wednesday if you can?'

'I'll let you know. I hope we can make it.'

Now she had opened it there was no point in locking the street door again. She turned the sign to 'open'. Mr Khoury had come out and was putting down his sunblind. Inez liked to see this just as she liked seeing café tables go out on the pavement—even if she dreaded the sight of the couples sitting at them. It meant summer was on the way. Mr Khoury never waved but dipped his head in a kind of court bow in her direction.

She went back into the shop and phoned the police.

As far as Will could remember, he had never been down here before. Everything was unfamiliar. The children's home had been in Crouch End, in the London

Borough of Haringey, Becky lived in Primrose Hill and
Inez in Paddington. These three locations bounded his
London and he knew no other. It was a departure for
Keith too, whose work was invariably in St John's
Wood, Maida Vale and the environs of the Edgware
Road, though his family home was in the district to
which they were heading. But they turned off long
before they reached Harlesden.

The block of flats in which they were working wasn't
quite in Ladbroke Grove but in a street which turned
out of it. Keith had a parking pass from the Royal
Borough of Kensington and Chelsea, so there was no
need to feed meters or keep moving the van to elude
wardens. The work they were to do, painting living
rooms and bedrooms in three one-bedroom flats, was
for a landlord, not an owner-occupier, and Keith had
been instructed, with a wink and a nudge, to keep the
costs down and not do too painstaking a job.

'So I said to him,' said Keith as they toiled up the
stairs, carrying their equipment, 'I said to him, "It's not
in my nature not to do the best I can. If you don't like
it," I said, "you'd best look elsewhere for some cowboy to
do the job. Suit yourself," I said. He looked down his
nose a bit but he never said another word. You'd think
they'd have a lift in a place like this, wouldn't you?'

Most of what Keith had said was incomprehensible
to Will. The lift part he understood. 'Right,' he said.

'Greed is what it is. That's what's wrong with folks
today. You look around you, you'll find everybody's on
the make, that's the cause of crime, that's what makes
them all do'—Keith sought for a way to end to his sentence, could only come up lamely with—'the things they
do. Say what you like'—he looked over his shoulder, suddenly nervous on this empty staircase of free speech—
'there was something to be said for the Communists.'

Will had nothing to say for the Communists, so remained silent. They let themselves into the first flat with the landlord's key.

'Smells like it's been shut up for six months,' said Keith. 'Get the windows open, will you?'

Crippen and his sidekick were already there by the time Zeinab arrived. He had brought Zulueta with him. Handling it with gloves on, the detective sergeant was sitting at Inez's desk examining the cross and chain through a magnifying glass.

'What's going on?' said Zeinab, kicking off her stilettos.

'I found that.' Inez pointed at the desk.

'Is it *the* one?' Zeinab looked over Zulueta's shoulder, her cheek close to his hair, treating him to a gust of Jo Malone's Tuberose eau de toilette.

'Looks like it,' said Zulueta.

'Makes you go cold all over seeing it like that. My— er, a friend of mine reckons that chain's what she was garrotted with. Is that right?

Neither officer answered her but Zulueta looked shocked at such appalling indiscretion or possibly at its close proximity to the truth.

'Now, Mrs Ferry.' Crippen perhaps felt that he had lost the control over this small gathering he ought by rights to have. He reasserted himself. 'We shall have to conduct a search of these premises. If you object I shall have no difficulty in obtaining a search warrant.'

Inez stood up. She had had enough. No one had thanked her for informing the police about the cross, all they had done was reproach her for not calling them at nine the previous evening. In her opinion she had been treated at least as the Rottweiler's accessory from the moment the two officers arrived and now she was angry. 'I have no objection at all,' she said coldly. 'I don't know why you assume I'm obstructing you. Nothing could be further from my thoughts.' Their behaviour was a far cry from the courteous way in which Forsyth had handled helpful witnesses. 'If this goes on I shall put in a complaint.'

'And I'll sign it,' said Zeinab, always loyal. 'Treating you like you was a criminal.'

'I'm sorry if I put your back up,' said Crippen, making things worse. 'Give the station a bell, Zulueta, and see if you can get Osnabrook and Jones over here for the search. Now, Mrs Ferry, if you've calmed down a bit, who comes into your shop? I mean, I want to know who could have put that necklace, ornament, whatever, in here.'

'Hundreds,' said Inez.

'At least twenty a day.' Zeinab turned on Crippen the full force of her shining black eyes. 'More some days.'

'You don't make twenty sales a day?' The incredulity in his voice was another insult. 'They don't all buy stuff?'

'Half do,' said Zeinab, not altogether truthfully.

'Then there are your tenants. I've seen some of them in here.' He made it sound as if Inez were running a brothel. The street door swung open and Morton Phibling marched in. 'Is this another tenant or a customer?'

'This is my fiancé.' Having had the forethought to wear the right engagement ring this morning, Zeinab flashed it in Crippen's face. 'Mr Phibling.'

Although Morton looked a lot like the public perception of a gang leader in his blond alpaca coat, with his tussore cravat and Rolex watch, his air of wealth rather impressed Crippen. 'I doubt if we shall need you to help us in our enquiries, sir,' he said.

Morton ignored him. 'What happened to you on Saturday, my rose of Sharon, my lily of the valleys?'

'You may well ask,' said Zeinab. 'My dad wouldn't let me out. You know what he's like. He locked me in my bedroom.'

'And there am I, heartsick and alone, waiting for you at my solitary table in Claridge's, too distressed to eat, too disappointed to do anything more than sip brandy. Are there no telephones in your father's mansion?'

Whatever answer Zeinab might have made to this was cut off by the scream of a police siren. The message sent to Osnabrook and Jones had been distorted in its passage and both were under the impression they were being called to a robbery with violence. Once there and enlightened, they set about searching the shop with Zulueta's help.

'Now the tenants,' said Crippen. 'Just let me have their names, will you?'

'Mr Cobbett in one flat on the second floor and Mrs Gogol in the other and Mr Quick on the top.'

'Then who has the first floor flat?' Crippen asked his question in a very suspicious way as if she were attempting to conceal a felony.

'Well, oddly enough, I do. Or did you imagine I slept on the floor down here?'

They found the fob watch. It too was on a table top in another darkish corner, lying on a green plate in the shape of a cabbage leaf and concealed behind the row of toby jugs. It was by then nearly midday. Crippen wanted to know what time the tenants came home from work and Inez said that since Ludmila and Freddy never went out without passing through the shop, they must be at home.

'Why didn't you say so before, madam?'

'You didn't ask me. Mr Quick should be home by six and Mr Cobbett earlier than that, about half past four probably.'

Inez didn't like telling him about Will, but if she hadn't he would have found out from some other source. Will was vulnerable, he would be frightened of a man like Crippen, he wouldn't know what to say, he wouldn't *understand*. Should she try to explain? Better not, better leave it. She could just imagine the inspector's reaction to hearing someone was—well, what was Will? Autistic? Not really. Mentally defective? Certainly not. The politically incorrect phrase sounded deeply offensive these days. He had a mild chromosomal problem, that was all. Surely Crippen would realise and be gentle . . .

In spite of insisting she wasn't obstructive, she asked them to ring the bell outside for Ludmila, rather than go upstairs by way of the interior door. Osnabrook stayed behind, stubbornly certain that he would find the keyring and the cigarette lighter if he only searched for long enough. Having the police about wasn't good for business, Inez thought, or having a police car parked outside wasn't.

Zeinab had gone out to sit with Morton in his car, where they appeared to be arguing. She came back, flushed and annoyed, and set about repairing her make-up which their heated exchange had brought to meltdown point. 'I should never have mentioned my dad,' she said. 'Now he wants to meet him and ask for my hand in marriage. That's what he says. It's expected of him, he says. Over my dead body, I told him. If he tries that one it's all over between us.'

'It's your own fault,' Inez said robustly. Though sure Osnabrook was out of earshot, she lowered her voice. 'You've presented yourself as an old-fashioned girl, not to say medieval. I mean, you haven't—well—*slept* with him or Rowley, have you?'

For good reason shocked by this suggestion, Zeinab flushed underneath the foundation and cheek gel. 'Absolutely no way.'

'Well, then. Girls do, you know, these days. Certainly when they're engaged. You said yourself, Rowley told you engagement was the modern marriage. I don't suppose he meant wearing a ring and putting a notice in the paper. Don't they pressurise you?'

'What do you think? All the bloody time.'

Inez laughed. Looking aggrieved, Zeinab changed the subject. 'You do realise, don't you, that the Rottweiler must have been in here, *disguised* as a normal customer. Maybe he bought something. He *spoke* to us. And all the time he was sneaking about putting them dead girls' things in your shop.'

'Oh, yes, I realise.' Inez turned the inevitable sigh into a cough.

Crippen and Jones came back at five thirty. By then Will had been home about half an hour. Leaving Zeinab in charge of the shop until they closed at six, Inez went upstairs as soon as she saw them get out of their car. It wouldn't have occurred to Will, who was already watching television, to offer a visitor a cup of tea, so Inez directly asked him. She would make it, she said. He mustn't mind, everything would be fine, but two policemen were coming to talk to him about the girls' murders—did he know what she was talking about? He nodded, though he didn't, not really. She'd be there, she said, feeling like a suspect's solicitor called to the police station, but she'd be in the kitchen at least until they'd been there a few minutes.

Will seemed accepting, not nervous. He turned off the television at Inez's suggestion. As the sound was cut off the outer doorbell rang. Will knew how to handle this. He picked up the entryphone, said hello, then pressed the keypad to unlock the door. The two officers came upstairs and Will said what Inez mouthed at him to say, 'Come in, please.'

'Mr Cobbett?'

Will nodded, though no one ever called him this. Outside in the kitchen, Inez watched the kettle come to the boil.

'Have you ever seen this before?' Jones produced from his pocket the silver cross, still inside its sterile bag.

Will looked at it, shook his head, said, 'I've never seen it.'

'Do you know what it is?'

Among the far more glorious jewellery in *The Treasure of Sixth Avenue* had been a gold cross of much the same size. Will remembered it well, as he did most details of the film. 'It's a cross.'

'It was the property of Gaynor Ray whose body was found in Nottingham last week. You remember that, don't you?'

This was a cue for Inez to declare her presence or let a noise obviously made by human agency declare it. She clattered the teacups and when Crippen said, 'There's someone in there,' came out with an innocent smile.

'Would you like a cup of tea, Mr Crippen?'

'Thank you but no. I was under the impression we were alone.'

'Really? Tea for you, Mr Jones?'

Jones looked at his superior officer, looked away, flung off caution and said he would. Very much, thank you. Inez smiled a smile of triumph. She said airily, 'I'll drink my tea and then I'll go. I'm afraid I can never drink it while it's hot.'

'You're sure you have never seen this before, Mr Cobbett?'

'He told you he hadn't,' said Inez, sustaining her role as supportive lawyer.

'Thank you, Mrs Ferry. Go into Mrs Ferry's shop much, do you?'

'I never go in the shop,' said Will. 'I did one day.' He tried to remember the day of the week but he couldn't. 'One day I did, didn't I, Inez?'

'It was last week and it was the only time you ever did.'

As the words came out, Inez realised their implication, but what else could she have said? Will was always transparently truthful. Perhaps he was too innocent and guileless to know how not to be. He smiled uneasily.

'All right, Mr Cobbett. That will do for now. We shall want to see you again. Come along, Jones, if you can't drink that tea you'll have to leave it.'

Assuring Will that she'd be back, Inez went with them, carrying her cup and saucer. Brutally, Crippen said on the stairs, 'What's with him? A bit weird, isn't he? A bit missing in the upper storey?'

Inez was outraged but she knew she had better not show it. 'Will Cobbett,' she said with dignity, 'is a normal young man who happens to have learning difficulties. He can read but not easily. I doubt if he ever sees a newspaper and I can tell you he never watches news programmes.'

'A bit missing, then, like I said. D'you reckon this chap Quick will be back by now?'

'I can't say.'

'We'll give him a bell, Jones, and if he's not home we'll wait in the car till he is.'

Upstairs again, Inez returned Will's cup and saucer and washed them up along with the rest. It was six o'clock and Will was watching a quiz on Channel Five. He didn't seem upset or in any way discomfited by the police visit. Inez heard Jeremy Quick's footsteps mounting the stairs, then the street doorbell. She returned downstairs just as Crippen and Jones were climbing up.

'All these stairs would be the death of me,' said Crippen.

Jeremy Quick impressed them as being a decent, respectable, eminently normal citizen. No *learning difficulties* there, no wilful refusal to take refuge in laziness and remain ignorant of what galvanised the whole country. Strangely enough, he commanded Crippen's respect because he offered them no refreshment. Anxiety to show hospitality to the police was, in Crippen's eyes, merely an ingratiation method, showing an anxiety to cover something up. And that nonsense about never going in the shop but once, for instance. The Cobbett chap was obviously on close terms with Inez Ferry. Was it reasonable to suppose he'd only once been in there? Once, and that at the crucial time? A few days before the cross was found and just after the unearthing of Gaynor Ray's body and the revelation of what was missing from her bag.

Quick, on the other hand, was perfectly frank about his friendship with the Ferry woman. He dropped in every morning on his way to the station and she made him tea. Probably fancied him. Most women would, Crippen thought, tall, upstanding, well-dressed bloke like him. He didn't at all dislike Quick looking at his watch, saying, 'If you're happy with what I've said, I do have things to do . . .' nor his curt, 'Goodbye. Close the door on your way out.' No sucking up there, no guilt making him want to get in well with the authorities.

'We may want to see you again, sir,' he said. It was routine. He doubted if they would.

When they had left, Jeremy watched their departure from the window until he saw their car disappearing round the corner into Norfolk Square. His sense of smell was acute, more like a dog's than a human being's, he had sometimes joked and now he sniffed with distaste the lemony scent 'with a hint of aromatic herbs' Jones had left behind. A well-known men's cologne, he thought, cheap and nasty. A smallish vodka and tonic in his hand—people said vodka had neither smell nor taste but he knew differently—he walked out on to his roof garden. The clocks had gone forward and it would be an hour before the sun set. Its late afternoon warmth, golden and benign, was bringing into flower his tulips in their green-painted tubs and his yellow jonquils. One of the little bay trees was in golden blossom, for the first time since he had bought it. On the table stood a blue and white pottery jar filled with pink and yellow and lilac freesias, beautiful things with a delectable perfume. He inhaled their scent, closing his eyes.

After a moment or two he opened the drawer under the table, took a sip of his drink, and lifted out from among pens and pencils, computer discs, rolls of adhesive tape and a small calculator, a black and gold keyring with a Scottie dog in onyx suspended from it, a silver cigarette lighter with the initials NN on it in red stones and a pair of silver hoop earrings set with tiny brilliants.

CHAPTER 9

Plans had been made and rejected for the disposal of these small objects. At first Jeremy had thought of dealing with them much as he had with the silver cross and the fob watch, by secreting them among the bric-a-brac in an antique shop. Not in Inez's this time, however, but elsewhere. Such shops abounded in Church Street and also in Westbourne Grove. He would have had no difficulty. But he had no legitimate reason for going into them, apart from as a potential buyer, and he might be remembered by the staff or proprietor, especially if the lighter and the keyring were soon found. The earrings, as yet, were rather a different matter. Another idea, more a joke really, had been to place each one in the immediate vicinity of where the girls had lain. This too was fraught with problems. Boston Place, for instance, where Caroline Dansk had died, was rather exposed to public view, even after dark. The long row of houses on one side of the street and the towering brick wall on the other, without a trees or any cover, made returning there at all perilous.

The lighter he had taken from Nicole Nimms was the second of these objects and he had taken it for a simple reason. He wanted to light a cigarette. These days Jeremy seldom smoked, it was unsuited to his second self, the other image he was then about to create preferring to present himself as fairly abstemious in most respects. Weeks had already gone by without his

smoking but that night, Nicole being his first victim
for a year and the one he thought might never be, he
had felt an overpowering need. So he had found the
cigarettes and the silver lighter, initialled NN, in her
bag and thus it became the precedent for further small
thefts. As a general rule, Jeremy abhorred stealing. It
was the British vice, he often thought, common now all
over the country. You couldn't leave anything out in
Star Street without someone snapping it up while your
back was turned. A disgusting petty crime. His taking
a small artefact from the girls was different, it had
become almost poetic, his sign, his benchmark, the way
to know him.

After Nicole he had taken on this second identity,
deciding to base himself in the district near where he
had killed her. From the first he had felt he was not this
man who killed, this garrotter, this Rottweiler, that was
someone else with another life and another name.
Alexander Gibbons, the conventional man, the *normal*
man, was himself, this killer quite different and beyond
his control. Jeremy Quick should be his name and his
home not a Kensington mews but the top flat over a
shop in Paddington.

If he killed again it would be in that name. Alexander
Gibbons, himself, his mother's son, the computer
expert, the self-made successful man, would be innocent, clean, apart. It was that man who hoped his alter
ego wouldn't kill again, that whatever it was which
drove him to kill was satisfied with two deaths and now
would sleep in peace. Jeremy Quick, holding in his
hands the objects he had taken not from two but from
three out of the five he had killed, knew that nothing
could stop him. He knew it without anguish, accepting
it as horribly inevitable, something he did while he was
this other one living in this other place.

Jeremy Quick was arrrogant in a way Alexander Gibbons never was. He knew he was and was proud to be proud. There was something masterly in the way he read people's minds, as, for instance, the way he had read Inez's over that absurd business of Belinda Gildon's mother's age. As soon as he had said she was eighty-eight, or rather, having said that, as soon as he had said Belinda was thirty-six, he saw in the expression on Inez's face that he had made an error. A woman with any brain at all would notice that kind of thing. It was a stroke of genius anticipating her thoughts and pre-empting suspicious questions by slipping in that oblique reference to Belinda's being an adopted child. Inventing Belinda was necessary to make him seem companioned, a normal man, not one who spent his evenings in brooding solitude. A lesser imagination would have called her something like Jane Venables or Anne Tremayne, novelists' names, and novelette writers at that. It would make an interesting paper, part of a doctoral thesis perhaps, the subject of the names writers chose for their characters. You could group them into categories, from Trollope's onomatopoeic Dr Omicron Pie and Dickens's Sir Leicester Dedlock to the Carruthers and Winstanleys of the spy thriller, their wives invariably named Mary. Also clever was his telling the police he had seen the running man or woman and believed him or her out for an evening work-out. They trusted, even admired, him. He could tell.

He had finished his vodka and wouldn't have a second. Nor would he have a cigarette. It was Alexander who smoked, not he. Everything in Jeremy's life was organised, arranged to the smallest detail. Alexander was more casual. At twenty past seven he would go down and knock on Inez's door. Meanwhile, although tempted to go on thinking of ways, dramatic, significant, shocking, in which to dispose of the keyring and the lighter, he crushed these struggling thoughts, sat down in an armchair between the bay trees and took from the table Kant's *Critique of Pure Reason*, the place where he had left off reading it marked with a green leather and gold leaf bookmark. It was more difficult than Nietzche but also more satisfying. Long ago he had taught himself to concentrate on the matter in hand, whatever that might be, and here it was that his mind and Alexander's met.

At seventeen minues past seven, half an hour after he had put the lights on, he replaced the bookmark but this time ten pages on, took his glass into the kitchen and put it on the draining board, left a single lamp on and another in his small hall, picked up his keys and went downstairs. He rang Inez's bell and after a short delay she opened the door on the chain. Very wise. Usually he simply gave a light tap on her door. She had expected her caller to be another tenant, someone she wouldn't let in but would talk to on the doorstep, and she had left the television on. She took off the chain and, turning her back, quickly switched off the set.

He understood immediately what she had been doing. Nothing but some sort of car chase, gone in a flash, had been visible on the screen, but he saw the cassette sleeve on the shelf, on its spine a photograph of her late husband. Martin Ferry—Jeremy had never watched one of the productions he was in for more than five minutes but he recognised him from newspaper photographs. Inez was blushing. What a fool she must be, pathetic and sentimental, maundering on in this ridiculous way over a man who had been dead three years.

'I'm so sorry to disturb you, Inez,' he said in a voice which was perhaps too compassionate, for she gave him a faintly suspicious glance.

'That's all right, Jeremy. What can I do for you?'

'It's a bit awkward. But I came down intending to explain to you and I will.'

'Would you like a drink?'

He shook his head. 'May I sit down?'

'Of course. You're not coming on Wednesday, is that it? Belinda can't get away?'

He had prepared his story and it was as well he had. Inez was looking annoyed—well, impatient. This was the right moment. 'I'll come straight to the point. Belinda and I have—well, not split up. Not quite that, though doubtless it will come. We've decided we both need'—he must get the absurd phrase right—'some space,' he said. 'We need time to think about our situation. The fact is— I may as well tell you—she says I resent the time she spends with her mother and I couldn't deny it. I said I didn't want to be married to someone who always puts her mother before her husband.'

Inez nodded. 'Her mother is going to live, then?'

'It looks very much like it. Probably for years. What is that going to mean for Belinda and me? I believe in absolute loyalty between marriage partners, don't you?'

'I suppose I do.'

'A woman should put her husband first.'

'And a man his wife, surely?'

'That goes without saying,' said Jeremy.

'Well, I'm sorry. I hope you can find a way to come together again. From what you've said, you seemed so well-suited.'

Inez was won over—or was she? Possibly it was only that she wanted to get back to her maudlin reliving of the past or whatever it was she got out of watching a dead man in a second-rate video. 'Still, if I may come on my own on Wednesday, I'd love that.'

'I don't think so, Jeremy. I'm going to take this

opportunity to go and see my sister. She hasn't been well and I haven't seen her for weeks.'

She didn't smile or even look at him. Perhaps it was only that she was tired or the events of the day had frightened her. He had expected her to want to talk to him about them, discuss the implications, ask him what the police had said and be able to tell him perhaps what they had said to Cobbett and that girl with the Indian name. But she got up out of her chair, the most dismissive gesture that can be made to a guest. He had no choice but to leave and no choice had no place in his life programme. Choosing always played a big part in his existential philosophy. Hadn't he chosen this second identity as a safety valve for his sanity? In only one respect was he without choice . . .

Outside, by now, it was quite dark, but nowhere in this immediate vicinity was an unlit place or space. Jeremy enjoyed absolute darkness. Even Hyde Park, not too far away, had lamps on at this hour, but most London squares had a garden in their centre that lay under a pall of blackness. Not Norfolk Square, which was too small, he thought as he reached it, turned southwards and crossed Sussex Gardens by the Monkey Puzzle pub. No moon tonight. The stars were always invisible up there in the dull reddish-black sky.

Sussex Street formed one side of Gloucester Square. It was far from brightly lit. No doubt the elite residents objected to chemical lighting on tall concrete stilts. That was for the poor, that was for council estates. Jeremy walked along the railings in the centre of the square until he came to a gate. Of course it was locked, it would be, and all the residents had keys. Choosing a corner the least overlooked by the windows in the tall terraces, he laid his raincoat over the spikes on top of the railings and climbed over.

Bushes and trees inside, a path going round a grassy area. These squares were all the same. Probably there was a seat. His eyes growing accustomed to the darkness, he walked along the path, found a seat and sat down. An icy chill from the stone crept up through his buttocks and his back, making him shiver. It was almost pain. The pleasure of being there overcame it. It was extremely unlikely that anyone would come into this garden now. Only in these quiet squares, under the trees in the scentless soundless dark, could he ever feel truly alone and at peace.

His thoughts turned to the keyring and the lighter. He could just send them to the police. That was what a lesser man would do. Wearing fine latex gloves, he could wipe them clean, drop them into a new hitherto untouched padded bag, do the label on a computer, and send them to Paddington Green Police Station. Once it would have been easy. Not now, with all these methods of detection. These days they could probably tell where the padded bag had been bought and where the label had, what sort of gloves had been worn and certainly through which post office it had been dispatched. Not the computer yet, though. As a computer consultant in his Kensington mews office, Alexander spent a good part of his time working towards the discovery of a method whereby forensics could isolate individual IT systems and thence the individual hand that had used them. A fortune awaited the inventor, if invented it could be. It would hardly do for him to discover it now . . .

Still, he wouldn't send the objects to the police, he wouldn't put them in other antique shops. Of course, he could drop them down a drain or even, without fear of detection, into a rubbish can. But this failed to satisfy something artistic in him—or was obviously less risky. He shivered, and not from the cold. Plant them on

someone else? That fool Freddy Perfect or the idiot in
the flat next to him? Fun but an over-the-top risk. He
would have to borrow the spare keys from Inez's office
behind the shop and get them back again. He could do
it but did he need the hassle?

Jeremy got up and walked round the garden in an
anti-clockwise direction. Then he walked back clockwise.
The square was very quiet. A car drove down one side,
another down Sussex Street, but they were big expensive
cars and they were driven slowly. He climbed the railings
again and began to walk back by a very circuitous route
that took him into Bryanston Square and up Seymour
Place. It was in a mews off York Street that he had strangled Nicole Nimms, taken a cigarette from her bag and
the lighter. She had been going home to the tiny house in
the mews she shared with two other girls. This was the
place, or rather, that was the place down there under the
stone arch. He noticed a cellophane-wrapped bouquet of
daffodils lying on the cobbles. Of course! Yesterday had
been the first anniversary of her death. He hadn't forgotten but it hadn't meant much to him.

Minute by minute it seemed to be growing colder.
The sky had cleared, the moon had come out. There
would be a frost. He walked briskly up Seymour Place,
turned left and took the Old Marylebone Road. A girl
on her own came out of Harcourt Place, not looking
nervous but walking fast towards the Edgware Road. He
watched her progress, smiled, though to himself not
her, when she looked twice over her shoulder to check
his whereabouts. She was safe with him, if she did but
know it. Whatever it was that his victims had which
drew him to them, she lacked it; even close to her and
in the dark, he knew that. It must be odd, awkward, to
be a woman and afraid to be out when daylight was
gone. But he couldn't imagine being a woman. He

could more easily have pictured himself as some fine animal, a noble dog or a beast of prey. The jaguar in Inez's shop when it was a living hunter in the pride of its strength. Or even a Rottweiler?

The time was coming up to ten when he crossed into Sussex Gardens and turned down into Southwick Street. No one about, not a soul. It had still been lively in the Edgware Road, lights bright, crowds of teenagers everywhere, Middle Eastern men sitting outside the cafés in the cold, smoking hookahs, the Lebanese restaurants crowded and the little shops doing a brisk trade. Star Street was just as quiet. He preferred it here where all was still. He always had liked silence and calm. Look what had happened when, uncharacteristically, he went into a 'nightspot', a noisier place than anywhere one could think of. If he hadn't, perhaps the cycle of deaths might never have begun . . .

A boy of about sixteen turned into Star Street ahead of him but on the other side. His origin was evidently somewhere in the Asian subcontinent, in the south probably, for his skin was a dark bronze, his shoulder-length hair black. He wore a pin-striped suit which was odd in itself. Just before he reached the turning that would take him into St Michael's Street, he crossed the road and stood on the corner in the lamplight as if waiting for someone. Jeremy, as he came to the street door of Inez's house, glanced across at him and saw that his finely chiselled face was more Caucasian in structure than any European face, the mouth thin-lipped, the cheekbones high, the nose long, straight and sharp. Their eyes met, the black ones and the pale mauvish-grey. Jeremy looked away and went indoors.

Like the two young men in the Leopold and Loeb play, he told himself that Jeremy killed out of curiosity, to see what it felt like. But *Rope* was written before psycho-investigation of the human mind had had much impact on literature and it is doubtful if such a motive would convince today. Alexander knew that and although he went on giving this reason in inner colloquies, he supposed there must be something else as well. But what? If, of course, he had Repressed Memory Syndrome, if such a thing existed, he might never know. It would have to be fetched out of him. Yet he believed that in the event, say, of some male relative having abused him as a small child (a most unlikely eventuality considering his mother never let him out of her sight and managed to delay sending him to school till he was seven) or some nanny beating him in secret (he hadn't had a nanny) or even his widowed mother neglecting him (she adored him and even more after his father's death) he would know when he dug deep down. Much digging had been done and had yielded nothing.

Of his early childhood he had no memory, and from his extensive reading in psychiatry, he knew that it was in infancy that a trauma would occur. It had also taught him that few people had much conscious memory of events before they were three. But what event could there have been with his mother always watching over him? When, eventually, he went to school he had encountered no bullying, nor had his teachers used draconian methods.

Should he be looking for unhappy incidents with women? There had been none unless you counted his marriage. This had taken place when he and the girl were both in their second year at the University of Nottingham. She had said she was pregnant and in those days it was still obligatory, in such circumstances, to marry. No baby came. After a couple of months she claimed to have had a miscarriage. Alexander was so

ignorant that he believed her but after a time he began
to doubt as there had been no signs of pregnancy and
no signs either of its coming to an end. As far as he
could tell sexual relations had always been satisfactory
and he would quite contentedly have settled for things
going on as they were, even though he admitted to himself that he didn't much like his wife or enjoy her company. But it was the sex she began to complain of and
in an offensive insulting way, shouting at him that what
happened was all to please him while he was indifferent
to her feelings. Quarrels grew more frequent and after
two years they separated.

Alexander went back to live with his mother. He took
a series of jobs, all in computers, slowly climbing the ladder, and on one course he met a woman who became his
girlfriend. She had a flat of her own, he moved in with
her and for a while he was happy. His girlfriend was both
more experienced than his wife had been and less
demanding. But while he was with her he made a discovery about himself. He disliked touching and being
touched. No doubt this phobia, failing, peculiarity, whatever it was, had contributed to the break-up of his
marriage. He faced up to something else too: he had
found that it was possible to have sex with a woman without touching her with his hands. Discussing this with his
girlfriend was impossible for him to do and he wasn't
altogether surprised when she decided she preferred the
boyfriend she had left for him and he was once more
alone. This he found he didn't at all mind. He liked the
freedom and peace of being alone, and if he missed
the home comforts his mother provided, he realised he
couldn't bury himself in a country village for the rest of
his life. He moved to London and a flat in Hendon.

For computers and their complexities he had a special aptitude and when he was thirty he went back to

university (not Nottingham) to get a degree in computer studies, a relatively new course subject. A much better job awaited him when he graduated and he began to make money. A knack for appearing genial and pleasant made him popular and he was asked to dinner parties. Acquaintances rang him up and asked him to charity receptions and fund-raising events. Underneath his warm exterior he remained cold and reclusive, and this, he told himself, was by choice. He bought a much bigger flat, in Chelsea this time.

Once, after he had been to see his mother, he drove into Nottingham. It was the first time he had been back since he broke up with his girlfriend, years and years before. He was simply curious to see in which ways the city had changed. Going to clubs in London had never interested him. His life was quiet, solitary, his entertainment the theatre, the opera, a little select television, reading and shopping for the expensive things he needed for the mews house he had bought not far south of Kensington Gardens. But, just as he had been curious to see this city which had been his metropolis when he was young, so now the bright lights and the noise, while they repelled him, also exercised over him a strange attraction. Visiting what he believed must be called a 'nightspot' would do no harm.

This was about two years ago. He found himself in a club that was underground, a sordid flashy place where girls did titillating semi-strips and sat on men's knees. He made it plain enough he didn't want any approaches from the girl he later came to know as Gaynor Ray. The night dragged on, he was bored and tired but still he stayed. His behaviour became incomprehensible to him.

At midnight he started serious drinking, something he had never really done, not even when he was student. Just before three he left, went back to the Mercedes, which he had parked in a makeshift car park adjacent to a building site, and took a blanket from the boot, intending to sleep there. He stood for a while on the pavement, in the belief that the night air would take away the dizziness and the headache he was beginning to feel. Three girls came out of the club. They were the dancers going home. One, only one, of them was the girl for him. Why? How did he know? They were all young, pretty enough, provocative in the club, weary now. The one standing nearest to him was the one for him, the only possibility, a girl who must bear some invisible sign, a scar or branding or badge, but a mark that no one could see. Even he thought he couldn't see it, he wasn't sure, but he knew he could feel it.

A terrible excitement seized him. He could feel his blood pressure shoot up, distend his veins and drum in his head. Sweat broke out on his chest and soaked his hands. If anyone—well, a doctor, a psychiatrist—had asked him to describe how he felt he would have said it was as if he were going to explode. He watched the girls. No, he watched *her*.

She said goodnight to the other two and came in his direction alone. She stopped, smiled at him, said, 'Are you staying in a nice hotel?'

'Maybe,' he said.

'Then you'll want to take me with you.'

'Get in,' he said.

She got into the passenger seat rather elegantly and in practised fashion, displaying long legs in high-heeled shoes. From her bag she had taken a silver cross on a chain and she fastened it round her neck, as if it were an amulet, a protecting charm. He came over to her side as if to shut the door, leaned over her instead, grabbed the chain in both hands and drew the two sides together, crossing his hands, pulling as tight as she could. Even then his fingers didn't touch her skin. It never even occurred to him that the chain might break, and it did so only when she was dead and her prominent blue eyes, more prominent by then, stared hopelessly at him. Her face had gone blue, the way they said in books that faces did. He put the broken chain in his pocket, pulled the girl out of the car, threw her on to the building site and, using a spade workmen had left there, began covering her with shovelfuls of bricks and rubble and concrete dust. There was no one about. His had been the last vehicle in the car park.

It would probably have been quite safe to stay there all night, but he didn't. Drunk as he was, he drove off for about a mile, found a silent suburban street and settled down there, sleeping until eight in the morning. The footfalls of a boy delivering papers woke him. He bought a bottle of water in a corner shop and drove back to the building site to check. Workmen had begun unloading rubble from a dumper truck on to the pile he had begun. A piece of luck. He drove back to London. Only when he was in the Chelsea flat did he look at the chain with the silver cross attached to it, but he came to no resolve or plan as a result.

Nicole Nimms had been the result of just such another inexplicable impulse, such a thunderous upheaval of his whole body—of Jeremy's body—specifically directed at this one and only to her. When he thought about their deaths at his hands and analysed what he had done, he broke out into a sweat and had to restrain himself from screaming aloud. It was as an escape from this that he had become Jeremy Quick. Being called the Rottweiler by newspapers and, following their example, the public, made him angry. He had never bitten anyone. He doubted if he was physically capable of biting into human flesh, for this was touching of the worst kind. He would vomit before he did so. The idea of himself as a mad sadist who bit his victims was made worse by the fact that he hadn't wanted to kill, he hadn't meant to. Why had he? And an equally mystifying question, why had it happened to him so comparatively late in life? Why had 'it' waited until he was in his forties?

Until he knew the answers, he would go on, because knowing was the only way to stop.

CHAPTER 10

'You can learn a lot,' said Freddy Perfect, 'from doing what I do. I mean, pottering about in shops like this one. Notice I never said "junk" shops, Inez. Antique shops. Yes, like I say, you can learn a lot from just quietly examining little bits and pieces. This vase, for instance, and this little box.'

'Yes?' Inez was reading in the *Guardian* about the continuing search for Jacky Miller or her body. 'Put that box down, please, Freddy. It's fragile.'

'I shan't harm it. I've got very delicate fingers, Ludo always says. I'm thinking of becoming an auctioneer, I reckon I may have a talent for it.'

'Possibly.'

The police had a theory and Jacky's parents another. It appeared that she had been an Internet enthusiast, had exchanged e-mails including photographs with a man the police had tried to get in touch with and failed. He too was missing from home. Was it possible she had left of her own accord and gone somewhere to meet this man? In that case, said Jacky's father, why not tell her mother, who wouldn't have tried to stop her, she was over eighteen and a free agent. His theory and his wife's was that she had gone on holiday to some resort on the Red Sea. This was less far-fetched than it sounded at first. A friend had wanted her to go with her and two others on a package tour but Jacky's mother had, in this case, done her best to stop her.

With the present situation in Israel, it was too dangerous to pay a visit to the region. On this question Jacky
had been mutinous, even saying she would go anyway,
though her parents had heard no more about it.

In spite of this, the newspaper had several articles on
the subjects of serial killers, young women as victims,
parallels between the Rottweiler, Jack the Ripper and
the Yorkshire Ripper, What Was To Be Done About It?
and the possibility of reintroduction of the death
penalty. Earlier, Jeremy Quick, drinking his tea, had
brought more doubts to Inez's mind concerning his true
character by remarking that he was all in favour of execution for those guilty of murder.

Zeinab arrived at the same moment as a phone call
came from Detective Inspector Crippen to tell her to
expect Zulueta and Jones at ten a.m. in quest of the full
names and addresses of her assistant, those of her tenants the police hadn't yet interviewed and any other
regular callers at the shop.

'I've nothing to hide,' said Freddy when she told him.

Zeinab had a new nose stud. This one was very obviously a real diamond. When she moved her head, toss-
ing back her long black hair, the lights reflected from
the diamond flitted up and down the walls. 'I couldn't
say the same for Morton. He won't want them around
his place in Eaton Square.'

'That's supposed to be the best address in London. Is
that where you're going to live when you're Mrs Phibling?'

'If,' said Zeinab, 'and it's a big if. Don't you let Inez
see you waving that Meissen plate about, that's two
hundred years old.'

Inez put the paper down. 'That's enough, Freddy.
Now, I'll be over at my sister's tomorrow evening so if
you and Ludmila are going out I'll give you the burglar
alarm number. I'll write it down.'

'That's a new departure,' said Freddy with the air of one about to begin an interesting conversation. He took the scrap of paper with the number on it out of Inez's hand. 'I've never known you to put that alarm on in all the years I've—I mean, Ludo's—been here.'

'Less than two, in fact. Off you go now, Ludmila will be wondering where you are.'

Ambling reluctantly towards the back of the shop, Freddy was still only halfway there when Zulueta and Jones arrived. As the least respectable-looking person present, he was homed in on by the hatchet-faced Zulueta. 'And you are?'

'Mr Perfect,' said Freddy, picking up a piece of Japanese porcelain and studying it dreamily.

'Are you trying to be funny?'

Suppressing a laugh, Inez said, 'I assure you, that really is his name.' But as soon as she had spoken, she wondered if she knew that for a fact. How did she know any of them—always excepting Will—were who they said they were?

'Well, Mr Perfect . . .' Zulueta put a wealth of irony into the name. 'Well.' He referred to the notebook in his hand. 'What might your full name be?'

'Frederick James Windlesham Perfect.'

'You live on the second floor, am I right?'

'No, you're not,' said Freddy. 'That's where my lady friend lives. Naturally, I am a frequent visitor.'

'Then where *do* you live?'

'Twenty-seven Roughton Road, Hackney, London, E nine.'

That was the first Inez had heard of it. Perhaps he had made it up on the spur of the moment. There was probably some penalty for giving the police a false address. Now for Zeinab who was looking distinctly uneasy. Jones hastened Freddy's departure by opening the interior door and holding it open for him to pass slowly through.

'Your full name, please?'

'Zeinab Suzanne Munro Sharif.'

Where did the 'Suzanne Munro' part come from, Inez thought. Simply an invention, perhaps. But when Jones asked for Zeinab's home address her expression became rebellious.

'I don't know what you want that for. It's none of it nothing to do with me. I haven't been strangling girls with silver chains.'

'You're not accused of anything, Miss Sharif. This is just for routine purposes.'

'If I tell you, you won't go around there involving my dad? He'll kill me if you do that.'

'It's merely for our records and absolutely confidential.'

Inez already had an address for Zeinab on her books. In case she came up with a different version, she listened with interest as Zeinab gave a number in Redington Road, Hampstead. It was the same one as her assistant had given Inez when she first came to work for her. A fine address near the west side of Hampstead Heath, if not quite up to Eaton Square.

'Now, about the gentleman you said was your fiancé . . .'

'He *is* my fiancé. And I'm not telling you where he lives. You'll have to ask him.'

She looked very flushed and rather dishevelled from running her hands through her hair. While Inez gave Zulueta the names of a few regular customers but refused to do the same with their addresses, Zeinab began combing her hair and restoring her make-up in front of the gilt-framed mirror. The girl was certainly hiding something, though what Inez couldn't tell. Did everyone she knew— always excepting Will, her sister in Highgate and a few friends—practise deception? Jeremy Quick probably, Zeinab and Freddy certainly. Ludmila with her variable accent and her claims of Russian descent, very likely. How about Rowley Woodhouse? She had once had a man pointed out to her across the street and been told by Zeinab that was who he was. But he hadn't crossed over to speak to her or indeed taken any notice at all of her. Did that mean you had to be . . . well, have learning difficulties before you could be transparently honest? Was she herself a deceiver?

Absolutely not, she thought as she closed the street door Zulueta and Jones had left swinging open on their departure. Then she thought of the videos, concealed from all visitors, the television switched off when someone arrived and, once or twice, the lies she had told as to what she had been watching when Jeremy or Becky called. With Will alone had she been honest . . .

He had spent Friday evening at Becky's and the whole of Sunday. She was so demoralised and so weary that when he asked, while eating his supper in front of the television on Friday evening, if he could come to lunch on Sunday, she lacked the strength to say no. It had always been unlikely that James would phone her, would ever phone her again, but a shred of hope remained and she clung to that, while at the same time foreseeing her embarrassment over Will, her prevarications and her pretences, if he did.

Will's pleasure in being with her, and especially in being allowed to come back two days later, went some way to consoling her. During the course of Sunday afternoon she had gone into the kitchen to make tea and, standing there waiting for the kettle to boil, she had seen Will come out of the living room and pause in the hall on his way to the bathroom. He opened the study door and looked inside. Of course, he had often not only looked inside the study but been in there, yet it seemed to her that this scrutiny of the room was different. She was sure he was making an assessment of the place, saying to himself that a single bed could easily be put in there without much disturbing the rest of the furniture. Why shouldn't it become his bedroom?

Pouring water on the teabags, lifting the large chocolate fudge cake out of the fridge, she rehearsed silently what she would say if he asked her. I need to work in there, Will, sometimes as late as midnight I have things to do in there. You know I have to earn my living, don't you, Will, the same as you do, you know that. It sounded feeble. It sounded like what it was, someone desperately snatching at excuses.

In fact, Will had been thinking somewhat along those lines. But Becky was wrong when she calculated he might ask her for the room or even that he might suggest it to himself as a possibility. The presence of the desk, the chairs, the computer and its attachments, the photocopier and shredder made it clear, as far as he was concerned, that there was no room for him. Besides, she had told him so and what Becky said was his law. Poor Becky hadn't enough money to share her home with him.

A couple of weeks before, he had been thinking that when he had the treasure all would be changed, he and she could share the money, buy *their* house, live together for ever and ever. He had written 'Sixth Avenue' on the back of an envelope, which had had a pizza restaurant advertisement in it. In order to do so, he had asked Inez how to spell it and had painstakingly printed the words with a ballpoint pen. It was to show people he asked in case they didn't understand.

But now he had almost lost hope of finding the place. He had asked everyone he knew and shown them the envelope, and they all said Sixth Avenue was in New

York or 'some other place in America.' At first he hadn't
accepted that. Reasoning wasn't something Will was
really capable of. Cause and effect eluded him and he
had never ventured into the mystery of the deductive
process. If someone like Jeremy Quick had said to him
all numbered avenues are in America, Sixth Avenue is a
numbered avenue, therefore Sixth Avenue is in
America, he would probably have laughed and agreed
but he wouldn't have known what it was about.
Without the need for any of that, he now sadly and
reluctantly half accepted it. One thing kept his doubt
going. That was the sound of the police sirens. It *had* to
be somewhere here because the sirens were the ones he
heard lying in bed at night. He heard them making that
noise, braying and yodelling, as police cars or ambu-
lances or fire engines roared down the Edgware Road or
charged along Sussex Gardens.

The difficulty was that none of those other people he
had asked had seen the film. He had tried to get Keith
to see it and he tried again on Monday while they were
sitting on the floor in the Ladbroke Grove flat, eating
their sandwiches.

'I can't go out in the evenings, Will, I can't leave the
wife alone with the kids when she's had them all day.'

'They could go too,' said Will.

'No, they couldn't. You don't know what boys of two
and three are like. And we can't keep asking Kim to
babysit.' He paused to see if Will showed signs of embarrassment at his sister's name but there was no reaction. 'I
reckon she's a bit disappointed she hasn't heard a word
from you since you two went to the pictures.'

Keith thought Will's silence and concentration on
the Kit-Kat he had brought with him in his lunch box
a sign of shame and awkwardness. He always overrated
his companion's mental capacity. Having an almost

superstitious fear of anything approaching brain damage, he would never have encouraged his sister to go out
with Will if he had truly understood his limitations.

'Well, if you're worrying you've upset her you just
give her a bell and I reckon you'll be surprised.'

They packed up at four. Rain had begun and, as soon
as Keith started the van, began to lash against the windscreen. In the Harrow Road he remembered an errand
which had slipped his mind. 'I told the wife I'd bring in
a cut loaf and a pound of tomatoes. If I squeeze the van
in here I'll leave you to move it if the warden turns up.
It's a double yellow line.'

Will had passed his driving test with no trouble five
years before. A short while later the written test was introduced, a measure which would have precluded him from
ever having a licence. He was an efficient driver who
wished he had more chances at the wheel. Now he half
hoped the traffic warden would come so that he could
take the van round the block while he waited for Keith.

It was parked on the corner where the Harrow Road
was joined by a residential street. After sitting there a little while Will got down from the cab and, the rain having slackened, wiped the wing mirrors with a cloth.
Looking up, his eyes lighted on the plaque on the opposite wall, bearing the name of this side street. Sixth
Avenue. He looked away because he must be dreaming
but when he raised his eyes again the name was still
there, Sixth Avenue, easily recognisable from the print-
ing on the envelope. Sixth Avenue. Not a hanging sign
on a lamp post as it had been in the film but attached
to the wall and quite high up. They must have moved it
since the film was made, that would be the answer.

Will would have gone across and stared more closely
at the sign but for Keith coming back at that moment
with his loaf and his tomatoes.

'I was wiping the mirrors.'

'Good lad. The wife's always saying prices are going through the roof, but you don't credit it, do you, till you see for yourself.'

'You need to see for yourself,' said Will, nodding but not thinking about loaves and tomatoes at all.

Sure he had made a good impression on the police, Jeremy had few qualms that they might come back and search the place. If they did he could, of course, make them get a warrant, but he knew what effect that would have on a man like Crippen or any officer, come to that. The assumption would immediately be made that he had something to hide. As, indeed, he had.

At least, he should leave the incriminating objects in the drawer no longer. In the living room cupboard he had a strongbox, the kind of thing hotels provide in guests' bedrooms, very simply operated and functioning on the principle of keying in a four-digit code. He had never yet used it but had already decided that when he did, he would avoid the kind of codes most people favoured, their birth date or an abbreviation of it—so in his case, as Alexander's birthday was 4 July, the number might appear as 4755. It was too obvious. A policeman, even one with a low IQ, would soon cotton on to it. Would Jeremy have the same birthday as Alexander? Perhaps not. At his house in the Kensington mews he had used his birth year, 1955, as the code in the burglar alarm, but the same had applied there, and he had changed to the date Jeremy had killed Gaynor Ray, his first victim—14 April 2000—1440. Should he use that again? No. They might establish that date, though he couldn't think how.

He took the lighter, the fob watch and the earrings out of the drawer in the roof garden table and put them inside the strongbox. It was a while before he closed the lid. Wasn't it foolhardy to keep them at all? But he had to run some risk, he told himself. *He had to get something out of it.* To call it 'some fun' would be ridiculous and not express what he felt. Since he was stuck with this compulsion, this almost disease, he must introduce into it some element of a game, a puzzle, an enigma. If not, he sometimes thought grimly, he might as well kill himself now. He had contemplated that often enough, in his low moments, thinking that to do so would rid the world and its women of a lethal menace. But Alexander didn't want to die, not yet, though he often reflected that his death might be the only way out. All he wanted was for Jeremy to die.

A number for the strongbox, a combination. Not his mother's birthday, not the number of her house plus her postcode number. He could remember neither his wife's birthday nor his girlfriend's. Best would be to find a date that meant something only to him or one he took out of the air. 1986 had been a good year for him, the year he got his degree, moved from Hendon to his first Chelsea address, the King's Road, got rid of his old Austin and bought his first new car, a blue VW. That had been in March, he could remember it, though not the day. It wasn't important. Make it the third, that would do. He keyed into the strongbox 3386, then opened his address book at the second page. There he wrote, King, Austin, and what would appear to be a phone number: 0207 636 3386. He added, to make it more convincing, a fictitious e-mail address: kinga@fitzroy.co.uk.

With the money Alexander had begun to make at that time he could do anything, go anywhere, have almost everything he wanted. And he had. Wonderful holidays abroad, expensive theatre seats, his flats beautifully furnished, his clothes the best, the beginnings of a fine collection of first editions. Then he had *projected* Jeremy who killed girls. In the midst of contentment and plenty he had begun to kill girls. He had killed five. The enormity of it hit him, as it sometimes did. It was so dangerous, so big, so out of the common run of activities that not so long ago men had been hanged for it. Men and women still were hanged for it, gassed, electrocuted, shot, in the United States. But when he thought of killing those girls, when he considered each individual case, he felt no more of a thrill than he had at the time, before, during or after. It had just been an act Jeremy had to do, and he realised something that had never really occurred to him before, that the feeling he had after it was performed was precisely the same as that which he had experienced after sex: relief. No more than that, simple relief. And all the time he never lost touch with reality so far as to believe that he was really two people, one who killed and one who was innocent. There was only one.

Finlay Zulueta was ambitious. He had done well in his career so far and aimed to be a detective inspector before he was thirty. Hard work was the answer, Crippen always said, and worrying at every niggling little doubt like a Sealyham with a bone. (Apparently, the inspector's wife bred Sealyhams, which Zulueta, who hailed from Goa, had learnt were small white terriers.) Zeinab Sharif was a lovely-looking woman, in his opinion, in surely every red-blooded man's opinion, but nevertheless a liar. More than a purveyor of niggling doubts, an out-and-out liar. Something in her manner had told him so. Why should she lie to the police unless she was up to no good? It was obvious she had also lied to her employer.

In fact, Zulueta was beginning to think there was something fishy about the whole of that house, Star Antiques included. That fellow Perfect, for instance, always poking his nose in where he wasn't wanted, the builder's labourer who pretended to be half-witted, Inez Ferry herself. Zulueta thought it very unlikely she had just come upon the silver cross and keyring in the course of dusting the place. It was more probable that someone had sold them to her and she had been going to sell them on till she got cold feet. And what was a builder's labourer doing living there? He, and Crippen too and their superiors, were all convinced someone in that house or connected with that shop was in on these murders up to the neck. As for the girl . . . He would be like the Sealyham and worry at that bone. He would go up to Redington Road and check if she really lived there. Phoning was no good. All he got was that impersonal British Telecom answering service.

The house was huge, a palace in its own grounds, one of those places that come on the market for five or six million. Zulueta expected something complicated about the gate, that he would have to punch in a code to open it or state his name and business to a disembodied voice, but it opened easily, at a gentle push. There were bars at the downstairs windows but no other security arrangements, no closed-circuit television, no dogs and no notices saying dogs were about. Zulueta, who disliked any dogs larger than Sealyhams, was relieved. He rang the bell at the front door.

If a uniformed maid had answered he wouldn't have been surprised but the man who came to the door was plainly the owner. He was very large, tall and stout, with a red face, wearing an open-necked shirt and jeans.

'Mr Sharif?' said Zulueta, producing his warrant card.

'Do I look like Mr Sharif?'

Zulueta thought this a racist remark and wondered what he could do about it, if anything. But he was bound to say that with his snub nose, light-blue eyes and the remains of fair hair, this red-faced householder could not reasonably be taken for anyone born east of Athens.

'There is no one in the house called that?'

Perhaps his putting the enquiry in the form of one expecting the answer no was what slightly softened the man's manner. 'Absolutely not. My name is Jennings and apart from me, my wife and son live here. They are called Margaret and Michael Jennings. May I ask what made you think a Mr Sharif lived here?'

He could ask but he wouldn't get much of an answer. 'Information given us, sir. Obviously false information.'

'Obviously. Good evening.'

'Good evening,' said Zulueta.

Crippen was pleased, though remarking that he might as easily have got it off the electoral register.

'I wanted to make assurance doubly sure, guv.'

'Quite right.'

The two of them went round to Star Street in the morning. It was twenty past nine but Zeinab wasn't there.

'Not done a bunk, has she?' Crippen said to Inez.

'This isn't particularly late for her,' Inez said patiently. 'If she's not here by ten you can start worrying.'

Inez was alone. Jeremy Quick had come and gone, while Freddy and Ludmila had passed through half an hour before on their way to take the bus to St Paul's and walk across the newly opened Millennium Bridge to Shakespeare's Globe. Though both had been in London for years, they still behaved like tourists, anxious not to miss out on any of the capital's latest attractions.

Crippen sat down in the grey velvet armchair but Zulueta wandered round the shop, behaving much like

Freddy but differing in one respect. He picked up a very ugly Victorian amber and pinchbeck necklace Inez had always disliked and asked her, not for the price but how much she wanted for it. The subtle disparity wasn't lost on her.

'Forty-eight pounds,' she said.

'Forty,' said Zulueta.

'I'm sorry but I'm not in the business of bargaining. That's the price.'

Zulueta looked about to argue but at that moment Zeinab arrived. She stopped just inside the door, unable to hide her disquiet at the sight of them. Crippen got up, his eyes fixed incredulously on her earrings.

'Who d'you think you're looking at?' said Zeinab in the street-honoured style of the young pub customer spoiling for a fight.

'It's not "who", it's "what". Where did you get those earrings, Miss Sharif?'

'It's not your business but my fiancé gave them to me.'

Which one, Inez wanted to ask, but she said nothing. 'Those earrings,' said Zulueta, the amber necklace forgotten, 'look very much like the pair Jacky Miller was wearing when she went missing.'

'You must be joking. These are real diamonds.'

'Well, Miss Sharif,' said Crippen, 'perhaps you'll be good enough to take them off and let us try them against a photograph we have of the missing pair. And while we're about it, give some explanation of why you gave us a false home address.'

Zeinab, for some reason suddenly more cheerful, advanced across the shop, kicked off her shoes and slipped her feet into high-heeled narrow strap sandals. 'OK, my dad used to live there but he's moved. Him and my mum live at 22 Minicom House, Lisson Grove now.' As far as her mother was concerned, this was true. Crippen looked as if about to say her family had come down in the world, hadn't they, but thought better of it. 'If you want to know where my earrings came from you can go and ask Mr Khoury next door. That's where my fiancé bought them.'

Crippen nodded and the three of them trooped off. It must have been Rowley Woodhouse's gift, thought Inez. Morton Phibling wouldn't have considered patronising a jeweller in the relatively humble circumstances of Mr Khoury. While they were away, Keith Beatty's van drew up outside and Will got out of it. Forgotten something, Inez supposed. He came in by way of the side door as usual and emerged again, carrying a package that might have been his lunch, just as Crippen, Zulueta and Zeinab came out of Khoury's. Not quite knowing why, Inez opened the street door and stood there. Triumphant now, having obviously succeeded in proving the provenance of the earrings and perhaps their superiority to the missing pair, Zeinab said a gracious, 'Hi, Will. How are you? I haven't seen you for ages.'

Will looked scared. He always did when Zeinab spoke to him. Muttering something, looking over his shoulder, he almost ran round the van to the passenger side. Zulueta stared suspiciously after him and Inez had to admit his behaviour made him look guilty of some misdemeanour—the very last thing to apply to simple, innocent Will. The van moved off.

To Inez's relief, even though she had failed to make a sale, instead of returning to the shop, the two police officers went off to their car. Zeinab began laughing as soon as she was inside. She stood in front of 'her' mirror repairing her make-up in preparation for the arrival of Morton Phibling.

CHAPTER 11

Unused to deviousness, Will disliked the idea of asking Keith to drop him off at Sixth Avenue on their way back from Ladbroke Grove at four fifteen. He couldn't have said why he wanted to be there in case Keith guessed why, so he might have had to make something up, say something untrue. This was too complicated and difficult, besides being wrong. Will might not have had a first- or even a fourth-class mind, but like a serious child he had a fairly well-developed moral sense. It extended to lying and truth-telling, and to be being polite and kind, but not to speculating about who truly owned the treasure, the people who buried it, or the public, or the jewellers from whom it had been stolen. These questions were far too difficult for him. Besides, although he hadn't formulated this, treasure truly belonged in the world of fairy tales, where rules about property, not stealing other people's and not believing finders were keepers no longer applied.

So he said nothing to Keith except that he'd see him in the morning when they would be starting on a new job. Coming back earlier because he had forgotten his sandwiches, he had had an unpleasant experience seeing those policemen he didn't like and Zeinab who made him feel shy. But they were all gone now. Unobserved, he went upstairs, made himself a cup of tea and ate a Danish pastry. Now the clocks had changed—Will didn't know how, backwards or forwards, Inez had altered his two clocks and his watch—it would still be light at seven thirty. Did it have to be dark for what he needed to do? Not really, though it had been dark in the film.

He decided to have his evening meal before he went out. At about half past five Freddy and Ludmila came back from their day of wandering about the South Bank and put on their CD player for some music. It was nearly always Shostakovich that Ludmila played, though Will didn't know this. But he knew it made a very loud noise, which he didn't mind, though he would have preferred a pretty tune or a voice singing. He didn't hear Jeremy Quick come in, his footfalls were always soft, and anyway quite drowned by the Battle of Leningrad. Will beat up three eggs with a fork and because they didn't look enough, added a fourth. He made toast and buttered it, opened a packet of crisps and a new bottle of tomato ketchup and sat down to eat. Becky had given him a bakewell tart for dessert, of which he ate two slices with double cream. The light began to fade and shadows crept across his windowsills.

When he had washed the dishes and left one light on, the way Becky told him to in order to stop burglars coming, Will put on his thick duffel coat and, double-locking the door, went downstairs. He took nothing with him. That would come later. Noticing that black-haired policeman with the funny name sitting in his car at the kerb took him aback. But he remembered how he had seen him and the important one coming out of Mr Khoury's shop that morning and Will decided Mr Khoury must have had burglars. He was quite proud of himself for thinking that. The one with the funny name was there to see the burglars didn't come back.

Will went down Star Street into Norfolk Square and up past Paddington Station into Eastbourne Terrace. He walked over Bishop's Bridge above the Great

Western line, through the underpass and into the
Harrow Road. The new buildings of Paddington Basin,
half-completed towers, concrete and glass structures,
fantastic shapes and curves and arches, all dominating
the old canal, lay in glittering darkness below him.
Seeing the sign Sixth Avenue gave him as much pleasure
as it had the first time, if no surprise. There had been
nothing in the film to indicate the number of the house
in whose backyard the treasure had been buried but
Will thought he would recognise the place from its own
appearance and its proximity to the car parking place.

Sixth Avenue was a long street of houses in long terraces. It was in most cases impossible to see what the
backs of these houses were like. Still, where a terrace
ended and another began the space between the last
house in one row and the first in the next afforded him
a glimpse of grass, bushes, part of a shed. There had
been a shed in the film, perhaps grass and certainly
bushes. Some of these end houses had side gates. Will
knew that if he went closer he could open these gates
and get a sight of backyards, but people lived in the
houses—lights were on behind drawn curtains and
some on where the curtains were not drawn—and they
would take him for a burglar.

There was no car park. That was something he
couldn't understand. But he knew there were some
things in life he couldn't understand and never would.
He needed Becky to explain them to him and he tried to
think what Becky might have said about the car park not
being there. This tactic was always difficult for him. If he
had been able to tell himself what she would have said,
he wouldn't have needed her, and now he needed her
very much. All he could do was think of her being with
him, explaining things and making everything clear, but
still he couldn't imagine what she might have said.

Shaking his head in frustration, he walked all the way up to the end, wondering now how to overcome the difficulty of looking into back gardens without the people seeing. He was a little way down the opposite side, coming back, when he came to a house he hadn't noticed before. It had no lights on. It had no curtains either and looked as if empty of furniture. But what interested Will most, what was most familiar, were the heaps of builder's materials in the front garden and blocking the side way from which the gate had been removed. Builders were working on this empty house, perhaps making an extension but by now, of course, they had gone home, leaving piles of bricks and heaps of sand and their cement mixer behind.

Will had encountered no one in his walk up the street and halfway back. As far as he knew, nobody was about. The man who was following him was too practised at this kind of thing and too careful to allow himself to be seen. But when Will stepped over the sand heap and edged round the mixer he slipped in behind him, crouching down in the deep shadows. The absence of a car park forgotten, Will was too excited by this time to notice anything but the area which lay behind the side way. Hard to tell in the dark, but the cracked concrete, the strips of bare earth sprouting weeds, the dilapidated shed, looked the same. Light was shed from a window next door but it fell on a small lawn and none of it penetrated here. The other side was in darkness but for a faint light, as from a candle burning in an upstairs room.

Will made his way to the bottom of this ruined garden. He tried the door of the shed but it was locked and there was no key. Spades and shovels lived in sheds and he had hoped to find one. Peering through the broken window-pane, he could see nothing but two plastic sacks filled with something solid and, beside them, what looked like a heap of old clothes. He would come back tomorrow.

Walking slowly towards the Harrow Road, he began thinking about acquiring something to dig with. Keith had spades but of course they only used them on outside jobs and he couldn't borrow one because Keith would want to know why. Will hadn't got a garden and Becky hadn't got a garden, facts which Keith knew. He would have to buy a spade, Will decided. Tomorrow, after work.

In Zulueta's opinion, Will Cobbett's visit to the house in Sixth Avenue and his efforts to get into the shed in the backyard clinched his guilt. After Will had gone, Zulueta made an attempt on the shed himself but, able as he was at other kinds of police work—shadowing someone, for instance, without being detected—he had never been any good at undoing locks without their keys and he failed again. The window was too small to admit even a thin man's body. Zulueta, though he had a torch, could see very little. He would dearly have liked to know what was in those sacks and what was under that pile of old and dirty overalls, anoraks and other indefinable garments. Jacky Miller's body? Other incriminating evidence, such as Jacky's earrings or some of her clothing? Some other girl the police didn't even know was missing because she had been alone in the world?

Certain Will had left Sixth Avenue behind him and was on his way home, Zulueta went to seek his car, which he had left parked in Star Street. He walked through the almost empty streets, the darkness and the unearthly chemical light, down to Paddington Green and under the flyover. Will had disappeared, using perhaps some back way or short cut home. What next, Zulueta wondered.

He had had his suspicions of Will ever since Gaynor Ray's silver cross turned up at Star Antiques. It wasn't only that, but the other man's furtive manner and not very effective attempts at appearing a simple innocent. Zulueta, who had a psychology degree, could see through that. Then there was the glance he and that Sharif girl had exchanged outside Khoury's shop that morning, Cobbett looking abashed when Sharif asked him how he was and said she hadn't seen him for ages. A likely story—she didn't even sound sincere. They would have to do a better job than that between them to pull the wool over Finlay Zulueta's eyes.

So were they somehow in it together? Crippen had been gunning for Sharif on account of that false address business. That afternoon Osnabrook had been round to Minicom House, which was one of those rainbow-coloured blocks of Westminster council housing in Lisson Grove, and found she had been telling the truth about her parents living at number 22. Half the truth, that is. Her mother lived there but when Osnabrook asked about the girl's father she'd said, 'He buggered off twenty-five years ago,' and laughed. But even Crippen would sing to a different tune when he heard about the house in Sixth Avenue and the shed.

Cobbett and Sharif might be in it together but Cobbett was the mastermind. That they were both exceptionally good-looking helped to clinch their guilt. Zulueta had a theory, developed in an essay he had once composed on psychology and the Hollywood movie, that beautiful people are attracted to one another. There was evidence too that the Rottweiler was in the building trade. Cobbett was in the building trade and no doubt he had been working on that site. That's what gave him the idea of concealing Jacky Miller's body there. He had concealed Gaynor Ray's body under a heap of rubble, so why not this one?

He was clever. Only a really clever man could assume that air of foolishness and innocence and sustain it. Zulueta wondered where Jacky Miller's body was now. His mind full of ideas as to where Cobbett might have hidden it, he began walking the long dreary route to where he had left his car.

It was quite by chance that Jeremy Quick had seen them both. He had got into the habit of taking a walk most evenings. At first, when he had killed Nicole Nimms and knew that having done it a second time he might do it again, he had told himself that he must never go out after dark in case the urge overcame him. This thought was succeeded by another, taking the opposite view. He must not condemn himself to a lifetime's curfew but instead go out and when temptation came, resist. Next time, in the half-dark, he fought with himself to control the impulse, and he succeeded, but at the cost of trembling and sweating, finally throwing up in the gutter. After that he brought the curfew into operation once again. What put an end to that was his garrotting of Rebecca Milsom in Regent's Park, and if not in broad daylight, long before it grew dark. He could kill, then, at any time, darkness was not the rule, and once more he began to walk whenever the fancy took him.

That evening he had made his way towards Paddington Basin and the vast area of new building. Even without the phantasmic Belinda Gildon as his promised bride, he must seriously think of moving this year. It was time. The flats at the Basin coming up for sale sounded pleasant and they would be new. Both his present homes were old and therefore more time-consuming and expensive to clean and maintain.

Getting into the Basin was, however, impossible. It was still closed off to all but the contractors working on the site. Jeremy was disappointed. Presumably, he would have to make an appointment with an agent who might have access, to view a show flat. Or would it be wiser to move a long way away, perhaps even to South London? From attempting to get through between Paddington Station and Bishop's Bridge, he came up a side street into the roundabout and almost bumped into that thickie, Will Cobbett.

He stared at Jeremy as if he had never seen him before and didn't like what he saw. He looked, for God's sake, *frightened*. Amused, Jeremy thought how if he did but know it, he was the wrong sex and the wrong size to be afraid of meeting him on a dark night. Still, being looked at like that wasn't pleasant for the recipient of that stare and Jeremy felt anger rise in him. He said a sharp, almost admonitory, 'Good evening.'

Cobbett didn't reply. Leaving Jeremy at the bus stop, he began to run, once looking over his shoulder, in the direction of the Edgware Road. Jeremy was furious. The man had treated him as a well-brought up boy of ten might treat a child molester. Slowly he turned away and, determined to continue his walk, made for the under-pass. It brought him up at the point where Warwick Avenue meets the Harrow Road. And there, coming towards him, was another Star Street acquaintance, Detective Sergeant Zulueta.

Each said good evening to the other. If Jeremy had made some excuse for being in this deserted, rather lonely place after dark Zulueta might have had his supicions awakened but Jeremy, dully conventional, said only, 'A mild night for April.'

His head full of the mysterious and doubtless criminal activities of Will Cobbett, Zulueta nodded, said he must be getting along. They parted on the corner, Jeremy taking the shortest route straight back to the Edgware Road. He had intended to extend his walk with an exploration of Maida Vale, but he wanted the company of Zulueta no longer than was absolutely necessary. He watched the policeman cross the canal bridge and disappear from sight down Blomfield Road.

CHAPTER 12

At no point in his life had Jeremy Quick or his alter ego Alexander Gibbons shopped for women's clothes or jewellery. When he married he had been too poor even to consider buying an engagement ring, even if it had occurred to him, and he had no reason to change his mind while living with his girlfriend. Since then there had been no occasion for going into women's shops. Now the time had come.

First of all, he had fully intended to use Jacky Miller's own earrings in his game, but he found himself, incomprehensibly, unable to do this. Early in the morning, he took them out of the strongbox, along with the keyring and the lighter, and experienced a powerful reluctance to part with them. It was suddenly as if they were of enormous value, the kind of precious jewellery the woman who owned them would have copied in silver and paste actually to wear them. Very probably they were composed of silver plate and brilliants, and worth at most fifteen pounds. Copied, he thought, that was it! He wouldn't have them copied, he'd *buy* copies. It would be easy, for they were obviously fashionable, that Zeinab girl had been wearing an almost identical pair, though hers were gold.

Careful not to keep too many newspaper pieces about the case, he had nevertheless two or three cuttings he felt were essential to him. One of these was an artist's impression, actual size, of the earrings Jacky had been wearing when she vanished. Jeremy studied this picture. About an inch in diameter they were, silver or something that looked like silver, studded with—how many brilliants? About twenty, it looked like.

Where should he go to do his shopping? Nowhere in this neighbourhood, certainly. A tease was all very well but that would be pushing things. When it came to buying cheap jewellery, he was out of touch. It was the expensive districts he knew, notably Savile Row and the Burlington Arcade where he bought his own clothes. Knightsbridge wouldn't do, nor would Bond Street. Eventually, memorising the appearance and dimensions of the earrings, he decided on Kensington High Street. First he dropped in to see Inez. Because it was a sunny morning, promising an unseasonably warm day, he had put on his new dark-grey suit with its discreet, only just visible, blue line, a snowy shirt, fresh from the Star Street laundry, and blue tie with purple chevrons. Alexander dressed far more casually, if in Armani.

Inez looked at him approvingly. Or so he thought at first, perhaps because he was accustomed to thinking this way about her. For a long time, with a quiet satisfaction but a certain amount of contempt, he had believed she fancied him—some hopes! As if he would give her a second glance. But as she went out to the tiny kitchen area to put the kettle on, he thought again about that look she had given him. It had been there these past few days as had the slightly dry note in her voice and her less than welcoming manner when he made his regular visit for his cup of tea. He could date its beginnings. That look, that tone and that manner had started the day after he had told her of his break-up with Belinda. He must have made his announcement of the split with less than his usual finesse.

Admitting to this, even silently, was unacceptable, as

was all criticism of himself by himself as much as by others. Telling her of his patient wait for Belinda to choose between him and her mother had been done with his usual artistry, perhaps more than usual, for he had made a studied effort to ensure it was perfect. Probably Inez was simply offended because he had twice refused her invitation. How vain she must be to think a man like him would want to waste a whole evening in her company.

The jaguar was looking at him with its baleful golden eyes. For the first time he noticed its scrubbing-brush whiskers and they made him shiver. She came back with the tea but remained unsmiling. Lately, she had been in the habit of telling him about the latest visit of the police and of the speculations of the people she talked to as to the fate of Jacky Miller. This morning there was none of that. In fact, there was silence until at last, lifting her head from the scrutiny of a ledger, she asked him what plans he had for the Spring Bank Holiday.

Jeremy had forgotten that this would fall on Monday week, 4 May. He had no plans but as she waited, drinking her tea, for his answer, the idea came to him of visiting his mother. Of the entire population of the United Kingdom, indeed of the world, the one person Alexander Gibbons loved was Dorothy Margaret Gibbons. It would be several weeks now since he had been to see her. Not exactly with a pang of conscience but certainly with surprise, he calculated that he hadn't been to Oxton, where she lived, since March. 'I shall go up to see my mother,' he said.

'Oh, yes, she lives somewhere in the Midlands, doesn't she?'

'Market Harborough,' said Jeremy, which was a lie but not much of one. His mother lived in the adjacent county of Nottinghamshire. Let her think Jeremy

Quick's mother lived somewhere else. She could never find out. 'How about you?'

'I always go to my sister and her husband that Monday. They're only in Highgate.'

Short of enquiring into the holiday plans of Zeinab Sharif, Will Cobbett and his aunt, Ludmila Gogol and Freddy Perfect, Morton Phibling, Rowley Woodhouse and Mr Khoury, there seemed nothing more to be said. Jeremy finished his tea, thanked Inez and set off for Paddington tube station, the Circle Line that would take him to Kensington High Street.

His first estimate of Inez's changed feelings towards him had been accurate. Suspect him of being what he actually was she did not. Such a thing was as far from her mind as could be, but she was sure he had been lying to her about Belinda and Belinda's mother, afraid he must be just as much a fantasist as Zeinab and a good deal worse than Ludmila. It was true that for a while she had entertained the beginnings of romantic feelings for him. She had thought, and still thought, that he had shown her a greater warmth than she had seen him extend to anyone else, and she remembered the interest he had taken in her unusual Christian name. Perhaps she misinterpreted the signs. But simply, in an old-fashioned phrase, she had thought him an honest man and she was disappointed.

It was not worth regrets and recriminations. She took the cups out into the kitchen and washed them up, carried the book rack and the books out into the street. No fewer than four had sold yesterday—a record? She hoped the police wouldn't come today, she was tired of them, Zulueta's cockiness, Crippen's boorish manner.

As it happened, no one came, not even Zeinab. Inez saw Freddy in the street, walking along in the company of that friend of his, Anwar something—an inappropriate relationship if ever there was one. She had no doubt at all that it was entirely innocent, Freddy filling the role of father figure to Anwar who seemed to be fifteen or sixteen. How had they met and what had attracted them to each other? Both, of course, belonged to what were clumsily called 'ethnic minorities', but that, in an area where people predominated whose origins or their parents' were in the Asian subcontinent, the Caribbean or the Middle East, was hardly enough to bring them together. Such things were often a mystery.

Just after ten, when Zeinab still hadn't appeared, Inez called her mobile number. It was switched off. She waited another few minutes. Then, remembering the address Zeinab had given the police, she looked up the Sharif family in the phone book. A woman answered. Inez rightly took it to be Zeinab's mother and she asked where her daughter was.

Reem Sharif was still in bed. 'They say it's a virus,' she said, her mouth full of cream-filled chocolate egg left over from Easter.

'You mean she's ill and she's not coming in to work?'

'You got it. I'll be going round later. That all?'

'Perhaps you could ask her to give Inez a call.'

'Yep. Bye now.'

What did that mean, 'I'll be going round later'? Going round where? Was it possible that in the two days since she had told Crippen her parents lived at Minicom House, Zeinab had moved out and moved in with Rowley Woodhouse or Morton Phibling? Inez was thinking about phoning Morton at his home in Eaton Square, if he wasn't ex-directory, when he arrived, driven in his Caribbean-lime-coloured Peugeot. In recognition of the fine warm weather—Inez had left the street door wide open—he was wearing a white suit with black linen shirt, open at the neck and showing his chicken gizzard throat.

'Where is she that my soul loveth?'

'I wish I knew, probably in bed with a virus,' said Inez, purposely making Zeinab's circumstances sound like a dirty weekend in Clacton. She wasn't usually bitchy but events of the morning were fast testing her temper. Still, she drew the line at advising Morton to speak to Mrs Sharif.

'No doubt she will be in touch.' He added rather mournfully, 'I was all geared up to take her to Knightsbridge to a fitting for her wedding gown.'

In *my* time, thought Inez indignantly, in working hours. 'Well, that, I'm afraid, will have to be post-poned.' He was looking so downcast that Inez took pity on him. 'I'm sure her illness is nothing serious,' she said.

'You're very kind,' said Morton and, probably for the first time in his life, 'I won't keep you.'

As the bright-green car moved away, Will Cobbett, who was perhaps also taking the day off, went past towards the side door carrying what looked like a spade, half wrapped in two plastic bags. Inez heard him go upstairs. It couldn't have been a spade—what would he want one for? Surely not to attempt digging the iron-hard clay in her own poor apology for a garden. Perhaps Becky had one . . . As Inez was beginning to wonder what was the point of her just sitting there, a potential customer appeared. The customer didn't buy anything, but the next one put down a deposit on a grandfather clock and said he would come back for it later with a van.

Freddy reappeared without Anwar Ghosh. As usual, if he came in at this time, without any preamble or greeting, he launched into a description of his morn-ing's occupations, from his waking to see the sun streaming into the room and reminding him of happy days in Bridgetown, Barbados, to his glass of fruit crush with Anwar in the Ranoush Juice.

Then, observing the 'sold' label on the grandfather clock and opening its door to examine the works inside, 'Where's young Zeinab?' he said.

'Please don't touch the pendulum, Freddy. She's off sick. Some sort of virus.'

'Dear, oh dear. You're all on your lonesome then?'

Inez could see it coming. Helplessly, she let it come.

'I'll tell you what, I'll give you a hand, take her place.' He must have seen her look of dismay but misinterpreted it. 'Don't you worry, I won't want paying.' He looked over his shoulder in case Department of Social Security spies were lying on the pavement with their ears to the crack under the door. 'Between you and I, I mustn't be paid, or I'll lose my Benefit.' He added hopefully, 'Unless you and me can think of some way to outwit them.'

'I can manage on my own, Freddy, really,' Inez said feebly.

'No, you can't.'

Such argument was bound to degenerate into a pointless no-you-can't-yes-I-can wrangle and Inez gave way. 'I'll just nip up and tell Ludo,' said Freddy, opposing the action to the word by strolling towards the inside door with extreme slowness, examining small ornaments on his way.

Feeling a need for fresh air, Inez went outside to stand for a while in the sunshine. Mr Khoury, who had the same idea, was already there, smoking a large cigar heavily scented with oriental spices. Tuberose and spikenard, thought Inez, coughing, cardamom and coriander. Morton Phibling's speech patterns were infectious.

'You will notice, madam, that the one-time white van is back,' said Mr Khoury, 'the van that is dirty and it is forbidden to clean for the scientific experiment.'

By now it was so dirty that Inez wouldn't have known it was white if she hadn't seen it before. 'Who does it belong to?'

Mr Khoury shrugged, blowing out tuberose fumes. 'He has RP but does he display the proof in his windscreen? No, he thinks him very funny. When the warden comes he show the proof and tear up the PT. This I have seen.'

Interpreting RP as residents' parking and PT as a parking ticket, Inez said the owner must be crazy.

'Many, many are crazy,' said Mr Khoury sorrowfully and, pointing again, 'Here is another.'

Another white van, he meant, not another madman. The purchaser of the grandfather clock had come back, all smiles. Welcoming him in, Inez hoped Freddy hadn't damaged its pendulum.

Will hadn't been taking the day off but was going in late, having been sent by Keith to order supplies from the builder's merchant. While there he had bought a spade, taken it home and walked down to the new job they had in Kendal Street. The evening was fixed for digging operations to begin.

The radio was, of course, on, Keith's indispensable background to making good and plastering, a dull beat and throb, and occasionally a human voice keening miserably or in manic bliss, which Will didn't even notice, he was so used to it. But he noticed the weather forecast at midday and he turned the sound up. Not everything that was said was comprehensible to him.

'Does he mean it's going to rain here?' he said to Keith.

'Search me. The south-east is here, presumably. They never say London, do they? Norwich and Kent and Bristol and whatever but they never say the place most people live in. He says it'll be raining in the south-east tonight.'

'A lot of rain or not much?'

'What do you want to know for, anyway? You going somewhere exciting?'

Will hoped to be going somewhere very exciting, the most exciting somewhere of his whole life. But he mustn't tell Keith where or what he would be doing. It had to be a surprise to everyone. He didn't answer the question but finished his sandwiches in silence and while Keith made his daily protracted phone call to his wife, returned to his task of sanding-down doors.

They went home as usual at four. Coming this way, Will had to pass the window of Inez's shop. Neither Inez nor Zeinab was anywhere to be seen and Freddy Perfect, dressed in a brown overall, was sitting behind the desk. Will didn't question this or even think about it very much. Many of the ways of those he still thought of as 'the grown-ups' were strange to him and he accepted them the way children do without wanting to enquire further into them.

Once more in his own domain, he made himself tea and opened a packet of lemon curd tarts. Eating, particularly sweet things, was one of the great delights of his life and eating in Becky's company the primary pleasure. Although he could afford an entirely adequate diet, he knew there were deficiencies which finding the treasure would remedy. At present he couldn't buy Belgian chocolates or real cream cakes (not every day, anyway) or whole cheesecakes and glazed strawberry tarts of the kind he saw in the windows of expensive patisseries. Will found it hard to pass these shops without stopping and pressing his nose in longing against the glass. When he had the treasure he wouldn't have to do that, he would be able to go inside and buy.

Not *all* of it would go on Becky's house. He thought of it now as 'Becky's house'. Enough would be left over for him to eat the food he took delight in. While he was thinking along these lines and carefully washing up his cup and plate, the phone started ringing. Hardly anyone phoned him but Becky. He would have approached the phone in trepidation had he believed it could be someone else but as it was he thought it would be Becky telling him which day to come at the weekend, or even which *two* days, if he was very lucky. He picked up the receiver and said, 'Hello, Becky.'

A woman's voice said, 'It's not Becky, whoever she is, it's Kim. Remember me?'

He remembered her. She was Keith's sister. She had been with him when he first heard about the treasure. 'Yes,' he said.

'Well, I thought . . .' Almost anyone else would have noticed how awkward this was for her, how much she needed encouragement. 'I thought—sorry, I'm finding this quite hard, but would you—well, would you like to come to this party I'm going to? I mean, it's this friend of mine, she's going to be twenty-one and she said to me to bring someone and I thought, why not you? It's on Saturday night.'

'I'll be at Becky's on Saturday.' He might not be, it might be Sunday or even Friday, but saying he'd go somewhere on Saturday was a risk he couldn't take. 'I can't go out on Saturday.'

Some childhood memory returned to Kim. He sounded like her friend next door had, years and years before, saying she couldn't come out to play. What was it with him? 'Some other time, then,' she said, and now the disappointment in her voice did penetrate.

'I do like you,' Will said earnestly, for he could tell he had hurt her. 'But I mustn't go out on Saturdays.'

He remembered that terrible day when Becky hadn't invited him at all—because he had been out on a Saturday?—and that could happen again. He said good-bye to Kim rather sadly, for he was grateful to her. If it hadn't been for her suggesting it he would never have gone to the cinema nor learnt where the treasure was. The phone rang again almost immediately after he had put the receiver down. This time it was Monty, wanting to know if he'd fancy a drink in the Monkey Puzzle one evening this week.

'I can't go out this week,' Will said. 'I'm busy.'

'Some other time, then,' Monty said, using the same words as Kim had. Anyone but Will would have noticed the relief in his voice.

When Becky did phone, about an hour later, he was examining his new spade and looking out of the window at the now softly falling rain.

'Would you like to come over on Friday evening, Will?'

Fridays he didn't like because he couldn't be there very long and he couldn't have lunch but he said yes, so as not to miss the chance, and then, daringly, 'Can I come on Sunday too?'

There was silence. Something like a little sigh made him think poor Becky must be very tired. 'Yes, of course you can.'

So that was all right. Better than all right. He might take three visits to Sixth Avenue to unearth the treasure if it was buried deep or he couldn't find it at once. That would be tonight and Wednesday and Thursday, which meant he would be able to tell Becky all about it on Friday. Will went to the window. It was still raining.

He couldn't start work in this. He and Keith had once done an outside job, digging up someone's drain, but when it rained heavily they had had to stop. Where you dug filled up with water and the soil turned to mud the spade couldn't budge. But he went downstairs to check, taking the spade with him and opening the tenants' street door, where he extended a hand to feel the frequency of the drops.

All this was witnessed by Finlay Zulueta, sitting in his car on the opposite side of Star Street. A very pleased Crippen, all broad grin and approval, had detailed him to do this with the occasional help of Osnabrook. He had seen Will Cobbett buy the spade and watched him walk down to Kendal Street. Keith's van outside told him Cobbett's business there was legitimate. But buying a spade couldn't be. Keith Beatty must have spades enough for anything above-board. And here was Cobbett standing outside in the rain now, spade in hand. Still, there was nothing much the chap could do tonight, not in this rain. The car windows were getting steamed up on the inside and obscured by streaming water on the outside.

And Will himself, though bitterly disappointed, unwillingly accepted that the rain had increased even in the short time he had stood here on the doorstep. It was coming straight down now like rods of glass, pounding on the pavement and defying the gutter to contain it. A passing car sent up a spray that drove him back inside. He would have to give it up for tonight, start tomorrow instead. After watching from the shelter of the doorway for a moment or two, noticing Zulueta in his car but seeing nothing significant in his being there, Will went upstairs and began to prepare his evening meal.

It was rare but by no means unknown for Jeremy Quick to come through the shop on his way home from work.

He had no such intention that evening, particularly as he was later than usual, having worked an hour longer on account of losing the time in the morning while he was buying the earrings. But Inez was still in the shop and the lights were still on, so Jeremy went in, conscious that it would be wise to reinstate himself in her good opinion, but with another purpose in mind as well. He might have stayed away and used the tenants' street door if he had known Freddy Perfect would be in there, bustling about, not so much fingering the ornaments as flicking a feather duster over them. He wore a brown overall, of the kind favoured by very old-fashioned ironmongers.

Inez couldn't imagine where this overall had come from. Did Freddy have it handy in case of a chance of working in the shop? Would he have a uniform if offered a job somewhere as doorman or a tailcoat if a vacancy for a butler came up? She was not very pleased to see Jeremy and told herself that if he was expecting tea at this hour, he could forget it. What she would have liked best was to be left alone to watch Zulueta, apparently watching this house. For what? If only Zeinab hadn't been so stupid as to give a false address . . .

'You see I've got myself a job, Jeremy,' Freddy was saying. 'Under-manager. I've no objection to that, I'm not proud.'

Jeremy loathed being called by his first name—or his alternative first name—by such lowlife as Freddy Perfect but he wasn't going to make an idiot of himself by saying so. 'You're open late.'

'We're not really open,' Inez said and, with one of the sighs she had so nearly succeeded in banishing, 'I did ask you at least half an hour ago to turn the sign to "Closed", Freddy.'

'I know you did, Inez, but we'd just had those two nice ladies in who bought the Big Ben snowstorm and

the little glass vase. I didn't care to discourage custom in
these difficult times.'

Times had never been easier but Inez dreaded pro-
voking an argument. 'Do it now, will you? And then
you'd really better go back . . . er, upstairs.' That often-
repeated platitude about Ludmila wondering where he
was had lost its impact.

By now desperate for something pleasant to say,
Jeremy offered to buy a Crown Derby plate. It would
look nice on his living room wall. 'Please don't bother
to wrap it.'

While Inez turned away to write his receipt and
Freddy ambled reluctantly towards the inside door, he
slipped the earrings out of his back pocket and dropped
them silently on to the green baize surface of the jewellery table.

CHAPTER 13

It was Freddy who found the earrings on the following morning. He had come down to the shop much earlier than he was needed, just after eight and long before Jeremy Quick's arrival for his morning tea and at much the same time as Will left in Keith Beatty's van. Inez had to admit afterwards that Freddy working for her had some advantages. If Zeinab had been there it might have taken weeks before anyone came across them. On the other hand it was horrible having Crippen and Zulueta in the shop yet again.

'Things are starting to look very serious,' said Crippen gloomily.

'I quite agree.' Inez didn't like the look he gave her.

'That makes three of these missing articles that have been found on your premises, Mrs Ferry.'

'What do you expect me to do about it? I didn't put them there.'

'Four, actually,' said Freddy. 'Seeing as there are two earrings.'

He was ignored. Osnabrook arrived and he and Zulueta began once more searching the shop.

'We may have to close you down.' Crippen was shaking his head, something he had been doing spasmodically ever since he walked in five minutes before. 'It may be necessary to get an order.'

What kind of order wasn't specified. 'What good would that do?' Inez asked. 'Whoever is doing it would only take them somewhere else.'

'That's true.' Zulueta, who had come out from the back where he had been going through jewellery drawers, whispered something to Crippen.

'I see what you mean,' said Crippen, suddenly brightening. 'Let us see what the day brings forth.'

They left abruptly, abandoning the search.

'What was that all about?' Inez's enquiry was rhetorical but Freddy answered it all the same.

'They are on someone's track. No doubt, someone who lives in this neighbourhood. It's someone who has got it in for you, Inez. I wouldn't be surprised if it was that Jeremy.'

'Don't be ridiculous.'

'I wouldn't be entirely astounded.'

'Then why didn't you say something to Inspector Crippen?'

'Betray a fellow tenant? I haven't sunk as low as that, I hope.'

Inez saw that she had offended him, probably for the first time. She had thought it an impossible feat. But Freddy had stalked to the street door and gone outside to say hello to Anwar Ghosh who happened to be passing. They stood and chatted, Freddy enjoying a restorative cigarette. It was amazing what unlikely things upset different people, Inez thought. She didn't know how many times she had told him not to be silly, to stop picking up things in the shop, and once at least come near to accusing him of theft. None of that had riled him but suggesting he might rat on Jeremy Quick, a man he scarcely knew and one who had never been even commonly polite to him, had got under his skin. Anyway, it was all completely absurd, the suggestion and Freddy's ruffled feathers.

The day was dry and clear, and where they were to be seen, grass and leaves were of a fresher green after many hours of steady rain. Near as it was to Hyde Park, Kendal Street had far more in the way of lawns and trees than any areas further up the Edgware Road. Will, who liked fresh air and would have been happy in the country, went out for half an hour at lunchtime and walked into the park and across as far as the Peter Pan statue in Kensington Gardens. He liked that statue with its animals and fairylike people, and he stood in front of it for a full five minutes. Then he had to hurry back to avoid being late. All the time, except when he was looking at Peter Pan, he had been thinking about Becky's house and how maybe it should be in the country, only then she wouldn't be able to go to work. But she wouldn't need to go to work when he had the treasure. You could see it wasn't going to rain today, the sky was all wrong for it, and he'd be up in Sixth Avenue by eight, as soon as the sun was gone.

He had forgotten all about Kim Beatty till Keith reminded him. 'You've given up on my sister, then?' Keith didn't look too pleased; he had been quieter than usual all morning. 'I mean, you're not going out with her any more?'

'I don't know.' Will didn't know what else to say.

'You're wrong there, you know, Will. You're making a big mistake and I'm not just saying that because Kim's my sister.' Keith turned down the radio. 'Now, I'm a lot older than you and a family man and all that, so you'll know this is for your own good, else I wouldn't say it. You've got the looks all right but you're not every girl's cup of tea, I reckon you know that, but Kim really likes you and she's a good kid, she's not one of these scrubbers that'll go with anything in trousers, or out of them, I should say.' He smiled at his own wit and, if the truth be told, at his own worldly wisdom. 'Now, why not give it a rethink, eh? A chance like this may not come your way again.'

Scarcely a word of this had been understood by Will. The cup of tea and trousers metaphors were completely lost on him. Any circumlocution always was. He didn't know what to say, so he said, 'All right.'

'Good. That's what I like to hear. I wouldn't have said it, you know, if I hadn't your welfare at heart. And now I've got that off my chest I'd best give the wife a bell. Look at the time.'

Will gave little more thought to any of it. He understood vaguely that Keith knew he had told Kim he couldn't go out with her on Saturday because he was going to Becky's and, for some reason, didn't like it, and understood too that he really could have gone because his visits to Becky were now arranged for Friday and Sunday. It troubled him a bit that he had said something untrue. Was that why Keith had at first seemed cross with him? Anxiety didn't last long because he had other more important things to think about.

The look of the day was entirely different from yesterday when he got home. The sun was shining, the air still and warm as midsummer, and there was a feel in the atmosphere of settled weather to come. Will longed to be outdoors again and to get on with the job in hand. But now was not the time to start digging up a garden. People would be about everywhere, working outside, sitting in deckchairs or on front steps, and no one must know his secret until Becky did. He must wait. Leave it till at least eight. Making his tea and setting a chocolate croissant and an almond slice on a plate, he gave himself up to dreams of the weekend ahead. If it was still fine, maybe he and Becky would go up on Primrose Hill or even up on the Heath, as they had done once before on a summer's day, walking from Kenwood to Highgate, and when they were there he would tell her about the treasure and her house, giving

up her job and living in the country, just the two of
them for always.

He was too excited to eat much supper, just a scram-
bled egg on toast. The sun was setting, colouring the
western sky over the park a soft orangey-pink. He
wrapped up the spade in carrier bags and fastened them
with elastic bands. Zulueta's car wasn't there but another
one, which he recognised because Crippen was in the
passenger seat, was further down the street. Will didn't
think much about it. He set off for Sixth Avenue on foot,
enjoying the calm of the evening and the warmth which
still lingered.

One or perhaps two of the bags would do to put the
treasure in. He wouldn't need the spade any more, he'd
have no further use for it, and if he ever wanted another,
to work in their country garden, for instance, he'd have
so much money he'd be able to buy all the tools he
wanted. But he mustn't rush ahead so fast. It might take
more than one evening to find the treasure and unearth
it. He tried to suppress his excitement but failed. Self-
discipline was something he was no more able to exercise than was a child, so that by the time he reached the
house the builders had been working on, the tension in
his body was extreme, his hands were shaking and when
he found himself in the back garden he began jumping
up and down.

There was work to be done. He must try to remember exactly where the treasure had been buried and he
conjured up the film once more. The shed was over
there—someone had mended it a bit since the film was
made—and in front of it were a lot of flagstones, only
the ones here were more broken and cracked, and there
to the left of the shed was the strip of bare earth, just
like here, and a bit further in, nearer the next-door
wall, that was where they had dug to make the hole.

Then he noticed something he hadn't seen that first time. A piece of board and half a dozen bricks lay on the bare earth, more bricks than in the film, he thought, but that was unimportant.

It was getting on for nine and most of the light had gone. Will had brought a torch, the lantern kind, and making sure no one was in the house to see him and no one, apparently, watching from next door, he switched it on and stood it, pointing downwards, on the eaves of the shed. Then he unwrapped the spade, carefully flattening and setting aside two of the plastic bags. They would serve for carrying the treasure home in. With another hasty glance at the house and the houses on either side, he set the spade to the heavy clayey soil and began to dig.

By this time Crippen and Zulueta were inside the house, which they had entered by simply removing a flimsy baton, loosely nailed across the back door. They had put no lights on. Indeed, they couldn't. The electricity supply was disconnected. Wary of using torches, they found the darkness impenetrable at first, but after a minute or two their eyes were used to it. Will's own light supply gave them a perfect view of him and his endeavours. Young and very strong, he had soon dug a trench three feet long and a foot deep. He was turning towards the shed now, taking the torch and, on his knees, shining it into the cavity he had made. At this point Crippen turned to Zulueta and nodded. They made for the back door, put on their own powerful torches and advanced on Will.

He was preoccupied in wondering why, having dug this far, there was no sign of the treasure, not a jewel or gleam of gold. Two blinding beams of light appeared from nowhere, directed first into his trench, then on to his face as he turned round, rising slowly to his feet.

'William Charles Cobbett,' said Crippen in a loud frightening voice, 'I am arresting you on a charge of entering upon these premises for an unlawful purpose and concealing a body.' He would simply have said a charge of murder if he had seen the girl's corpse, if he even knew where it was. 'You are not obliged to say anything . . .'

The caution completed with more ominous words, Will said nothing. This was because he could think of nothing to say as he had no idea what was going on. Completely bewildered, he looked from one policeman to the other and, still clutching his spade, decided to run for it. It was, in fact, hardly a decision, more an instinctive reaction and the only thing to do. Somehow, he knew these men wanted to punish him and if you could, you escaped punishment. You ran. He ran to the side of the house, squeezed past the cement mixer and into the arms of Crippen's reinforcements, three officers from the uniformed branch, who had just left their car.

He put up no more resistance. They manhandled him into one of the cars between Zulueta and an officer in the Metropolitan police uniform which had always, since he was little, overawed him. One of the ladies at the home, when she took a group of children out, used to say to them that if they weren't good that policeman over there would get them. In all innocence, Will repeated this one day to Monty. After that, for some reason, they never saw the lady again, but it was too late and he was left with a permanent fear of men who wore dark blue with silver buttons and blue and white chequered caps. The man in the car next to him was dressed like that and Will soon became rigid with fear.

In a bleak room at the police station they sat him at a metal table and the one called Zulueta, who couldn't be a policeman because he didn't wear a uniform, offered him a cigarette. Will had never smoked and he wanted to say no, thank you, but he couldn't get any words out. Crippen came in, Zulueta pressed a switch on something a bit like Keith's radio and said, 'Interview commenced at twenty-two thirty hours. Present are William Charles Cobbett, Detective Inspector Brian Crippen, Detective Sergeant Finlay Zulueta and Police Constable Mark Heneghan.'

Will thought it wasn't so frightening because there was no one else there, but when he looked over his shoulder he saw a policeman standing just inside the door. He wasn't wearing a hat but he had the uniform on and a belt with something that looked like a heavy stick hanging from it. The sight made Will shake, though his body was stiff and tense.

'Where is she?' Crippen asked him. He said it with a sigh as if he were very tired.

Will didn't know who 'she' was. When he tried to ask, the words wouldn't come. The one in the uniform brought him a glass of water and Will drank some of it but his voice didn't come back.

Crippen asked him the same question, using the same phrase and then he said, 'Where is Jacky Miller? What have you done with her?'

All Will could do was shake his head. Zulueta asked him what he had done with a girl's body and then wanted to know where the girl had been, alive or dead, when he took off her earrings. When did he put the earrings in the shop? Was her body in the shed in Sixth Avenue? (They knew it wasn't because they had searched it before Will got there.) He couldn't answer any of this, not just because of the absence of voice but on account of not knowing what any of it meant. He sat silent, not looking at any of them, but keeping his eyes fixed on a hole in the skirting board. It looked like the kind of hole a mouse might make. Will liked mice, though he had mostly seen them only on television, and would have liked one to put its head out while he was watching. If he kept on looking at the hole and thinking about the mouse, perhaps they would let him go home.

'Keeping quiet like this', said Crippen, 'isn't going to do you any good, you know.' Why at least hadn't the man asked for a solicitor? Well, he wasn't going to tell him about his right to one or the one phone call he could make, if he wouldn't ask. 'You're just making things worse for yourself.'

Zulueta wanted to know if Will had been digging a grave. Who was the grave for? If it wasn't for Jacky Miller, what was the purpose of it?

If Will had been able to speak he would have told them about the treasure. Even if it meant sharing it with them. But he couldn't get a word out. Perhaps it was best, his surest way of keeping the treasure for himself and Becky. He went on staring at the hole but not thinking of the mouse any more, thinking about the treasure. Why hadn't he found it? Where was it? Could someone else have been there and dug it up? He didn't think so, for the earth had been hard as iron, untouched by a spade for years . . .

Two hours went by. They had tea and biscuits. While they ate and drank they bombarded him with questions. He couldn't eat or drink anything. It was after one in the morning when Zulueta said to the machine that was a bit like a radio that the interview was terminated. Trembling because he was handed over to a real policeman, the one who had stood inside the

door, Will was taken to a cell with a bed in it and a
table and a covered bucket. Glad to be alone, he sat on
the bed, then lay down.

It was rather cold. He pulled the thin blanket over
him. Tears trickled out of his closed eyes and he
squeezed them more tightly shut. He was too big to cry.
In the home they used to say that. A great big boy like
you crying, we can't have that, they used to say. The
tears dried on his cheeks as he fell asleep, thinking of
Becky, knowing Becky would come and please come
soon. Let him wake up and find Becky there, ready to
take him back to her house, and don't, please don't, let
the policeman come back.

CHAPTER 14

Four of them were in Anwar's room in St Michael's Street, discussing the proposed break-in and passing round a spliff prepared by Keefer Latouche. Keefer was thought the most highly skilled at filling and rolling joints, on the grounds that he was older and had once been threatened with jail 'next time' by DC Jones for being in possession of a white powder. For about five minutes Jones thought the powder was cocaine, but it turned out to be a substance for dissolving in water to treat splitting nails and the property of Keefer's then girlfriend. The other two people were a black boy called Flint Edwards and the girl, who had been Keefer's girl-friend, the manicurophile, and was now Flint's. Her name was Julitta O'Managhan, pronounced O'Moin. Keefer, at eighteen, was the eldest and therefore known to the others as Grandad.

'So I reckon on May sixth for B Day,' said Anwar, who never smoked anything.

Keefer and Flint looked at him uncomprehend-ingly but Julitta said, 'My auntie's got a bidet in her bathroom.'

Already high on his mixture, Keefer and Flint rocked about laughing, into which Julitta joined, rolling about on the floor. Keefer began tickling her under her arms and round her waist.

'You take your dirty white hands off her,' said Flint, laughing no more.

Anwar looked at them despairingly but he wasn't one to let things slide. 'Will you shut the fuck up, the lot of you? Or do I have to make you?'

'You and whose network?' said Flint but he said it half-heartedly and, sitting up again, took a long indrawn gulp on the joint.

'I call it B Day,' began Anwar, already at sixteen an accomplished chairman, 'because that's the day we're going to do the job, the break-in. B for break-in, see, as I don't suppose there's one of you fuckers can spell. The folks'll all be out all day. It's what's called the Spring Holiday, right? Come over here.' He had moved to the window. Pulling down the sash and letting in the mild night air made Keefer double up with coughing. 'We'll go in the back way, providing Grandad lasts that long. I've drawn a plan and I'll show you how in a minute. The burglar alarm number is 2647 and I want you to memorise that—if Grandad's shit hasn't fried your brains.'

They all contemplated the backs of houses in the parallel street. Large old sycamore and plane trees intervened, making clumps and fronds of darkness between this window and the bright amber rectangles in the brick expanse. Those who could interpret what they saw would have detected from the pairs of fiery yellow points in the leafy mass below a dozen cats squatting and watching.

'We going in one of them windows?' asked Flint.

'By then I shall have a key to the back door.' Anwar didn't specify how he would acquire it and no one asked. They knew that if he said he'd have a key he would. 'Me and Ju'll do the top floor, Flint can do the middle—and remember, nothing from Flat 2— Grandad and me Flat 1. I'll give him a hand when I've done the top.' He rounded on Julitta and barked at her, 'What's the alarm number?'

'I do not give a fuck, as all alarms suck,' said Julitta, a reply which prompted screams of laughter, as her rhymes and jokes invariably did.

'Oh, what's the use?' Anwar slammed down the window, the noise scattering the cats. 'Fucking moggies,' he said. 'Maybe it's best if you don't remember. It's enough that I know it. There's a week to go to the sixth. Balaclavas or black stockings'll do. Trainers, obviously.' He eyed the four-inch heels on Julitta's cowboy boots with disapproval and turned his gaze with equal distaste on Keefer's hands, busy with a fresh mix. 'Meet again here Sunday night. On the sixth we go in at noon sharp, so it may be just possible for you lot to keep off the grass for the morning. And the juice.' This was for Flint, a well-known vodka connoisseur. 'You can all fuck off now. I'm going to bed.'

Shocked into forgetting her role as comedienne, Julitta said, 'What's with you, An? It's not midnight.'

'I'm younger than you, remember? I'm a growing boy and I need my sleep.' He yawned hugely to prove it, hustled them towards the door, pushing at the air with his hands like someone driving away a brood of hens. Down the uncarpeted woodworm-eaten staircase they clattered, shouting and shrieking, waking up the tenants whose rooms they passed, blowing cannabis fumes under doors. They tumbled out into the street and into Keefer's filthy white van with the notice about not cleaning it in the rear window. Before moving off, Keefer turned on the radio to a garage channel at full volume and opened all the windows.

Anwar closed his door very quietly. First he made himself a cup of cocoa with full-cream milk, his favourite drink. Leaving it to cool a little, he took off the suit he wore, dark grey with a pinstripe, and hung it on a hanger in the cupboard. His white shirt he

dropped on the floor for the laundry tomorrow. He possessed no jeans, T-shirts, leather jackets or boots.

Aged sixteen but looking younger, he was the only
son of a doctor who had come to London from Bombay
when a boy, and his wife, a teacher in a sixth-form college. They also had three daughters and, being comfort-
ably off, lived in a large detached house in Brondesbury
Park, not far from the premises of the group practice of
which Dr Ghosh was a member. Anwar, his parents had
been told, had a phenomenally high IQ, was certainly
tipped for Oxford and would very probably manage ten
GCSEs and sit for his A Levels a year early.

But that had been eighteen months before and the
GCSEs had not been taken. It was uncertain whether
the friends he associated with had corrupted Anwar or
he had corrupted them. His parents didn't enquire
because most details of the life he led were unknown to
them. Of course, they were aware of his truancy because
his school told them about it and they knew it was
impossible to say if he had fallen behind in his work
because he was seldom there to do any. But the room he
rented in St Michael's Street, Paddington, and the successful crimes he and his cronies committed, of all that
they were ignorant. He was so polite to them, so clean
in his person, so clever and talented, that apart from his
seldom attending school, there seemed no fault to find
with him, yet both of them remonstrated with him continually about this failure.

He must go to a university. It would be absurd if he,
of all his contemporaries, a natural for Oxford or
Cambridge, should miss out on this vital stage of education while even the dimmest C-streamers were off to
some former polytechnic somewhere. There was even a
period when Dr Ghosh drove him to school and
parked at the gate to see that he didn't come out again.

Anwar, naturally, got out through the gym, across the car park and, lying very low, by way of someone's back garden. All that was a year ago. Once he became sixteen no one could compel him to attend school. He wouldn't even have to live at home and he could get married if he liked—but of course he didn't like. Almost the only thing he couldn't do was vote, and who cared about that?

At first he had explained his overnight absences by saying he was staying with a friend. Perhaps they only believed that because they wanted to. They wanted to think he did something ordinary and normal, that other boys did. It wasn't as if he never came home. He often did for a night or two, a tallish boy, very thin, immaculate in one of his dark suits, smelling of the coconut soap he used in his shower. Mena Ghosh would happily have washed his shirts and underwear had he brought them to her but he had them all done at a laundry in the Edgware Road. His parents were sociable and when they went to a party or a dinner he would often accompany them, courteously addressing elderly relatives as 'auntie' and 'uncle'. He helped his sisters with their homework and escorted them to friends' houses if they went after dark. He always had plenty of money.

Dr Ghosh told himself that his son was prudent, well able to manage the modest allowance he made him. But the handmade shoes made him wonder and so did the ring with what looked like a genuine diamond in it. Now Oxford had gone by the board, he spent a lot of the time Anwar was at home in nagging him at least to 'do something vocational'. Becoming a plumber or an electrician would at least be a means of his earning a living. Anwar always went off again after a couple of days. He had 'some friends' in Bayswater, he said. This was quite true, for Julitta and Flint had a room at the Sussex

Gardens end of Spring Street. His own place, as he referred to it among his cronies, he rented along with half a dozen other people, each of whom had single rooms, from a Turkish man. Mr Sheket ran a sweatshop in the basement, where fifteen women worked at sewing machines in twilight conditions for twelve hours a day.

No word had ever come from James. For the first few days after he had gone, leaving her on the doorstep with Will, she had felt only a bitter resentment. What a shallow conventional man he must be to abandon her simply because, through no fault of her own, she had a relative who appeared to be a street sleeper. To go like that, without even waiting for an explanation and without any promise of getting in touch. He had been *frightened* of Will, she thought. And not only that. He had been wary of any closer involvement with her, fearing that any at all might lead to his being drawn into some kind of caring for Will, helping him, perhaps even spending money on him. For a little while she managed contempt for someone who could be so selfish and so cowardly.

The passing of time without a sign from him should have hardened those feelings until she was able to dismiss him altogether. After all, it wasn't as if this had been a full-blown love affair. She had spoken to him a few times on the phone, twice been out with him. Her pride might be hurt but that was all and by now she should be well on the way to forgetting him. She couldn't. He had been so nice, so charming, on their two dates, funny, sensitive, interested in her, obviously admiring. And she had been mildly, then strongly, attracted to him. On that scanty level of intimacy, she would have said—on their way home from the party, say—that he was the last man in the world to behave like that. Obviously, she hadn't really known him at all. Or was it rather that there was something she hadn't understood about him? Could it be that his leaving her like that was not a sign of a lack of sensitivity but *because* of it? He had known she wouldn't want anyone else around while she dealt with Will, so ever-tactful, he had made himself scarce?

In that case, why hadn't he phoned her that evening or next day? So her thoughts went round and round, condemning him, then making excuses for him, finally coming to a conclusion that the only way of laying these speculations to rest was for her to phone him. She had nothing to lose by phoning him. He could put the receiver down when he heard her voice, he could tell her he didn't want to see her again, in which case her initial feelings would be confirmed and she would know there was no use in maundering after him. Or he could give her a second chance, agree to come over and discuss the problem of Will.

Her heart sank, though, when she thought of the weekend ahead. Tired, too weary of the whole Will business and too fond of him to make a stand, she had agreed to let him come over on both Friday evening and Sunday. For the whole day on Sunday. If she phoned James and it worked, he wanted to see her and arranged a meeting, she'd have to stipulate Saturday as the only possibility. Why not? She didn't have to have her wandering-round-the-shops morning. It was beginning to trouble her conscience, anyway, as trivial and almost shame-making.

She would phone him. She finally made up her mind as she was driving home from work on Wednesday evening. But coming to a decision was one thing, carrying it out quite another. She drew back, she cringed, from the idea of phoning this man she had known so briefly and doing what amounted to asking him for a date. Several times she approached the phone, put her hand to it, retreated. At last, when it was nearly nine, she poured herself a stiff gin, let it take effect before she lifted the receiver, then quickly dialled his number.

Of course he was out. His voice on the answering machine brought him back before her eyes, his good looks, his pleasant easy manner. She left no message but tried again five minutes later. Had she ever given him her mobile number or her office number? She couldn't remember. In any case, it was unlikely he still had it. Suppose he had forgotten her, even her name . . .

After the long beep, she said into the phone, 'James, it's Becky Cobbett. Please give me a call. I'd like us to talk.' She gave her home number, then those for her mobile and her office. The effect of the gin had been so stimulating, so self-confidence building, that she had another, immediately wishing she hadn't.

Early in the morning, she woke up with a headache. Two aspirins helped but they also stunned her. She would have liked to fall back into bed and sleep for hours, but she couldn't, she had to be in the office early. There were no messages for her from her own answering service. What had she imagined? That he was so longing to speak to her that he'd call in the small hours?

By eight thirty she was at her desk, and in the morning conference that was the cause of her early arrival by a quarter to nine. Becky was too good at her job to allow herself to be distracted from the important matter in hand by thoughts of a remotely possible but improbable love relationship. That was dismissed until the conference ended at ten thirty. Back in her own office, she resisted dialling into her home number to pick up any messages there might be, but drank the coffee her secretary brought her, made half a dozen essential phone calls and took twice as many—each time hoping it might be James—turned her attention to the rough draft of the marketing plan she was compiling, and at one went down the road to the little bistro for lunch.

She couldn't eat. It was all ridiculous, to lose one's appetite from tension over will-he-phone-won't-he-phone. At her age too, when she ought to know better. She longed for a stiff drink but knew this was the brink of the slippery slope. All her adult life Becky had had to resist the lure of hard liquor and occasionally had yielded to it, never bingeing and never totally abstaining, but drinking a little or quite a lot every day. She had long ago fallen into the precarious situation of needing a drink before undertaking any big enterprise, meeting any challenge or encountering alarming departures from the norm. To this temptation she often refused to give in but the struggle exhausted her, leaving her drained. She meant to fight it now but tired as she was, the headache not entirely gone, she found the battle too much for her and she gave in.

The gin, vodka and whisky bottles in her office cupboard had never been kept secret. Along with tonic and sparkling water, they often came out when a guest or colleague arrived to discuss something—so long as the time was after five thirty. Her secretary knew about it and she and Becky sometimes partook at the end of a hard day. Becky got out the brandy now and poured rather over an inch into a glass. It would serve both as bracer and hair of the dog. She swallowed it quickly, poured another for more leisurely absorption and, trying to empty her mind of emotion, dialled home for her messages.

There was only one, and that not from James but from Inez Ferry. Unlike most people, Inez had given the time of her call, no more than half an hour before. As Becky listened she had to sit down, it was such a shock.

'Becky, it's Inez. This is urgent. It's Thursday the twenty-fifth of April and the time is one forty-five. I knew you wouldn't be at home but I haven't got your office number or your mobile. Listen, Becky, Will's been arrested, they've been holding him since last night. The police were in here and the detective inspector told me. Call me back as soon as you can.'

Inez had tried to explain to Crippen that Will was not quite—well, of course he wasn't retarded, you didn't use that term any more. He ought to know that, she said indignantly, fixing him with a resentful look.

'All right, all right, keep calm,' said Crippen. 'As a matter of fact, he seems quite normal to me. He doesn't speak but there's nothing new in that. A lot of them have got silence off to a fine art.'

'Will isn't capable of getting anything off to a fine art, as you put it. What's he charged with? Have you got him a lawyer?'

'There's no need to get heated, Mrs Ferry. I don't know why you're so upset. Cobbett hasn't asked for a solicitor and he hasn't asked to make any phone calls. You ought to appreciate that on our part, very—er, very, what's the word I want?'

'Stupid?' put in Freddy. 'Ignorant? Bigoted?'

In spite of her dismay, Inez couldn't help laughing and her feelings warmed to Freddy. 'I suppose you mean magnanimous,' she said. 'Anyway, I don't agree. You don't seem to realise that you're holding a man with the mental age of a little boy and treating him like some—some old lag. What's he supposed to have done, anyway?'

'That we can't tell you,' said DC Jones who had accompanied Crippen. 'Suffice it to say that we are currently conducting a comprehensive search of the Queens Park–Harrow Road area for evidence.'

'What evidence?'

Neither policeman answered her but Freddy said lugubriously, 'Some poor girl's body, I expect.'

Agreement to or rejection of this suggestion were cut off by the phone ringing. It was Becky Cobbett. Inez spoke to her, covered the earpiece while she said to Crippen, 'His aunt wants to come to the police station and have me with her. I suppose that's all right with you?'

Jones lifted his shoulders, dropped them. Crippen said cryptically, 'If you must.'

The visit to the police station was quite useless. They weren't allowed to see Will, were told nothing and largely ignored. A friendly sergeant in uniform eventually took pity on them, and brought them tea and chocolate chip biscuits. Inez was on tenterhooks because she could smell the liquor on Becky's breath from a yard away. Becky had picked her up at the shop and driven her here, and all the time Inez had been afraid they would be stopped and Becky breathalised. Some time or other, maybe not till the evening, Becky would have to drive them back again—please God, with Will—and surely then the police would detect what she had detected from the first. In spite of being in Inez's opinion quite far gone on what smelt like brandy, Becky had been on her mobile at least half a dozen times, talking to the office.

Inez thought about Freddy whom she had left in charge. Everything would probably be all right, though she would have been easier in her mind had it been Zeinab. Freddy was honest, she was sure, and though not stupid, deeply *silly*. If she had been asked to explain—after all, didn't the two terms mean much the same thing?—definition would have defeated her. Perhaps she meant he trusted people too much and he looked at the world from the point of view of an innocent who believes himself to be sophisticated—a dangerous illusion. Becky had gone up to the sergeant's counter to ask if they had come up with an answer to her question of whether Will could have a solicitor. Couldn't she get one for him? Presently, Zulueta appeared, said that since Will hadn't uttered a word he didn't need a lawyer and, sitting down with them, asked them what was Will's connection with Sixth Avenue, Queens Park. Why had he bought a spade? Why had he been digging up the garden of an empty house?

Becky was completely mystified by this. As far as she knew Will had never set foot in Queens Park unless he had worked there with Keith Beatty. 'Look, how long can you keep him here?' she asked. 'It must be twenty-four hours by now. This is outrageous.'

'Actually,' said Zulueta, looking at his watch, 'it's just twenty. He can be held in custody for thirty-six hours and then—you may be sure of this—we can get an extension. In this case, without difficulty.'

Bored on her own and not the kind of woman who likes going about without a male escort, Ludmila had come down to the shop soon after Inez's departure. She was proud of her continuing blondeness, which she swore was not touched up, and her emaciation, so she usually arranged herself to show off both these advantages. In a skin- (or bone-) tight floor-length dress of dark-green silk with a mauve pashmina draped over her arms, she reclined in the grey velvet armchair, her legs crossed and her hair spread across the chair back like an antimacassar. The pashmina she had just ironed, leaving a burn on the hem by the fringe, but the brown mark she had artfully folded in over her elbow. Her pose was not designed for any man's entrapment, Freddy being trapped already, but when Anwar Ghosh strolled in for a word or two with his mate, she stretched herself more sinuously.

Anwar took no notice of her. 'What's with the old woman?' He looked about him as if Inez might be hiding behind one of the cabinets.

'Doing business with the police,' said Freddy importantly. 'I'm in charge.'

'What business?' Anwar didn't much like the sound of that. It was to his advantage that the police took the minimum of interest in Star Antiques.

'It concerns that backward boy who lives next to me,' said Ludmila in a curious Baltic accent.

Longing to justify his existence by actually selling something while Inez was absent, Freddy said, 'Nothing to do with us. You going to buy something now you're here, An? Things are a bit slack this afternoon.'

Anwar looked anything but keen. 'Something like what?'

'How about that nice bust of Queen Victoria? Though why "bust" I'm sure I don't know. More head and neck, I'd say. Or that lovely glass cat? Look great in your flatlet, that would.'

'I'm a minimalist,' said Anwar, shaking his head. 'I'll be back in a tick. I gotta find a toilet, I need a slash.'

He disappeared in the direction of the Edgware Road. 'Going to the one in the Metropole Hotel,' said Freddy admiringly. 'Nothing but the best for that young man.'

'Is he gay?' Ludmila asked only because she could hardly believe anyone heterosexual could be proof against her charms.

'He's too young for that,' Freddy said incomprehensibly, but then he often said things that seemed to have no logical or experiential basis.

'Why were you in his place, anyway?'

'I never was, Ludo.' Detecting something threatening in her expression, he said, 'I swear on my mother's head!'

'You have no mother, you fool.'

Freddy was about to say that, like everyone else, he did once have a mother and had only said that about the bust and the cat because these ornaments would look good anywhere, when Ludmila said in scolding tones, 'Have you picked up our weekend vouchers yet?'

'I'll pop up to the travel chap right now. You'll look after the shop, won't you, sweetheart?'

'Well, I'm here, aren't I?'

The travel agent who was making arrangements for their weekend break was just round the corner in the Edgware Road. When he had been gone about a minute, Ludmila stood up, stretched and the pashmina fell off her arm, revealing the burn mark for anyone to see. This reminded her that she had left the iron on. With a hasty glance up and down the street to check no one was heading for the shop, she went out by the interior door and up the stairs.

Anwar, who hadn't been near the Metropole but watching from the alley opposite, sauntered into the shop and, much more swiftly, into the back. He took the key from the back door and let himself out again by the tenants' street door. The best place and quickest for the job he wanted was down in the underpass beneath the Edgware Road where it was crossed by the east-west flyover. To the people of the neighbourhood, especially the women, this underpass provided both safety and danger, safety from the relentless unceasing traffic pouring down the A5, but danger from the dubious characters who congregated in the passages and the occasional menacing loiterer. Easier, really, to cross above ground on the lights. But Anwar had no fear of the underpass. People were afraid of *him*.

The man who ran the place where they mended shoes, engraved tags for dogs' collars and cut keys, was always affable and pleasant but Anwar suspected him of total honesty. That was enough to make him suspicious. Still, he never asked questions as to why one wanted a key copied and he didn't ask now.

'Half an hour?' said Anwar, laying Inez's back doorkey on the counter.

'Oh, come on, son. I'll need an hour.'

'Three-quarters?'

'OK. But not a minute under.'

It was just after six when Crippen appeared and said to Becky in a surly tone, 'We're letting Cobbett go home.'

She jumped up. 'Where is he?'

'He's coming. I've had a doctor see him.' Crippen spoke in the manner of a responsible person piously proud of doing his duty. 'The doctor can't account for his refusal to talk.'

Becky turned away. How different would Forsyth's conduct have been, thought Inez, in similar circumstances. For an instant, vividly, she saw Martin's face as he showed that tender empathy with the aunt of the poor boy his men had wrongfully arrested. Tonight, when at last she got home, she would put all this behind her and watch *Forsyth and the Forlorn Hope*, she'd forget Will and Becky and Freddy and Zeinab, and indulge in her therapy . . .

They brought Will in. Like a zombie, he walked mechanically, his legs stiff, his head hanging. Becky ran to him and threw her arms round him. He let himself be hugged, staring blankly over her head at the window and the long slanting sunbeams of late afternoon. Then, with a wondering slowness, as if learning the move for the first time, he brought up his hands and laid them against her back.

Not a word did he utter even when they were in the

car, Inez in the back, he in the passenger seat next to
Becky. One good thing, thought Inez, Becky's body
must have processed the alcohol in her blood by now.
The police had seemed unaware of it. The traffic was
heavy, nose-to-tail queues from Maida Vale down to
Marble Arch and not much better going up. 'Thursday
evening,' said Inez. 'Late shopping in Oxford Street.'

'Of course I shall take Will home with me,' said
Becky. 'He can't be alone.'

To her shame, Inez was enormously relieved. Instead
of luxuriating in Martin's company for a couple of
hours, she had imagined herself up and down the stairs,
checking on Will, feeding Will, continually obliged to
phone Becky.

'I suppose he'll have to take time off work?'

'*He* will? I should think that's the least of our worries.
What about me?'

'Becky, I'm so sorry. Did you find out anything
about what they suspected him of doing? Why he'd
been in—wherever it was—Queens Park?'

'They said they'd want to see him again, but I expect
they always say that. They found him digging in a garden and when they asked him he wouldn't answer. Of,
course the truth is he couldn't answer. He can't speak.
Very obviously, I'd say, he's lost the power of speech.
They've had masses of them digging up all the gardens
round there and searching through sheds and garages.
They told me that but they wouldn't say why. Looking
for Jacky Miller's body, I suppose.'

Will remained silent, his face not so much
inscrutable as empty. The last Inez saw of them as
Becky drove off along Star Street was his head and
shoulders in profile, expressionless, rigid and inani-
mate as the marble bust Freddy had tried to sell to
Anwar Ghosh.

Quite properly at this hour, the shop was closed. Inez
let herself in and found on the desk a note from Freddy,
written in marker pen, smeary and fingermarked:
*Custermer that bawt grandad clock say does not work, pen-
dullum funny, will bring back tomorer. Luv, Freddy.*

Freddy himself was certainly responsible for damage
to the clock. There was nothing she could do about it
tonight. She checked that the front door was once more
locked, left the note where it was and went out into the
back hall. The wheelie-bin that lived in the backyard
had to be out in the front for the rubbish collection
before eight in the morning. Inez was weary but she
knew she'd have to do it. The backdoor was locked and
the key in the lock as usual. Only it wasn't quite as
usual. The key, with its asymmetrical head, could be
turned once to lock it or one and a half times, in which
case it would still be locked. From habit or some compulsion, she always turned it one and a half times.
When that was done the hole in its uneven-sided head
would be at the bottom; given one and a half turns, at
the top. Freddy must have gone outside for something,
that was all. That made two things to ask Freddy about
tomorrow . . .

CHAPTER 15

Not anticipating the worst, Becky had done nothing to prepare her study for Will's reception. It was as she had left it two days before, the laptop open, books and papers strewn about, waste paper basket half full. She told herself she must be optimistic. This trauma and its effects would pass, he would regain the power of speech and within a few days return home to Star Street. It surely wasn't necessary to remove all her things from the room and refurnish it. Becky knew that however you guarded your privacy, if you lived in London you must have somewhere for a friend to sleep in an emergency, and the sofa already in there was designed to convert into a comfortable bed. Having led Will up the staircase and into the flat, providing him with tea and cakes, she set about converting the bed. It was a more difficult task, requiring greater physical strength, than she remembered, and when it was done she thought how it wasn't something she would want to do often.

The desk and the workstation with computer and printer could remain where they were. And the photocopier, the dictionaries, the paper shredder and the large wicker basket. If she had to take the chairs and the table out she would have to find somewhere to put them. Where? There really wasn't room in the rest of the flat.

Will was sitting in silence in the living room. He had eaten the meringue but left the piece of fruit cake—unheard of for him. He didn't smile at her, he didn't even

look up. Roundly, but in her mind, she cursed the police
officers who had done this to him. After a while, a despairing few minutes, she switched on the television to one of
the noisy quizzes he usually so much enjoyed. This time
he did raise his head. He fixed his eyes on the screen but
it seemed to her that the loud voices and raucous singing
of the group who diverted viewers from intellectual effort
every few minutes, made him flinch a little, and she wondered painfully if for some reason these people reminded
him of Crippen's and Jones's barked enquiries.

At least he was occupied. She got up to pour herself
a drink—had she ever needed one so much?—and
crossing to the cabinet noticed the light on the phone.
In the horror of it she had forgotten her earlier stress
and the message left for James. Now she was almost
afraid of what might be waiting for her. But she lifted
the receiver and listened to her messages. One was from
Inez, another from Keith Beatty wanting to know where
Will was. The third was from James.

'Becky,' he said, 'it's James. You asked me to call you,
but I've tried your mobile and it's always engaged.' That
would have been in the afternoon when she was making
all those calls to the office from the police station. 'I'm
sorry I left that day. It's been on my conscience and then
when I decided to phone you I thought you'd be too
angry to speak to me. I'll call you at nine tonight,
Thursday the twenty-fifth, and maybe we can meet.'

Absolutely plausible, quite reasonable. She ought to
be elated, she *would* have been if he had called before
lunchtime. With a second drink in her hand because
she had gulped down the first one on hearing the message, she sat down beside Will once more. He put one
hand up to his lips and she knew he was trying to tell
her he couldn't speak, he didn't know why, the words
wouldn't come.

'Never mind,' she said cheerfully. 'You'll be able to talk again. Tomorrow, I expect. Don't worry about it. Look, there's that man on the TV you like.'

To her horror, she saw that his eyes had filled with tears. She took his hand, squeezed it, sat there thinking of his plight and, equally, of her own. James was forgotten. If Will's speech didn't come back, or didn't come back for weeks, what was she going to do? She couldn't go to work and leave him here alone. Could she even go out to the shops? A carer? But Will would hate a carer, would be made worse by anyone being here but herself.

She phoned Keith Beatty, told him Will was unwell, wouldn't be in again before Monday. She heard Will go to the bathroom and shuffle back a few minutes later. Her drink on the kitchen counter, she stood in front of the fridge, looking for something to give him for dinner. Eggs, bacon, mushrooms, she supposed, and there were always chips she could defrost. A can of fruit, ice cream, more cake if he wanted it. Luckily, she had already got the cakes in for the visit he had been due to make next day. Not only James, but his nine o'clock phone call were forgotten. She piled food on the tray for Will. For herself she could fancy nothing but she sat with him while the worst television could offer that evening dribbled out of the screen.

At nine sharp the phone rang and getting up to answer it, she wondered before she heard his voice, who it could be.

No one returns to work after an illness on a Friday, but Zeinab did. As she was half an hour late as usual she wasn't expected and Freddy was taking her place. An hour before Jeremy Quick had come in for his tea and when Inez handed it to him she asked if he had been out into the garden before she came home the previous evening.

'I thought tenants weren't permitted to use your garden, Inez.'

'They're not but people do strange things around here.'

'I hope you don't think I'm one of them,' said Jeremy, looking genuinely shocked.

Inez didn't quite like to say he was—what could be stranger than inventing a girl friend and her aged mother?—as quarrelling with a tenant wasn't the happiest start to the day. Briefly, she wondered if he flinched from any woman's touch or if it was just hers. 'Someone did.' She wasn't going to tell him how she knew. A few secret weapons were always required by a woman in her position. 'Someone went out there between three in the afternoon and six thirty when I got back.'

'Is it important?' He asked his question gently but still Inez didn't like it. Of course it wasn't important to *him*.

'Perhaps not. Shall we change the subject?'

'Gladly.'

'I suppose you've heard that the police found Jacky Miller's earrings in this shop?'

The change in his expression was tiny but, observant woman that she was, Inez noticed it, the minutest twitch to his lips, a point of light in each eye. 'Jacky Miller?' he said.

'The missing girl, the one they're searching for.'

'Ah, yes,' he said. 'I must go. Thank you for the tea.'

Freddy came soon after he went. 'Another glorious day, Inez.' He rubbed his hands together. 'It makes you glad to be alive.'

'Possibly. Did you go out into the garden yesterday afternoon, Freddy?'

'Oh, no,' said Freddy obsequiously. 'Tenants aren't allowed.'

'But since you aren't a tenant, perhaps the rules don't apply to you?'

'As you say, Inez.' Freddy sat down on the arm of the grey velvet chair and wagged one finger like the needle on a metronome. 'As you say, I am not a tenant. Ludo is the tenant. I am domiciled in Walthamstow.' Inez eyed him suspiciously, almost sure that last time it had been Hackney. 'But still I regard myself as Ludo's *representative*. Or perhaps her agent. In other words, if she had an urgent need to go out into the garden but no wish or ability to do so it is possible I might do so for her. I hope I make myself clear. On the other hand, yesterday I did *not* go out into the garden, nor would I . . .'

'All right, Freddy, that's fine. You ought to have been called to the bar. Unlock the door, would you, and turn round the sign?'

If Inez had asked Ludmila the question she had asked Freddy she might have been told about Anwar Ghosh. Ludmila hated Anwar for various reasons, his scorning of herself, as a possible rival in Freddy's affections and his treating her as a shop minder. She would happily have made trouble for him. But Inez rather disliked Ludmila and never spoke to her unless it was essential. Not because of any diffidence but to avoid more long-winded speeches and explanation, she postponed asking Freddy about the pendulum on the grandfather clock but pondered instead whether she should take it back meekly or refuse to refund the money paid for it.

A few minutes after nine she phoned Becky to enquire after Will.

'I never thanked you for coming with me yesterday, Inez. It was very kind and I am grateful.'

'How is he today?'

'Well, he's up and he's eaten his breakfast. He still doesn't speak.'

'Will you be able to manage?'

'I hope so. I'm going to phone the office in a minute and say I'll take a week of my leave. I'm hoping a week will be enough, Inez.'

She sounded a lot less despairing, Inez thought. Next she planned on phoning Mrs Sharif to enquire when Zeinab would be coming back, but instead she sat thinking about the oddities of the people she daily encountered and wondering particularly what Will had really been doing digging up a garden in Queens Park. It was impossible, even in his case, to imagine any law-abiding motive. Though you might be somewhat . . . well, intellectually handicapped, you surely didn't go after dark to an empty house in a district you didn't know and where no one knew you and dig a deep hole—three feet deep, one of the officers had told her—if you were an honest person. You didn't, since you hadn't money to spare, buy a spade for that sole purpose. And what had he hoped to dig out of the hole or, perhaps more to the point, put into it? She shivered a little and thoughts of Will's activities brought her back to her own garden, the back door and the key.

Someone had gone out there and, whoever it was, it couldn't have been Will. Was it possible that the last time she had been in the garden, probably a week ago, she had turned that key only once instead of one and a half times? She was asking herself this question, examining her memory, when the street door swept open and Zeinab came in, escorted by Morton Phibling.

'Here is my beloved,' declaimed Morton, 'turned up like a bad penny, though it goes against the grain to call so much beauty a bad anything.'

Zeinab gave him a look which might have denoted disgust or merely resignation to an inevitable fate. She appeared to be very well, blooming with health in a new black suede skirt some ten inches above her knees and a new white silk shirt, her eyelids painted gold and the diamond nose stud in place. Her black hair, newly washed and smelling of tuberose, hung down her back like a satin cloak.

'What do you think of my engagement gift?' Morton laid a finger like a pork sausage on a diamond, roughly the size of the koh-i-noor, which hung from a gold chain round Zeinab's neck. 'Beautiful, eh?'

'Very beautiful,' said Inez. 'I don't want to put a dampener on things but I don't think you should wear that out in the street around here.'

'Oh, I shan't. I was OK in Mort's car. Mort took me for a fitting for my wedding dress yesterday, Inez.'

'Really? I thought you had a virus.'

'The worst was over by then.' Zeinab floated a kiss on the air half an inch from Morton's face. 'Run along now, darling. I'll see you tonight.'

'That's the first time I've seen you wear one of his presents,' said Inez, 'apart from your engagement ring. Tell me something. When I phoned your mother you didn't seem to be there and she said she'd be going round to you later. What did she mean?'

But Zeinab had seen Freddy for the first time and noticed his brown duster coat. He was standing behind Inez's desk, contemplating the expenditure book. 'What's he doing here?'

Freddy looked up and said with dignity but an unfortunate mixing of metaphors, 'You going sick like that left Inez in a hole and I stepped in.'

Suppressing laughter with difficulty, Inez said, 'Freddy has been helping me while you were away, that's all.'

'All! It looks to me as if some people have been plotting to take away other people's jobs. I call that a low-down underhand trick.'

Freddy's life was probably easier now than it had been at any time since he left Barbados when he was an adolescent. Since then he had been dogged by near penury, racist insults, loneliness, callous sackings and utter disrespect. It had done nothing to damage his basically sweet nature but it had taught him how to fight and give as good, or as bad, as he got. 'And there's some people,' he said, 'who'd sell their own grandfathers for a giro. The last thing they need is jobs when flogging the gifts of same grandfathers with more dosh than's good for them is all in the day's work.'

'Don't you dare speak to me like that!'

'A tart is what you are and not even an honest one.'

'Be quiet,' said Inez in a voice not to be defied. 'Be quiet, both of you. I will not have you quarrelling in here.' They stared at her mutinously but they were silenced. 'Thank you very much, Freddy, for your help but Zeinab is back now and you know you were only working here in her absence. I'm sure Ludmila will be pleased to have you back with her.'

Slowly Freddy took off his coat and folded it up. 'First I shall go down the road and enjoy a restorative glass with my friend in the Ranoush Juice. I hope you won't regret taking that one back, Inez. Me and Ludo wouldn't like to see your business come to grief through a criminal assistant.'

'You and that Russian cow would be out on the street if I had my way,' Zeinab screamed as the door shut after him. 'You'd know all about criminals, on the Benefit fraud like you are!'

Inez hadn't sighed for weeks but she sighed now. Until the fracas over Freddy, she had been going to ask exactly where Zeinab lived and with whom, but she was daunted by the prospect of more lies and prevarications. 'I had better remind you'—as if the girl needed reminding—'that Monday is the Spring Holiday. Tomorrow, of course, we'll be opening as usual. So,' she added, unable to resist, 'no taking time off for further wedding dress fittings, please.'

'Oh, Inez, is that fair?' Zeinab managed to look near to tears. 'I've always done things like that in my free time, haven't I, or when I was off sick?'

Inez gave up. She could see she had other things to argue about. The street door had opened and the clock complainant was coming in, he and two friends carrying his purchase, which they set down in front of the desk with a bump, causing it to chime resonantly. For form's sake Inez argued with him a little but in the end it was easier to give him his money back. She'd have it out with Freddy next week.

Zeinab was in front of her favourite mirror, repainting her eyelids. 'I promise I won't be more than exactly one hour, Inez, but I did say I'd have lunch with Rowley. It'll only be the Caffe Uno, I promise.'

'You'd better not let him see you wearing Morton's present.'

'No, I won't. Pity, though, I do just love it.'

They had a busy morning and the next time Inez looked at her, she had taken off the pendant.

Becky had told him something of her relationship with Will. Someone to talk to about him was all she wanted, someone to tell about Will and his childhood and her guilt, an ear to listen even if after five minutes it got bored. She might have imagined the touch of impatience in his voice after less than that.

'He's here with me,' she ended, 'and I don't see any prospect of him going anywhere else. And I feel bad enough even thinking like that. I do love him, you see, and I'm so sorry for him and somehow I feel it's all my fault. I know I shouldn't drag you into it, so if you like, just say you won't see me again and I'll understand.'

'I thought maybe I could come over tomorrow,' he said. 'Maybe in the afternoon around three?'

That had been the previous evening. It cheered her a lot. Even if being with Will frightened him off she would still have been comforted by his phoning and by what he'd said. Into her head came some lines she had once read: *Two is not twice one, two is two thousand times one* . . . It went on to say that was why the world would always return to monogamy. She didn't want monogamy particularly and she certainly didn't want marriage but the prospect of being two even for just one Saturday afternoon was so inviting that she slept that night without waking.

'You and your lady friend going somewhere nice for the weekend?' asked Anwar, perched lightly on a high stool at the counter.

Freddy, next to him and roughly twice his weight, was more precariously balanced. 'We've got ourselves a weekend break at a five-star hotel in Torquay. Very relaxing, Torquay, I'm told.'

'Depends what you mean by relaxing.' Anwar put on a serious face and said virtuously, '*I'm* told it's known as the cocaine capital of Western Europe. When you coming back?'

'Monday night.' Anwar hadn't asked, he was too subtle for that, but Freddy told him just the same, 'Inez is going to her sister for the day, the diamond geezer on the top floor'll be at his mum's and poor William's at his auntie's.'

'Why "poor"?'

Freddy went through the outdated pantomime of tapping the side of his head with two fingers. 'The Bill knocked him around so now he can't speak.'

'Is that a fact?' Anwar was uninterested.

'So what you doing for the weekend?'

'Business as usual,' said Anwar, and piously, 'I'll be going to the temple with my mum and dad, then there's a family wedding in Neasden. It's all go.'

'That white van that's not to be cleaned for scientific purposes—know the one I mean?'

Anwar, who knew very well, said he hadn't noticed it. Did Freddy want another mango juice?

'Yes, please. Very refreshing. It's outside the shop again, that van, and I was thinking—d'you know what I was thinking?' Anwar shook his head and ordered two more juices. 'Well, I was thinking, if there was any criminal activity, like a mugging, say, or the nicking of some girl's mobile, there'd be a witness who'd say they saw this dirty van parked with a notice in the back about not cleaning it and the Bill'd be along before you could say "car wash".' Freddy chuckled at his own wit.

'Maybe,' said Anwar, 'I don't know.' He looked at his Rolex watch. 'I gotta go. See a man about a van.'

Freddy laughed. 'Don't you want your mango juice?'

'You drink it,' said Anwar, and Freddy did.

Anwar made his way back to Star Street where, at a house well-known as a squat since the eighties, he rang the ground-floor bell. Keefer was still in bed, said the slatternly woman who answered the door.

'Lead me to him,' said Anwar dramatically.

He pulled Keefer out of his bed, a mattress on the floor among half a dozen other mattresses. 'Get up, mate,' he said. 'A job for you. Take that vehicle of yours to the car wash in Kilburn—no, the one in Hendon's better, and then get rid of that shit in the rear window. It was only funny for about five minutes.'

'Wash my van?' said Keefer, as if Anwar had suggested something serious like having a bath or getting gainful employment.

'That's what I said. You'd better put it through the wash twice and do it *now*.'

Anwar pressed a ten-pound note into his hand.

CHAPTER 16

Alexander was in Oxford Street, buying presents for his mother, having left Jeremy behind in Star Street. It would be her birthday next week but, in any case, he always bought things for her when he went to see her. The big present was a CD player and fifty new CDs of her favourite kind of music. The player and CDs could be delivered as they were far too heavy for him to carry unless he brought the car to Paddington. Parking outside would be possible on a holiday Monday when restrictions would be lifted but so far he had avoided his car being seen by fellow tenants and he thought it a good idea to keep things that way. The main gift settled, he bought a large box of chocolate truffles, Krug champagne, a green orchid growing in a ceramic pot and a bottle of Bulgari perfume.

When involved in the business of self-analysis, trying to find out why Jeremy killed girls, it amused him in a dry kind of way that experts would say he was taking vicarious revenge on a mother who had bullied and dominated him. He loved his mother dearly. She was probably the only person he had ever really loved. His parents' marriage had been happy but neither of them had a strong character. An only child, he had ruled the household from the age of eleven when he won spectacular results in the examination that would admit him, at a very low cost, to a public school. Before that they had loved him unstintingly, afterwards they worshipped him. If they had had a different sort of son his father's death would have come close to killing his mother, but she had left to her this paragon, this kindly loving genius who took all responsibility out of her hands, who saw to everything and, even when he no longer lived with her, directed her from afar.

The flaws in his career and lifestyle—she could scarcely admit they were flaws—did nothing to turn his godlike feet to clay. She could find better excuses for him than even he could himself but afterwards she never mentioned the flaws or the excuses. His success at business and particularly in working for himself earned her continued encouragement and praise. With his wife and his girlfriend she hadn't got on because of course they weren't good enough for him, and now she never asked when he was going to settle down and get married.

She longed for his visits and accepted his presents with extravagant delight, telling him in her charming way that really he shouldn't but it (whatever it was) was so lovely she was glad he had. And she had the gratifying habit, common to few, of continuing to refer to the flowers, the chocolates or the perfume throughout his visit with such comments as, 'Aren't they beautiful?' and 'What good taste you have to choose those!' Only twice in all his life had she spoken in a way he disliked and that was when, fondly referring back to his teenage years, she remarked with a tender smile on the brace he had been obliged, rather later than most children, to wear on his teeth. This brought back in a frightening way, a way disproportionate to a simple reminder of what a big percentage of children endured, his shame about it, his hatred of it. Sternly, he had forbidden her ever to mention it again. She had flushed and apologised. Never again was it mentioned between them.

Sometimes she remarked on what she supposed his lifestyle was, the big spacious office, the secretary, the

parties, receptions and theatres, the visits to his tailor, to
Ascot and (for some unaccountable reason) the Chelsea
Flower Show. It made him smile, though affectionately,
when he contrasted imagination with present reality
and his walking the streets waiting for a dreadful desire
to possess him . . .

When he was with her, in her pretty little house in
one of those quiet closes on a village perimeter, listening
to her gentle prattle about local activities, his mind concentrated more on the girls he had killed and those he
would kill than at any other time. Why? His mother so
hated the idea of murder that she watched no crime dra-
mas or documentaries on television and wouldn't have a
detective story in the house. And though he would
inevitably think about it while sitting with her, he
wouldn't speak of what everyone in the whole country
would at least mention this weekend, the disappearance
of Jacky Miller and the failure so far to find a trace of
her. His mother would go white and start shivering if he
so much as uttered the girl's name. Then why all the
time would his brain be seething with the memory of
killing her? Why did he kill her and those others? What
was in it for him?

Perhaps because they failed to match up to her standard as women. But she was sixty-eight and all of them
were young. And this failure applied to all women, but
he felt no compulsion to kill Inez Ferry or the next-door
neighbour in the mews he had seen but never spoken to.
Once he had asked his mother if, as a small child, he
had ever had a nanny or some young girl to look after
him while his parents went out.

'Oh, no, darling,' she had said, shocked. 'I wouldn't
have left you with anyone else. I couldn't have trusted
anyone. Your father and I never went out together in the
evenings until you were sixteen. I sometimes think

that's why I never had another baby. I would have had
to go into a hospital, maybe for days, and you would
have had a stranger to look after you.'

Carrying his packages, some of them gift-wrapped in blue
and silver, the orchid pot in the crook of his arm, he took
the bus back to Kensington High Street and walked southwards. Maybe there had been some young matron caring
for the boys at his school? But he had been a day boy—his
mother would never have allowed him to board. The
young and pretty mother of a friend who, instead of seduc-
ing, had scorned him? He had a clear memory of every
friend he had ever had—they had been few—and all of
them had mothers of an unbelievable hideousness. One, he
remembered, waddled splay-footed like a duck, another
had a face like Mao Tse-tung. So what had happened to
him to leave him with this feverish, all-conquering and
passionate need when he saw, after dark or in a lonely
place, an appropriate young woman?

He couldn't even say what made her appropriate,
how it was that he *knew* when he saw her that this was
the next one. They weren't alike. Gaynor Ray was little
and pretty with curly ginger hair, Nicole Nimms was
fair and very thin, Rebecca Milsom dark to the point of
swarthiness, Caroline Dansk also dark but facially quite
different and much slimmer, and Jacky Miller over-
weight, her hair the palest blonde, her skin pink with a
perpetual flush. All he could do to categorise them was
to say that all were young and none was Asian or
African. That wasn't to say a suitable one never would
be. He was no racist, he thought rather bitterly, laughing drily at his joke and congratulating himself on
retaining his sense of humour.

He let himself into the house and went straight to the
office. He disliked working on Saturdays but there was

no help for it if he was to take Monday off. Probably he would sleep here on Sunday night so as to make an early start in the car. But getting down to work was difficult. It always was, *anything* was but that one thing, when he had been thinking about the girls and especially about their appearance. That must be why his mind filled with them when he was with his mother and had nothing to do. Not why, though, he wanted to kill them in the first place. Not why, when he saw the next one, the one that absolutely *had* to be, he became in a flash nothing but an adrenalin-charged machine with one sole function. No, not quite a machine, for during it all he was conscious of his own blood coursing in his veins, of the beat in his head and the roar in his ears, of his skin tingling, of saliva dried, of a tightness in his chest and a closing of his throat. His whole body then became light, floating but controlled, like a dancer's.

It wasn't sexual. In sex he had never had feelings of this magnitude. Besides, the way he felt when about to kill was different in kind as well as degree from desire. And doing the deed, he touched only the skin of the neck and, if he must, where the object he was taking was. Only in the case of Jacky Miller's earrings had he been obliged to touch flesh, for Gaynor Ray's silver cross hung against the silk of the top she wore. The memory of that, comparable to another man's feelings on touching rotting offal, would always be with him . . .

So why did he kill them? Why did he have to kill them? And why had this compulsion come into being only two years ago? They walked in a procession before his eyes, shadowy shapes but all remembered as if they had been his lovers. There was nothing accusing in their faces, only an impish teasing, as if they had won. In this contest he had failed and they had triumphed because *he didn't know why*. In sudden rage he slammed his fist

down on the desk, making the laptop jump and the
pens rattle in their jar.

When James arrived Will was watching a British film
from the thirties on television. Increasingly nervous
about the coming visit, Becky had done her best to
make him at least change channels but Will, whatever
his shortcomings in other areas, was highly skilled
with the remote, and as soon as her eyes were turned
away he reverted to his chosen programme. James
came with flowers and a bottle of wine, and was introduced, Will getting up and shaking hands like a normal person, but still, of course, not speaking. Becky
desperately wanted them to get on. She was proud of
Will's appearance, especially when contrasted with last
time, the white shirt she had ironed for him, the blue
tie. There was nothing wrong with his looks and now
he had had several good meals and nights of sleep, he
looked particularly handsome. She was still wondering
whether to tell James about the police, their suspicions
and Will's detention—but what other reason could she
give for his speechlessness and continuous presence in
the flat?

'It's the rugby in a minute,' James said. 'All right if we
turn over?'

Will looked doubtful but nodded, the channel was
changed and he made no attempt to change it back.
They sat in silence while Becky made tea. She had
hoped to talk to James while Will concentrated on his
film, she had so much to explain, but she could see that
James was endeavouring by this move to create a rap-
port with her nephew and she was thankful. The tea was
drunk and the cakes eaten, at least by Will, and an hour
had gone by when James at last came out into the
kitchen, took her in his arms and held her close.

Becky was anxious and extricated herself unwillingly. Suppose Will were to come out and find them embracing—what would he do? Would he mind? He had never seen her in a man's company until that day he fell asleep on the step.

In spite of what had happened before, 'I have to tell you about him,' she said. 'I have to tell you about him and me, and why he's here.'

'You don't. Not today, anyway. I'm quite happy to accept.'

'I'd rather', she said, 'get it over.'

She started with her sister and Will's birth but after she got to the accident it all came out, what she called her refusing to face her responsibilities, her guilt, his love for her and the latest sad event in his life.

'But what was he doing in that garden?'

'I don't know. I expect he knows, he probably has some quite logical explanation—I mean an explanation which would seen logical to someone of his mental age. But whether he has or not hardly matters because he can't speak.'

'He's dumb?'

'Oh, no, no. He lost the power of speech while with the police. They terrified him. Horrible, isn't it?'

'Yes, it is,' James said very seriously.

He took her hand, lifted it and held it in both his. That was how Will found them when he came out into the kitchen. The rugby was over and he was looking for company. He found Becky with her back against the counter, James holding her hand up near his face, and the two of them gazing into each other's eyes. The inarticulate noise he made wasn't the first sound Becky had heard from him since he came to stay with her, there had been several such grunts, but this was the most expressive. As for the look in his eyes, that she had never seen before and it turned her body cold. Will didn't look unhappy or bewildered or hurt. He looked angry.

'Let's all go back in the living room,' she said heartily. To do what?

Will settled that. He turned on the television, looking at her and patting the sofa cushion next to the one he sat on. James sat in an armchair at the other side of the room. A cartoon, very brightly coloured, very noisy, exploded from the screen, and animals unknown at any period on this planet, green animals and purple, scaly and horned and winged, fell upon each other in furious combat. Will was smiling. Fabulous beasts fighting never upset him. Perhaps, even to him, they were too unreal. It was curious, Becky thought, noticing how he had turned his back on James and was three-quarters facing her, how she had worried that he would be unacceptable to James but never that James might be uncongenial to him. Despair made her slump into the cushions. James had taken up the newspaper, found a pen on the table and started to do the crossword puzzle.

Off for their weekend break, Freddy and Ludmila passed through the shop at lunchtime on Saturday, he carrying the two enormous cases she considered indispensable for two nights in an English seaside resort. Ludmila herself carried her hatbox and her dressing case. Over her pale-blue chiffon dress she wore a fur coat, chinchilla and apparently very old, its moth-eaten patches inadequately covered by an orange pashmina. Both of them kissed Inez, something which had never happened before, as if they were going away for ever instead of just for the weekend. Zeinab, entering by the inside door, stared at them and turned her back, pretending to examine the damaged grandfather clock.

'We shall be back before your return on Monday, Inez,' said Freddy, 'so you can rely on me to turn off the burglar alarm. Two-six-four-seven's the number, right?'

'Why don't you shout it down the street?' said Zeinab, turning round. 'Tell all the lowlife around here? Might as well give them the key.'

'All right, Zeinab.' Inez anticipated another full-blown row before Freddy and Ludmila went off to get their coach from Victoria. 'But it's not a good idea to make that number public, Freddy.'

'I wouldn't do that, Inez,' said Freddy virtuously. 'Come to think of it, I reckon I may be wrong thinking everyone in here is beyond reproach. I'm too trusting, that's my trouble.'

'And what's that supposed to mean?' Zeinab advanced a few steps towards him.

It was to be a long time before Inez fully realised the truth of his remark. 'Please, Zeinab,' she said and to Ludmila, who had lit a cigarette, 'Off you go, the pair of you. I don't know when your bus goes but I'm sure you haven't time to spare and you're going to miss it.'

Freddy opened the door with a flourish and picked up the cases. In the doorway, Ludmila turned round to deliver her parting shot. 'Pity you're not coming with us, Miss Sharif. You could bring grandad in his wheelchair.'

In fact, Zeinab intended to spend Sunday with Rowley Woodhouse and Monday with Morton Phibling. Once she had recovered from Ludmila's jibe, she told Inez all about it. Rowley had wanted her to come away with him that evening to Paris and Morton had suggested a weekend in Positano.

'I vetoed all that. I know it's old-fashioned, Inez, but my virginity is precious to me and it's bloody precious to my dad. They wouldn't respect me if I gave in to them before the weddings.'

Digesting this outdated view as best she could, Inez said, 'But there aren't going to be any weddings, are there?'

'Absolutely not, but they don't know that, do they? Rowley and me are going to Brighton for the day and Morton says he's taking me on the river on a luxury boat he's hired for lunch and dinner.'

Inez remembered going on both these excursions in the company of Martin, only it hadn't been a luxury boat—and none the worse for that. Tonight she'd watch *Forsyth and the Scarab*, it was one of her favourites. Her sister had all the *Forsyth* series on video too, she happened to know, but on Monday they would be hidden away. Miriam was too tactful ever to let them come within Inez's field of vision. She sighed—turned the sigh into a cough—not at the memories, nor even her loss, but at misunderstandings. Even her own sister, kind, delicate-minded, thoughtful, had never understood that she *wanted* to be reminded, she wanted to see his image, wanted to talk about him, lest she forgot or memories grew dim.

She and Jeremy Quick were alone in the house throughout Sunday and, more significantly, over Sunday night. This had never happened before; it made Inez uneasy. She hadn't previously understood how reassuring was the presence of Will Cobbett and Freddy and Ludmila between her and him, but the last time she had thought about it she had had no reason to distrust Jeremy. Some would say she was giving the matter undue prominence. After all, he had done no more than invent a girlfriend and her mother, and fill into the story their biographical and circumstantial details, no more than recoil from her touch on his arm. Put like that, it amounted to very little. Hadn't these women been dreamt up simply to avoid accepting her invitations? Still, she told herself, as she got ready for bed, normal men in their forties didn't fantasise in this way and talk about their fantasies as if they were real. If he told her, a mere acquaintance, surely he must have told other people as well. And if he fantasised Belinda and her mother, how much of the rest of his life was a manufactured story, a lie?

He was an accountant, he said, and he went to his place of business on a tube line from Paddington. He had a mother, he had never been married, he possessed no car. Some of that might be true and some of it not but she had no way of knowing. Sitting up in bed, she found herself unable to concentrate on the novel she had bought in paperback. Jeremy was up there—she had heard him come in from his evening walk an hour ago—but she had heard no other sound from him. The name he called himself by might not be his real one. For the first time she wondered if she should attach any importance to the fact that while Ludmila paid her rent by cheque and Will's was paid in the same way by Becky, Jeremy's always came in cash, in fifty- and twenty-pound notes. It could simply be designed to enable her to avoid declaring it to the Inland Revenue—something she had never done—but on the other hand, there was a possibility he paid in this way because 'Jeremy Quick' was not the name on his bank account.

She passed a restless night. Between her and sleep kept intruding the idea that he was not asleep but waiting and listening some fifteen feet above her bed. Of course, she knew very well that night terrors and other products of a heightened imagination mostly disappear in the morning, but knowing that never made the fear vanish and it didn't now. Fortunately, at this time of year darkness endured for only a few hours; it was light by half past four and she slept a little. Making her coffee at eight and swallowing two aspirins, she heard

Jeremy come downstairs and the soft click of the front door as he closed it quietly out of consideration for her.

Never before had she watched one of her tenants from her window but she watched Jeremy now, her mug of coffee in her hand. It was a surprise not to see him head for the tube at Paddington or Edgware Road but walk up Bridgnorth Street. He was wearing his dark-green sports jacket and carrying a suitcase, though he had said he was going to his mother's only for the day. She lived in Leicestershire, so Inez would have expected him to get the Circle line tube or, failing that, a taxi, to King's Cross. A taxi with its light up, a very unusual sight at this hour, came towards him along Bridgnorth Street but he didn't hail it. He must intend to walk to King's Cross, quite a long way if you were carrying what looked like a heavy case.

By now Inez was very interested but there seemed no prospect of finding answers to her questions as within a moment he would have reached the far end. Instead, as she was about to move away, he turned left up Lyon Street. Was he going to call for someone? A *real* girlfriend? Some friend who would also be visiting Jeremy's mother? He had disappeared from view and now she would never know. But she continued to stand there, sipping her coffee, soothed by the emptiness and early-morning silence. The sky was a pale blue sprinkled with tiny spots of cloud, the sun weak and distant. A cat crossed the road soundlessly, stood up on lean hindlegs to examine the contents of a litter bin. The newsagent's boy emerged from Bridgnorth Street, pushing his trolley laden with newspapers, when a car came out of Bridgnorth Street and headed for the Edgware Road. It was followed by another, this time from different side turning further up Star Street and nearer Norfolk Square, going slowly in the same direction. Jeremy Quick was at the wheel.

Afterwards, Inez thought she couldn't have sworn in court that it was he but still she knew it was. The man driving wore a dark-green jacket, he had Jeremy's profile and Jeremy's sleek mouse-coloured hair. Of course, she would never have to swear to it anywhere. She watched until his car too had turned into the Edgware Road and then she went thoughtfully back to the kitchen. By eleven she was ready to leave for her sister's, having spent most of the intervening time, while she was having her bath and dressing, in speculating as to what Jeremy was up to. It was almost understandable that a man might invent possession of a car when he hadn't actually got one, nearly inconceivable for anyone to say he hadn't a car when he had—and a large, high-powered Mercedes at that. And say he couldn't drive?

Was it Jeremy who had been into the garden in her absence and when he came back, turned the key not one and a half times but once only? He had denied it but that obviously meant nothing. She checked the back door and the key again, and put on the burglar alarm. As its braying died away, she walked across the road to the car she made no secret of possessing and drove up to Highgate.

CHAPTER 17

'Easy-peasy,' said Anwar to himself as he climbed over the wall between the garden of the house where his room was and that of Inez's. There was nothing covert in the way he did this. He knew better than that. Over his suit trousers and shirt he wore a pair of paint-stained workman's overalls—he had spent an enjoyable hour daubing on the paint himself—he carried a bucket coated with dried cement and a roller, and used a ladder to help him. His story of sizing up the situation prior to an exterior redecoration job he had ready if anyone questioned him, but no one would. They were all watching the football at this hour of a Bank Holiday afternoon and, although it was bright sunshine, some of them had drawn the curtains of the windows behind which were their televisions.

Ever the artist, Anwar stood for a moment clutching his paint roller and contemplating the back of Inez's house just in case some nosy neighbour happened not to think soccer the most vital ingredient of British life and looked out. No one did. He inserted his key in the lock on the back door and opened it. A nasty thought had come to him that in the time intervening between his returning Inez's key and today, some prudent busybody might have attached bolts to the top and bottom of that door. The ease with which the lock yielded set his mind at rest. Her key wasn't even there on the other side to be poked through.

The moment the door gave and he set foot over the threshold the alarm started braying. It was on the wall just inside the street door. Anwar punched in two-six-four-seven and the noise stopped. He listened. The house being part of a terrace, neighbours on either side might have heard the alarm but if they had, the noise it made being of such short duration, they would only think one of the tenants had come in, set it going and almost immediately turned it off. There was no key to the interior door into the shop. Anwar went in, opened Inez's desk and extracted what he had hardly dared to hope would be found so easily, a key to each flat in the building.

His team were to come singly and as he stood there waiting, Julitta rang the bell. Anwar let her in and two minutes later, Keefer. Flint came last, after fifteen minutes, just in case anyone might be watching and wondering why Inez was suddenly entertaining all these young people.

By prearrangement, Anwar himself was to do the top floor where the 'diamond geezer' lived, Julitta Inez's flat, Flint the shop and Keefer the two flats on the middle floor. Those were the least important. To Anwar's disgust, Keefer smelt of the forbidden cannabis and couldn't be trusted with anything significant. If he had had to confide in Freddy, Anwar had decided to promise him and Ludmila that their place would be left inviolate, but there was no need for it, the back door key having practically dropped into his outstretched hand. Therefore Freddy was as vulnerable as the other tenants. Not that he was likely to possess anything worth taking, but Ludmila might. After Anwar had made an unkind remark about him looking even older than his years, his brains fried beyond saving, Keefer was told to put on his gloves and get going.

Also gloved, Anwar went upstairs. The man called Quick might be wealthy but at first glance he seemed to have little worth taking. The tall teakwood racks were full of CDs but none of them the sort of music favoured by Anwar and his team. He left them. Drawers were rather a disappointment, though there was a driving licence in one of them in the name of Alexander Gibbons. This, along with the gold watch he found on the dresser in the bedroom, he put into his pocket. No cash anywhere. Then he opened the tall cupboard in the kitchen, looking merely for a tin with change in it, the kind of thing you keep for paying the milkman. Instead, he found Jeremy's strongbox. You had to be really good at guesswork to open a safe like that without actually breaking into it, a difficult if not quite impossible task. The combination might be the man's birth date—it usually was something like that— or the last four digits of his phone number. Or it might not. The only thing to do was reason that it wouldn't be there and locked up unless it contained something of value. God, it was heavy! The carrier bag he found to put it in split as soon as he lifted it off the floor, so he took a canvas backpack from the bedroom, put the safe inside and carried it downstairs, carefully relocking the front door behind him. Of course there was no sign of anything having been disturbed.

On the other hand, chaos prevailed in Ludmila's room.

'It was like that, I swear,' muttered Keefer. 'I never done it. There's some people live like pigs, you know that.'

'You included. What you got?'

An elaborate heavy necklace of what might have been, and Keefer said were, rubies set in gold.

'Those are glass,' said Anwar contemptuously, 'and that is shit called pinchbeck. You wouldn't give a fiver for that down Church Street market. But we'll have those wedding rings—how many times has she been married, for God's sake?'

'Maybe they're her dead mum's or her auntie's.'

'Yeah, maybe. Take the pearls too and let's get going.'

In the shop Julitta, who should have been upstairs, was standing by a long gilt-framed mirror, holding up to the light a chain from which hung a large diamond.

'That's a diamond, innit, An?' Anwar examined the pendant Morton Phibling had bought for Zeinab. It consisted of a single large stone of emerald cut, suspended from a thin gold chain. 'It'd be worth thousands and thousands,' he said. But he spoke excitedly, not at all in his usual laid-back fashion. 'Maybe fifty thousand.' Now the look of wonder on his face, an expression that had briefly turned him into a child again, changed to one of doubt. 'It can't be. Who'd leave a thing like that in here for anyone to pick up?'

'Yeah,' said Flint, 'maybe it's a trap.'

'What the fuck's that supposed to mean?' Anwar rounded on him. 'I suppose there's a needle on it going to give me a shot of cyanide, is there? Or a microchip sending a code to the pigs at Paddington Green?'

Not very quick at the best of times, Flint could think of no answer to that. Anwar wrapped the pendant up in one of the pieces of Valenciennes lace Inez sometimes sold to antique dress connoisseurs and put it in the bag with the safe. 'Why aren't you upstairs like I told you?' he said to Julitta.

'I done her flat. There's nothing in the jewellery line but costume and you said not to mess with costume. Oh, and there's hundreds of videos, TV crime shit.'

'No cash?'

Her 'Oh, no, An' came so readily that, meeting her eyes in a disconcerting way, he said roughly, 'Come on, give it here.'

Four twenty-pound notes and two tens were unwillingly put into his hands. He would have searched her himself if she hadn't handed it over, inflicting the maximum pain. 'Thief,' he said. 'You get your share when the time comes, you know that,' and then, 'Is that all?'

'I swear it, An.'

That amounted to very little, but if she wanted to keep a fiver and a few coins, who cared? Some people were irredeemably crooked and couldn't even stick to the code of honour among thieves. 'Time to go,' Anwar said as Keefer appeared at the interior door. 'Leave as you came, one by one. Not carrying anything, are you?'

They weren't. He watched them go, making sure of a full ten-minute gap between Julitta's departure and Keefer's. Then he put the backpack, which now also held Ludmila's wedding rings, into the cement-coated bucket and the notes into his overall pocket, punched six-two-four-seven into the burglar alarm keypad and left by the back door. As he was closing it the alarm began making its siren howl. Anwar locked up, but instead of taking the key he had had cut away with him, he pushed it carefully under the door. What she had done with the original he had no idea, taken it with her, he supposed. Leaving his behind was not only an artistic gesture but a kindly one. A householder could always do with a spare key, especially one she didn't have to pay for.

He listened to the alarm till it stopped, then went back the way he had come, over the wall. If he hurried he would be in time to get to his cousin's wedding in Neasden.

CHAPTER 18

A van was parked outside the shop when Inez got back. It was yet another of those white ones that seemed so popular with a certain type of young man, but surely a newcomer to the neighbourhood. Some days had passed since she had last seen the dirty, fingermarked and graffiti-coated van with the once-amusing notice in its rear window.

She put her key in the street door lock and let herself in. The alarm starting up told her she was the first of the household to return, for if any of the others had come in they would hardly have reactivated it. With a glance into the shop to make sure nothing was amiss, she went upstairs to her own flat. Intending to settle in front of the television with a glass of wine and a *Forsyth* film—needed after a day with her sister and brother-in-law behaving as if she had never been married at all, so excessively tactful were they—she stopped halfway across the room and stared at the untidy pile of her videos on the coffee table. She would never have left them like that, she was a neat, methodical person. At least they were all there and otherwise untouched . . .

Was it possible Freddy had in fact come home already and been in here? He knew there was a key to her flat in the desk. But why would he and why touch her videos? Besides, Freddy was an honest man, she was certain of that. Silly and trusting but honest. She didn't put the video on but she poured herself the drink, carried it back into the living room and looked about her. Nothing else appeared to have been touched. In the bedroom what not-at-all valuable jewellery she had, apart from her wedding and engagement rings which were on her finger, was all in place. There was money in the tin in the kitchen, kept there for household shopping, dry-cleaning and so on. As soon as she picked it up, she knew the tin was empty by the weight of it. Even the small change was gone as well, of course, as about a hundred pounds.

Forgetting the burglar alarm, Inez remembered the incident of the key. Recall sent a cold shiver through her and she swallowed the rest of her wine at a gulp. She always *knew* she hadn't given it a mere single turn. It was still in her handbag where she had put it this morning after checking the back door was locked. Sure by now that no one else was in the house, she went downstairs and felt a little relief at the sight of the locked door and no key. But wait a minute . . . A key, like her own but brighter and shinier, lay on the floor between the bottom of the door and the edge of the mat. She picked it up, examined it, not that there was much point in that. Some visitor to the shop in her absence must have . . . Still, he, whoever he was, had let her down lightly, but what of her tenants?

One of them was coming in now. She walked down the little passage towards the street door. It was Jeremy Quick.

'I'm sorry to tell you we seem to have had a burglary,' she said.

'What, the shop, you mean?'

If that didn't take a national award for selfishness she didn't know what would. His tone had been positively eager.

'No, not the shop, oddly enough. They've been in my flat, raided the cash tin in the kitchen. I imagine they went over the whole house.'

He had gone white. Not just pale but a sickly almost greenish-white, the bones of his face standing out and his eyes staring. There must be something up there he didn't want anyone, anyone at all, knowing about. Hard pornography? *Child* pornography? Stolen goods? She knew suddenly that there was nothing she'd put past him. 'I'd go straight up and check if I were you,' she said. And then she remembered she should have called the police. Dialling the number, she wondered which of them would come or would it be someone unfamiliar?

Jeremy took the stairs two at a time. The inside of his flat looked undisturbed. He closed his eyes, took a deep breath and opened the cupboard, hoping against hope the weight of the strongbox would have deterred them. It hadn't. Although he had expected that empty space on the shelf, it was still such a shock that he had to sit down. Was there a chance they might find it so hard to open they would abandon the attempt and throw it away? Drop it over one of the bridges into the river? Not much chance, he thought, facing things. They would be sure a safe so securely locked contained valu-able items.

An unfamiliar feeling invaded him. He didn't want to be alone, he wanted the company of his fellows. Inez and however many of the others were at home would have to be told what the thieves had taken from him, and it would be wiser not to mention to them, and certainly not to the police if they came, that his safe was missing. Better say money and jewellery, cufflinks, a watch, some-thing like that. He had left his other watch on the dress-ing table in the bedroom, he remembered, running in there. The watch was gone. He went downstairs.

Ludmila marched up and down the shop, making a big scene about the robbery and the mess her flat had been left in.

'The place ransacked,' she kept shouting, 'and all my wedding rings stolen! All of them! Jan's ring and Waldemar's, these I mind most, all of them gone!'

'I never dreamt', said Freddy, looking troubled, 'you'd been married so many times, Ludo. It puts a different complexion on things.'

She took no notice of him but began tearing at her hair as if she wanted to pull it out by the roots. Inez went to the window, watching for the arrival of the police officer who had promised to come 'within the next half-hour'.

'You had much nicked?' said Freddy when Jeremy came in.

'Not much. A watch I rather liked. Some cash.'

'I've been lucky,' said Freddy when it was clear Jeremy wasn't going to ask. 'All my valuable property is safe in my home in Stoke Newington.'

'Moved again, have you, Freddy?'

While Inez turned towards him to ask this irresistible question, a car drew up outside and DC Jones got out, followed by a uniformed officer. Suppose they've already found my safe, thought Jeremy, suppose they found it discarded and empty . . .

Planned to be eaten at a table in the open air and overlooking the river, lunch had instead been taken indoors in a restaurant where the management had to turn the heating on. It was a bright day on the whole but from time to time hailstones burst out of the sky and rattled on the elaborately cobbled pavements. James had seemed uneasy and Becky was anxious, no matter how she tried to relax. Will was staying at home. They had left him a cold lunch of a pork pie, hard-boiled eggs, quiche and pickles, and promised to be back by three thirty at the latest. Becky had prepared the lunch, knowing he wouldn't eat salad and afraid to leave him anything hot, while James did the promising.

He was quite good at this, or he thought he was, but Becky knew that telling Will he wouldn't want to spoil his aunt's pleasure and it was good for her to get out of the house sometimes was not the way to win him over. Will thought Becky's greatest joy came from being in her own home with him. To her dismay, she could tell he didn't like James. Of course, he still didn't speak, and though childlike, was sufficiently not a child to control his facial expressions. He would never pout and frown as a real nine-year-old might but was a master of the amiable nod and smile.

She could read his face expertly—she had had plenty of practice—and she saw his unease with James in the way his unhappy eyes followed her every move, shifting them only to look at James with a hard implacability. The second time she had seen that glance, directed this time at James's back, she almost said she wouldn't go out, it wasn't the nice day they had been promised and they would do just as well at home. But the thought came to her that if she did that it might be weeks before she ever went out again without Will, might not be until after he had recovered his speech and his confidence, and gone back to Star Street. It was of all this that she had been thinking in the restaurant as they ate their asparagus and drank their Sauvignon.

'We have to talk,' James said, words which struck her with a cold shock.

'Do we?'

'I really like you, Becky. I'm very attracted by you and I'm more sorry than I can say that I deserted you for those weeks for no good reason.'

'It doesn't matter now,' she said.

He made no answer. 'If I'd known you for a long time, if we'd really got to know each other, perhaps I'd understand and I'd be willing to share you with a—a dependent nephew. If it was like that and it had happened that Will had to move in with you for a time I'd accept that and—wait. But it's not, is it? I've never even been alone with you at home in your place or mine for a couple of hours. As for staying the night . . .'

Ridiculously, at her age, she found herself blushing. She had looked at him, willing him to stop. He didn't.

'As for staying the night, I think you'd say that's not possible with Will there. I *know* you would.'

'Yes, I would.' Unwillingly, the words were forced from her, 'I don't know what he'd do..'

Their main course came. She had no appetite for it but she knew that somehow it was for her to mend things, make 'we have to talk' a profitable, not a negative, exercise. 'James,' she said, with no confidence in what she had to say, 'it won't go on. It's just unfortunate you and I happened to meet at the same time as the police put Will through—well, all they did put him through. He'll get better. He'll go home and the most I'll have to see him is once a week.' In all her years of guilt, had she ever felt as guilty as she did now? Had it ever weighed on her so heavily that she felt she had betrayed Will even more than when she let him go to that home? 'I really'—she had been going to say she loved him but she amended that—'am fond of him. He's my responsibility, especially at the moment.'

'He's not mine,' said James with a harshness that hit her.

She had thought she might have to leave the table, go outside and be sick. A superhuman effort controlled that. 'Give me—two weeks,' she said and, hating to plead but pleading, 'Please. Just two weeks and things will be quite different.'

'All right,' he had said. 'All right. At least we've got everything out in the open now.' Oh, you don't know, she thought, you don't know. 'Let's talk about something else.'

Her lunch had been spoiled but she had never had much hope of its success. The time pressed on her and while she talked absent-mindedly, she thought of Will at home alone, perhaps of his lunch being a disappointment, of the television refusing to obey the remote—was its battery still good?—and of the phone ringing in her absence. James seemed very unwilling to go back. They could walk, he suggested, along the South Bank as far as Westminster Bridge. Had she ever been in the aquarium? They might do that.

'We said we'd be back by three thirty.'

'Ah, right. We'd better go, then.'

Will was fine. He had eaten the food she had left and even washed the dishes. The television was on and he was happily watching an old black-and-white film. Becky made tea, produced the pastries which Will loved and James looked at as if she had offered him a plate of maggots. He picked up the paper for today's crossword but either couldn't do it or hadn't the heart to make a serious attempt, and sat staring out of the window as if in the depths of rather boring thought. Becky reflected miserably that if he was going to go on like that for the next two weeks—if he stayed the course—she might come to dislike him and never want to see him again. That would solve all their problems.

At six, when the television had been on for three hours, he got up and said he must go. He had promised to call in and see his sister, but he would be in touch, he'd ring her. A smile of relief and positive

THE ROTTWEILER 237

pleasure spread across Will's face and when James had
gone he relaxed into the cushions, laughing uninhibit-
edly at the screen and flashing conspiratorial glances at
Becky. Once he winked, something she had never seen
him do before.

She had been unable to eat any supper but Will had.
In spite of having lazed on the sofa all day, he was voraciously hungry for his favourite meal, the eggs, bacon,
chips and fried tomatoes she cooked for him. When the
doorbell rang at eight she thought it might be James
come back, that he was sorry he had sulked and been
less than kind, but all would be different for the future
. . . Not James but Detective Constable Jones, whose
appearance in her living room struck some chord in
Will, reminded him of his overnight-in-the-cell experience or simply shocked him.

Whatever it was, it restored his power of speech, so
that he burst out, jumping up, 'No, I'm not coming! I
won't come, I'm staying here!'

'It's not that I don't love it to bits, darling,' Zeinab was
saying to Morton Phibling. 'But you know what Inez
said. Don't wear it in the street, she said. It wasn't as if
you was coming to pick me up in the Lincoln, was you?'

'I would have if you'd let me come to your home.'

'I've told you a million times my dad'd kill me. And
you.'

Instead of the boat trip, they were in Kew Gardens.
Morton had remembered that boats made him seasick.
Zeinab hadn't wanted to go to Kew. She liked flowers,
especially orchids and arum lilies, but gardens left her
cold. Morton had only been keen on the visit because
when he was at school he'd learnt a poem about going
down to Kew in lilac time, it wasn't far from London.
Zeinab thought it was much too far from London and

told him so several times. She wasn't worried about the diamond pendant, which she thought she remembered leaving on a shelf in the bathroom cabinet at Dame Shirley Porter House. Her engagement ring (the big one, not Rowley's more modest affair) was on her finger and she flashed it proudly whenever anyone was looking. There was nothing else to do in here.

Morton went some way to retrieving the day by taking her to tea at the Ritz. Zeinab, who never put on weight, ate two chocolate eclairs and a large slice of strawberry tart with cream. Despite this, she was giving serious thought to breaking things off with Morton. It was nearly time, before all this wedding dress business and fixing the date and inviting guests brought things to a crux. She wanted to get one more large present out of him first, though. The Jaguar took them to Hampstead where Morton's driver was imperiously told to stop on the corner and let her out in case Mr Sharif was watching.

Morton was driven back to Eaton Square, of course, while Zeinab had to get a couple of buses to Lisson Grove. Algy and the children were watching *Mary Poppins* on television. An uninvited and unexpected guest, Mrs Sharif sat in the most comfortable chair, eating Godiva chocolates.

'What a day I've had,' said Zeinab, hoping her mother would think she was the only woman in Marylebone who had been at work this holiday Monday. 'It's all go.' Her mother's opinion was of no importance to her but if she disapproved of the goings-on with Morton and Rowley she might refuse to babysit. Thinking of Morton reminded her of the diamond pendant. She went into the bathroom and looked in the cabinet. The pendant wasn't on the shelf. She must have taken it out of there and put it in the bedroom. Crossing the hall, she was hindered in her search

by Algy who said he had something to say to her he
would prefer Mrs Sharif not to hear.

'If it's about me going about with Morton and
Rowley,' said Zeinab, 'don't bother. I don't get any fun
out of it either and it's bloody hard work. I'll have you
know Morton's friend Orville Pereira who's a billionaire
asked me out but I said no. On account of you. So there.'

'It's not about that. It's about the exchange.'

'What d'you mean, exchange?'

'This couple phoned. They'd seen my ad and they've
got a flat in Pimlico they're giving up on account of
wanting one around here. It'd be free of hassle, Suzanne,
it's the same council, it'd be quick.'

'I don't know, Alge. It's a big decision. I don't even
know where Pimlico is.'

'I do. I could show you. Your mum'll stay with Bryn
and Carmel, and we could go down there and have a
look. We could look at the outside, at any rate.'

'OK,' said Zeinab. 'I don't mind. But while we're
about it, let's have a meal somewhere, might as well
make an evening of it. First I've got to find that necklace thing Morton gave me.' His black look made her
giggle. 'I've got to find it to flog it, haven't I?'

The pendant wasn't on the dressing table or inside it,
it wasn't in the drawer where Zeinab kept her jewellery
and it wasn't mixed up with her cosmetics—two big
drawerfuls. What had she been wearing on Friday? Her
usual costume of clingy white sweater and black
miniskirt, she supposed. She always did, she was *now*.
Her leather jacket would be worn only if the weather
was very cold while Zeinab would rather have got pneu-
monia than cover herself up in a topcoat. She looked in
the pockets of the jacket. The pendant wasn't there, not
surprising as she hadn't worn it since last Friday, not,
indeed, since March.

What had she done that day? Come in to work with Morton, shown off the pendant, had that row with Freddy, he'd called her a tart and she'd called Ludmila a Russian cow, then there'd been some customers, then— she remembered suddenly—she'd told Inez she'd be having lunch with Rowley and Inez had said to take off the pendant and she had. But what had she done with it? Nothing that she could recall. Just put it on the table, the top of which met the base of the mirror, while she redid her face. She must have left it there. Forgotten all about it and left it in the shop . . .

Well, it would still be there. She'd get it tomorrow. Back in the living room, Reem Sharif was grudgingly agreeing to Algy's proposal.

'If them kids eat any more of my chocolates they'll be sick as dogs. And if I'm stopping here half the night I'll want a meal. Where you going to eat?'

'Chinese,' said Algy.

'You can bring me in a lemon chicken platter, then, and egg-fried rice—oh, and sesame prawn toast to start. Not a minute after ten, mind. I'll be starving by then.'

The police hadn't taken Will away, Becky told Inez on the phone, but they'd questioned him on and on about some break-in. Had there been one at the shop?

Inez told her about it. 'But that's preposterous thinking Will had something to do with it. He hasn't been here for a week.'

'I don't know if they really think it,' said Becky, 'but that was the drift of what they said. They wanted to search my flat but I put my foot down, I said absolutely not, and they went away, this DC Jones said to get a warrant, but that was last evening and no one's been back.'

'I know Jones,' said Inez. 'Not as well as I know

Zulueta and Osnabrook, not to mention Crippen, but I do know him.'

Becky said she was sorry, she ought to have asked if Inez had had anything taken. She listened while Inez listed the things that were missing, making her laugh about Ludmila's wedding rings.

'Will's got his speech back,' Becky said. 'Last night. The shock of seeing Jones, I expect.'

'Then he'll soon be coming back here?'

'I hope so, Inez,' she said, and Inez detected a wist-ful note in her tone.

The phone call had come while Inez was waiting for Zeinab to arrive. She was no later than she always was. For the first time on a weekday morning since last October when he had stayed in bed with a bad cold, Jeremy hadn't come into the shop for his tea. It hadn't been a formal arrangement but just the same he could have given her a call, stopped her putting an extra teabag in the pot. She suspected he hadn't gone to work. Seeing him at the wheel of that car yesterday morning came back to her. Instances of incongruous behaviour were always occurring in his life recently. He must have told her at least three times that he had no car, wouldn't have a car in London, considered it antisocial to pollute the atmosphere with fumes. Of course, it was possible the one she had seen wasn't his at all, but that he had hired a car to go to his mother's. But he'd also said he couldn't drive. Being with the police so much must have infected her with their way of thinking, for she found herself wondering why she hadn't noted down the registration. Still, she knew what the car looked like, a silver Mercedes.

Zeinab rushed in at a quarter to ten. People who were incorrigibly late, Inez had noticed, were always in a hurry, always breathless and panting when they did arrive. Without a word to her, with scarcely a glance, Zeinab rushed to what everyone called *her* mirror and the console table below it. Inez saw her face, aghast, incredulous, in the mirror and her hands scrabbling among the little ornaments on the adjacent display tables. She turned round, holding up her hands as if about to pray. 'It's gone!'

'What's gone?'

'My pendant Morton gave me. I left it here on Friday when I went out to lunch with Rowley and I— I forgot it!'

Inez knew the pointlessness, despite the temptation, of telling someone in Zeinab's situation that she should have been more careful. She would know that now or else she never would. Now to break the news, but gently. 'I'm very much afraid we had some trouble yesterday.' She paused for this to prepare the way. 'A break-in, I'm sorry to say. Things were taken from everyone. I suppose—well, it seems likely they took your pendant.'

'Oh, my God, oh, my God, what am I going to do? What am I going to say to Morton?'

Inez happened to believe, as Martin had, that telling the truth is always best. No prevarication, no 'white lies', and no putting off the evil day. But saying so would sound sententious. 'Perhaps you won't need to tell him anything yet,' she said, though it went against the grain. 'The police may find it.'

'What am I going to do if he asks?'

'He's never asked about the other things he's given you, has he?'

'There's always a first time,' said Zeinab. 'The police won't know it's missing, will they? I'd better go down there and tell them.'

'Phone them,' said Inez, intent on preventing Zeinab from avoiding her job for another hour or two.

'Ask for DC Jones. And I'd like a word with him too. I want to tell him about the dirty white van with the notice in the back that always used to be outside. It may be important.'

The search of her home was worse than an actual burglary would have been, thought Becky. Jones and a PC in uniform went through every room, investigating drawers and emptying out the contents, peering into wardrobes, feeling in coat pockets, taking out books one by one and searching behind them. Any book that was particularly thick Jones opened, looking for one of those secret compartments. Her own jewellery was closely examined, particular attention being paid to her mother's worn and scratched wedding ring. In the study, now Will's bedroom, they found in a drawer in the workstation a pair of woollen gloves. They were hers, bright red and almost too small for Will to get his hands in, but Jones seemed to look on this find as very serious, the allegation being that Will had worn the gloves while raiding Inez's house.

They found nothing else to bear out this theory but they went on searching methodically, inspired and energised by the discovery of the gloves—why had she ever put them there and when?—moved into the living room where they hunted all round Will who sat, fearful and hunched, in a corner of the sofa. When they began on the books and sleeves of videos, he made a whimpering sound and ran out of the room to seek refuge, not in the study but in her own bedroom. There he lay face-downwards with his face buried in the pillows and there Jones saw him when he put his head round the door, looking for Becky. Jones said nothing but pursed his lips and raised his eyebrows, a grimace there was no one to witness.

Half an hour later, the search complete and nothing found but the gloves, the wedding ring and a man's watch which she occasionally wore because it had a large clear face, Jones asked her if she and Will were really aunt and nephew.

'What's that supposed to mean?'

'He seems very familiar with your bedroom.'

Perhaps Becky should have told him to mind his own business. She didn't. 'I can prove it if you'd like to see my birth certificate and his mother's and his. I deeply resent your suggestion.'

'OK, Ms Cobbett, keep calm. That'll be all for now. We may well be back.'

Will was still on her bed, his fingers stuffed in his ears, though neither officer had made much noise. Suppose he refused to move all day? Suppose he wanted to stay there all night? If she and James had a real relationship, if this had become a love affair, she could have phoned him and asked his advice or help. The terms they were on at present were too fragile for that. There was no one really she could go to and ask for aid. She realised when the morning was nearly over that for the first time since she took Will in, she hadn't been in touch with the office or sent any e-mails or faxes. And next week she was due to return to work.

She went back to her bedroom. He had fallen asleep where he lay, but it was a restless sleep in which he muttered and twitched, his hands opening and closing like someone intent on restoring feeling to numb fingers. That sensation of panic overwhelmed her. She went back into the living room and poured herself a large whisky.

CHAPTER 19

Opening the strongbox was even more difficult than Anwar had supposed. He started by taking it to a motor mechanic friend of his who seemed to have the tools needed, but although the friend tried everything, its door remained shut. More subtle means would have to be used. But Anwar knew very well the near impossibility of trying numbers to fit a code combination. It would run into millions of attempts, billions, before you succeeded.

He and Keefer went back to St Michael's Street in Keefer's now spotless white van. Anwar took Zeinab's diamond pendant from under his pillow and put it in his pocket. Later he'd take it to a jeweller he knew, an Indian though not a relation—he wouldn't risk trying anything on with relatives—who wasn't exactly crooked or even bent but a little bit, as his father might say, 'on the skew'. So tired he could hardly keep his eyes open, a trickle of spit trailing out of the corner of his mouth, Keefer sat on the floor in a corner, doing a line of cocaine to wake him up. Anwar would have thrown him out, only he knew his friend in this mood. He was liable to stand out on the landing, beating at the door and howling. Since coming into money, Keefer's indulgence in Class A substances had been unrestricted.

Anwar sat on the bed with the strongbox. He tried Inez's burglar alarm number, the birth date of Alexander Gibbons—whoever that might be, obviously someone

of significance in Quick's life, possibly Quick's own
pseudonym—which he got from his driving licence:
7 July 1955. A man about Quick's age, then.
Interesting—but the four digits didn't make up the
right code. Quick's phone number next, Inez's phone
number and the number of the shop. Nothing worked.
Maybe he should stop for now and pursue some other
line. He'd set Flint to tailing Jeremy Quick, follow him
when he left in the morning, see where he went. If
Alexander Gibbons and he were one and the same he
must presumably take on Gibbons's character from time
to time, resume being him. And Gibbons would be his
real name, Quick the pseudonym. He, Anwar, would
have found a way to have a driving licence in another
name if he'd wanted to, but Jeremy wasn't as clever as
he. Few were.

Keefer was jumping galvanically, his legs twitching
and his feet drumming on the floor.

'That's what comes of taking a cocktail of that shit,'
said Anwar. 'You'd better stay here. I'm going out in
the van.'

He was too young to drive but he could. The van was
uninsured and he had no personal cover. Neat in the
pinstriped suit, he drove up to Brondesbury Park and
his parents' house. His sister Arjuna was at home, also
skiving off school, he supposed, but both his parents
were working, 'to keep you children in the style to
which we were never accustomed', as his father put it.

'Hello, stranger,' said Arjuna, more like one's old
auntie than a fourteen-year-old.

'Hi.'

Anwar wasn't going to waste time on her. He went
upstairs to his bedroom where he had a computer with
Internet access. There, he quickly entered the London
electoral registers website, knowing his efforts might

take him hours but determined to be patient. Almost two hours passed before he found what he wanted. Luckily, the place where the man lived, or was supposed to live, was as nearly central as Star Street but in the Royal Borough of Kensington and Chelsea. Chetwynd Mews, 14, Gibbons, Alexander P. No need now to tail Jeremy Quick. He would go there himself and spy out the land.

By this time Uma and Nilima had also come home.

'Mum's been asking where you are,' said Nilima accusingly.

'You can tell her I've been here, can't you?'

'I suppose you're going back to your friend in Bayswater. It's a girl, isn't it?'

'Wouldn't you like to know, nosy Nilima?' said Anwar, slamming the back door as he left.

How often would Quick go home and become Alexander Gibbons? Maybe every day, maybe only occasionally. And why did he? One thing was sure, if he could afford to keep two homes going and one of them in a Kensington Mews, he truly was the diamond geezer Freddy had said he was. Therefore, no more time must be wasted before that strongbox was opened. It might well contain something as valuable as the pendant. Suppose he couldn't get it open, would he then try bringing pressure to bear on Gibbons-Quick to open it himself? In Kensington, though, not here.

Anwar parked the van in St Michael's Street and walked back to the Edgware Road, where in a newsagent's he bought a paperback A–Z London guide. In his room Keefer had reverted to his somnolent state and was lying on the floor foetus-fashion. Anwar kicked him in the ribs, for no reason but his own personal satisfaction. Keefer didn't stir. I hope he's not dead, thought Anwar, not out of affection for his friend but imagining attempts to get the body down the stairs unseen and out of the house.

The London guide showed him that Chetwynd Mews was a turning off Launceston Place, W8. Drive or take the tube to Kensington High Street. Easy-peasy. Now to have another go at the strongbox. After a couple of fruitless hours, Julitta and Flint appeared. They looked dispassionately at Keefer, whom they had seen in this state before.

'Do you wonder', said Julitta, 'that I told him to fuck off? Who needs that around the house? Haven't you got that open yet?'

That was not the way to speak to Anwar. 'You try then, bitch. You couldn't open a can of beans let alone a safe.'

'OK, I only asked.'

'Was there something you wanted? If not you can piss off and take him with you.'

It took all three of them to get Keefer on to his feet. Julitta took one arm and Flint the other. Anwar heard them thumping down the stairs, Julitta's heels clacking, Keefer muttering and swearing, his booted feet kicking the treads. Back to the strongbox. It was beginning to look as if he'd have to get Gibbons-Quick to open it himself. Torture him a bit—oh, yes, easy-peasy, he might open it but he'd go to the police the minute they left with descriptions of them all. It was important to Anwar to keep his unblemished record and his reputation, as yet only sullied by school truancy.

Now he was trying any combination. One-two-three-four and five-six-seven-eight. All four digits the same, six-six-six-six, eight-eight-eight-eight. Nothing worked. Just for fun, for nothing but liking to see it because it was his, the number he'd never use for a safe code, it was too obvious, and certainly the number

Gibbons-Quick had no possible reason to use: three-three-eight-six. His own birthday and birth date, the third of March 1986. Wasting time, he admonished himself, but he keyed it in.

The strongbox emitted a low growl, then two clicks and its door slid open.

'I don't believe it,' Anwar said and he closed his eyes. When he opened them again the door still stood ajar. 'Come on, get yourself together. You've done it.'

But what was this? A pair of cheap earrings, a lighter and the kind of girl's watch you pinned on. The disappointment which came at once faded as he began to realise. Those were *the* earrings, Jacky Miller's, that lighter belonged to one of the other girls and the watch to a third. It had been in the papers and on telly day after day. Two murdered girls and a third who had probably been murdered. Gibbons-Quick had their property, or had had it. That must mean he'd killed them. He was the Rottweiler. What other explanation was possible?

Anwar Ghosh was old in villainy but still he was only sixteen. He came from what his head teacher would have called 'a nice home' and had grown up in an Indian middle-class tradition of hard work, protracted education, careful husbandry and the importance of family life—hugely extended family life. The thought that he, the son of professional people and destined for great things, had broken into the flat of a serial killer and robbed him turned him cold all over. It was as if the icy spray from a shower head where there is only cold water had hit him with a nasty shock. For a moment, but only a moment, he considered dumping the strongbox and its contents, telling the others it contained no more than costume jewellery junk and a few notes, and then dropping it over one of the bridges into the canal.

But the strongbox was a potential money-maker. And in no small way. It might make thousands, tens of thousands. Remember Gibbons-Quick is loaded, he told himself. Remember he's got two homes. He's a diamond geezer. What to do about it? Sit here in the quiet and think. Think about the next step. And he must never forget the man was very dangerous.

Just before five Anwar was in the mews, sitting in the white van. He didn't dare leave the van in case the traffic warden who had been prowling about in here, but was on his way out just as he arrived, came back. He had parked outside number nine but on the opposite side, where there was a brick wall with creepers all over it, from which number fourteen could be easily kept within his sights. The house incorporated a garage and when Anwar looked through its small window he saw a silver Mercedes inside. Unlike Inez in similar circumstances, he noted down the number.

His discovery hadn't yet been fully realised, hadn't become part of the day's work, or just one of those things. Every time he thought of those objects being inside there, sweat broke out on the palms of his hands and his forehead, and he found himself asking if he was dreaming, it *couldn't* be. But it was, it was. And now he was going to capitalise on it. Hold on to that, he told himself every time that dreaming stuff came back, hold on to that.

Gibbons-Quick was in the house. Anwar hadn't seen him go in but he'd seen him at a window. Easily recognisable if encountered only twice, one of those times when the man was returning home—well, to one home—after some evening trip out, the other when walking up the Edgware Road and he and Freddy were coming out of Ranoush Juice. Just now G-Q had appeared at an upstairs window, looked down into the mews and drawn the curtains. And that was the guy who had killed all those girls, put a garrotte round their necks and pulled it till they were dead! It was unbelievable. No more of that, said Anwar sternly, it happened, right? It's him.

And here he was coming out of the house just as the traffic warden reappeared at the other end of the mews. Where was he going? Back to Star Street, via Kensington High Street tube station, it looked like. For part of the way Anwar followed him until it became impossible, there was too much traffic and all wanting to go as fast as possible. Having no driving licence and no insurance, Anwar knew the folly of attracting attention to himself while at the wheel of Keefer's van.

On the drive home, he reflected on his researches into Gibbons-Quick's life. A double life, obviously, therefore one—or two—with much to hide. A man who could disappear from one life and reappear in the next, and one with a bizarre sense of humour. For two days now he would have known that his strongbox had gone and that the thieves would succeed in opening it if they tried hard enough or had his kind of staggering luck. Only the exceptionally stupid would get bored with trying and dispose of the box unopened. So the Rottweiler must be expecting some kind of approach, maybe even an approach from the law.

The next step, thought Anwar, would be to gratify his expectations—but prepare the ground carefully first.

Will was a frightened child. All the thin veneer of grown-upness built over his inner self by the encouragement of friends, of Becky and Monty and Keith, seemed to have been peeled away by the police. Sometimes he lay face-downwards on Becky's bed, sometimes he huddled in a corner of the sofa, staring into space or gazing at the sky out of the big window. Television still provided entertainment, so long as it was totally anodyne, gentle quizzes purposely designed for the low IQ, it seemed to Becky, children's cartoons, historical comedy. But even this last often contained scenes of violence, duels, the rough handling of prisoners, punishment and death, and all this made Will quail and bury his head in the cushions. Detective series, war films, news programmes, all these were out of the question. The sight of a uniformed policeman on the screen or even a plainclothes man in raincoat and soft hat, caused him to whimper aloud and run from the room to the sanctuary of her bedroom. She had given up sleeping there, leaving it to him, and moved into the study at night.

True to his word of giving it a trial, James continued to come. He might have been a social worker himself, compiling a case history, for all the closeness there was between him and Becky. He kissed her when he came in much the same way as she kissed Will, helped her get tea, told her about events at the office, offered her a second television set for her own use in the study.

'Thank you very much but it's not worth it,' she said with more optimism than perhaps she felt. 'Will must go back to his own place in the next week or two. I've had two weeks off and I've got one more. After that I have to go back if I want to keep my job.'

James had become addicted to *The Times* crossword. He did it every time he came and Becky, glancing at it before dropping it into the recycling, saw how his facility with it had improved. Seldom now were there blank spaces where he couldn't solve a clue and find a word. When he left he kissed her on the cheek and said he would 'look in' again in a day or two. Before he arrived and immediately after he left, she swallowed a gulp, or two gulps, of whisky straight from the secret bottle she kept on a hidden shelf in the kitchen.

Another visitor was Keith Beatty. It brought Becky dismay to see the shock on Keith's face when he saw Will and she realised how she had grown used to his deterioration. For a few minutes Keith didn't know what to say but he rallied, made an effort on which she silently congratulated him, and talked about the current decorating job, his wife, his children and his sister.

'Kim's really missed you, Will. She keeps asking how you're getting on, said you were going to get in touch and fix another date, and then this. She hasn't much time for the police after this, I can tell you.'

Becky marvelled that he still seemed to think—as he had thought from first acquaintance with her nephew—that Will was a normal person who happened to be rather reserved and for some reason had missed out on essential schooling. Was that the sister's attitude too?

'I might bring her over to see you, if that's all right with Miss Cobbett, I mean Becky.'

'Of course.'

What else could she say? And Will, who was always suspicious of James, visibly improved in Keith's company, speaking a little, answering his enquiries and smiling much as he had smiled before the police found him digging up that garden. Perhaps he would be the same with Kim. Becky saw it as a kind of therapy. This might be the way to get Will restored to his old self.

Keith evidently believed he had simply been physically ill, had had flu or a virus. She should be grateful to Inez, she supposed, for creating this belief among Will's acquaintances. As for her, almost for the first time since he was born, she had ceased to feel guilt. By giving up her life to him, her future and her very self, she had rid

herself of guilt, but only for him. It was there in strong
measure over her job, failure to work from home as she
had intended, her career and her once-potential lover.
No doubt it was part of her nature and if she banished
it from one area it only resurfaced in another. Drinking
had become an essential part of her lifestyle, and the
worst kind, the secret, covert, conspiratorial sort, and
the conspirators were her ego and her unconscious.

None of that introspection solved the terrible difficulty of what to do when she was due back in her office.
If she wanted to keep her job she must go back. She was
twenty years away from retirement and she had
intended, in any case, never to retire.

Near despair, she listened while Keith chatted about
his small son starting nursery school and Will nodded,
smiled and said 'Good boy' or 'He's big now', and
thought how she was caught in the carer's cage, in the
trap with no escape hatch, the thankless, unpaid, labo-
rious and mind-numbing boredom of looking after
the unfortunate.

That same week the body of Jacky Miller was found in
the front garden of a house in South Kensington. The
house had been gutted and, although a good deal of the
debris had been collected and removed, an area in the
front where once had been a lawn was again covered
with bricks, battens, chunks of fibreglass, broken glass
and wrenched-up floorboards. The fibreglass was
unpleasant and perhaps dangerous to handle because
the thick fuzzy yellow stuff was made of fine filaments
of glass. Bare hands thrust into it came out covered with
innumerable hair-thin scratches. It was therefore the last
of the piles to be taken away and when it was, the driver of the builders' waste truck uncovered a dead girl,
fast decomposing.

Her mother who, for the past month, had lived in alternating hope and dreadful fear, identified the body in the mortuary; approaching, staring, turning away like a woman sleepwalking.

All this time Jacky had lain there no more than two streets away from the mews where Jeremy Quick lived as himself, as Alexander Gibbons. Driving his car through the West End was something he seldom did but he had done it on the night Jacky left the club she had been to with her friends. As it was long past the restricted hours, he had parked in a rare empty space on a single yellow line because he saw the girls. Four of them, all a little drunk, merry and now perhaps tired. It was Gaynor Ray all over again.

He approached them and was no more than a yard away when he turned into a phone box and pretended to make a call. Already excited, tingling with it, he remembered Gaynor and her silver cross, the willingness with which she had accepted his offer of a lift. What was happening to him he could no more understand now than he ever could. Analysis of his feelings deserted him while he was looking at the girl he would next kill. His intellect was subsumed in this stronger faculty, which wasn't sexual or anger or something fools called bloodlust. Was it an overmastering desire for revenge?

Three of the girls went off, down Tottenham Court Road, perhaps seeking an all-night bus. The one he had singled out—why? He didn't know—turned down a side street and waited at the kerb, for a taxi, it must be. It was twenty past one and there were no taxis. There were no people either, not in this narrow darkish street.

The greyish-white light of a single street lamp glittered on the earrings she wore. Brilliants set in the silver like diamonds in white gold—some chance! He started the car. If he had stayed there he would have been sick, have had to get out and retch into the gutter. Once before, when he had tried to resist this impulse and had only succeeded because the girl had unlocked a door on to the street and gone inside, he had actually thrown up. Not this time.

Immaculate as usual in dark suit, white shirt and blue tie, he doctored his accent as far away as possible from the Nottingham tones he grew up with. A public school drawl replaced it as he pulled up where the taxi she wanted might have stopped, and said, 'Where are you going? Don't look like that'—she wasn't looking like anything, only surprised—'I'm really not a strange man. I've got a daughter of my own your age and I'm absolutely safe.'

'Wandsworth,' she said, and she named the street. 'It's by the common.'

'Sure you feel OK? You wouldn't prefer to wait for a cab?'

'There aren't any. Were you going there yourself?'

'Balham,' he said. 'It's on my way.'

He had driven her southwards, almost passing his own house, into Chelsea by the World's End and down the Wandsworth Bridge Road. They talked all the way, she about the friends and the evening they had had; he, congratulating himself on the scope of his imagination, had invented a wife who was a doctor, a daughter at Oxford, a son taking A Levels. When they were nearly at Wandsworth Bridge, he turned off into an even lone-lier and emptier side street.

'I don't think this is the way,' she said, not fearfully but as she might say those words to a friend who had taken the wrong turning.

'I know. I wanted to do like the taxi drivers and look it up in my guide.'

He unfastened his seat belt and leaned across her to open the glove compartment. But instead of taking out his London guide he had put his hand over the length of electric lead which lay inside.

When it was done he didn't even move the body from where it still sat. Passers-by, if there were any, would suppose his passenger asleep. It was a risk but taking risks lifted it above the inexplicable and the sordid. Perhaps taking risks also made it seem more like a game, less real. However, she couldn't stay there for long. On his way to the mews, where he had in any case meant to stay the night, he passed the dumped waste in the front garden. Huge houses here, all separate, all with gardens full of dense shrubs and tall trees. A few lights were still on but none in this house, of course, and none in those of the immediate neighbours. Usually he didn't bother with hiding a body but something told him this time that concealment might be wiser. He had taken off her earrings the moment he knew she was dead. As he had told himself before, it was Gaynor Ray all over again . . .

Passing that way on foot a week later he had been gratified to see the layers of fibreglass which had been her sole covering were half-buried now under bricks and sand and broken wood. It might be a long time before they found her. It was.

The discovery briefly distracted him from the worry which never really left him now: speculation as to what had become of his strongbox. A happy outcome was, of course, possible. Apart from the thieves growing fed up with it and discarding it somewhere unopened, there was the chance the objects inside might not be recognised for what they were. And if they were recognised those who had taken the strongbox might decide it was better to do nothing, it was safer. Were they not just as

criminal as he? The likelihood of people in their situation going to the police was small.

As each day passed and nothing happened, his mind
grew easier. Perhaps his best course would be to vanish
back into his true identity and become Alexander
Gibbons for ever more, as he had intended to do when
he planned to marry the fictitious Belinda. Since the
burglary the flat in Star Street had become less desirable
to him. He sensed that the astute Inez had become dis-
trustful. Not that she suspected him of his true offences,
he was sure of that, but of lying and prevarication she
did. Being alone with her was no longer pleasant or
amusing, and he had begun avoiding that cup of tea and
chat in the mornings. Once or twice he failed to go to
work in the mews house but stayed all day in the
Paddington area, walking about, sitting in cafés drinking coffee, always wondering if someone was following
him. Sometimes he was sure he had a shadow who
dogged his footsteps along the Bayswater Road, up
Westbourne Terrace and over the bleak and lonely
hump of Bishop's Bridge. But long before he reached
home the man or woman behind him turned out not to
have been following him at all but merely going the
same way as he was and at the same pace.

The newspapers were full of the discovery of Jacky
Miller's body, of interviews with her mother, her relatives and friends. One of these, with the particular
friend who had given her the earrings, alerted him more
sharply to his danger, for the girl, shown the pair he had
bought and planted in the shop, denied these had been
her gift. The hoops of her earrings had been studded
with twenty brilliants, she had made a point of counting them, while the pair the police showed her had only
sixteen. Somehow, a pair identical to the ones she had
bought were found in a jewellers and a photograph of

these beside one of the pair he had bought appeared in
every paper as well as on television.

This must be bad news for him, Jeremy thought, up
in his flat, again absenting himself from work and today
from his rovings around north-west London. If the
thieves of the strongbox saw this story, and they would,
of course they would, things would be worse for him.
They would know, if they hadn't before, that the earrings in the box had twenty brilliants in their hoops and
were identical to those in the photograph. Why, oh why,
hadn't he thought to count those glittering glass frag-
ments before buying the substitute pair? Because it
wouldn't have crossed his mind, he wouldn't have imagined the number might have any significance. Did that
mean he despised women who adorned themselves with
cheap jewellery? Or even that he looked down on and,
more than that, loathed, women? Perhaps. He couldn't,
at the moment, think of one he knew that he liked.

Except his mother. Of the rest it was true. Besides—
and he seemed to have made a strange discovery—his
mother wasn't exactly a woman, she was unique, *his
mother.* Outside categories, outside sex. This delving
into his inner self left him feeling exhausted and he was
sitting in his chair, half asleep, when the phone rang.
Few people knew this phone number. The other tenants, of course, Inez, now, presumably, the police.

He let it ring, five times, six times. Then he lifted the
receiver.

CHAPTER 20

The voice was a woman's, the accent, Jeremy thought, what you might expect from this kind of lowlife. The words were unreal, or perhaps surreal. He wondered if man or woman had ever asked this question before of anyone.

'Is that the murderer?'

He made himself speak. 'What do you mean?'

'It's the Rottweiler, innit?'

This time he didn't reply. He hated that sobriquet.

She said, 'I got your safe and the shit in it. You wannit? You better answer. Not talking's not doing you no good, *Mister* Gibbons.'

He wouldn't admit even to himself that this frightened him. Alerted him, he thought. How did she know? How *could* she know? 'What is it you want?' he said.

Following the time-honoured style of the blackmailer, she said, 'You'll see. I'll call again later and you better be there.'

That she knew his name was, for the moment, the most alarming thing. Of course it wasn't just she alone, there would be others, certainly one other. Somehow they had broken open his strongbox and cruelly taken their time in approaching him. He marvelled at his use of that word 'cruelly' even in his thoughts, silently, internally, in the silence of his mind. Cruel, he repeated to himself, cruelly, cruelty, cruellest. The way she had spoken his real name was cruel. Besides that, he couldn't understand how

she knew it. He had brought no documents here for
intruders to find. His insurance policy, share certificates,
passport, car insurance, current tax return, credit card
statements, driving licence and all the rest were securely
locked up in his desk at 14 Chetwynd Mews. But wait a
minute . . . Where *was* his driving licence? Not this last
time but back in March when visiting his mother, he had
been stopped for speeding. Only five miles per hour over
the limit but this officious motorcycle cop had stopped
him. Of course he hadn't his driving licence on him but,
obeying the rule to produce it within five days at the nearest police station, he had done so, pocketed it and
returned to Star Street. What had he done with it? In spite
of that woman's telling him not to leave the house—he
wasn't going to take instructions from a woman, especially
one with a voice like hers—he went out, walked up to
Norfolk Square and took a taxi to South Kensington.

Halfway there the thought came to him that his
mother had never, not through all his infancy and boy-
hood, told him what and what not to do, she had never
instructed him. She had loved him. His second thought
was, what if by some horrible coincidence or some find he
couldn't identify, they had also broken into 14 Chetwynd
Mews. But he was letting nervousness bring him fantasies.
The burglar alarm was on as usual and everything inside
inviolate. In the desk he found all the documents he had
enumerated—with the exception of the driving licence.
Then it came back to him. He had meant to bring it here
but had done what is so easily done, put it in a 'safe place'
in the Star Street kitchen, the drawer where he kept
brochures telling him how to work the microwave and the
dishwasher. Why would they look in there?

He didn't know why but they had. No driving
licence. He went out into his roof garden, a bower of
bliss on this fine day, the first geraniums out, little trees

in pots putting out new leaves, the tree fern fresh green, its fronds unfurling. He scarcely noticed it, he scarcely noticed the scent of the hyacinths, but sat down to await that woman's call.

'I've told him', said Zeinab, 'I've put it in the bank till after the wedding. Then it won't matter what he thinks, it'll be too late.'

She reminded Inez of those girls in Victorian novels who married rich men, only confessing their load of debts to the bridegroom after the ceremony. But marriage was an irrevocable bond in those days . . . 'You're going through with it, then?'

Instead of answering directly, Zeinab said, 'The wedding's June eighth at St Peter's, Eaton Square. I hope you'll come.'

'It doesn't seem very appropriate, considering he's Jewish and you're a Moslem.'

'It's all the same God, isn't it?' said Zeinab in a pious voice and she contemplated her engagement rings, one on each hand, the small diamond Rowley Woodhouse's and the huge one Morton's.

'Where are you going for your honeymoon?' This from Freddy, who had walked in from the street.

He and Zeinab seemed to have settled their differences and decided to let bygones be bygones. 'Bermuda,' she said and corrected herself. 'No, that's with Rowley. Me and Morton are going to Rio.'

'You can't marry both of them.' Freddy didn't wait for her reply. 'I'm thinking of getting married myself.' Since no longer working for Inez, he had resumed his old habits of examining and occasionally dusting the pieces on sale. Striking an orator's attitude, clutching a soapstone camel in his left hand, he began to hold forth. 'Marriage is an institution I feared was falling into disuse, but not a bit of it, it is rather on the up and up, in other words, becoming the fashion. Mark my words, in a few years, cohabiting, all this living together without benefit of register office, will be a thing of the past, not to say frowned on by them in the know . . .'

'What about you living with Ludmila, then?' said Zeinab.

'Living with her is not correct, Zeinab,' said Freddy with dignity. 'As is well known among them as matters'—a friendly glance for Inez—'Ludo is a tenant in this house, while I am resident in London Fields. Mark my words . . .'

Inez had marked them long enough. 'Freddy,' she said quietly as a customer came in and Zeinab glided gracefully to serve him, 'Freddy, while you were looking after the shop that afternoon I was at the police station with Becky, are you quite quite sure no one went into the back? Not some friend of a tenant or casual caller?' Her mind roved over Rowley Woodhouse, whom none had ever seen, and Keith Beatty and his family, and, as an orange car pulled up outside, Morton Phibling. 'Are you sure?'

'Cross my heart and hope to die,' said Freddy. 'I swear on my mother's head.'

'And you never left the shop unattended for a moment?'

'Never!'

Knowing him, Inez was inspired. 'Or attended, come to that?'

'Ah, now that's a horse of another colour.' While Freddy nodded sagely, she put her hands up to her face, disbelieving. 'Ludo was here. I nipped down the road,' he said, 'to pick up our documents.' Inez didn't care what documents, listened in near-screaming impatience while he outlined how he and Ludmila

needed this voucher and that certificate from the agent
in order to maximise the benefits of their heavily dis-
counted weekend in Torquay. 'Ludo was left in charge
for five minutes.'

'And she didn't leave and was there when you got
back?'

'Ah, now I didn't say that, Inez. You're putting words
into my mouth. What I said was that she was left in
charge, right? What happened in point of fact was that
Ludo recalled while waiting for my return that she
had inadvertently left the iron on in her apartment and
she . . .'

Morton came in, trotting jauntily, and his suddenly
youthful smile made Inez wonder once more where on
earth she had seen him before. The few seconds he took
to remove the baseball cap he was unaccountably wearing
gave Zeinab the chance to slip Rowley Woodhouse's ring
into a drawer. 'My beloved is a lotus in the garden of
Allah,' he declaimed, in a possible reference to Zeinab's
religious persuasion, and planted a kiss on her cheek.

It was all too much for the customer who made a
quick excuse and left.

'You'll lose me my job,' grumbled Zeinab.

'So what, my treasure? You'll be resigning anyway on
seven June.'

They began whispering, Zeinab irritably, Morton
with his arm round her and a soppy smile on his face.
Inez took up her interrogation of Freddy where she had
left off. 'So no one was here for some minutes? Anyone
could have come in?'

'Not "some", Inez. Not "anyone".'

She gave up. She would have to tell Crippen or
Zulueta and then they would be back. Meanwhile,
Freddy might as well make himself useful. 'Look, if
you've nothing to do, would you mind taking my watch

in next door and getting Mr Khoury to put a new battery in it?'

It was unfortunate but somehow not unexpected in the general gloomy scheme of things, everything going wrong all the time, that James, Keith Beatty and his sister all happened to arrive together. This was something that might have been avoided if even one of them had phoned her first but none had. James scarcely bothered to conceal his dismay, and worse his distaste, for the Beattys. He and Becky were in the kitchen, while she found drinks for all the company, beer for Keith, orange juice for Kim and Will, wine for him and her.

'I suppose this is to be a home-from-home for all his mates, is it?'

'I'd no idea they were coming, James.'

'Why do I bother? It makes no difference as far as being alone with you goes.'

He went back into the living room without another word. No doubt he had already picked up the crossword puzzle, she thought, as she poured herself a generous glass of whisky and drank it down, a swig from the bottle being inadequate in these circumstances.

The girl had seated herself on the sofa next to Will and was talking to him in a friendly, easy fashion. If he said nothing himself, he hadn't made one of his gestures of rejection, turning his back or moving to an armchair. She was a pretty girl and seemed nice, Becky thought, her skirt not too short and her make-up sparing. Why was she suddenly thinking like someone twice her age, she asked herself. Was this the effect of staying at home being a carer, with little prospect of her servitude coming to an end?

The television was, of course, on and showing its usual late-afternoon–early-evening fare. Neither Will nor the Beattys seemed to find anything to object to, for all three of them it was the obligatory background to home life, as normally present as light and air and an equable temperature. Will alone was really watching it. Keith and Kim chatted, glancing from time to time at the screen, occasionally addressing a meaningless remark to James, who looked up and nodded or raised his eyebrows. Becky watched Kim gently take Will's hand and expected to see hers pushed away, but Will kept hold of it and in quite a strong grip. Well, support might be coming from that unexpected quarter . . .

How long were they going to stay? Her thoughts were moving in a way that made her dislike herself. *These people*, these *sorts* of people, never knew when to leave, they didn't know how to make a graceful departure. She would probably have to tell them tactfully. But instead, principally because she needed another drink, she went out into the kitchen, gulped down the whisky quickly before James came out to find her and began thinking about food. If they were here much longer she would have to feed them. Eggs, she supposed, it always came to eggs in the end, or she could phone for food.

The door opened and she expected James, but it was Kim.

'I was wondering if I should order a pizza or maybe Chinese takeaway. What would you like?'

'Oh, we aren't stopping. I've had my tea and Denise'll be expecting Keith. Becky, I came out to say— well, I've had an idea. About Will, I mean.'

A flush had come into her cheeks and now she looked very pretty. Becky noticed how beautifully cut her hair was and how clean. But, of course, she was a hairdresser . . . 'What sort of an idea, Kim?'

'I really like Will. I don't know if you know that but I really like him. I know he's been ill, he's had a sort of

breakdown, hasn't he? Your friend said you had to take
time off work to look after him and he really ought to
go home and I thought, you know, why don't I sort of
move in with him and look after him for a bit?'

'You?'

'Yes, well, I mean, you know, I really like him. I
know he's shy and he never says much but he's sort of
nice and gentle and, you know, most blokes aren't.
When I say "move in" I don't mean like *partners*, I mean
I'd just be there at first, and maybe one day . . .'

'There's only the one room.' Becky felt her head
spin. With the shock of this or the whisky? Both, probably. 'But it's a big room.' And with the put-you-up
turned into a bed and a screen . . . 'There's your job.'

'It's not far. I could get home at lunchtime. And he'll
go back with Keith, won't he?'

She could go back to work. She'd be free again. And
Will would *like* it. James and she would be able to see
each other properly, go out, he could stay the night, and
once a week Will would come for the day as he used to,
Will and *Kim* would come . . . She was letting her
thoughts run away with her.

'I'd like to think about it.' She would tell James, ask
him.

'Your friend left,' said Kim. 'He said to tell you he
had to go.'

'We'll keep him on the edge,' said Anwar. 'Let him sweat.'

'Dirty murderer.' Flint had a pious look, all disapproval and conscious virtue. 'Deserves all he gets. The
gas chamber'd be too good for him. Give him a lethal
injection and make it slow.'

This display of familiarity with execution methods
brought a snarl to Anwar's mouth. 'Shut the fuck up,
can't you?' he said.

Julitta, their spokesperson, had gone home for the day to see her mum in Watford and wouldn't be back before midnight. It was hard to say if Jeremy, had he known this, would have been comforted by it or more dismayed. He felt only that it would be unwise now to go far from the phone. It might be three when it rang, it might be nine or later. He wanted nothing to eat and he was afraid to drink lest alcohol send him to sleep. What did he want? He asked himself that, thinking a true answer might be of help, but if he were absolutely honest—and there was no point otherwise—he wanted to run away and hide. Only there was nowhere to hide.

He found some books, new ones he had bought but hadn't yet looked at, and began on a reputedly wonderful biography of Winston Churchill. When he found he was looking at the print and taking in the shape of the words but not their sense, he gave it up and tried a novel. That was worse. A new translation of Suetonius managed to hold his attention because the dissolute lives and excesses of those Roman emperors continued to fascinate, perhaps because, however wicked and evil one might be, they were always worse. Killing a few young women would have been all in the day's work for Tiberius, say.

The book kept him going till the afternoon, though after he had laid it down, if anyone had asked him to specify what it was about, he could only have given a vague reply. He had begun to will the phone to ring, but in vain. The sandwich he made he couldn't eat. He managed a glass of orange juice with a wineglassful of vodka in it. The weariness he feared came and he fell into a troubled sleep.

The phone ringing woke him. He reached for it and knocked over his empty glass. It was a wrong number, the scolding voice blaming him for not being the person she wanted. He was wide awake now and it was only three thirty. The girls came into his mind, Gaynor Ray, Nicole Nimms, Rebecca Milsom, Caroline Dansk, Jacky Miller. If he could find something they had in common he might be some way to finding out why he did what he did. They were all young or fairly young, all single (though he hadn't known that) but for Gaynor who had a man she lived with, and all walking down the street alone. That was all.

He re-created the sensations he had when he saw them, always the same sensation, and always felt for this particular girl. Not for the hundreds of others he might see in the course of a day, though these, or individual ones, might equally well have been alone in a lonely street and he alone behind them. It always happened when he was behind them—was that significant? Something they had about them was what drew him, something in their walk or stance or backward glance or posture. And when he recognised it, or some inner eye of his did and unconsciously, his whole body and soul—yes, his *soul*—swelled and shook with desire, an excitement intolerable unless he used it for its only purpose. For sexual it was not. No act of sex would have exhausted it or satisfied it. The object which had aroused it had to be—annihilated.

As far as this, or almost as far, his inner investigations invariably brought him. He must go one step further, or several steps back, to uncover the rest, the cause, but he never could. Occasionally, he had played analyst and analysand, taking both parts, had lain on his couch and his shadow-self sat in his chair, asking the questions and giving the answers. He might as well do it now, pass the time. He lay down, on his back, and closed his eyes. The analyst asked him to go back, back beyond his father's death, beyond school, into his early childhood. Many times he had tried this before and always, at the age of about three, came a blank. The part of his mind that was neither analyst nor analysand knew that some authorities said memory was virtually lacking from before a child could speak coherently, for we think and remember in words.

He surprised himself by saying, 'It's too far back.'

Surely, in these curious sessions, he had never said that before?

'Go to the time, then,' the analyst said.

'I can't.'

'You can.'

'It's school,' he said. 'I'm at school. I'm twelve or thirteen. I'm happy, I'm all right. My dad's ill, very ill, he's going to die, but I'm happy and guilty too. Guilty for being happy. Oh, I can't, I can't do this!'

'You can.'

'I've got friends. Andrew is my friend.'

'Go on.'

'My mother's very unhappy because my dad's dying. I love her. Andrew's mother goes with her to see him in hospital. I love his mother—I mean, I love my mother . . . I can't go on, I can't, I can't . . .!'

He was crying now and the analyst was crying, both of them sobbing, breaking their hearts, merging into one man sitting up, weeping into his single pair of hands.

Television documentaries he sometimes watched, those and political programmes. There was something on about Jung but that seemed too near the bone after his experience of the afternoon. You could damage your mind like that, some said, literally drive yourself mad. And that was how it had felt. He would never do it again. The programme on Tibet sounded possible but once he had turned it on he became very nervous.

Although the sound was turned quite low and he wasn't deaf or anywhere near it, he was afraid he wouldn't hear the phone when it rang. Much the same applied to going outside on to the roof garden, though it was lovely out there, the sky a tender lilac-blue, still coloured at the horizon by the last of the sun, and not at all cold. He saw a large moth alight on the table and spread flat its brown ring-marked wings.

He made himself watch two news bulletins, and 'watch' was right, for the sound was so low it was no more than a faint whisper. When the phone call hadn't come by eleven, he took his clothes off, put on his dressing gown and cleaned his teeth. Flossing in front of the mirror brought to mind the brace he had once worn to correct his dentition. As he thought of it he found the girls returning to his mind, especially one girl or woman who wasn't one of *them*. He held on to her, suddenly short of breath, but she faded as fast as she had come and he spat toothpaste and saliva into the basin. He went to bed. The extension was plugged in and on the bedside cabinet. He sat up for a bit, reading Suetonius, pausing sometimes to reflect how riveted he would have been without this dread hanging over him. The light out, he lay in the dark, wide awake. The same feeling as he had had over the television sound returned, only this time he had a neurotic fear he wouldn't be able to hear the phone bell in the dark. Of course the light had to go on again. He wouldn't sleep, anyway.

Midnight, one o'clock. Suppose they had given it up, whatever they planned to do, got cold feet and taken the stuff to the police? Or even suppose the police had found them, raided their hideout and discovered the earrings and the rest? But they wouldn't, not for a petty burglary. You don't know if it was petty, he muttered to himself, you don't know what Inez had down there or

that ridiculous Russian woman. Someone like that
might have a fortune in jewels. Two o'clock. If only he
could run away, run to his mother . . .

Just before three the phone rang. He picked up the
receiver.

'Surprise, surprise,' said the voice he had heard that
morning. 'Me again.'

CHAPTER 21

He had agreed to everything she asked because he had no choice. In all areas of life, most people have some sort of choice. It depends, of course, on what they have done and what the threat may be. A few dirty photographs fallen into the wrong hands, an infidelity possibly disclosed, these can be dealt with by a resourceful man or woman or the consequences bravely faced, a 'publish and be damned' stance maintained. When the threat is to reveal, or by irrefutable implication reveal, a series of murders, the killer has no recourse but to submit. Revelation is worse than any compliance with threats, however costly.

She asked for £10,000. She was alone, she said, but he didn't believe her. When she said she hadn't done the burglary alone, she was in this with one other, her boyfriend, but he hadn't seen the strongbox and what she had found inside, when she said her father had broken it open but had never realised the significance of its contents, then he half believed. Only a woman, she said, would recognise and appreciate what those objects were and what they meant, and that he understood. It might be true. She wanted £10,000, she was poor, she and her boyfriend needed the money for the deposit on a flat, they had to have somewhere in London and London prices were through the roof. All right, she might want more, she couldn't guarantee she wouldn't, a little more. There was a frankness about this which almost convinced him. Whether it convinced or not, he had to pay, he had to meet her and pay, to play for time and because he had no choice.

She would call him next day to name a time and a place.

'Don't take too long about it,' he said, hating to plead, but dreading the effect on his mind if he had to pass through another day like this one. 'In the morning, please.'

'OK, I'll try.'

After she rang off there was a terrible silence. It seemed to him, in the middle of Paddington, in the heart of a great overcrowded city, that London had never been so quiet. He began talking to himself aloud. 'She phoned,' he said, shouting in the stillness. 'She did phone. At least the waiting's over. It's over, I know the worst and I can sleep.'

He couldn't. He lay in the dark for a while, then with the light on. He thought about it, about himself. He didn't particularly want to live, not if he or someone he deceitfully called his other self went on killing women. But if she went to the police he wouldn't die, he would live for years incarcerated. That was what he couldn't face. Death would be fine but death was not so easy to get. He lay face-down, then on his side, then on his back. At some point, half dozing, he told himself she would phone at six in the morning, at seven. He should have known better. People like that go to bed in the morning, at six or seven she would be settling down to sleep somewhere till it was time to get up at three. Three in the afternoon was her morning. At eight he got up, drank water, fell on the bed and slept heavily until midday. The events of the previous day rolled back and he relived them all, heard her voice in recall, remembered his decision to pay. Getting up, afraid even to take a shower, he sat in his dressing gown, waiting for her to call.

Becky phoned Kim at the hairdresser's. If she was sure, if she hadn't changed her mind, they could give it a try. Will had been consulted, gave little sign of being pleased or displeased with the idea, but she could tell he wasn't aghast. In some ways he was pleased at the idea of being back in his own home in Star Street, and if he said once or twice that he'd like it best if Becky came too and stayed with him, she didn't repeat his words to Kim. She packed his things and set off early in the car, to stop on the way at the big Sainsbury's in the Finchley Road to stock up with all the things Will liked to eat and some things she thought Kim might like.

Everything was happening early, as it always does when you want something very much, the getting to the airport when you long to be at your destination, the arrival at the meeting on which your whole future seems to depend so that you pace for ten minutes in the street outside the venue. Becky got Will to Star Street by four, knowing Kim couldn't get there till five. They went in by the street door and up the stairs. The place had been shut up. It was close and airless and dusty. Becky opened the windows and dusted the surfaces. She made tea and set out the pastries she had bought. Guilt returned, the guilt that had been absent all the time she was doing her duty, and she asked herself what her sister would have thought of her, longing as she was to be rid of this poor child, her only relative, the little boy left behind motherless and—not quite like other little boys.

Kim rang the bell loudly and repeatedly at exactly five o'clock. Becky ran down and opened the door.

'I'm not late, am I?'

'You're absolutely on time.' Becky wanted to say, you're not catching the only train that runs today, you're not going for the interview of a lifetime, but Kim would no more understand than Will would. She smiled instead.

Now, of course, she knew she couldn't go immediately. She had to stay and show Kim where everything was, explain things, tell her about the burglar alarm, the other tenants, she had to stay simply not to look as if she was longing to leave. It finished with her cooking a meal for them, pork chops and mashed potatoes and carrots and peas. Kim kept saying how lovely it was, how she loved the flat. She marvelled at the size of the room, the large bedroom area the curtained-off section made, the comfort of the makeshift bed. The dismal Russian music keening in from next door passed over her unheard.

By the time she left it was nine, Kim and Will were in front of the television and the sounds from Ludmila's flat had ceased. Becky got into her car, wondering if she were right to go. Should she rather have taken Will away with her for just one more night? But after all, what could happen? She had told Kim to phone if he seemed distressed, to call her at any time and she would come. The night passed and, strangely, she slept, her sleep visited by dreams of her sister and by Will as a baby, but otherwise undisturbed.

Jeremy hadn't been in for his tea since the burglary. Morning after morning Inez had set out the two cups as usual but only one had been used. She knew he was up there. She had heard his feet on the stairs and, from the street, seen him at one of his windows. Evidently he had decided to drop her—if you could drop someone you rented a flat from and who lived in the same house. Her pride was a little hurt but not her feelings. It would be unsurprising if this absenting himself from the shop in the mornings was a lead-up to his moving out. One day he would just walk in and hand her his notice.

'William has come back,' said Freddy, strolling in by way of the interior door. For some reason, since the burglary, he seemed to have decided Inez must never be left alone in the shop, so for the three-quarters of an hour or so between nine o'clock and a quarter to ten, he had determined to be there to 'help' her. 'And he's brought a young lady with him.'

'You mean Becky?'

'Oh, no, Inez, a really *young* lady. She must be his paramour. She stayed the night. I heard her voice last thing last night and first thing this morning. Those walls are paper-thin, you know.'

Inez didn't know. When the conversion had been done she had had the walls insulated with sound-proofing material. Freddy's news astonished her. Will with a girlfriend! Was she expecting to live there with him while he continued to pay the same rent, or Becky did? Was this Ludmila and Freddy all over again? At any rate, Becky might have told her.

As she was reflecting, rather indignantly, about this, the phone rang and it was Becky to tell her.

'It's a temporary thing, Inez. They're not living together. She's there to look after him just till he's better.'

Inez hadn't heard Becky sound so happy for months

'He thinks you're going to marry him on June eighth?' Algy was aghast. He sat down heavily. 'And the other one, Rowley whatever, thinks you're going to marry *him* on the fifteenth?'

A rumbling sound, rather like a tube train passing subterraneanly beneath one's feet, came from the depths of one of the armchairs. It was Reem Sharif laughing.

After a late babysitting she had stayed the night and was now occupied in wiping breakfast off the faces of Carmel and Bryn.

'I don't know what all the fuss is about,' said Zeinab. 'I'm not really going to marry them, Alge.'

'Don't you see you're on thin ice? All hell'll break loose if one of them finds out. It's time to stop, break it off before it's too late.'

'At least I never took up with Orville as well. And not for want of asking.'

Zeinab was looking particularly ravishing this morning in a new black linen miniskirt and, in accordance with the current fashion, a white muslin frilly peasant blouse. An engagement ring was on each hand. 'You want to look around you, Alge, at what it's done for us. Digital TV and the kids' bikes. Them chandeliers. And have you seen our joint account since I sold Morton's diamond and sapphire job?'

'I'm too scared to look,' said Algy. 'You still haven't told me what was in that dirty great box as was delivered here yesterday. There was two guys brought it in a great black van with gold all over it.'

'You could have looked. I don't have nothing secret from you, you know that.'

'May as well tell him what it was, Suzanne.' Reem undid her handiwork by stuffing a chocolate into each child's mouth and pushing them away. 'Jealousy is the pits. Put the poor sod out of his misery.'

'D'you know what I think? I think you ought to marry me. Specially now we're getting a new place to live. That'd stop you marrying anyone else. Now are you going to tell me what's in the box?'

'OK, I don't mind. It was my wedding dress, so there. The one what I'm wearing when I marry Morton. I mean, I'm supposed to be wearing. My God, look at the time. I should have been at work half an hour ago.'

He didn't have to wait so long this time. She phoned at three. Nothing she said surprised him, unless it was a certain sophistication about her directions. Unmarked notes, and however he obtained them, directly from his bank or from cash dispensers, the money must come from several different places. When he had accumulated five thousand he was to change half of it, choosing small outlets, the kind that were found at the back of jewellers' shops around Paddington Station, into euros. The remaining five thousand he must draw, using credit cards, from various London bank branches. If the limit on his cards was inadequate for this—clearly she thought this unlikely—he was to draw a cheque and support it with a card.

'It'll take weeks,' said Jeremy.

'I'll give you one week. Wednesday, twenty-nine May. I'll call you again, this sort of time, make arrangements.'

'Wait,' he said, 'I have to know more, I have to . . .'

'Ciao for now,' she said and put the phone down.

He went out on to the roof garden with a gin and tonic and a bread and cheese sandwich. It was something like thirty-six hours since he had eaten anything. The hyacinths were over, their waxy flowers sticky and their scent the smell of decay. Think, he said to himself, think this through logically. If he didn't pay up this woman would take the keyring, the lighter and the earrings to the police. The fact that these were truly Jacky Miller's earrings would be apparent to them since that friend of hers had identified the pair he bought and put in the shop as containing the wrong number of brilliants. How would she say she had got hold of them? Of course, she wouldn't show them the strongbox. The robbery was known to them—yes, but not that an occupant of the house in Star Street kept the missing keyring, the lighter and the earrings in his kitchen cupboard. Somehow she would have to make the police connect them with him, and that she could only do by telling them the objects had been taken from his flat.

She didn't have to take them in person, though. She could send them and with an anonymous covering letter. Something like, *Found in Jeremy Quick's flat. Why not ask him where he got them?* They might distrust it, even be disgusted, but they couldn't afford to ignore it. Crippen and co. would come and indeed ask him where he got them. Of course, he would deny all knowledge, he had never seen those things before. But suppose they had his fingerprints on them? He had never wiped them, never considered doing so while he handled them, though he had wiped the earrings he bought before putting them in the shop. If they asked to take his fingerprints he would have to agree.

He also had to face the fact that this girl most likely had no reputation to lose, no record she would want to keep clean. If they charged her with robbery and maybe this boyfriend with her—he didn't want to think about the boyfriend, another potential blackmailer—if they did that, why would she care? She'd get no more than probation or a few weeks' community service. He was beginning to see he couldn't win. Unless . . .

Later in the afternoon he went downstairs to spy out what money exchange places there were in the area. Up until now, whenever he needed foreign currency, he had bought his dollars or deutschmarks at the airport. Like anyone who always uses a specific agency for his transactions, he had never noticed that there were other options. But now, as he crossed the pavement, he saw that a sign, hanging from chains, outside Mr Khoury's offered 'currency exchange at competitive rates'. A thousand times he must have passed that shop and never seen that sign or, if he had, taken in what it meant.

As a kind of rehearsal, he went in, spotted the little window and grille at the back, and stood there looking about him for signs of life. After a moment or two he rang the bell on the counter and Mr Khoury came out from the back. Seeing Jeremy, he went behind the grille and said, 'How may I help you, sir?'

'I want to buy a hundred pounds' worth of US dollars.'

'Certainly. I will make a computation.' The jeweller did something to a calculator and named the sum. 'Taking perhaps a pleasant vacation in Florida?' Getting no answer, he said, 'Perhaps you will be so kind, sir, as to tell Mrs Ferry her watch is ready.'

Jeremy very nearly gaped. The man knew he lived next door! Often in the past he had wondered about that illusion some people had that no one in London knows their neighbour's business. He said brusquely, 'Well, thanks, but I've changed my mind.'

Mr Khoury watched him go with that silent inscrutability that has led to the fallacy that everyone born east of Suez is calm, fatalistic and resigned to *qismet*.

Still, Jeremy thought, he now knew how it was done. Did that mean he meant to submit to the girl's demand? Without any specific aim, he began to walk westwards and, taking Norfolk Street, made his way towards the Bayswater Road and Kensington Gardens. He needed fresh air just as he had needed food, and whatever the degree of pollution on the congested streets, the air in the royal parks was always fresh.

Crossing the big thoroughfare, he walked along one of the paths in the direction of Kensington and the Round Pond. It was sunny and quite warm, even hot. Until now he hadn't noticed. Couples and single people lay everywhere on the grass. In these places there always seem to be more young girls than any other section of the population. Don't they have jobs or babies or occupations apart from trailing desultorily in here, some linking arms, others walking side by side, chattering? Dozens of them had passed him but not one had aroused in him that fearful and terrifying excitement. He threw himself down on the grass among them, smelling its green warm smell.

CHAPTER 22

She hadn't consulted James but presented him with a fait accompli.

'You'll never regret it,' he said and she wondered at his insensitivity.

Hadn't she been at least half regretting ever since? Guilt, which seemed assuaged for ever, had come back and, it seemed, more painfully and urgently than ever. She was back at work but there had been scarcely a moment in her day when Will hadn't been in her thoughts. Determined not to phone, she had yielded at last and spoken to Kim an hour before James arrived. They were fine, Kim said, they were watching TV. She had decided to take Will out for a meal and he said he'd like that. 'Don't worry,' she said, but of course she didn't really know what there was to worry about.

Looking at herself in the mirror, Becky realised that for the past two or three weeks she had paid very little attention to her appearance. Her hair was rough and shaggy, her face aged by anxiety, and all the drink had brought an increase in her weight. She looked her age and more. A long hot shower, a face mask, shampoo and conditioner, did a lot to help. She sprayed herself all over with Bobbi Brown perfume, rubbed cream into her hands, put on a dress she had never previously worn because when she got it home the neckline seemed too revealing and the colour too bright.

Five minutes before he was due, she made herself a

large gin and tonic, plenty of gin and not much else. Necessarily, it had to be swallowed fast. She washed away the evidence with a foul-tasting mouthwash.

James praised her appearance, said how wonderful it was to be alone with her at last, but they had not been in each other's company for more than half an hour before she began to suspect that he intended to punish her. Somewhere in his head the idea must be circulating that he had suffered and because of her.

They went to a restaurant in Hampstead, a fashionable place much written about by trendy food columnists. Drinks were ordered and when they came they toasted each other.

'I wonder how many men', James said reflectively, 'would put up with what I have these past weeks.'

She felt like saying that he didn't have to come so often. At the time she had sometimes thought there was something masochistic about him, relentlessly visiting, sulking when there, obsessed with that crossword. Aloud she said, 'I know how hard it was.'

'I'm not sure if you do.' He smiled to take the sting out of his words, covered her hand, which lay on the table, with his. 'You're going to have to make it up to me.'

If he meant what she thought he meant (in that male cliché which always made of lovemaking a threat), surely they both took that for granted. Wasn't it what they had been waiting for, ever since they found Will asleep on the steps? Now was the moment to change the subject. She talked about her pleasure at going back to work, about her first days back, and he listened, making appropriate comments. Things were going to be all right. After all, he was a man, and men, she had often thought, need to be appreciated more than women do.

Impulsively, she said, 'Thank you for being so supportive, I really am grateful.'

His reply chilled her. 'I was wondering how long it would take you to say so.'

All that time, weeks, he had sat in the corner in silence for hours, frowning over the paper, speaking to her, on the few occasions when he did, only to nag. She looked at him, into his eyes, and saw a handsome man, none the worse because he was so obviously a product of a lifetime of expensive medical and cosmetic care— perfectly capped teeth, faintly tinted contact lenses, hair cut by an expert, nails attended to by a manicurist. Often, with other women, she had felt plain and ill-groomed beside them, not as well-dressed, not as honed and polished, but never before with a man.

The desire she had known off and on when he came to her flat was still there, but it seemed to be shrinking into the kind she might have for a good-looking young labourer or even an actor on television. No meeting of minds, no dawning reciprocal tenderness. She was thankful she still wanted him.

Several times during dinner he referred back to his sacrifices and her failure, in his eyes, to recognise his selflessness and patience, but he talked of other things too, of his work, his parents and sister, and of his house which, though two years in his possession, he was still furnishing with great care. And by the time they had driven back to Gloucester Avenue, she felt both were in the mood that had been so horribly disrupted by James's first encounter with Will.

Going to bed with a man for the first time should ideally be natural, a spontaneous consequence of accord, mutual attraction and, sometimes, too much drink. Even this last would have been preferable to a

contrived coupling. It must have been rather like this
for her grandparents' generation, bride and groom self-
conscious and awkward with each other, on their wedding night. But James wasn't awkward, and because she
had schooled herself not to expect a miracle the first
time, her expectations were exceeded and afterwards,
briefly, she felt at peace. Unable to sleep, she got up after
about an hour and went into the kitchen. There she did
what she hadn't dared do in front of him, when he and
she had been decorously drinking Sauvignon, poured
herself a large measure of whisky and, for some reason,
sighed with relief as the warmth and the thrill of it slid
down her throat.

Still, now Will had gone and James was at last her
lover, she would gradually wean herself off the drink.
There would be no need for that kind of stimulus
and support.

Going downstairs just before eight thirty, he had to pass
the front doors of Ludmila Gogol's flat and that of Will
Cobbett. Only from two a.m. until about now could no
music be heard from the Russian woman's place. It was,
of course, what is called 'classical' and therefore, Jeremy
had often noticed in other contexts as well as this one,
regarded by those forced to listen to it as nowhere near
as reprehensible as pop, soul, hip-hop or garage, and by
those playing it as irreproachable. He paused for a
moment to listen outside the other door, heard a
woman's voice, then Cobbett's own, and the woman
suddenly giggling. So Cobbett had a girlfriend—wonders would never cease. He speculated as to whether
Inez knew. As he went on down, he heard from behind
him a heavy thumping and a succession of majestic
chords, like a thunderstorm breaking out afresh after a
peaceful and sunlit lull.

He tapped on the door at the foot of the stairs and, instead of the usual invitation to come in, heard, 'Who is it?'

For answer he opened the door and went in, forcing himself to smile and look jovial. 'I'm a bit of a stranger, I know, but these things happen.' Never apologise, never explain . . .

He noticed the single teacup and the tea dregs at the bottom of it. 'I've already had mine,' Inez said, and in a voice that sounded anything but keen, 'I can make you another if you like.'

'Please don't bother,' he said, but he forced himself to stay and sat down, as he always had, in the grey velvet armchair. 'Mr Cobbett has a girlfriend, I hear.'

'So I believe.'

'One wonders what she thinks of Shostakovich booming through the wall at all hours.'

'Does one?' Inez said frostily.

This was much worse than he had expected. Perhaps it was only that she was having an off day. Hardly PMT at her age. The woman-hating remark coming into his mind unbidden reminded him of how he had decided he found no woman likeable . . . What was it the Italians said? *Tutte le donne sono putte eccetto mia madre ch'è una santa.* Probably that wasn't correct but its meaning was clear: all women are whores except my mother who is a saint. 'Well, I must be on my way,' he said.

Inez looked up and gave him a small restricted smile.

He walked down towards Paddington Station, hating her. What gave her the right to believe she had him at her beck and call? His next thought was to wonder why he didn't kill women like her, old, ugly women, no use or ornament to anyone. No, he had to choose the young against whom, as far as he could tell, he had no personal animus. His conscious mind might hate Inez and her like but his unconscious directed his energy against a certain kind of youthful femininitiy. Not only did he lack knowledge of why he did it, he didn't even know why this one and not another. His thoughts reverted to the fact that he was always behind his victims. It was always the ones in front of him, the ones whose backs were towards him, that he killed, never those approaching him.

Further than that he was unable to go in his mind, except to understand that this was why he used a garrotte. Like the practitioners of thuggee in India, he had to attack from behind. Beyond that realisation came a curtain, a closed blind that very nearly threatened to obscure what had come before. For the time being he would think of it no more.

There were jewellers down here but only one of them had opened. *Bureau de Change*, a sandwich board on the pavement announced. He went in, this time bought euros to the value of a thousand pounds, a transaction which left the account very short of funds. The long straight stretch of Sussex Gardens brought him back to the Edgware Road. On the way he thought what a suitable victim for a mugger, and they abounded round here, he would make. All those euros on him and the two hundred in sterling, but he would give any mugger who tried it on a—literal—run for his money. He would enjoy that.

It was supposed to be unwise to use the cash dispensers down here unless you kept your wits about you. Jeremy liked to think he always did that. He inserted his card, keyed in his pin number and asked it for £500, hoping letters wouldn't come up on the screen to tell him the account couldn't stand it. Of course, he had far more than that on deposit and in securities but he couldn't touch them immediately. He would probably have to go and see his bank, have invested money transferred to his current account—and hope they could do it fast. However, the dispenser produced £500 and this he took further down the street to the more respectable end, the bit that came into Marble Arch, and changed it into euros at a place that had no jewellery department but only changed money.

A branch of his own bank was in Baker Street. Somehow the idea of going there and taking funds that earned interest into an account where it would lie unprofitably enraged him more than anything he had done so far. Did these people ever earn anything for themselves? Or did they live entirely by theft and fraud and blackmail? And there were thousands like them. Crime in this city outraged him, the grabbing and destruction of other people's property, the disregard for rights of ownership, the sheer wanton *immorality* of it. But he turned into George Street just the same and walked, fulminating, to his bank.

Becky left it another day before phoning to see how they were getting on. Of course it was Kim who answered. She sounded cheerful and calm, full of how nice the flat was, how much pleasanter than living at home with her parents, and what a good meal she and Will had had when they went out to eat at the Al Dar. Becky felt satisfied enough, she wouldn't have bothered to suggest she speak to Will if Kim, after enumerating all the dishes on offer at the Lebanese restaurant, hadn't done so.

He took the receiver, said hello in that neutral voice she associated, for no good reason, with his discontent. 'I'm OK,' he said.

'Are you going back to work with Keith?'

She heard him ask Kim, 'Am I going to work with Keith?' and her answer, 'You know you are, love. On Monday.'

'I'm going to work with Keith on Monday, Becky.'

'And you're happy with that?'

If he had had to ask Kim if he was happy, she didn't know what she would have done. But he replied for himself, saying again, 'I'm OK,' and 'I've got to go back, haven't I, Kim?'

Her answer she didn't hear. She heard his next remark all right, it rang in her head. 'I wish I was with you, Becky. When can I come and see you?'

'How about Sunday?' she said. 'For the day, for lunch and supper?' Did she have to ask Kim too? She waited, but neither of them suggested it.

'I'll come on Sunday. I *love* coming to you, Becky.'

She had been obliged to phone but she wished she had put it off till another day. One thing, she had seen James for two evenings (and two nights) in succession and she'd see him tonight, so she need not ask him on Sunday. As she helped herself to her first gin and tonic of the evening, needed after that phone conversation, she wondered what she was doing, what on earth was she playing at, being thankful because her new lover, at the start of her new love affair, would *not* be coming to see her.

He walked home with a young woman in front of him. She was just about the right distance ahead, about fifteen feet, and they were moving at the same pace. She turned into Star Street and he followed. Though the sky was overcast, it was warm and bright, and any attack made on her would be sure to be witnessed. Even if she had exercised that indefinable attraction on him, that mysterious force so strong as to pull his heart out of him, he couldn't have killed her there, in broad daylight, and would have suffered from the deprivation, been made ill by it. The point was rather that he didn't feel that attraction, he didn't want to harm her.

Now he believed he had followed her to test himself, to see if being, so to speak, in her company, in the right position, the compulsion would rise and grow. It hadn't. Nothing had happened. He would have liked to know why not. She seemed about thirty, was tallish, slender but not thin, fair-haired—still, he knew none of these things, except perhaps being of roughly suitable age, made much difference. He could smell the perfume she left behind her on the air, sweetish, floral, warm. The something else always eluded him. He watched her cross the road and continue her walk up to Norfolk Place and, when she was out of sight, went into the corner shop by the tenants' front door.

He sat out on the roof garden and counted the money. Just over four thousand and he had four days to go, only Sunday didn't count. He had Monday and Tuesday, really, because he would have to be here on Wednesday to take her call. Was he actually going to give it to her, all that money? He'd kill her first, he thought. He'd kill her, even though she wouldn't have, or was most unlikely to have, the required qualification. But he couldn't kill her. It wouldn't save him, it would make matters worse. If no one else was involved, the boyfriend would be, and maybe her father. Kill her and they would go straight to the police with the earrings, the lighter and the watch. They could say they'd seen him drop those things into a litter bin, had retrieved them and given them up to the law. Blackmail? The girl had spoken to him only to say she had found his property and was returning it . . .

By coincidence, they were back. From where he was, he saw what he thought was Zulueta's car coming along Bridgnorth Street, and when he went back into the flat and looked out of one of the front windows, there he was in the act of parking—with impunity, no doubt— on the yellow line. Another DC was with him. They sat, watching the corner shop. But Jeremy knew he had nothing to worry about there. It was Will Cobbett they were watching.

He continued to look, saw a turquoise Jaguar arrive and Morton Phibling get out. Would those two, Zulueta and—Jones, was it?—would they do anything about the car on the residents' parking? Probably it would be beneath their dignity to sink to traffic cop level. He had to go out and get more money. As he emerged into the street once more, he saw he had been wrong about Zulueta and Jones. They cared less about status than he thought, for there they were at the driver's window of the Jaguar, haranguing Phibling's defenceless chauffeur.

He shivered a little. *He had been wrong.* Was this the shape of things as they would now be? Was it coming to an end, his rightness, his success, his double life, his inviolability? Two lines came into his head from a play he had seen long ago in Nottingham. Which play he couldn't remember but he said the lines in his head. 'The bright day is done and we are for the dark . . .'

I am for the dark.

CHAPTER 23

She had been forced to ask James to stay away.

'I thought we were going to spend our weekends together.'

'James, I'm sorry, but now Will isn't staying here any more I do have to see him sometimes. I have a duty towards him, I can't just drop him.'

'I understand that,' he said. 'Does it have to be at the weekends?'

'If it were a weekday, it would be for the evening only now I'm back at work.' She knew the next thing would cause an explosion. 'Will likes to have his main meal at midday.'

'And I', James almost shouted, 'like to have mine in the evening, like all civilised people. Like you. Why does everything have to give way to his ridiculous working-class rules? His detention centre timetable?'

'It was a children's home,' she said, trying to keep her patience. 'His habits were formed by it just as yours were by the parents who brought you up. Will didn't have any parents, he had social workers.'

'As you repeatedly tell me. Why you didn't adopt him and have done with it beats me.' The unfairness of this almost took her breath away. 'And do you realise that's what we mostly talk about? Will? It's Will this and Will that until I sometimes wonder if he isn't closer to you than you make out. But you needn't worry. I shan't come round on Sunday. I'll make a point of staying away.'

He made a point of staying away on Saturday too. Becky lacked the heart to resume her old Saturday morning habit of leisurely shopping, shop-gazing and buying odd little luxuries. Perhaps she would never do it again. She was beginning to think she could never do anything that wasn't criticised by James. He wanted to change her into someone else. Not only in the matter of Will but her physical appearance too. Why don't you have a manicure, he had started asking, a facial, why not have a proper haircut? She was too old and too independent to change. Several times she wondered unhappily what he had meant by Will being closer to her than she had admitted—that he was her lover or really her own son? She went for a walk on Primrose Hill and stayed out for quite a long time, feeling more lonely now than before James came into her life.

Becky had once, years ago when she lived in a ground-floor flat with a garden, had a cat. He was a very affectionate animal, a large handsome tabby, and when he died, aged seventeen, she had resolved never to have another. The wrench, the real pain, of his death was not to be repeated over and over in her life as it is in the lives of inveterate pet owners. When he was about five he had disappeared. He went out as usual one day and failed to come home that night. She put the usual notices up on walls and lamp posts, rang the neighbours, phoned the local vets and the council's lost animal service. Nothing helped and after a week of anxiety and misery, she gave him up for lost. Friends, hoping to comfort her, said that he must have found a home he liked better, as cats will. Others believed he had jumped into someone's car and been driven away. Only Becky knew he would never have found a home he loved more than his with her and that he disliked cars so much he would avoid them as he avoided dogs. On the eighth day of his absence he came back, jaunty as ever, bright-eyed, swift, bursting through the cat flap and coming straight to her for instant affection. He was thin but otherwise healthy. She never found out where he had been.

Will's return was rather the same. In her eyes, he too looked thinner. In other respects he was like the errant cat, greeting her with joy, throwing his arms round her, his eyes shining. Like the cat too, he ate a huge lunch and, watching television afterwards, fell into contented sleep. Of his days with Kim he said nothing until she asked him. It was uncanny the way, at first, he seemed to have forgotten who Kim was, staring at her with puzzled eyes. Then some kind of realisation seemed to dawn. 'She's all right,' he said.

'It must be nice for you, having someone you like with you.'

Could anything be more banal? Still, he seemed to be giving the matter serious thought. She knew what his thinking would achieve, she knew what he would say, though she expected less vehemence.

'It's better here with you. I'd like it better, I'd like it lots and lots better, if you'd come and live there with me.'

Later, when it was almost time to take him home, he astonished her with a revelation and an explanation. 'I was looking for a treasure,' he said, 'when I was digging that garden. When those men found me and took me away. I knew the treasure was there, I saw it in a film, and I bought a spade and dug and dug but I couldn't find it.'

She had nothing to say.

'It was jewels, worth millions and millions. When I found it I was going to buy a house and you and me would live in it, there'd be room for us both, not like

here or my place. I was going to buy it. But there is
room here really, isn't there, Becky? There is.'

Morton Phibling came in every morning now and he
and Zeinab, regardless of how many customers might
arrive, sat side by side in a corner discussing wedding
plans. Zeinab's ploy about the diamond pendant
appeared to have allayed any fears Morton might have
as to its whereabouts, for Inez, having failed to persuade
a visitor to buy an early nineteenth-century French
horn, a sale she was sure Zeinab could have brought off,
heard him tell his fiancée to get it out of the bank on
Friday the seventh in order to wear it at Saturday's ceremony. Meanwhile, he had presented her with a diamond and emerald bracelet, which she had put on and
flashed about, the rays from it when it caught the bright
sunlight making rainbow spots up and down the walls.

'So you've made up your mind, have you?' Inez asked
as Morton was driven away.

'Made up my mind to what?' Zeinab sounded
abstracted, as if imagining her sumptuous future as Mrs
Phibling. In fact, she was wondering where she could
take the bracelet to get the best price for it.

'To get married, of course.'

'I reckon I shall have to.'

To Inez it seemed as if she were coming back to
earth, had awakened from a dream, while though
Zeinab had indeed regained equilibrium, it was from
the realisation that if the bracelet fetched what she
expected, she and Algy would have halfway enough to
buy the kind of house they wanted. Make the flat
exchange first, as soon as they could, to get her away
from here and her two fiancées, then start phoning
estate agents . . . She got up, served a customer who was
looking for genuine old Venetian glass and another in

search of 1930s jewellery. It was amazing, Inez thought, how she could sell anything and not only to impressionable men.

'Then I suppose you'll be giving me notice?'

'Do I have to let you know now?'

'Well, you do if you're leaving on Friday week. It's Monday now.'

'Yeah, well, a week's will do, won't it?' Zeinab swiftly changed the subject. 'Have you noticed how those murdered girls have taken a back seat?' The grotesque picture this presented to Inez was quite enough to take her mind off her assistant's wedding plans. 'It's like they've found them all now and they've found Jacky Miller's earrings, so they're not bothered.'

'They haven't found the lighter and the watch.'

'No, you're right. I never asked you what that Zulueta wanted last Friday. It slipped my mind.'

'Oh, more nonsense about Will. Was he ever alone in the shop? Had I ever seen him digging the garden here? That sort of thing. Jones even said that girl he's got with him might be in need of protection. I told him I thought that Anwar had been in here sniffing about while I was at the police station but he didn't seem interested.'

'I'm not going to tell her,' Algy said, 'and I'm counting on you not to say a word.'

Reem, sharing a greasy bag of chips with her grandson, said with her mouth full, 'You know me, Alge. I never do say much, don't seem to have the energy. I see this move as one step up the ladder to you getting your own place with a nanna annexe for me, eh, Bryn?'

'Bryn *love* nanna,' the little boy said fervently, climbing on to her lap.

'That's a good boy.'

'I've scheduled the move,' said Algy rather grandly, 'for Friday, June seven.'

'Suppose she don't play?'

'My two mates'll come with the van half-seven, and by the time she wakes up half the stuff'll be out on the pavement.'

'Good thinking.' Reem's rumbling laughter rocked the little boy up and down and up and down pleasantly. He laid his cheek against the vast billows of her bosom and closed his eyes.

By Tuesday evening Jeremy had amassed all the money. He was impatient to get on with things. If he had to give them £10,000, he wanted to get it over, and he tried not to think about their receiving it and then coming back for more. Their call would come, he calculated, learning their habits, around three in the afternoon, and they would name a place for the—did they call it the 'drop'?—for that evening or the next day. Briefly, he thought with envy of those people who, facing blackmail, were in a position to tell the police the nature of the threat and secure their help. For him that had always been out of the question.

A letter from his mother on the Wednesday had a request for him to buy her a certain kind of perfume. Not for herself but for a present for a young friend, a girl who sometimes did errands for her. His mother would of course reimburse him when she saw him on Monday, a promise which made him smile, it was so absurd for her even to think of it. On Saturday morning he'd visit some big store and buy the stuff, and he noted down the name.

In spite of being sure the phone call wouldn't come before the afternoon, he still found it impossible to go out. But he had accustomed himself sufficiently to this particular kind of tension to be able to sit outside in the roof garden without being afraid of not hearing the bell. Ever since he read the letter he had been thinking about his mother, her uncritical love for him, her ultra-sensitive mind, her consideration. Unless he had invited himself for this coming Bank Holiday Monday, she would never have presumed to expect him. As it was, when he had asked if he could come for the day, she had said tentatively, 'Are you sure you can spare the time, dear?' And when he had assured her he was looking forward to it, 'It's very nice of you to say so.'

How would it have been if his father had lived? Jeremy, aged thirteen, had been with him the day before he died, or so his mother assured him when he told her he couldn't remember. Sometimes, if he concentrated, if he tried to pierce the curious swirling dark mists which had to be penetrated to reach it, he thought he could see his father's yellow cadaverous face on the hospital pillow, but he only *thought* so and couldn't be sure. He was afraid to ask his mother if his father had had jaundice that day he had been there.

Once, and only once, re-creating that macabre picture, he had seemed to see another figure present and it wasn't his mother. A woman or a man, he couldn't tell that either, except that it wasn't his friend Andrew's frumpish mother either. And as he brought thought and reason to bear on it, it vanished as if it had never been—and perhaps it had not. Gradually, he reconciled himself to the certainty that he was never going to remember. Why did it matter? He had loved his father but had come to dislike him, had wiped the deathbed at which he had nearly been present clean from his memory, that was why. And there was another reason. He was beginning to wonder if his motive for killing those girls had its origin in the last scenes of his father's

life, those forgotten scenes, which might yet be vital to
track down.

The sun was warm, the lilac in bloom in its tub and
the snowy philadelphus in the wide-mouthed green
vase. Their mingled scents, quite different yet equally
exquisite, drifted past him when the little breeze blew,
and he fell asleep in the cushioned cane chair—to be
awakened, with a start and an exclamation, by the
phone bell.

'I'm not doing it on me own,' Julitta had said. 'He
might murder me. He done the others and they hadn't
done nothing.'

Anwar had already thought of this in all its aspects,
from the point of view of Julitta's safety and that of
expediency. If Alexander Gibbons—even in his own
mind he had no patience with aliases—strangled her in
his habitual fashion, he, Keefer and Flint would have an
even greater hold over him than they now had. But on
the whole, he decided, the hold they had was more than
adequate. He wasn't going to tell her she was right, that
wouldn't do at all. 'No question of that,' he said. 'I shall
do it myself.'

'The geezer'll know you again,' Flint objected.

'Leave that to me.'

They all turned their eyes on Keefer, who sat miserably in the corner of Anwar's room, on the floor
because there was nothing else and the rest of them
were on the bed. He sat with his arms wrapped round
his bent knees, the skin of his face and neck greenish
and running with sweat. A trail of something viscid
dribbled from the corner of his mouth. From time to
time he let out a whimper of pain and, unwrapping his
arms, thrashed them about. At the moment he was
quiet, somnolent, and Flint and Julitta had both

remarked, in various picturesque ways, that he looked on the point of death. When they referred to him, they spoke of this process of coming off hard drugs by one of the dozens of slang terms in current use, but Anwar called it 'being rehabilitated' and managed to give the phrase a sinister ring.

Now, poking one toe into Keefer's flank, as one might attempt to shift a sleeping dog, he pulled Zeinab's diamond pendant out of his pocket and laid it on the bed between himself and Julitta. 'It belongs to that girl,' said Anwar. 'The beautiful one.' He said this casually, as someone else would refer to 'the dark one' or 'the thin one'. To a student of character like Inez it would have revealed either the intrinsic coldness of his nature or a budding appreciation of feminine beauty or perhaps both.

The others were used to his strange habits of speech. 'How d'you know?'

'My mate that's the lover of the old Russian woman told me. She's engaged to a funny old fucker that's got five cars. Another diamond geezer. He gave it to her. We gotta be very careful how we dispose of it, that's all. No good getting any ideas about taking it to Hawker down North End Road.' Anwar fixed his eyes once more on Keefer, whose find this receiver of stolen goods was, and stared at him aggressively, though he was obviously incapable of ideas about anything. 'You'd best leave that to me too. You get on the phone to *our* diamond geezer, Ju, and say to him he's to bring what we're asking for to the recycling bins in Aberdeen Place, St John's Wood. You got that? Aberdeen Place and the bins are on the right side opposite Crocker's Folly. He's to bring the dosh in a white bin liner, not a black bag, and when he gets there he's to look inside the bin that's for old clothes, but he's not to put the bag in. It's mostly full, that bin, and it'll be full when he gets there. The clothes bin's a bit apart from the others, there's a door in the wall next to it and then the bottle bank, right? He's to put the bag on the ground between the clothes bin and the doorway.'

Julitta nodded. Her relief at not having to be present at this transaction was so great that she would happily have done anything else he asked her. 'He'll want the things. He'll ask about the earrings and whatever.'

'And he'll get them—only the earrings'll be different. You don't say that, right? You say he'll find them taped to the inside of the clothes bin lid. After that he can go. He's to do it nine sharp tonight. Tell the bugger to go by way of the footpath by the canal and home down Lisson Grove. He won't, he'll stay and watch but that's OK, that's all to the good.'

He let it all sink in, then barked at Julitta, 'Now repeat what I told you.'

She did so, not stumbling much, and Anwar shooed her and Flint out with instructions to Julitta to make her phone call within the next hour. Keefer was asleep. He wouldn't sleep long but would wake up, thrashing about and screaming for the heroin he could now easily afford. Since he was coming off the hard stuff on his instructions, Anwar decided to get him some methadone if he could; he didn't want the guy breaking the place up or otherwise attracting too much attention to them. Leaving, he locked the door behind him.

All his sisters were at home in the house in Brondesbury Park. They regarded him much as young Victorian girls saw their brother, as one who through chance happened to be male and therefore untrammelled, away from parental constraint and free. This, notwithstanding the fact that their mother and father were enlightened people who required no more of their daughters and expected of them no different standard of behaviour than of their son. But tradition dies hard and each of these girls, exposed to the views of elderly relatives, had yet to put ideas of the sheltered life, the long skirts, the chaperoned outings and the arranged marriage, behind her.

'I should be so lucky,' said Arjuna, at the sight of Keefer's van parked at the kerb, though there was nothing to stop her borrowing a friend's car and driving it, except the law, and that applied equally in her brother's case.

He reminded her of this and while she was thinking up a suitable reply, asked her if Mama's friend's old *abaya* was still in the house. Nilima, the eldest girl, had once worn it in a school performance of Flecker's Hassan.

'What d'you want it for?'

'Not your business. Where is it?'

'If you can't tell me why you want it I'm not telling you where it is.'

Anwar looked at his Rolex. These girls wasted so much time. 'What you saving up for, Arj? There must be something.'

'Telly in my bedroom. If Nilima can have one why can't I?'

'OK. How much more d'you want?' He took a wad of notes out of his pocket.

His sister eyed them. Fives and tens they were. If he had twenties and fifties he wouldn't show them to her. 'Fifty,' she said.

'Twenty-five.'

'You must be joking. Forty.'

'Thirty-five,' said Anwar, 'and that's my last word. I can find the thing myself only it'll take me a while.'

'OK. Thirty-five.' She rolled up the notes and pushed them into the cleavage revealed by her low-cut

T-shirt. It was a movement she was perfecting for more worthwhile company than a brother. 'It's in the loft, in the big trunk, inside one of those plastic things the dry-cleaners give you.'

Anwar went off up the stairs, carrying a pair of steps, the more easily to reach the trapdoor in the ceiling which was the entrance to the loft.

CHAPTER 24

Although he knew there would be at least one further demand, it was still a relief. The money itself was very little to pay as the price of safety and impunity. Of course, it wouldn't be if multiplied but he would face that when the time came. If there was anything that seriously worried him it was how he was to receive back the fob watch, the lighter and the earrings. The girl had said he would find them there, in an opaque plastic bag taped to the pull-down drawer at the top of the clothes bin. But suppose they weren't there? What then?

He left home much too early. It was inevitable in his situation. As he came out of the tenants' street door he looked about him, certain they must be watching. If they were, it wasn't out in the street. No one was about and none of the cars had an occupant in any of its seats. Earlier in the day it had rained, but the clouds had shifted away at sunset and the pavements were slowly drying. Jeremy carried the money inside the white plastic bag, as instructed, in a small blue backpack he had once used but not in recent years. A briefcase was more his style but he thought that might look conspicuous in this neighbourhood in the evening. He walked up the Edgware Road and under the flyover. The usual crowds of men were gathered outside the Lebanese restaurants. Very few women were to be seen and those who ventured out at this hour wore the scarf or in some cases the *chador*, that all-enveloping black robe that conceals all but the points of the toes and the eyes.

Nearly at the top he crossed on the lights into Orchardson Street and entered Aberdeen Place by way of Lyons Place, a rather more discreet approach than directly from the Edgware Road. One or two people, braving the damp chill of evening, sat at tables outside Crocker's Folly. Jeremy thought of them vaguely as potential witnesses. But witnesses of what exactly? And who was to be confronted with their evidence? He was a murderer and could therefore tell the tale of his wrongs to no one, ever, let alone call witnesses.

His watch told him it was still only ten to nine. Better do as they said. After all, he had done the rest, the worst part, so why quibble about ten minutes? But how slowly they passed! If anything could have convinced Jeremy that time doesn't move along at the same rate, or at any rate at all, but remains still while we move in it, it was how sluggishly it seems to pass in some circumstances and how swiftly in others. All illusion, all self-deception . . . He walked up to the St John's Wood Road, past Lord's Cricket Ground, up Hamilton Close and back, and it was still only five to. Back down Northwick Place, trying to drag his feet, and at last it was a minute to. He waited to hear a church clock chime somewhere, heard nothing and went up to the old clothes bin. Drawing a deep breath, he lifted the lid. There, taped inside as promised, was the small opaque plastic bag containing—what?

The men outside Crocker's Folly weren't looking at him but he slipped into the narrow defile called Victoria Passage just the same and in there, in the shadows, looked inside the bag. Earrings, fob watch, lighter. Good. Well, he had better get on with it. He took the white bin liner with the money in it out of his backpack, came out of the passage, and dropped the bag between the clothes bin and the doorway in the red brick wall. Back into the passage to wait and watch.

She came within five minutes. She was tallish, slight, as far as he could tell, for her figure was covered from head to foot in a black garment. Only her eyes showed, large, black, fringed in thick black lashes, their lids violet-coloured with eyeshadow and painted with kohl. She picked up the bag, burying it somewhere inside the voluminous folds of the black robe, and disappeared the way she had come, down the steps on to the canal bank. Jeremy followed but by the time he reached the head of the steps and the sluggish yellow waterway lay beneath him, the figure was nowhere to be seen. Only his backpack, open and empty, lay at the top of the iron stairway.

'I've never been married,' said Freddy and, as was his way, settled himself down in the grey velvet armchair to elaborate on his subject. 'It will be a new experience. I ask myself how I shall find it. Less congenial than the present arrangement or more blissful?' He began to wag his right forefinger as he spoke. 'Ludo, of course, has been married before. I'm not at all clear how many times, but all that is behind us. Marylebone Town Hall is the venue, June first the date and eleven ack emma the witching hour. The honeymoon will be another of our favourite weekend breaks, this time in a place called the Isle of Man. It will be a magical mystery tour for me, in more ways than one. Have you ever heard of the Isle of Man, Inez?'

'Of course I have. It's off Liverpool, in the Irish Sea. I went there once with my first husband.'

'Another lady of multiple marriages, I see,' said Freddy, meaning to be polite. 'Is it anything like Barbados?'

'I've never been to Barbados, but I shouldn't think so, certainly not as far as climate goes.'

'I shan't mind, I am always ready for a change. In for a penny, in for a pound, I say, or should it be "in for a euro"?' He got to his feet as Zeinab came in, whether as gentlemanly behaviour or because he intended to get moving Inez couldn't tell. 'Good morning, Zeinab. I was just telling Mrs Ferry, or Inez as we are all privileged to call her, that me and my fiancée will be tying the knot next Saturday.'

'Tying what knot?'

'He means he'll be getting married,' said Inez.

'Is that right? The week before as me and Mort.'

'So my next move this morning—I am up to my eyes in it—must be to buy a wedding ring and I'm sure one can be found here. No need for fresh woods and pastures new, eh?'

'Let me help you,' said Zeinab.

This morning, Inez noticed, she was entirely jewel-free, not a diamond or sapphire about her. This must mean both Morton Phibling and Rowley Woodhouse—if he really existed, no one ever saw him—were out of town for the day. She had already heard Will Cobbett and his girlfriend leave the house by the tenants' street door and see them walk up Star Street towards the Edgware Road, carrying shopping bags. The girl was holding Will's arm and it was plain to see he was doing no more than acquiesce in this, passively allowing her hand to remain hooked on his elbow. Was it generally true, then, that there is always one who kisses and one who lifts the cheek? It hadn't been so for her and Martin. Would the day ever come when almost any event, serious, disturbing, ludicrous, ordinary, no longer served to remind her?

After his attempt to return to a place in her regard, Jeremy Quick hadn't come into the shop. Nor had his behaviour in other respects been normal. For instance, he hadn't been to work every day. He had gone out but come back to the house several times before staying at home for the afternoon and evening. Now, as she sat looking out of the shop window waiting for custom, while Freddy and Zeinab scrutinised the stock of plain gold rings, she heard Jeremy's feet on the stairs and the tenants' street door closed with almost a slam. He walked in the opposite direction from the other two, heading for Paddington Station or St Mary's Hospital or just Hyde Park.

He would be visiting his mother on one of the Bank Holidays, the Monday or the Tuesday, she guessed, and probably was off now to buy her a present. A good son, whatever might be his other shortcomings.

'Can he take this lot upstairs for Ludmila to see which one fits?' Zeinab asked her.

Five wedding rings, one of them with a lover's knot and 'Albert and Moira, entwined for ever' engraved inside it, lay on a jeweller's black velvet tray.

'She won't want that one,' Inez objected, picking up the engraved ring.

'Unfortunately,' said Freddy, 'I fear that may be the only one to fit her slender finger.'

Fearing the worst, Jeremy had nevertheless not looked closely at the earrings. He was experiencing the coward's retreat into that state where what you don't know for sure, when a doubt lingers, you can't worry over it. Except that you can, but hope still remains and the knowledge that if things turn out well by a miracle, the postponement will have been worthwhile. Eventually, of course, you have to leap upon the thing in question and examine it quickly. This he had finally done at one in the morning. He had awakened in intolerable anxiety, jumped out of bed and torn the bag open. Still a vestige of hope was there. He closed his eyes, opened them, and counted the brilliants in the silver metal. Sixteen, of course, only sixteen, not twenty. His blackmailers—he was sure now there was more than one—had bought a similar pair to the ones he had placed in the shop. They were probably in every cheap jeweller's in the country.

Their reason had to be that they would come back to him for more money. Not today, perhaps, not even next week, but around 10 or 11 June, that was when he should expect a call. No more sleep for him that night, though what had happened was only what he had dreaded since he untaped the package from the bin lid. But he acknowledged the inevitability of things. He could no more have stayed in bed and slept again without getting up to look and check than he could have refused their demand in the first place. He had no choice and what was happening to him now was the beginning of his fears about the bright day being done and the dark coming.

All this he thought of as he walked up Star Street and turned towards Sussex Gardens, choosing a pleasanter if more roundabout way of reaching Oxford Street than the Edgware Road. There were trees here, laden with the dense foliage of spring becoming summer, window boxes on Georgian houses, troughs of flowers outside smart little pubs. He would never go to prison, he would kill himself first, but his heart sank a little when he thought of his mother, bereft of him for ever.

It was to buy this perfume she wanted that he had come down here. Tourmaline was its name, some kind of semi-precious stone, he had thought, but it must be very challenging thinking up new names for scent, there were so many on the market.. Four big stores were to be found in Oxford Street between Marble Arch and the

Circus, the nearest being Selfridges. At Selfridges he would make a start.

It was a long time since he had been there. Since his last visit the perfumes and cosmetic departments had grown much larger. He would never have considered himself well-informed in matters of the kind of scent and beauty aids women used, but the big names were familiar to him. Some of these were still there but the firms he remembered his mother patronising when he was a child, all these were gone or their counters reduced in size and exiled to a corner. New names were everywhere. Photographed women, girls, surely the world's most beautiful, beamed or pouted at him from every wall and pillar. Their flawless skins and gleaming hair left him cold. He wanted neither to kiss them nor kill them.

But he was bemused. Women looking very different from the cosmetic company's models wandered about gazing or marched purposefully to their prearranged goal, but he felt himself lost in a mysterious dreamlike emporium with no idea where to go or even what to look for but that elusive name, Tourmaline. Last time he had bought perfume for his mother he had seen what he needed in a pharmacist's window at the Marble Arch end of the Edgware Road, had gone in, pointed, said he wanted that one. Perhaps he should have done something like that this time, gone into a little shop and handed the assistant a piece of paper with the name written on it.

Tourmaline was nowhere. He would go up Oxford Street and try the next store. This time he would ask instead of wandering around. He made his way towards the nearest exit, or tried to do this, but he found himself impeded by a crowd of young women who stood staring at a girl seated on a high stool having her face made up

by a beautician. Impatiently forcing his way through
them, he had come out into a relatively empty space with
watches and jewellery ahead of him and then the street
door. But just as he calculated he could reach the door
without further hindrance, a young and beautiful oriental girl with long dark hair stepped into his path, holding
up a spray bottle and asking him if he would like to try
this particular scent. It was an old perfume, out of use for
years but so many requests for it had been made that the
perfumier had brought it in again two years ago.

'By popular demand,' she said in her seductive per-
fumed voice. 'It used to be called "Yes" but that's outdated, so we renamed it. Would you care to try?'

He saw the name in gold letters but without reading
it, shook his head, muttered 'No, thanks', too late, for
she had let fly a jet of it over the hands he had raised to
ward her off. The effect on him was cataclysmic. He
stepped back and as it assailed his nose, felt an earth-
quake shake him from head to foot. His first reaction
he never quite knew, only that he cried out, some
strangled string of words coming out, but after that the
floor rose like a lift. He sank through it as if it were
made of jelly, viscid and glutinous. Its quivering walls
closed in and he fainted.

When he came round he was lying on some sort of
makeshift stretcher, being carried out of the department.
Keeping his eyes shut and his body still, he feigned continued unconciousness. He didn't want to come to, he
didn't want to talk or be questioned, and if given a
choice, he would have preferred the total extinction of
life and the long rest which would come afterwards.

But, as in the previous night, he had no choice. The
stretcher had been set down. He struggled into a sitting
position, saw they had brought him into an office and

laid whatever they were carrying him on across two chairs. A man was bending over him, asking if he should call a doctor. Jeremy said he didn't want a doctor. This was normal, he lied, what had happened to him, a kind of epilepsy, only it had never before happened in a public place. He was fine, he would leave and go home. Was there anything he wanted? At that moment a woman brought him a glass of water and finding himself suddenly parched with thirst, he drank it down.

'I was looking', he said, 'for a perfume called Tourmaline . . .'

'Nothing easier,' said the woman, and she was back in two minutes with a red casket, the name printed in gold on its side.

Jeremy paid for it, allowed them to call him a taxi. Sitting back in his seat, he found himself silently reciting over and over again the words on a small notice in front of him: *Thank you for not smoking, thank you for not smoking.* He couldn't stop saying it and he even said it aloud to the driver as he got out. 'Thank you for not smoking—I'm sorry. I mean, how much is that?'

The man gave him a strange look, occasioned perhaps by his repeating the phrase which had become a mantra or by the reason the cab had been ordered for him. Men don't faint. Women may do but men don't.

Why had he? He knew the answer to that but he still had to think about it all, go out on to his roof garden and think.

What had happened to him at the time of his father's death had not come back to him in complete unexpurgated form in the moments between smelling the scent and passing out, but only the salient incidents. There had been no illusion of seeing a film rapidly run nor that experience, the favourite of old wives' tales, of his whole past life flashing before his eyes. Now, though, as he sat among his flowers, under a benign blue and white sky, he thought of himself at thirteen, already very tall, already well into puberty, the hated brace on his teeth. He was accompanying his mother to the hospital where his father lay in the extreme last stages of lung cancer. All his life James Gibbons had been a smoker, as had his wife, as his widow still was, in her late sixties and apparently fit. Then she was young, distraught with misery, telling her son over and over that he would soon be all she had left to live for.

Her reaction to these bedside sessions became more and more violent so that by the time of this visit, when her husband lay stunned with morphia, she was on the verge of hysteria. He knew his son and managed for Jeremy a faint ghastly smile but he seemed no longer to recognise his wife. His seeing but uncomprehending eyes turned on her with bewilderment in their dark depths, he seemed not to know who this woman was. It was enough to provoke a storm of tears and with a murmured, 'I'll see you at home, darling,' to Jeremy, she had run out of the room.

Later he was to wonder if the woman who came in would have done so if his mother had still been there, if she had perhaps looked through the little porthole in the door to check first. He recognised her as a one-time friend of his mother's who had dropped out of their lives when she moved house some two or three years before. She was younger than his parents by a dozen years and very good-looking. In those days he had a fast-developing eye for female beauty—that was long gone—and he appreciated this woman's shapely figure, short and trim blonde hair and long stockings-advertisement legs. In fact, the sight of her stirred him in a way he had never known before but hoped to know again. In his eyes, though certainly fifteen years older than he, she was a girl just enough his senior to be exciting.

At first she took no notice of him. She stopped a yard into the room, saw his father and drew in her breath. He thought he heard her murmur, 'Oh, God.' Then she went slowly up to the bed and fell on her knees, taking his hand and covering it with kisses. Jeremy might not have been there, or been a wheelchair or a folded-up bedspread for all the notice she took of him. His father turned on her a look so full of love that even Jeremy, young as he was, recognised it. To recognise was one thing, to understand another. He was confused, not knowing what he was witnessing, feeling dreamlike sensations, unsure by what mystical or supernatural means he had stumbled into this scene.

'Tess,' his father said in his whispery cracked voice, 'Tess,' and then, with a huge effort, 'Lovely of you to come.' Even those few words exhausted him and he gasped, closing his eyes.

Lost for a while in his memories, Jeremy came back to life in Star Street, got up, stretched his legs and his arms above his head. He went back into the flat and poured himself a stiff gin and tonic. The first sip he took before returning to the roof garden. When you considered how wonderful that first taste was, how it buoyed you up, how it infused you with energy and a kind of inspiration, it was hard to understand alcoholism, for nothing that came after equalled in intensity and sheer excitement that first sip.

He stood on the roof looking across Inez's garden and the one that joined the end of it. Everything was richly green now and thickly overgrown. A shrub was covered in great snowy bracts of flowers, another he identified as a lilac. The house the garden belonged to must be in St

Michael's Street. From an upper window a bronze-skinned face he vaguely recognised—from where? In what circumstances?—looked back at him before slowly retreating.

He sat down again, unable to close his mind to Tess and his father. There was something miraculous about recovered memory, which, previously, he had never believed in. Another life was lived in that past. He had slept through remembrance of it and now, suddenly, because of a perfume, recalled it all.

She had stayed at his father's bedside for perhaps half an hour, mostly not speaking, the two of them simply contemplating one another. On her face a look of need and concupiscence, in his father's a terrible weariness and a kind of hopeless longing.

'Shall I go now?' he had asked. He was too young to be anything much but embarrassed.

'Alex,' his father said, for that was what he always called him, 'please stay. Stay and take Tess home. I'll feel better if she's got you to look after her.'

He look after her? At thirteen? But he stayed and at last Douglas Gibbons fell asleep. Jeremy was never to see him again. He looked at Tess and she at him, and simultaneously they nodded. He didn't smile, he kept his lips closed because of the brace. As for him taking her home, it was she who took him back to her house, for she had a car with her. She lived in a house on the outskirts of the city. To himself he called it 'a nasty little house' because he was a snob, as most children are in one way or other.

Indoors, she asked him if he'd like tea or coffee but when she fetched the drinks it was sherry she brought, rich, brown and sweet. He had never tasted it before and it went straight to his head. That was when he really noticed her legs and he suddenly saw them as

quite different from men's legs, just as her breasts
(which he was almost afraid to notice) were something
no man had. She talked to him then in a way he recognised when he was older as something she should not
have done. It was as if she had forgotten that Douglas
Gibbons, her lover, was his father and that when he left
her it would be to go back to Douglas Gibbons's wife,
his mother. She told him they were passionately in love
and that his father would have left his home for her if
he hadn't fallen ill. She spoke, in only a thinly veiled
way, of their lovemaking and its wonders. Again he was
embarrassed but something else too. He was excited by
these references to the act of love.

After a while, when she had drunk a second sherry,
she said she must go upstairs and change. Her skirt was
too tight and her shoes pinched her feet. She was a long
time and he was reaching a stage of not knowing what
to do, go home, call out to her—she might have fallen
asleep—when she called out to him, 'Come up here a
minute, will you?'

Scent pervaded her bedroom. *The* scent, it must have
been, and as he smelt it in its full strength, he realised it
had drifted from her as she came up to his father's bed
and knelt down beside him. She was in bed, a quilt
pulled up to her chin. 'I was so tired,' she said. 'I was
quite worn out.'

He stood by her. She put out her hand for his hand
and as she sat up the quilt fell off her shoulders, exposing her naked breasts. Heat flooded his face and neck,
and he knew he must have blushed violently. He dared
not look at her breasts, yet it was impossible to tear his
gaze away.

'You'll stay with me, won't you?' she said. 'I'm so
lonely. I'll be lonely for ever now.' She meant when his
father was dead but even those words failed to chill him.

'You look a lot like Douglas. He must have looked just the same as you when he was young. Except for that awful teeth brace.'

He nodded, blushing, his mouth tightly shut.

'What I'd really like', she said, 'would be for you to come into bed with me and hold me. Just for a little while. Will you do that?'

He was so green, so naïve, that he thought she meant as he was, dressed in grey trousers and green checked shirt and school blazer. Even through all those clothes he imagined what her breasts would feel like pressed against him.

'Oh, darling,' she said in the voice she had used to his father, 'do get undressed.' She giggled. 'I won't look.'

It was ridiculous—or seemed so in retrospect. He went behind the dressing table, behind the mirror, took his clothes off, and covered himself with her bathrobe which lay across a chair, approaching the chair backwards. At that time he still thought all she meant was that he was to hold her and cuddle her for comfort, and he was ashamed of his erect penis which the thin robe barely hid. She put her hands over her eyes and he ran to the bed and got in beside her.

She began, in what he supposed later was a fairly expert way, to stroke his body. She touched his penis and held it and said it was lovely. Jeremy had never even kissed anyone *in that way* and now he discovered kissing was a revelation, a great deal more than just lips meeting. Her tongue ran across the hated brace and he didn't mind. She said, unwisely as it turned out, whispering it in a soft conspiratorial way, 'You won't tell your mother, will you? I don't mean about us, that wouldn't matter all that much, but about me and your father.'

She had moved herself on top of him, perhaps because she feared—and with justification—that he

wouldn't know what to do without aid and encouragement. But as she spoke, using those fatal words, he
thought of his mother waiting at home for him, already
mourning his father, probably trusting his father and
certainly wholeheartedly loving him, and his erection
weakened and slackened, so that his penis became a
flaccid tiny thing, curled up between his belly and hers.

'Oh, sweetheart,' she said, 'what's happened to you?'
She began to knead his penis and kiss it, and he, as the
quilt fell back and uncovered him, felt such shame and
indignity that if he had stayed there he thought he
would have died. He pushed her away roughly and
jumped out of bed.

'Trust me,' she said, reaching out to him. 'I can deal
with it. Just relax and leave it to me.' She began to
laugh, staring at him and pointing. Peals of laughter
shook her. 'You really are rather young for that to happen. I'd have thought at your age, obviously a first
time . . .'

What shouldn't have taken place at his age and what
she would have thought, he didn't stay to hear. The
scent caught him in a wave, released as the bedclothes
were loosened, and with his clothes held against his
body, for just as he had been ashamed of his erection, so
now he felt doubly disgraced by the lack of it. The bathroom door was open and he ran in, just making it to the
lavatory pan before being sick.

Saying goodbye to her, saying anything to her ever
again, were not options. He dressed, went downstairs,
let himself out of the house. No doubt she had intended
to drive him home—he was too inexperienced to envis-
age the assignation she might also have intended making—but he was dependent on the bus, which took a
long time coming and involved itself in a traffic queue
most of the way back to his village. He thought of what

had happened while he was on that bus, and as far as he knew it was the last time he ever thought of it or recollected it until today.

The mind will bury experience if the unconscious will is strong enough. Wounded though it is, it will grow scar tissue over the place and will it never to be peeled away. But the scent that girl had sprayed so liberally on him had stripped it bare, so agonisingly that the bleeding and the pain took away consciousness and for a moment or two laid him low.

He had rediscovered it all and now he knew. He knew that her words and her laughter, his failure and his shame, had so marked him that at the time his life was quite changed and he had entered more than a new phase: a new world. Just as he had that morning come into another world, different again, when he smelt the scent, hidden from him for a third of a century.

Thinking of it—he would always be able to think of it now—he understood why it was always when they were ahead of him and he walked behind them, that the impulse to kill those girls seized him. The scent they wore, all of them using that perfume she used—popular once, long out of production, revived two years before—drifted *behind* them as they moved, lingering and delicate or strong and pungent, on the air in their wake. And he was there to be caught by it, ensnared, captured, reminded, driven to dreadful things.

Now he knew, would he stop?

CHAPTER 25

Anxious not to fall into the habit of going to her sister and brother-in-law every Bank Holiday, Inez resolved this time to take herself to the cinema and spend the evening at home, watching a *Forsyth* video as antidote to the film which would probably be a disappointment. What a negative attitude to life, she said to herself, but she kept to her plan. Westminster and the West End would be full of sightseers in pursuit of the Golden Jubilee celebrations, so those areas she avoided and went to the Screen on Baker Street. A gloom she failed to shake off settled on her when she reflected that there were to be two days of holidays in succession this year, an unparalleled phenomenon in British history.

In the Isle of Man it was sunny but cold. Freddy and Ludmila went on a coach tour every day, avoiding any contemplation of beauty spots, visits to museums, churches and big houses, eschewing beaches and leaving their seats only to go shopping or eat huge meals of the pizza–burger-and-chips variety. Freddy told everyone on the trips and anyone else they encountered that he and Ludmila were just married, a piece of news that made them immensely popular. As Freddy said afterwards, he hardly had to pay for a single drink himself, but his bride's opinion was that it was ridiculous when you'd been married as often as she had, and who knew how many more husbands she would have?

Algy took Zeinab and the children and Mrs Sharif to
the Mall to watch the Queen and the Royal Family
come out on to the palace balcony. Reem Sharif was
enthusiastically patriotic and pro-monarchist, and wept
copiously into her binoculars when the national anthem
was sung. Algy was amazed. He had never seen her cry
before. Also in the crowd quite near them were Anwar
Ghosh, Keefer, Julitta and Flint, but although Anwar
recognised Zeinab he gave no sign of knowing her. He
was concentrating on winding his own black scarf
round Julitta's neck to hide the diamond pendant.

'What the fuck d'you think you're doing?' Julitta bel-
lowed at him. 'I'm too bloody hot as it is, I can't fucking breathe.'

'The girl it belongs to is over there.'

'What? Where?'

'Swallowed up by the crowd,' said Anwar.

'I told you not to wear it, you stupid bitch,' said
Flint.

'She won't after today.' Anwar was still peering about
in search of Zeinab. 'I'm flogging it tomorrow.'

He sounded confident but in fact he was wondering
if the man he knew in Clerkenwell would touch it. They
should never have taken something so obviously valuable. Well, wait and see. Enjoy the here and now. He
was a great believer in living in the present and if he'd
had to have a motto it would have been: Seize the Day.
The four of them had all been spending a lot of Jeremy
Quick's money and meant to resume spending it in
pubs and, later, in clubs and restaurants, once Julitta's
passion was satisfied and she had seen Prince William.

On Friday James took Becky out to dinner, came back
with her and spent the night in Gloucester Avenue.
Although she had warned him several days in advance

that Will would be coming on Monday, he forgot all
about it, stayed in bed on Monday morning and was in
the shower when Will arrived. As he muttered to Becky
later in the day, he would have gone home at once but
he had lent his flat to a couple of friends who had come
down from the north to see the Jubilee celebrations.

His behaviour in Will's presence, largely ignoring
him, sulking, absorbing himself in the crossword, com-
plaining to Becky whenever he could snatch moments
alone with her, had perturbed her from the start. But up
till now Will's behaviour in his company had been very
much what it was when he and Becky were on their own
or with Kim. On that Monday she noticed a change.

Of course, it was true that Will had been different
since his treasure hunting and consequent night in a
police cell, more fearful, less talkative and when he did
speak, saying odder things than he used. This was
another departure. The television inevitably on, he began
doing something Becky had never known him do before,
using the remote to flit back and forth between channels.
Unusually for him, James was showing some interest in
the screen, the World Cup being on during the whole
month of June, and although no play was taking place at
present, commentary on past matches, the form of various teams, whether this player or that had recovered from
injury, was almost continuous. Football, someone
announced, was more important than the Golden Jubilee
and far more than impending war between India and
Pakistan. Not to Will, who preferred children's programmes and game shows, and who, particularly when
James showed heightened interest in film clips of past
England victories or concentrated on Beckham's damaged foot, flicked back to a Tom and Jerry cartoon.

Witnessing some of this, Becky thought at first it
was innocent, Will having no idea of James's preference

but acting with a child's characteristic egocentricity. But staying in the room with them for a longer period than usual, she saw that this wasn't so. Will was doing it on purpose to annoy, handing James the remote, then taking it back and returning to his favoured channel. From time to time he cast sly glances at James, watching his exasperation with satisfaction, and Becky understood something up till this moment hidden from her. It was taken for granted that those with, to put it politically correctly, 'special needs', must be perfectly good and pure, their virtue co-existent with their disability. They were like those holy fools in nineteenth century Russian novels, their saintliness compensating for what they lacked in intellect. It wasn't so, it was false. Will had the same jealousies and resentments, the same desire for vindictive revenge, as anyone else, but in him it was more overt and more marked because he was a child in a man's body and, like a child, he showed his triumph in his face. When, finally losing the last vestiges of patience, James threw down the *Radio Times* and stalked out of the room, Will laughed out loud, rocking backwards and forwards on the sofa.

Jeremy fetched his car from the garage in the mews on Sunday evening and parked it, as he was permitted to do at weekends and holidays, on the single yellow line in St Michael's Street. Of all the street's residents, it was probably only Anwar Ghosh who was awake and up at seven thirty in the morning, drinking his mug of cocoa—he never lay in—and he was the sole observer of Jeremy's unlocking the car, placing a large flower arrangement, a bottle of champagne, a parcel that might have held a book or a box of chocolates, and a Selfridges yellow bag on the back seat, and driving off.

Making an early start, Jeremy was on his way to see his mother. Though always devoted to her, he had given more thought to her than usual since his experience of Saturday and now she filled his mind. It was almost impossible for him to imagine himself in her place, for he had never tried to understand women and now it was too late to begin. Had she ever known about his father and Tess—her surname he still couldn't recall—or had she been in ignorance of the affair? If she had known, how much would she have minded? Perhaps she had known but preferred to keep silent, fearing that if things came out into the open her husband would leave her. Jeremy could never ask her, never even touch on the subject. The best he could hope for was that she had never known or that time had dulled the memory as age took away passion and jealousy and the pain of rejection. Did it? He had read that it did but he didn't really know.

Driving up the nearly empty motorway, deserted by the Jubilee celebrants in favour of central London, he let his mind return to Tess and her bedroom and his escape from it, and the all-pervading scent. He could view it now without humiliation, without shame and self-castigation. He had been a child and she had used him unforgivably. It was the result of that immediately buried experience which concerned him now. No doubt a desire to kill Tess, a rage which must have followed his failure and her unconcealed amusement, had been buried with it, surfacing and resurfacing not when he saw a woman like her or of comparable age or with legs like hers, but when he smelt a wave, drifting behind a woman, of that unmistakable perfume. And now he recalled what the girl who sprayed him with it had said, how it was old but the brand revived 'by popular demand', that it had been called 'Yes' but recently renamed.

Those girls he killed all used it. Perhaps Gaynor Ray was still wearing the old version, bought from some small back-street shop, but the others, his later victims, had been persuaded by current fashion to use the renamed brand. This was the answer too to the enigma of why he had never been incited to murder in the long years between his teens and his mid-forties. The perfume wasn't there to be worn, had been withdrawn, almost as if—how fanciful, how ridiculous!—the manufacturers sensed its lethal potential.

When he smelt it, drifting behind these women, discernible only to someone with a superlative sense of smell, he must have been at once transported back to revengeful rage, unquenchable except by killing Tess in each of them. It struck him as quite funny, in a macabre way, that he didn't know what the perfume was called. He thought he knew everything, now, but not the name of the agent which directed him to murder.

When Will asked if he could stay the night, James announced he would go home. His friends were leaving in the evening; by the time he got there they would be gone. At the signs of his departure, Will didn't go so far as to cheer or say, 'Good,' but his satisfied smile did it for him. Becky had planned to take them out to dinner and was trying to think of a place which would have the kind of food her nephew liked, yet be acceptable to her lover, but now she could abandon all that, and she and Will go alone to a Café Rouge or even a McDonald's. If James had packed his things and walked out a fortnight ago, if he had said nothing to Will as he left and given her no more than a kiss on the cheek and a cold, 'Well, goodbye then,' she would have been very nearly distraught. On this evening she felt relief and if she had recourse, once James was gone, to the gin bottle, this was mere habit. Any evening would seem lacking, deprived, without a few swigs of strong spirits to prepare her for whatever might be in store.

If Becky wasn't going to cook for him—for the second time that day, it would have been—Will wanted to go to a fish and chips restaurant where she had taken him once before. He was in jubilant mood, positively crowing, and naturally making no effort to hide this, over James's leaving and Becky's agreement with his suggestion that he should stay till Tuesday.

'I don't like him,' he said as he got into her car. 'He's not nice. Don't have him here again, will you?'

'I'm not promising that, Will.'

'He sulks. Monty told me sulking is bad. Better get cross and shout than sulk, he says.' Will always talked about the children's home and its staff as if he were still there and their advice still being delivered to him. 'Why is what he wants to see on telly better than what I want?'

It was unanswerable. What would she have told a ten-year-old if he had asked that same question? Because he's grown-up and you're a child was barely permissible to a real child; to Will it would be outrageous. James should have given way, she thought, he should be the wise, understanding one. After all, it was only once a week—well, twice this week. Thinking like that made her shiver, she didn't quite know why. The consequences of it all were that she felt something like dislike for both of them, but for Will it was tempered with tolerance, with making allowances, while for James—her feelings for him were shrivelling, each time they were together declining a little more. Soon, she thought, as she and Will were shown to a table, anything she had once had with him would be gone.

Excited by the smell of frying, Will was doing his best to decipher the fortunately limited menu, hesitating

between plaice and rockfish. She ordered him a Coke. If
the restaurant hadn't been reasonably sophisticated she
wouldn't have come, despite Will's pleadings, and for
herself she asked for a large glass of white wine.

'Oh, what lovely things! You're so good to me, darling.'
    Thus Jeremy's mother when she arranged the flowers
in no fewer than three vases, unwrapped the chocolates
and removed the flask of Tourmaline from its yellow
bag. Jeremy basked in her approval, felt happier than he
had since the first blackmailing phone call. His mother
produced one of his favourite lunches, the kind of
Ascot–Glyndebourne picnic hamper she seldom offered
and he seldom had: smoked salmon, game pie and
salad, and strawberries and cream. She insisted they had
the champagne.
    After lunch she again departed from the norm by
talking about his father. As she produced a photograph
album he couldn't remember seeing before, it occurred
to him that it must have been some years since she had
so much as mentioned Douglas Gibbons's name. Was
that odd in an elderly widow? Or was it that in any long
life, a companion who had shared no more than fifteen
years of it must fade with the passing of time and lose
the great importance he once had?
    Jeremy was confronted by pictures of himself at
eleven, at twelve, and then the fateful age, thirteen. To
his middle-aged eyes, his young self looked like what he
was, an exceptionally tall schoolboy with a schoolboy's
untried, inexperienced face and innocent eyes. His
refusal to smile hid the hated brace. What had Tess seen
in him to make her desire him sexually? His father's
face? He was thinking along those lines, with a fair
degree of tranquillity, when suddenly she was before
him. There she was in the next photograph with his

parents and a man who might have been the husband
she had parted from, and two other people Jeremy
thought he recognised as next-door neighbours. His
calm was destroyed and he struggled not to show it but
was unable to resist closing his eyes against that too-
clear image of her.

At the same time, though he believed it to be purely
coincidental, his mother took the album on to her own
lap and closed it. 'You young people', she said, 'find old
snapshots a bit of a bore, don't you?'

Immediately he demurred. 'Not a bit, not a bit. It's a
very long time since I've seen a photo of Dad.'

His instinct was to say 'my father' but he managed
'Dad' because he thought it would please her. If it did
she gave no sign of it but sighed, rather in the way he
had heard Inez Ferry sigh, not from suffering or pain or
despair, but from loneliness, he thought. Yet she was
smiling at him, saying, 'Your father was a good husband'—and then spoiled it with—'on the whole.'

He was astonished, suddenly afraid to hear more.
What would he do if it all came out, Tess and possibly—horror of horrors—other women before Tess? But
he soon knew there was no danger. If the photographs
had reminded her of anything in particular, it seemed
unlikely to have been her husband's infidelity.

Then she dropped another few seeds of doubt into
his mind. 'You know, dear, I was brought up not to
expect too much from a man. I was taught that in some
ways they never grow up—not you, of course, you're
quite different. My mother used to say that if a woman
wanted something she might have to persuade and plan
and—well, scheme, to get it, but if a man wanted something he would simply take it as of right. And, generally,
I think, I found that.'

He was afraid to ask what she meant. But it left him

with a picture in his mind of his father grabbing anything he thought he had a right to, including women.

The subject of his father she abandoned after that
piece of philosophising and returned to praising his
flowers, his chocolates. It was a fine sunny day, quite
different from what had been forecast, and they went
out for a walk along the country lanes and took a footpath across meadows to the church, coming back by
way of a wood and another lane. This walk he had been
on a thousand times, as a child with his mother, later
on alone or with friends, but he looked at it with new
eyes, wondering if his father had ever met Tess in this
wood. In retrospect, she seemed the kind of woman
who would relish sex in the open air, especially when
an element of risk was attached to it. But Tess's house
had been at least ten miles away and this place was so
near his mother's home as to have been positively
dangerous . . .

They had soup and cold chicken for supper, and
Jeremy took his departure just before eight. The road,
he had thought, would be empty, no one returning to
London until the following afternoon, but he was
wrong and soon found himself in a traffic jam. He had
meant to take the car back to Chetwynd Mews and go
to Paddington by tube or taxi, but it was past eleven by
the time he entered the outskirts of London. He drove
straight to the Edgware Road and put the car back on a
yellow line, this time in Praed Street.

Inez's lights were still on. As he climbed the stairs he
was visited by an unfamiliar longing for company. All
the way home he had felt uncertain, insecure, in danger.
A new week had begun and in that week, maybe on
Wednesday, maybe later, he had decided that those
people, *that girl*, would come back to him asking for
more. He had more, a reasonable amount more, but

what was to stop them persisting and cleaning him out? Without much preliminary thought as to why his normal feeling of self-sufficiency had deserted him, he tapped on Inez's door. She didn't hear or was determined not to and he knocked again. Instead of speaking to him on the entryphone, she paused inside the door to view whoever it was through the spyhole. Then she opened it, though looking far from welcoming.

'I've just come back from my mother's,' he said. 'There's a crowd of kids in the street'—there wasn't—'and when I saw your lights on so late I wondered if they'd been bothering you.'

'No. Everything's been quite calm and peaceful.'

'May I come in?'

Although her expression told him that she would prefer him not to, her voice said, though coldly, 'Yes, of course.'

She had switched off the television but failed to hide the cassette sleeve with its picture of her late husband. It's almost a vice with her, he thought savagely, it's her kind of pornography. All his wistfulness, his desire for company, any company, was devoured by rage at her reception of him. Instead of sitting down, he stood in the middle of the room making anodyne replies when she asked him how his mother was, what the state of the traffic had been. She didn't offer him a drink but said, 'Well, if there's nothing I can do for you, I was on the point of going to bed.'

Liar, he thought, I bet you were playing with yourself over images of a dead man. Necrophile. Suddenly he loathed the whole household, that fool and the mad Russian woman, the moron next door to them and his girlfriend, as thick as he, and Inez most of all. He would have liked to murder her, garrotte her there in her own living room as somewhere a distant clock struck midnight. It was impossible. He knew he couldn't do it. She was inviolable, as any woman would be unless she walked ahead of him, trailing a cloud of the nameless scent. And perhaps even they had escaped him now he had solved the mystery and analysed the cause of his killer instinct. He had killed them because he couldn't help it, because a scent and a memory drove him on, but he wasn't sorry. He was glad because he hated them, all of them.

'Goodnight,' he said to Inez, and his voice to him sounded hoarse and throaty. 'I just thought I'd check you were all right.'

'Yes, thank you. I'm fine. Goodnight.'

The door closed rather too quickly for politeness behind him. When all this was over, and all his accumulated savings perhaps paid to that girl in the black thing, perhaps then, if he was still safe, he would give it all up, this double life, and go home and live with his mother for the remainder of her life. Why not? He loved her and she loved him. She was the only person he had been able to be with for long without boredom and disgust.

By now he should have been tired but if he went to bed he was sure he wouldn't sleep. He made himself the drink Inez had failed to produce and sat down to savour it, though, as by no means the first of the day, it lacked the lovely effect of a gin and tonic, say, drunk at noon. The newspaper, in its virgin state, lay on the coffee table. He opened it to be confronted by Jubilee pictures, the Royal Family in pastels or military uniforms, the sun shining on the bright foliage in the parks. Apart from the howl of a fire siren rising, falling, dying away, all was silent. Seldom was it quite as quiet as this. Ten to one in the morning and another Bank Holiday tomorrow—no, today. He would have a leisurely bath and that might make him sleepy.

Taking his drink with him, he was halfway to the bathroom when the phone rang. He almost dropped the glass. It could only be one person, no one else would call him at this hour. For nine rings he let it go on. Then he lifted the receiver and heard her voice, that horrible accent, that careless speech.

'You can't say I didn't warn you. You may have to give us more, I said. You will. Flats cost a lot and they're going up all the time. Five thousand and that'll be the end, I reckon. Can't be positive but it looks that way.'

'Wait,' he said. 'Let me speak to your boyfriend.'

'Why?'

'To prove he exists. Is he there?'

'No,' she said, 'he's not. I'll get back to you tomorrow.'

Unable to sleep, Inez sat up in bed worrying about things that would scarcely have caused her anxiety in the daytime. So far she had done nothing about a replacement for Zeinab when she left her job on Thursday evening, now in less than three days' time. She asked herself if this omission was due to her no longer really believing a word Zeinab said. No doubt, Morton Phibling intended to marry her on Saturday, but did she mean to marry him? The wedding dress, Inez thought, the engagement ring . . . But she had another engagement ring, allegedly given her by Rowley Woodhouse. If Rowley Woodhouse existed . . .

Thinking along these lines reminded her that Phibling hadn't, in fact, been into the shop since at least last Tuesday, perhaps longer. Had something gone wrong? Had Zeinab perhaps confessed to him that, due to her carelessness, the pendant had been stolen in the robbery? That would be enough to make a man angry but surely not sufficient to make him cancel his wedding. So should she begin looking for an assistant to take her place? If she didn't, Freddy would certainly offer, and not only offer but refuse to accept a 'no, thank you'. She didn't think she could stand another dose of Freddy five days a week for ten hours a day. From time to time her thoughts reverted to the problem of the key with which those people had got into her house. Freddy was absolutely honest, she was sure of that, but still he might have been taken in by some villain of a friend, though she could hardly see how.

At this rate she'd get no sleep at all. A blessing tomorrow—today—was another Bank Holiday. She put the light on, sat up and found on the floor beside the bed the *Radio Times* with the photograph of Martin in it. They were showing an old film in which he had a small supporting part, made years before the *Forsyth* series. He looked very handsome and very young. She resisted the temptation to kiss the picture, because that would be sentimental silliness. On Wednesday she would definitely ask Zeinab her intentions about her job and the wedding, and persist until she got a straightforward answer. Decisions were good, decisions helped to bring peace of mind. Martin had been very decisive. She said goodnight to him, put out the light and lay wakeful in the dark for a long time.

Julitta put the phone down and her feet up on Anwar's bed. It was a tight fit as Anwar and Flint were also there, Flint smoking a joint which he passed to Julitta. The air was blue and sweet with marijuana fumes. They had only been back ten minutes but Keefer had already fallen asleep on a bag of Anwar's dirty washing in the corner. Anwar alone was not absorbing anything stronger than a can of decaffeinated Diet Coke. He raised himself on one elbow to back away from Julitta's smoke and, looking down at her neck, said, 'Where's that diamond thing?'

Her hand went to her throat, she sat up and screamed.

CHAPTER 26

He was to go to the cinema, the Odeon at Swiss Cottage, and take the money with him, drawing it from banks and cash dispensers as before, and carried this time in a computer carrying case. The Odeon was one of those multi-theatre cinemas and the film he was to choose, *Bend It Like Beckham*, was showing in auditorium three. The performance he must attend was at three fifteen on Wednesday and he must be there by five past. Most of the seats would never be occupied at that unpopular time in the afternoon. He was to sit in the fourth row from the back on the extreme right-hand side, the last seat on the right if possible. In the unlikely event of the fourth row being full he was to go back to the third.

Jeremy was incensed at her choice of film and he wondered if she had come to know more about him in the past week, including knowing how any of the other productions at the Odeon, such as *Unfaithful* or *About a Boy* would have suited him better. She also seemed to know he had a computer business and that therefore a carrying case was something he could easily acquire. That presupposed that she, or she and the boyfriend, if boyfriend there was, was intelligent, and this he doubted. It must all be coincidence. The girl's final instruction was that after half an hour he was to place the carrying case under his seat, *his* seat, not the one in front, and leave. They would be watching, they would

find it. But he was not to linger and if he involved the
police . . . He, she, they, knew very well he wouldn't tell
the police.

The wearisome business of getting the money
together began all over again and he had only a day and
a half to do it in this time. As he walked from cash dispenser to cash dispenser to bank and back again, he
thought how slight a risk they ran. If he went to the
police—to Crippen, he supposed, or that Zulueta—he
would have to tell them what the burglars had taken
from his flat and that would be the end of him. After he
had given them another five thousand he would have
only a little over five thousand left, and that in invest-
ments. Those had been the extent of his savings and
after they were gone he would have to sell his car or
even his house. Don't think about it now, he told himself, go to the cinema tomorrow, hand it over and then
have a good think. Surely a man of his intelligence
could outwit a teenager in a black robe and her cretin of
a boyfriend, if there was a boyfriend.

Will had only been back in Star Street for an evening
and a night but Kim was moving out. On the previous
afternoon, having returned at lunchtime and expecting
Will back by three or four, she had set about making his
room and his kitchen immaculate, and in her mother's
word, 'homelike'. The place was clean enough already
but Kim got busy with vacuum cleaner, duster and
spray polish. She bought pink tulips and white lilac, and
arranged it in the only two containers she could find—
one was intended for waste paper. And then, rather like
a nineteen forties housewife getting ready for her man,
she had a shower and dressed herself in the diaphanous
summer frock she had bought on Saturday. In the nick
of time she remembered she hadn't changed the sheets

on Will's bed—vitally important in her plan—and set about doing it.

Her hair had been done that morning, by one of the assistants at the salon who came round to her mum's specially. Normally, she wore very little or no make-up but this afternoon she had done her face with care and paid more attention than usual to her nails. When she looked at herself in the bathroom mirror—the only one in the flat—she thought she looked a lot like Cindy Crawford, only younger.

Becky brought Will home three hours later than Kim expected. By that time the roast chicken was over-cooked, the oven chips blackened and dried up, and she had redone her face. Her anger was compounded by Becky coming in with Will. A man of his age didn't want his aunt running around after him like a hen with one surviving chick.

'You're very late.' Kim was conscious as she spoke of sounding just like her mother.

'I don't think we said any definite time, did we?' said Becky.

'Will said he wouldn't be late. He said it last Friday.'

Becky took a bottle of wine out of Will's fridge and drew the cork. She must have put it there herself because Will never drank wine and mostly Kim couldn't afford it. But she accepted the glass Becky offered her. She needed it.

'Seven is hardly late,' Becky said mildly. She drank her wine very fast, poured a second glass and remarked on the cleanliness of the flat. Kim liked that, she was calming down, but she wanted Becky to go all the same. What was she hanging about for? She'd got a home of her own and a boyfriend.

But Becky stayed and chatted, saying she was glad of a chance to get to know Kim better, and how nice she

looked, and though she thought she could smell something cooking, Will wouldn't need another meal as he
had had his before they left Gloucester Avenue. Kim
turned off the oven and as soon as Becky was finally off
and the front door closed behind her, tipped all the food
into the waste bin. By this time Will had had the television on for half an hour. He had smiled at Kim and
said hello but after that not said another word.

Despondently, she sat down beside him and watched
the serial. Since she had failed to see any previous
episodes, it was meaningless to her. Anyway, she scarcely
saw it. She was thinking about her plan. Surely she had-
n't been wrong about Will's feelings for her? This past
week, when they sat on the sofa together, she'd held his
hand and he'd seemed to like that. One evening, as they
were going to bed she'd given him a hug and he'd
hugged her back, very tightly, the way her brother
Wayne's boy did when she'd given him something. For
some reason that comparison made her feel uncomfort-
able, as if she were thinking of Will as a kid, which was
absurd and impossible in a grown-up man who had to
shave and was six feet tall.

She took his hand now and he turned his head and
gave her a lovely smile. The serial was succeeded by
another one, police this time instead of people in a pub,
and then by the news. Will never wanted the news, so he
played with the remote until he got a comedian and a
bunch of leggy girls in glittery bras and miniskirts.

'Aren't you tired?' Kim asked. 'It's late.'

'I want to see this programme. I'll go to bed when it's
over. Promise.'

It was another reminder of her eight-year-old
nephew. She wished she'd never thought about him
because now she couldn't get him out of her head.
Everything Will said—'In a minute, in a minute' and

'I'm coming, I *said* I was coming'– seemed an echo of Wayne's little boy. But at last the programme was over and obedient Will had turned off the set and gone to the bathroom. She put all the lights out but his bed lamp and pulled the curtains round her bed only to get into her nightie, a new one, short and pastel-blue. He hadn't seemed to notice her frock but perhaps he'd notice this.

But when he emerged in pyjamas, she felt suddenly shy and drew the curtain round herself quickly. Her heart was beating fast. She heard Will get into bed. The place went dark as he switched off the bed lamp. That was something she hadn't bargained for but she lacked the nerve to switch it on again. She almost gave up then, but thought, if I don't I won't be able to stay here, the way I feel. It'll be lovely once I've shown him I want it, maybe that's what he's been waiting for, five minutes and he'll be thrilled I showed him how I felt. She came out from behind the curtain, went over to Will's bed and whispered, 'Will, Will . . .'

'What is it?' He sounded half asleep.

'Shall I come in with you?'

She didn't wait for an answer but pulled back the cover and got in beside him. He would, he *must* put his arms round her. And she'd let him take her nightie off, he'd like that. She put her hands on his chest and lifted her mouth to his.

What happened was worse than anything she'd feared. He turned his head away so that his thick fair hair was in her face and shook her hands off him. 'I don't like other people in my bed,' he said and rolled over. His forehead was against the wall and his knees drawn up to his chin. 'Go away. *Go away.*'

So now, at seven thirty in the morning, after a sleepless night of incomprehension and shame, she was moving

out. Will would be leaving for work in an hour but she
wanted him to see her go, wanted him to understand he
couldn't get away with treating her like an unpaid cleaner
and cook when she wasn't his girlfriend. But he seemed to
have forgotten all about last night.

'I'm leaving, Will,' she had told him. 'I can't stand
any more. I'm not your mum to sleep in your room
when you're scared at night.'

'My mum's dead,' he said quite cheerfully, 'but I've
got Becky.'

She would have liked to attack him for that, beat him
with her fists and scratch him with her long nails.
Instead, she finished her packing and, since he didn't
offer to carry her cases downstairs, put them outside the
door herself. She'd take them to work and after work—
well, it'd be great if the three girls she knew would let
her move into the Kilburn flat with them. If not, it
would be back to her mum and dad in Harlesden.

'Goodbye, Will,' she said.

He was watching breakfast television and he didn't
look round. 'Bye-bye.'

To tell James she never wanted to see him again, Becky
had to get drunk. She had been in a bad enough way on
the return journey from Star Street. Twice she mounted
the pavement and once missed going into the back of
someone else's car by about a millimetre. The driver said
she had touched his bumper but there wasn't a mark.
Much worse was being told, with a lot of effing and
blinding, that she was 'pissed' and should be ashamed.

If she hadn't been drunk she would have understood
that it's not very brave, not to say badly behaved, to tell
your lover goodbye on the phone. But the pleasant
unsteady haze she found herself in, the room rising and
falling in waves, took away any ethical feelings. She

phoned James, said their relationship was over and please not to try to see her.

'Becky, how much have you had to drink?'

'Don't know,' she said. 'Not much. Not much at all.'

'You probably think I never noticed all those secret sips you were having but I did. Oh, I did.'

'I hate you,' she said, as Will might have done, and, as Will would never have done, slurring every word, 'You're a puri-puri-puritannical moraletic—mor-al-is-tic, moralistic, boring prude.'

She slammed the phone down before he could. He was all the things she had said, anyway, and nasty to Will, and impatient and—well, all sorts of other things. What things she didn't know because she had fallen asleep.

Next day she felt so ill she phoned the office and said she wouldn't be in, she had summer flu. With the help of aspirins, Alka-Seltzer and at last a hair of the dog, it still took her all the morning and most of the afternoon to recover. Shame and self-recrimination set in. Guilt too, as she wondered if Kim Beatty had noticed anything odd about her. God knows, she was justified in having a few drinks. Will, reluctant to leave the flat in Gloucester Avenue, had begun pleading with her, as soon as lunch was over, to let him stay, not to make him go back to Star Street. He had been so happy these past two days. There was plenty of room in her home, it wasn't true that she hadn't a second bedroom. It was big enough for him, he didn't want any more.

It had been a long time since she had last heard him whine as he was whining then. 'Please, please, go on, let me stay. Say I can, Becky, go on.'

'You're happy with Kim, aren't you? You're not alone.'

Before resuming his pleas, he had looked at her as if he hardly knew who Kim was. And she had been so sure

the arrangement was a satisfying one for both of them,
even wondering at one point if what was surely the
inevitable had happened, what she believed had really
been Kim's wish all along and perhaps his too, and they
were lovers. Now she was almost certain she had been
wrong. Had she been, only half consciously, pimping
for Will? The blood mounted hotly into her face.

'I do want to stay here with you, Becky. You won't
make me go away, will you?'

Recourse to the gin got her through the afternoon.
Sullenly, he watched television. She made herself raise
the subject again when he hadn't whined for half an
hour. 'Your staying here isn't going to be possible, Will.
Please don't ask me again. I'm going to cook you your
favourite meal, a big fry-up, and then I'm going to drive
you home.'

He hadn't replied.

The pendant was lost. Tired though they had been, they
had searched the room and been up and down the stairs
and into the street, but all in vain. The clasp must have
come undone and the chain and diamond fallen to the
ground when the three of them were among the crowds
in the Mall.

Julitta kept saying she wished she could put the clock
back and she'd give anything not to have worn the
bloody thing.

'You've got nothing to give now,' Anwar said brutally,
though Julitta still had her share of the ten thousand
and he had had no intention of letting her keep the pendant. 'It's too late anyway, so you can stop crying. I can't
be doing with a fucking woman crying.'

But Julitta continued to sob. 'Someone'll have picked
it up and kept it,' she bawled and, unconscious of the
irony, 'Fucking thieves.'

Flint dragged her home. It was three in the morning. When they had gone Anwar made himself a cup of cocoa on his gas ring and crumbled up a chocolate milk flake on the top. It helped him reflect. It was he himself, not Julitta, who had worn the *abaya* and picked up Jeremy's backpack from Aberdeen Place. As had been his intention, the diamond geezer had thought it was a girl. Perhaps he should do it again. On the other hand, it was their turn . . .

This time Flint could pick up the dosh and if they had the luck to succeed in a third attempt, it would be Julitta's turn. The geezer was too frightened to be anything but harmless. Keefer, who had succumbed to shooting up heroin again along with his methadone, a dangerous mix, had become so comatose and speechless that he and Flint had carried him downstairs between them, put him in the white van and dumped him on the steps of St Mary's Hospital. It only went to show, thought Anwar, who could be sententious at times, how the unfamiliar possession of money went to the heads of the weak-willed and those of low intelligence.

He finished his cocoa, got under the duvet and was asleep in two minutes. It was two in the afternoon before they met next day, and that was too early for Julitta who kept yawning. She seemed to have recovered from the loss of the pendant but it was hard to tell with someone who had her mouth open most of the time. They discussed plans for retrieving the second instalment of the money.

Flint wanted to disguise himself in turban and djellaba but felt humiliated when Anwar told him that the headgear and the garment each belonged to different cultures. He would do much better to wear his black hooded jacket and dark glasses.

'I could get a tache from the joke shop.'

'And my mum's got a wig,' put in Julitta. 'She had it for her alopecia.'

'Grow up, will you?' said Anwar. 'And for fuck's sake stop yawning. I'm pissed off with the sight of your tonsils.'

In the end Flint went off to the Odeon at Swiss Cottage dressed just as Anwar recommended, in blue jeans, black leather boots, a loose hooded jacket and shades like goggles, with a rolled-up Tesco carrier in one of his pockets. The geezer was instructed to enter the cinema at five past three but Flint wasn't surprised to see him cross the road from the bus stop, carrying a computer case, at three minutes to. There's nerves for you. He wouldn't dare leave before three forty-five. Flint went across the road for a coffee.

Sitting at the extreme right-hand end of the fourth row, the case on his lap, Jeremy looked around the cinema for a woman in a black robe. No one. The only other people were two middle-aged women together, a woman with a child of about six and several solitary men. The commercials and the trailers were still running when the half-hour was up. He looked around him again, uncertain whether there had previously been seven people in the cinema including himself or eight. Had the figure in the hooded jacket had been there from the start or had he recently come in? It made little difference. Was it a man or a girl? It seemed too slight for a man, even a very young one. Its hands, a sure giveaway of sex, were concealed in black gloves. Still, it must be the same girl. It was her height and, as far as he could tell, her shape. Suppressing a sigh, useless anyway in the circumstances, he put the computer case under his seat, got up and left.

Flint, who had once wanted to go on the stage—Hollywood, Bollywood, or just the TV—and still occasionally had dreams of acting, made a big display as of a laid-back girl sashaying out of the cinema. Behind the partition dividing the back row from the entrance and foyer, he paused, stared idly over the top of it at the screen for five minutes, then strolled a yard or two down the right-hand aisle and sat down where the geezer had sat. The film had started. Pity he had to leave, really, he was beginning to enjoy it, but when on a job stick to the job, he told himself virtuously. This was work, not pleasure. He pulled the case out from under the seat, put it into the Tesco bag and made his way out. No one seemed to notice or care.

Back in St Michael's Street, Flint and Julitta left the opening of the case to Anwar. He lifted the wads of notes out, counting them as he went. Five thousand pounds.

At the bottom of the case lay a sheet of A4 paper with print on it, obviously produced on a computer.

'*You have had £15,000 from me and that is enough,*' Anwar read aloud. '*If you plan to ask for more, think again. I will not, repeat will not, pay you dirty bloodsucking thieves another penny. Threaten all you want. You have had all my savings and there is no more.*'

'What's a penny?' said Julitta.

'A pence, you stupid cow. One of those little copper things.'

'Why would we want one of them?'

'Piss off, can't you?' said Anwar. 'Think again, he says. I'm thinking again and what I'm thinking is he'll fucking do what we say. Funny thing, but until that silly bitch lost the diamond, I'd almost made up my mind to call a halt.' He directed a warning snarl at Julitta, who had opened her mouth, presumably to ask him to translate. 'I shan't now. We need another five K. He's fucking asked for it and he'll get it. Or, rather, we will.'

'Good thinking,' said Flint.

CHAPTER 27

Of course she was going to marry him. Inez need have no fears about that. Hadn't she had her invitation to the wedding? Inez hadn't and, in any case, had no intention of going.

'I haven't seen him in here lately.'

'He's up to his eyes in last-minute preparations,' said Zeinab. 'What's happened to the Chelsea china clock?'

'I sold it. To a man who didn't haggle, just paid what I asked. At last.' In spite of feeling better about Zeinab than she had at the Bank Holiday, Inez couldn't resist a dig. 'At about a quarter to ten this morning. Before you got in.'

Remarks like that had no effect on Zeinab. 'Shame he didn't take that animal as well.' She stood in front of the mirror she called hers, studying her reflection, beautiful as always but neck, arms and ears jewel-free. The only diamonds she wore were in Morton Phibling's engagement ring. 'Shame about that pendant getting nicked,' she said. 'I never told him. Best make it a wedding night confession, I reckon.'

'We never heard another word from the police.'

'Useless bunch of layabouts, they are,' said Zeinab. 'And poor Ludmila lost all them wedding rings. You got a replacement for me? Or you going to take Freddy on again?'

It was unfortunate, in Inez's opinion, that at the precise moment she spoke those words, the interior door opened and Freddy walked in. 'I think that's understood, isn't it, Inez? Or, to coin a phrase, it goes without saying.'

'A pity you said it, then,' Inez said with more acidity than she usually allowed herself. Then, guiltily, she asked Freddy if he and Ludmila had had a nice honeymoon.

'Blissful,' said Freddy, seating himself in the grey armchair. 'Ludo was in cracking form and I must say, Inez, in spite of what you said in your disparaging way, the Isle of Man put me in mind a lot of Barbados.'

That girl and her boyfriend, if there was a boyfriend, wasted very little time. Jeremy wondered if it was his note which had irritated them and spurred them on to further action. Before the phone rang—at eleven p.m., early for them—he had been thinking about his blackmailers or blackmailer. These days he thought of little else, unless it was to view with ever-renewed astonishment his past and the cause of his killing those women. If that girl ever phoned him again, and he was sure she would, he would ask her if there really was a boyfriend, if there were any more of them, or if she truly was alone. That would mean either that she had managed to steal his strongbox without her companions knowing or, more likely, one of the men, of whom there must have been several, would have succeeded in opening it but hadn't seen the significance of what it contained. She alone had known that—precisely because she was a woman.

Of course she would want him to think others were involved, a boyfriend and maybe two or three more friends. That way he would believe that if he planned to do away with her at the next pick-up, others would still be there to continue extracting money from him or to tell the police what they suspected. But if he came to know she was entirely alone . . .

He had started on his last-thing-at-night gin and tonic, the first taste of which he found so exhilarating, when the phone rang. Able to think only that it could be Inez or his mother—was he really so lacking in friends?—he lifted the receiver, astounded and immediately furious at the sound of her voice.

'I told you in my letter,' he said. 'I haven't any more. You've had all I've got.' She said nothing. 'Didn't you read my letter?'

He thought her tone was stagy, put on for effect, shriller than usual. 'One of the others read it. There's a whole bunch of us know about this. Did you think I was alone? You should be so lucky, Alexander, or whatever you call yourself. It don't matter a fuck'—he winced at the word, he had always hated that sort of language—'what was in it. We want another five grand.'

'You won't get it. It's not there.'

'You can flog something, can't you? Your car, your nice little place in South Ken.'

Anger rose inside him in a tide which broke, spreading heat all over his body. 'I'm not doing that.'

'OK. The bank'll lend it. You know what'll happen if you don't. We can write letters too and we'll just put one in the parcel for the filth. I'll give you a bell Saturday.'

'Wait,' he said sharply. 'Let me speak to someone else.'

The line was still open but she was silent. He could hear nothing in the background, no movement, no voices. She rang off without another word.

The Saturday call would be for the venue. He felt the last thing he expected, a sense of relief. He had been sure before, meaning he had some doubts, but she had virtually told him: she was alone. He recovered her voice from his memory and heard the falseness: 'There's a whole bunch of us know about this.' Not true. She was either alone, he thought, or the boyfriend had been in on the early stages, but now she was acting on her own. She was greedy. Her greed would be her undoing.

What was he going to do? He didn't know—yet. Wait for the Saturday call. What a stupid illiterate phrase that was, to give someone a bell. He felt his mouth turn down in haste and he sweetened it with a sip of his gin. For some reason he remembered then how he had quoted to himself a sentence from something or other when he was feeling particularly low: *The bright day is done and we are for the dark.* The dark had receded again and light come in brightly, of all things at a time when for the third time money was demanded of him, money with menaces. She would never send those earrings to the 'filth' as she called them. He would see to that.

That Thursday night Zeinab had promised to have dinner with Morton Phibling who wanted to take her to the Connaught, but when she got back to Dame Shirley Porter House rather earlier than usual, Algy was waiting for her all dressed up in a new suit with a table booked for the two of them at Daphne's. A surprise dinner, he said. Her mum would babysit. In fact, she was already in the flat, a child on each bolster-sized knee, the three of them intent on a video of *The Others*, which had just reached the creepiest bit.

'Why's Nicole always got the same purple dress on?' said Zeinab. 'She's a big star. Why don't she have a big glamorous wardrobe?'

'Don't ask me.' Reem stuffed half a Bounty bar into each baby-birdlike open mouth. 'And shut up. We're watching.'

Zeinab thought she'd better go with Algy. He'd start being funny with her if she turned him down again, especially if she disappeared on a date with Morton. Somehow, she'd not have a problem with her conscience if she hadn't lost that pendant but could have sold it and handed over the money to Algy. 'OK,' she said. 'I'll just go and change.'

In the bedroom, getting into a black satin dress, embroidered with beads, that would have been the death of Algy if he had known what Morton paid for it, she phoned Morton on her mobile and, thankful he wasn't answering, left a message to the effect that she was too tired and mysteriously unwell to go out. Then, the film being over, she told Reem that if Morton phoned, to tell him she'd gone to bed and mustn't be disturbed.

'Right,' said Reem. 'They was ghosts, that's why.'

'That's why what?'

'Nicole had the one dress on.'

Algy and Zeinab left the flat and took a taxi down to Knightsbridge.

They had a lovely evening and Zeinab admitted to herself that she always had a much better time with Algy than she did with Morton or anyone else, for that matter. It was quite romantic, like before the kids were born. The only odd thing was that Algy seemed all the time to be on the brink of telling her something but he never did, so maybe it was her imagination. Reem was staying the night, which meant they could get back when they liked. Algy took her to a club and then on to another, and it was nearly two before they got home.

Algy got up early just the same. He had to. He
woke Reem at seven thirty because he was going to
need her help, got the kids up and reminded her she'd
promised to take them to school. Zeinab slept on,
which suited Algy very well. The removal van came at
eight thirty. Algy could afford a proper firm these
days. When they moved here he had driven the
Wheels van himself, and he and Zeinab had done the
loading. Of course, they hadn't so much stuff then.
He told the men to start in the living room and be
careful with the digital TV, and when they were busy
in there and Reem had gone lumbering off with
Carmel and Bryn, he woke Zeinab.

'What time is it, for God's sake?'

'Getting on for nine,' he said. 'You'd best get up.
We're moving.'

'We're what?' Zeinab screamed.

'You heard, Suzanne: Come on, you knew we was
going only not just when. Well, it's today, it's now.'

She got up, pulled on her new jeans—fashionably
faded about the knees, the hems frayed—and a cash-
mere sweater because it was freezing cold for June.
Moving was quite thrilling, really. Men usually gave in
at her slightest word, so it was a pleasant novelty to have
matters taken out of her hands in this way by masterful
Algy, whose high-handed action had been an exciting
surprise. It made her want to buy him something nice.
Maybe, once she was living in Pimlico, she'd flog her
engagement ring, the last jewellery, of everything given
her by wealthy admirers, that she still had.

One thing about Freddy, he was always punctual.
Rather too early, Inez thought, having barely put the
kettle on before he appeared in his cardboard-coloured
duster coat.

'In case you were anxious,' he said, 'I'd like you to know I have my wife's full permission to assist you in the shop.'

'I'm afraid I took that for granted, Freddy.' She poured tea into his cup and ladled in the sugar. 'Ludmila didn't object last time.'

'Ah, but now she's my wife things are different. A wife is in what you might call a sacred position. And, a rather delicate matter, Inez, now I'm here in what you might call an official capacity, not to put too fine a point on it, there'll be the little matter of my salary.' Freddy lifted one hand in an admonitory gesture. 'Not now. After we've had our tea will be time enough for negotiations.'

'In that case,' said Inez, 'there will also be the little matter of an increase in rent now you are a married couple living here permanently.'

The argument which ensued ended not very satisfactorily in Inez agreeing not to raise the rent while Freddy worked for her but paying him considerably less than what Zeinab had received. 'You won't forget to tell the Benefit office, will you?'

'Trust me,' said Freddy with a reassuring smile.

The morning was cold but bright and sunny, which meant nothing. It was always like that first thing and lashing down with rain by lunchtime. But she put the bookcases outside, making a mental resolve to keep an eye on them and the clouds which would gather in an hour or two.

Jeremy Quick hadn't appeared for tea on his way to work. It was several weeks since he had and at least a week, she was sure, since he had been to work. She had caught glimpses of him and he hadn't seemed ill, rather the reverse, in fact, scurrying up and down the stairs, marching off down the street towards the Edgware Road, returning half an hour later only to go out again after ten minutes upstairs. She was longing for him to give notice but she felt she had no justification for evicting him. He paid his rent, he wasn't noisy, he didn't have late-night parties. No objection to him could be found beyond her growing dislike of him, her distaste for his cold mauvish-coloured eyes and his lying.

Freddy must make rather a good impression on callers at the shop. This was a surprise because she had always considered him a liability, but now, entering from the street herself, she saw him briefly with new eyes and thought he looked quite professional in his working coat, holding a Venetian glass tumbler up to the light. A retired auctioneer, she thought, or some kind of craftsman in need of extra funds. Presently, a woman in a wintry felt hat came in and Inez watched with satisfaction as he sold her a Victorian barometer.

'Better than those weather forecasters on the telly,' he was saying as he wrapped her purchase up in brown paper. 'Nine times out of ten they get it wrong but this little chap can't fail.'

The next visitor was the kind of person they seldom saw, a man in his thirties, tallish and burly, in a leather jacket and jeans, his rather long ginger hair tied back in a ponytail. Inez was wondering what he was in search of, something flashy maybe, wax fruit under a dome or a painting of a nineteenth-century nude, when, after looking round him in a puzzled way, his eye lighted on the jaguar. 'That's a disgrace, that is,' he said loudly. 'Worse than a fur coat.'

'I didn't shoot it,' Inez said.

'It's a disgrace giving it houseroom. Poor thing. Doesn't it make you cringe just seeing it there, or are you so insensitive you don't *think*?'

Inez stood up. 'When you've finished abusing me, was there something you wanted?'

For some reason her words had a calming effect on him. 'I'm looking for Ayesha,' he muttered.

'There's no one called Ayesha here,' Inez said, though already having more than an inkling of his meaning.

'Lovely-looking dark girl, got long hair. About twenty.'

'Ah, I think I know who you mean. And may I know who you are?'

'The name's Rowley Woodhouse.'

Before she could stop herself Inez had come out with it. 'You *do* exist!'

'Of course I bloody exist. Where's Ayesha?'

'She terminated her employment here yesterday.' Freddy, who had been listening avidly, came up to them, greedy for drama. 'I'm sure she'll need today to get prepared in. She's getting married on Saturday. I was married myself last week, so I know how it feels, none better.'

Rowley Woodhouse was staring at him. Enough of the situation had been deduced by Inez to have steered well clear of that subject but either Freddy was being innocently insensitive or joyfully vindictive. Woodhouse said, 'I don't understand.'

'Look, you'll have to have this out with her yourself,' Inez was starting to say, and 'I can't . . .' when she saw Morton Phibling's yellow BMW draw up at the kerb and the driver get out to open the door for his employer.

Wild thoughts came to her of hiding Woodhouse in the little kitchen or even a cupboard, as if he were a clandestine lover in a French farce, but Morton was already in the shop, another man in search of his fiancée, then asking for her. 'Where is she that looketh forth in the morning, fair as the moon?'

He must learn all this stuff before he came, Inez thought irrelevantly. She didn't know what to say, then an idea came to her. 'Zeinab finished work here yesterday.'

Was it possible Woodhouse would think she had had two Asian girls working for her? 'I thought you knew.'

Morton, of course, was bound to give the game away. 'I remember now. What a fool! I must be losing my marbles forgetting my own wedding day.'

Woodhouse moved towards him. 'Are you talking about Ayesha?'

'Zeinab.'

'One and the same,' said helpful Freddy.

Woodhouse glanced at him, but spoke to Morton. 'Let's get this straight. Are you saying you're getting married to *my* fiancée tomorrow?'

'No, I'm getting married to *my* fiancée. The most beautiful girl in the world, Zeinab or Ayesha or whatever, it's all one to me. Today,' he continued rapturously, 'she looks like Miss World but tomorrow she'll be Mrs Phibling.'

Woodhouse hit him, a rather shaky left hook. Inez screamed. She couldn't help it, the sound involuntarily issuing from her open mouth. Morton staggered but kept on his feet. As Inez shrank away, retreating behind the desk, shouting at Woodhouse that his adversary was an old man, he shouldn't fight a man twice his age, Morton came at him with both fists. In spite of her distress, Morton's expertise amazed her. Then, suddenly, she knew who he was. All the time he had been coming into the shop she had wondered where she had seen him before. Years before, maybe thirty-five years, he'd been the world bantam-weight boxing champion. Her first husband had once or twice taken her to fights. He hadn't been Morton Phibling then but Morty Phillips. No wonder Woodhouse had fallen over.

'Phone the police,' she shouted to Freddy.

But before he'd lifted the receiver, Zulueta's car had drawn up outside. Inez had never been so pleased to see him. Morton and Woodhouse were once more going at it hammer and tongs but now there was no doubt Morton was the victor, Zeinab's other fiancé beaten to his knees, making feeble feints at the former boxer's legs. What was needed was a referee to intervene and one had appeared in the shape of Zulueta marching into the shop with DC Jones.

'What's going on here?'

Woodhouse fell on the floor and rolled over, making sad little grunts. Watching him from the grey velvet chair, which he had sunk back into, Morton wiped his face with a red silk handkerchief while a smile of satisfaction spread across his face. 'I don't seem to have lost my touch,' he said.

Jones was bending over Woodhouse who, unwilling to be an object of pity, especially when his rival was a good thirty years his senior, struggled to his knees.

Shaking his head as if in despair at the follies of humanity, Zulueta turned to Inez. 'The purpose of our visit, Mrs Ferry, is to enquire if you can give us the address of a Mr Morton Phibling who I believe is engaged to be married to the young lady who works here.'

'That's me,' said Morton, getting up as if to make himself more recognisable. 'Don't you remember me? When you came in about those murders I was here. Don't you remember?'

'The circumstances were rather different, sir.'

Woodhouse had got to his feet, pushed Jones out of the way and would have made a fresh onslaught on Morton if Zulueta hadn't grabbed him by the shoulders from behind. He shoved him into the chair Morton had just got out of and Woodhouse sank back into it with a groan of frustration.

'That's quite enough.' Zulueta had the air of a primary schoolteacher admonishing a class of five-year-olds.

'Now, you two gentlemen must call it a day and since neither of you is hurt, we won't take it any further.' He addressed Woodhouse with a frown. 'However, I'll remind you, sir, that there's some would construe the shove you gave DC Jones just now as an assault. So be warned.' Turning his attention to Morton and producing a notebook from his pocket, he said, 'Now it's our understanding, sir, that a valuable diamond pendant picked up off the street in the Mall, London double-you-one, last Monday is your property. According to Messrs La Touche-Chessyere, jewellers of Bond Street, same postal district, you purchased this ornament from them at the price of twenty-two thousand pounds'—gasp from Freddy and incredulous look from Rowley Woodhouse—'May'—he looked at the notebook—'twenty-second, two thousand and two.'

Morton was nodding, his smug expression suddenly wiped away.

'That seems to ring a bell,' said Zulueta, abandoning pomposity, 'so we'll trouble you to come back with us to the police station and identify this item.'

Woodhouse and his quarrel with him forgotten, Morton was now shaking his head in the same rueful way as Zulueta. 'My beloved must have dropped it off her lovely neck while taking part in the Jubilee celebrations,' He followed Jones towards the door. 'Never mind. What a delight for her when I restore it into her hands!' To the other officer he said, 'I'm quite ready to accompany you to the nick, but I'll go in my own vehicle if you don't mind.'

Up in the loft at his parents' house, Anwar was searching through the boxes of old clothes, source of the *chador*. Results were disappointing, so he climbed down the ladder and went into his parents' bedroom. Should

it be a sari this time or a *salwar* and *kameez*? Of the lat-
ter she had only one set and he had never known her to
wear it. Saris, and she had some magnificent ones, she
put on when attending grand dinners or fund-raising
receptions. With either he could wear a veil. It might be
necessary to cover Julitta's face with the corner of a
dupatta, she was very fair-skinned and would look odd
in a sari unless made-up. This, Anwar thought, might
be beyond him.

Which one wouldn't his mother miss? The pale pink
with the silver border he remembered her saying was
now too young for her, but he had never seen her wear
the dark-blue with the white pattern. It was cotton and
she probably judged it too simple for a dinner engagement. On the other hand, the wearer's face must be covered, he could see that now, and although a woman in
a sari might wear a *dupatta* she would surely not cover
her face with it. At the far end of the wardrobe he spotted something else: a long buttoned and belted coat, a
dowdy dark- grey garment such as Moslem women wear
in parts of the Middle East. His mother had bought it,
he remembered, some three or four years before while
she and his father were on holiday in Syria. It would be
warm, she had said when derided by her family, suitable
for wearing while out in the winter. She had never worn
it, as far as he could recall. Though not at all clothes-
conscious, this had turned out to be too unflattering
even for her.

Julitta could wear it with the *hijab*. Maybe a white
one, or better still, since even a scarf wouldn't hide her
face, a yashmak. Anwar doubted anyone's ability to
make one, but just winding a black scarf round her
head, across the bridge of her nose back again above her
eyebrows, and tying it in a knot at the back should be
all right. He bundled up the coat, found a long black

scarf in a drawer and went back to the van without again seeing his sisters.

Driving back to Paddington, his thoughts turned to the diamond geezer. They would soon have to find a new name for him. He wouldn't be spouting out diamonds much longer, the rate they were milking him. Where should he send him to meet Julitta this time? How about the gardens, the little triangle of grass and trees, between Broadley Street and Penfold Street? It was one of those rather shady areas, not a safe place after dark, yet as birds fly, not far from the grand dwellings of Crawford Place and Bryanston Square. Over the other side of Lisson Grove, Boston Place where the geezer had killed one of those girls, ran down past Marylebone Station towards Dorset Square.

Recalling the murder of Caroline Dansk as she walked past the railway wall, brought to Anwar what was probably the first chivalrous thought of his life. How pleased his father would be, though not, of course, by the context in which the thought had taken shape. Why not? He smiled to himself, reflecting that once again he would enjoy himself.

The man who had bought the Chelsea china clock came back in the afternoon. Inez thought he must have found something wrong with it, a chip out of the porcelain or the works going wrong, but that wasn't his reason. What that was he didn't reveal but walked about admiring things and talking to her. He was sixty years old, newly widowed, a retired solicitor living in St John's Wood. No doubt he expected her to remember the name he had given her for the invoice when he bought the clock. She racked her brains but couldn't recall it, nor could she exactly open the desk and get the invoice copy out to look at while he was talking.

Freddy came back about half an hour later than he had promised from his lunch at the Ranoush Juice with Ludmila, but Inez wasn't as pleased to see him as she had expected to be. Her visitor stayed only two or three minutes after that, saying as he left that he would like to come back on the Monday as there were more things among her stock he wanted to look at.

'It's easy to see he admires you, Inez,' said Freddy.

'Don't be absurd.'

'All right, have it your own way. Poor old Freddy's always wrong, as usual. But we shall see.'

That evening she had intended to indulge herself by watching not one but two *Forsyth* films. Yet, when the time came, when she had poured her glass of wine and was comfortable in front of the screen, she made no move to press the key on the video remote but asked herself instead if there wasn't something morbid in this cultivation of grief beyond its natural time of endurance. For too long she had wallowed in dreams of a past and perfect love, gone for ever. It was time, as the popular phrase had it, to move on.

She picked up and opened a book she had bought months ago but never since looked at.

CHAPTER 28

The garrotte he used had been different each time. The first girl he strangled with her own silver chain. It was the only means to hand because, of course, when he set out he had had no idea that he would kill Gaynor Ray or any woman. The next time, too, it was winter and he had used a length of electric cable he happened to have in his overcoat pocket. After that, although he had never set out on an evening stroll with the intention in mind of killing someone, perhaps he would hardly have gone out at all without the chance of it simmering below the surface of his mind, and he always carried something with him that would serve that half-contemplated purpose, a piece of rope, a length of picture cord, a strip of cloth. But he had never had in mind the distinct aim of following a girl and killing her with one of those tools of his method. It was just that the possibility was there and not to have had the means if there was a suitable encounter might have driven him mad. Sometimes he thought of trying to explain this to a policeman or a lawyer in the event of his being taken and how incomprehensible it would seem to the virtuous law-abiding who were never tempted. Not so long ago he had been law-abiding himself, so he knew.

This time the garrotte he took with him, a piece of electric cable, perhaps the most efficient means, was deliberately pocketed. One of those bags made of shiny synthetic fabric that are light to carry and cheap to buy, sometimes given away at conferences as a package full of

documents and brochures, was requested. Jeremy had to
buy his; as a self-employed person, he never attended
such gatherings. But he failed to comply with his blackmailer's request to fill it with five thousand pounds collected up from different sources. This time the chosen
container, jade green and black with an unidentifiable
logo on the front, held only newspaper cut up into
note-sized pieces.

Apart from wondering what disguise she would
adopt this time, he speculated very little about the girl.
The only risk, as far as he could tell, was that he had
been wrong and she had others to help her. But in that
case, would these others always allow her to collect the
blackmail money herself? Knowing his proclivities,
would they allow the same person, and a woman, to
expose herself over and over to a very real danger?
Would they not send one of them, a man? Wouldn't one
of them phone him and make the demand? She had
talked of her boyfriend, he thought, in a rather desperate way, as if she were willing him to believe. Why, if he
were present, hadn't he spoken and declared himself?
And if the answer to that was that she had always made
the calls on her own, why had she?

Because she was doing this on her own, had possibly
done something of the same kind before. If she died,
garrotted in a garden off a back street in Marylebone,
why should not the police and the media take it for
granted she was simply another victim of the
Rottweiler? To that end he would take from her some
small personal item, as he had done from all the others.
Disposing of her would be easy, she was slight and not
nearly as tall as he. And he had had plenty of practice.

This collection point was the nearest to Star Street of
the three, the time appointed hours later than either of

the others. Midnight—it would be dark, of course, even
at nearly midsummer it would be very dark, especially if
the sky was overcast. It was ten minutes to twelve when
he set off, not wanting to be forced to hang about as he
had last time.

He found Broadley Street rather a sinister place.
Perhaps that wouldn't be apparent in the daytime but by
night there was a loneliness and an emptiness about the
area, particularly in the narrow cross streets with their
blocks of local authority flats and the occasional tall
Victorian house. Lights were on in some windows, yet
there seemed to be no people about until a gaggle of
teenage boys erupted from Penfold Street, jostling each
other, letting out unearthly howls and kicking an empty
beer can from one to another like a football. They
passed on ahead of him, loping into the roadway without looking to the right or the left, up on the pavement
at the other side towards Lisson Grove. A car came
along too fast, its roof open and music of the thump,
beat and squeal kind pouring out of it at full volume.
After that the silence returned, seeming deeper now
than it had before the various interruptions.

He looked at his watch as he crossed the road, just
able to make out the time. Two minutes past midnight
but the girl wasn't there yet. No one was about in the
still silent garden which no woman in her senses would
enter alone at this hour. For this girl it was different—
or she thought it was. Then he saw her approaching
from Ashmill Street, or gliding rather, for she walked as
modest Asian women do, slowly as if she had all the
time in the world, her head held high, her face, head
and body entirely enveloped in clothing the colour of
the night.

There was no moon, there were no stars and few
street lamps, but he could tell her ankle-length belted

coat was dark grey and the scarf which was wound round her head, then round the lower part of her face and her forehead, was black. She gave no sign of having seen him but stood a few yards from the tree, under which he was to place the document case. But instead of advancing to the tree he stood where he was, staring at her, trying to meet her eyes but not knowing whether he had done so. Her eyes and eyebrows were uncovered, that he could tell, but not whether what light there was caught them and he fancied the lids were lowered. He sniffed, smelling for her, knowing he would get a scent of her even from this distance, but there was no hint of *that* perfume, of course there wouldn't be. If there was any smell it was of the grass, a lingering of tobacco smoke and, oddly, a whiff of coconut.

His hand in his pocket, he felt for the electric cable, closed his fingers over it. The case in his other hand, he walked very slowly to the tree, hoping by his apparently casual calm to unnerve her. She might have been watching him, she might not. He laid the case on the grass and turned, standing quite still to look at her. It would be easier, he thought, if she showed the nervousness she ought to feel, if she showed *something* instead of standing there like a statue. He was seized by a strange distaste for the act he had to perform, a reluctance he had never felt before. On previous occasions, as soon as he knew this was the destined one, the blood pounded in his head, his whole body pulsated and throbbed, yet his feet seemed to have springs on them and his hands to be charged with electricity. Why was that missing now when it was so much needed?

Realisation made him shudder. It was the scent, the nameless scent, which wasn't there, only the hint of coconut. He needed *that* scent to impel him, to be the mainspring of his actions. Never mind, he must do without it, he knew what he was doing, none better, and if he could do it when driven on by a compulsion he must be able to do it unaided and unstimulated. She had moved towards the tree, again with that graceful gliding gait. He saw her in the only light there was as the small pale street lamp shone on her passage across the grass, and he sprang, one end of the cable in each hand. She let out a deep roaring gasp, bent forward and kicked him. He held on, pulling hard, hoping the cable would still constrict the windpipe, through all those folds of thick black stuff. For a half-second he would have to slacken his hold. He did so and wrenched the scarf from her neck, falling back with a cry as his knuckle felt the projection of the thyroid cartilage.

Adam's apple. This was a man! A very young man with smooth olive skin, a rather long aquiline nose and eyes which, blank though they had seemed before, now glowed with anger or triumph or revenge. His upper lip curled back and he snarled. He came at Jeremy kicking, scratching with nails far too long for a boy, but Jeremy was taller and able to seize his blackmailer's throat with his bare hands. He squeezed, pushing in his thumbs, his finger ends. Surprisingly strong but gasping and retching, the boy managed to knee Jeremy hard in the groin. The pain was excruciating. Jeremy didn't fall but he staggered, unable to stop himself crying out, and while he struggled to keep his feet, the boy grabbed the case and ran. He was young and he could run faster, much faster, than a man of forty-eight, even while holding up the skirts of his floor-length coat. In pursuit but far behind, Jeremy saw him shed the coat and leave it lying in a heap on the pavement. The scarf he had already dropped on the grass, though he kept hold of the case.

Jeremy gave up. He had to, he knew when he was beaten. The boy who should have been a girl he could still see far ahead of him. He had run down into Penfold Street, Jeremy limping behind him, but he soon gave up. The boy had reached the comparative safety of the Marylebone Road, he could see him still running, heading as fast as he could towards Baker Street Station.

The pain in Jeremy's scrotum had ceased to stab and burn but the throbbing ache left behind was almost insupportable. He was forced to sit down on one of the wooden seats. After a little while, the pain cooled slightly, thought came back. He hadn't thought at all for the past ten minutes, only acted and suffered. As he got up to turn back the way he had come, he reflected on what he had done. The garrotte had bitten into the boy's flesh, must have been painful, depriving him briefly of breath, and when he discovered the mark or even the wound, he would be bent on revenge. He and the girl, his girlfriend no doubt. Would he go to the police? Probably, for Jeremy now understood that there would be no need to bring the earrings into this at all. He had only to go to the police with the evidence of the mark (or wound) on his neck and with the ability to describe and identify his attacker, for them soon to recognise the man he meant and come straight to Star Street . . .

At home he mounted the stairs slowly, unhindered in his progress by the sound of someone, a child surely, sobbing behind Will Cobbett's front door. The rest of the house was in darkness and uninterrupted silence. Jeremy let himself into his flat and flung himself into an armchair without putting lights on. To sleep seemed an impossible ambition, he would never sleep again. But he closed his eyes and lay back, thinking what to do. Stay there and wait for them to come?

The idea of that had no appeal. To his surprise and then to his shame, he found that he wanted to run home to his mother. That couldn't be. He might never see her again, or if he did, it would be in prison or at his trial. Don't think in those terms, he said to himself. He opened the drawer in the desk where he had put the false earrings, the lighter and the keyring and put them in his jacket pocket. Was there anything else incriminating in his possession? Not that he could think of. Carrying his key in his left hand, he went downstairs again. The sobbing behind Cobbett's door was still going on and now a line of light showed between it and the floor. Jeremy went out into the street.

It looked just the same as it always did by night, deserted, cars parked nose-to-tail along all the kerbs with only narrow spaces between. The driver's window of a newish Peugeot had been smashed, for the sake of its radio or mobile, no doubt. He seemed to remember that that window had been intact when he came in. At the lamp post on the corner was a waste bin but it had been emptied. The people two doors up Bridgnorth Street had already put their rubbish out for collection in the morning. Jeremy untied the string that closed the top of the bag and stepped back at the foetid stench. Another penalty of a superb sense of smell. He put the earrings, the lighter and the keyring inside and resealed the bag.

As he climbed the stairs once again he paused outside Cobbett's door. The light had gone out and the crying had stopped. Why did he care? Not for Cobbett, he thought, or whoever might be in there, child, ill-treated woman. The sobbing had somehow been for him, a lament for his life, a dirge because that life would soon be over in all senses that mattered. He went back into his flat, took off his clothes and lay sleepless on his bed.

You would think, Becky told herself at seven in the morning, that drinking the way she did and the amount she did, her body would gradually get used to a large intake of alcohol and she no longer suffer such acute hangovers. That was the rule; she seemed to be an exception to it. Once more she thought, as she thought every morning, that she must stop or drastically cut down. She would put her job in jeopardy, ruin her looks, make herself fat, grow old prematurely and destroy her liver.

She got up, staggering, her legs mostly obeying the directions they received, her head floating off towards the ceiling. The fierce headache wouldn't kick in for half an hour and then it would begin its draconian punishment. Her teeth cleaned and mouth rinsed, cold water uselessly splashed over her face, two aspirins taken in vain, she asked herself why. Why was she drinking so much now when she was free, had time on her hands, a good job and plenty of money? For no reason, and that was why it was time to stop.

The noises in her head were quite bad, a perpetual rustling that seemed to be on the left side and a rhythmic throbbing, a regular beat, on the right. Added to that was a ringing in the centre, directly above her eyes. She closed them, leaning against the kitchen table, and then she understood that the ringing wasn't in her head, it was real. 'Hello. Who is it?'

'It's Will. Let me in, Becky, *please*. I'm cold.'

She pressed the key with the picture of a key on it, opened the front door to the flat and sank down into the first chair she came to. Will looked as if he had been crying for hours, his face red and puffy, his eyes swollen and slit-like. He was carrying a suitcase that looked heavy and he dumped it on the floor. Becky recognised it as the largest of the three suitcases he had. He didn't speak. Oh God, Becky thought, has he lost the power of speech again?

He hadn't. 'Can I have a drink of milk?'

'Yes, of course. Help yourself.'

While Will poured the milk into a mug, she made herself a stiff gin and tonic in a tumbler. The only thing that would help, however bad for her it was, more intake of alcohol. 'What's wrong, Will?'

He wouldn't answer precisely. 'I've come to stay, Becky. I didn't want to go home on Saturday, I wanted to stay then, I always do want to because it's nice here.'

'Isn't it nice at Inez's?'

'Yes, but it's not like here.'

'What's in the case, Will?'

'All my things I need.'

He knelt down and opened it. Clothes there must be somewhere in its depths but all she could see were a toy truck—did he *play* with it?—a comic paper, the *Radio Times*, the video remote as if hers didn't work and he could use his here, a jar of humbugs, a red baseball cap with 'Man United' on it in white, a video cassette of *Spot the Dog*.

'I'll get my room ready myself,' he said. 'I'll do what you did. I'll take out all the chairs but one and put the computer somewhere else and make the sofa into a bed and put sheets on it.'

'What about work, Will?'

'You could phone Keith and say I'm not well.' The equivalent of the primary school sick note, she thought. 'You could say I'll be better tomorrow and to come here for me.'

He fastened the case and dragged it into the study. Her headache lifting but her body still weak, she heard him moving furniture about while he hummed the dwarfs' chorus from *Snow White*. He only sang, as she knew from old, if he was very happy.

What was to be done? If he went to work tomorrow she supposed she could too. He'd be alone for a couple of hours each afternoon but that wouldn't be too bad. She had sent her lover away and there would be no more. The television would be on all the morning and all the evening, day in and day out, every day. She would feel no more guilt, all that would be in the past. A kind of deadly peace would replace it, a lifeless calm with a sweet, wilful child ruling her and always *there*. For her goings out and her comings in, her meetings and her partings, her waking and her sleeping. Perhaps, with the guilt gone, the need to drink would go too. Perhaps. One day.

His coming here was inevitable. Maybe, somewhere inside her throbbing head, she had always known it would happen. All she had done was put off the evil day. But I do love him, she thought. The words had a hollow ring. Did she love him? Did she love anyone in the world?

Becky put her arms on the table and her head on her arms and wept. She wept for a car crash and a fragile chromosome and a callous society and for herself.

From the study came Will's voice singing, 'Heigh-ho, heigh-ho, as off to work we go . . .'

'You should have informed us last night,' said Detective Inspector Crippen, 'when it happened. Not waited till now.'

'I thought you'd be over the moon when I came to you with the best lead to the Rottweiler's identity you're likely to get.' Anwar wasn't really indignant. He didn't care. If the police did nothing after the evidence he was giving them, he would get hold of the media and see what they made of the law's indifference when presented with plain evidence of a garrotting attempt.

'Let's have a look at your neck.'

Anwar, who had covered it with a polo-neck sweater worn under his suit, not from embarrassment but the better to create a drama when his throat was bared, pulled down the dark-blue woollen stuff and extended his head.

Both policemen, Crippen and Zulueta, reacted almost as well as he had hoped. 'That's a nasty lesion you've got there,' said Crippen, recoiling a little from the bright reddish-purple ring encircling Anwar's olivine throat. 'I'll be very much surprised if that doesn't leave a scar.'

'You'd better get it seen to,' said Zulueta. 'That needs medical attention.'

Crippen was still shaking his head, perhaps at the evil tendencies of West London's humanity. 'Tell me again what happened.'

'I was walking home from Marylebone Station. I'd been visiting my auntie in Aylesbury.' He had been doing this, with his parents, on the previous Friday, but Auntie Seema would never remember which day it was, she'd always been a couple of cumin seeds short of a korma. 'It was around midnight when I came up Ashmill Street from Lisson Grove.' They wouldn't be able to fault that, it was the shortest way.

'You don't look much like a girl,' said Zulueta, 'or a woman at all.' He looked at Anwar in perplexity, at his boniness, his concave chest and skinny legs, the incipient growth of beard on his chin and cheeks, and his big, bold nose.

'Maybe he couldn't see very well,' said Anwar. 'It was dark and he was under a tree. I was cutting through the garden into Broadley Street. He came at me with this electric cable and before I could do anything it was round my throat.'

'What did you do?'

'I'm not a girl, am I? I fought him off, of course.'

'And you say you recognised him?'

'Sure I recognised him,' said Anwar virtuously. 'I don't know his name but he lives in the flat above my friend Frederick Perfect.'

Having won a hundred pounds on the Lottery, Freddy was in cheerful mood. He waved at Jeremy from the shop window and was pointedly ignored, though the tenant of the top flat had certainly seen him, had even met his eyes.

'He can't be going to work at this hour,' said Freddy. 'He doesn't look well, like he's sickening for something. I hope it's not infectious. Going out without a coat or an umbrella will make things worse. It's going to pour. I wonder where he's heading for. Maybe the doctor's. That will be it.'

None of these remarks seemed to require a reply. Inez smiled vaguely at Freddy. He had come downstairs very late this morning, following in Zeinab's footsteps, but for that, for this one instance at any rate, she was not sorry. Only just after she had unlocked the door and put the books out on the pavement, the man who had bought the Chelsea china clock came in. He had walked about, appearing to examine objects—but not really examining them, she thought—then walked up to her and asked her to have dinner with him. She was so surprised she said she'd like to, and when he had gone realised that, surprise or not, she would like to very much.

Not, of course, going to the doctor's, Jeremy was on his way to buy a gun.

A real handgun he wouldn't know how to handle. A replica would do or even a toy, so long as it looked like a pistol or a revolver from a distance. Toys were as frightening to bystanders as real guns so long as you didn't fire them.

He had passed a terrible night, finally falling asleep at seven in the morning. If asked, he was in the habit of saying he never had dreams or if he had them they were forgotten when he woke up, and this was roughly true. What he had were curious nocturnal visions or fantasies that recurred and recurred in wakefulness, breaking open in front of his eyes and teasing him with their apparent meaninglessness. There had been the time when he had seen the first girl he had killed, full-face, in profile, looking down, looking up, laughing and weeping, and later the procession, like Macbeth's kings, of varieties of garrotting means, rope, wire, cable, cord, string, tape, chain and twine, dancing and rolling down an endless stair. Last night, having not suffered this particular affliction for a long time, he saw flagons and phials and bottles of perfume but smelt nothing. The scent bottles, large, small and tiny, clear, golden, pink, green, blue, black, tossed and jumbled as if thrown from a height. He tried to resist them, closing his eyes, then forcing them open, getting up, putting lights on. As soon as he lay down again, light on or off, they began again, jumping and skipping, falling, falling, falling, but never reaching the ground, where mercifully they would have broken and been swept away.

Now they were gone, but not the memory of them nor the need they had left behind. His thoughts were full of *the* scent and how he didn't know its name. But he must get the gun before he gave way to this desire. There was a place along New Oxford Street, near St Giles's, where he thought he could get a replica. At Marble Arch he got on a bus going eastwards and after a slow journey that took a very long time in heavy traffic, he got off at the point where Shaftesbury Avenue meets New Oxford Street. The place that sold the replica guns had been next to the umbrella and walking stick shop but it was no longer there. It would have to be a toy.

A taxi took him back the way he had come and dropped him outside Selfridges. In spite of his need, he avoided the perfume department but went up in the escalator in men's fashions. Among the toys on the first floor he found a passable gun which would do. It was silver and black, and made of plastic but that wouldn't be detected by anyone in the street below. He bought it. Should he or should he not take a hostage? If the Asian girl who used to work in the shop were still there he wouldn't have hesitated. He must take someone to be sure his plan to commit suicide would work. No, not suicide, for he could throw himself off the flyover if that was what he wanted, but to be killed, to die at the hands of others.

Down on the escalator, he headed this time for Perfumes. He had to know. It mustn't take long, though. Unless the boy he had met last night had failed to go to the police, they would be with him soon. Phone first and when they got no answer . . . ? Come and wait for him, no doubt. His heart pounding and his palms sweating, he walked into the perfume department, his nostrils immediately attacked by scents, sweet or bitter-sweet, musky or fruity, but harmless to him in an area where one was far from harmless.

He was looking for the girl who had sprayed him with the lethal essence.

She had been beautiful in anyone's eyes, dark, black-eyed, with some oriental blood, he thought, no epicanthic fold on her upper eyelid, so that blood would be Far Eastern. The spray bottle had been black and gold.

At all costs, whatever happened, he mustn't let her spray him with it again. He was more afraid of the scent than of dying.

CHAPTER 29

He recognised her. Not tempting customers with perfume this time, but standing behind a counter talking to a girl of similar age but very dissimilar looks. Rather cautiously, he approached her, confused by the variety of goods in stands and on shelves. How did women cope with all this? Why did they? It seemed to involve unnecessary and ultimately useless labour. An underlying fear drove social comment away. Did the police know by now? The thought surfaced. It had been there for the past half-hour, buried under something spurious, unneeded, a fantasy question that if solved would contribute nothing to his well-being, his life, his peace. All that was gone for good. He wanted to know the name of the perfume before he died, that was all.

While he was crossing the floor, the dark beauty had disappeared. He looked around him, hoping to see her. There were dozens of girls everywhere, some as perfect as any model, all of them good-looking. He said to the pale, fair girl, 'Excuse me?'

She turned and he fancied the expression on her face, kindly, tolerant, understanding, was one she had been trained to assume when the customer was male. 'How may I help you?'

The ridiculous phrase, which had no place in ordinary day-to-day speech, for once failed to rile him. He said, almost diffidently, 'I was in here just over a week ago and your friend sprayed some perfume on me . . .'

'My friend?'

'The young lady you were talking to just now. I wondered if you could tell me what the perfume was called.'

'Well, Nicky doesn't actually work with our products. She's over there.' She pointed to another stand, another counter with a different array of packages and bottles and jars behind it. 'But she's in a meeting now.'

This excuse or apology, more often applied to the whereabouts of company chairmen or chief executives, took him terribly aback. He felt old and as if transported to a new and different world. Going back home now, defending himself, if necessary making an end to everything, seemed the only option.

Sympathy for him brimmed in her eyes like tears. 'Can you remember the date? What the—er, fragrance, looked like?'

'It was Saturday the first of June. In the morning. I think it looked—it was black and gold. She sprayed it on me, I needed—I want . . .'

'I quite understand,' she said, and all he could think of was how little she could possibly understand. 'I could find out for you. My name is Lara—have you got that? Lara. If you'd leave me your phone number . . . ?'

He had no business cards for Star Street, so he told her the number and she wrote it down. He would never hear from her, he knew that. In the unlikely event of her phoning him, of her not losing the piece of paper and forgetting him, it would come too late. He thanked her, aware that in the past few hours Jeremy Quick had been growing humble, his customary arrogance seeping away, as Alexander Gibbons quietly stepped into his place.

Star Street he must approach carefully. He was thankful for the rain that had begun while he was in the store. It was a fine drizzle, which hung in the air like a mist and increased the smell of diesel and fast food. Going home in a taxi wasn't to be contemplated, but it wasn't far. He decided to walk. If police cars were there, if Crippen's or Zulueta's cars was there—he would recognise the inspector's dark-red Audi and the sergeant's blue Honda from a long way off—he would retreat to work out a strategy. But it might not be those particular officers, they or one of them might be taking a day off or a completely different team have been transferred to the case. He walked up Seymour Place, turning left into George Street, the Edgware Road ahead of him.

It was fairly certain the boy in the black veil hadn't gone to the police on the previous night. If he had, they would have come for him first thing in the morning, something he had desperately feared as he lay wakeful, his sleepless fantasy running before his eyes. And what happened to his theory that 'these people', the boy and his girlfriend, went to bed so late that they never adjusted to daytime life until the middle of the afternoon? That obviously wouldn't apply in an emergency, not when she saw the mark on her boyfriend's neck from the garrotte. Then he wouldn't have waited until this morning . . .

By this time he was crossing the Edgware Road and he was very wet, having contemplated buying an umbrella but rejecting the idea. He was calculating which direction would be the safest to approach from. They would expect him either to come up Star Street from here or down it from Norfolk Square, so he would take St Michael's Street. He was quite unaware that he was watched from a window on the left-hand side, Anwar pointing him out to Flint as they stood in the hall, squinting through the glass panel in the front door.

'You gonna give the filth a bell?'

'I don't know. But, no,' said Anwar. 'I've given them enough fucking help. Let them do some work for a change.'

No police cars, no cars at all. Oddly for a mid-week morning, the residents' parking and the meters in the vicinity of the shop were all vacant. Jeremy hesitated outside the tenants' street door and went in through the shop instead. A scream or even a sign of shock from Inez would have told him a lot.

She looked up from her accounts book and said a not very friendly, 'Oh, hello.'

A grin from that fool in the brown overall. 'Well, good morning, Mr Quick. You *are* a stranger. Time was when you were always popping in to see the boss.'

That merited no answer. Jeremy screwed up his nerve. 'Has anyone been asking for me, by any chance?'

'I don't think so,' Inez said. 'Surely they would ring your bell, wouldn't they? Oh, yes, a call came from that policeman—Zulueta, is he called?—wanting to know if you were at home. I said I hadn't the faintest idea. It didn't sound important.'

It wouldn't. He thanked her, still humble, went out through the interior door and upstairs. The next floor throbbed with Rachmaninov. He fancied he could see the doors shaking. Inside his flat the phone was silent, but there was something about it (or about him) which told him it had been ringing and ringing, over and over. Perhaps he should have had an answering service but there had never seemed a need, and what good would it do him now to hear Crippen's recorded voice?

Out in the roof garden the first flower of the season had opened on his climbing rose. He couldn't remember its name. Its colour was an indifferent pale-pink but its scent, as promised in the catalogue, was exquisite, like ripe oranges and jasmine with a touch of nutmeg. He brought his face down to the flower, his nose to the heart of it. Yes, it was all they said it would be. It would be the last rose he was ever to smell, the last rose of his summer.

Yet the phone was silent, the doorbell was silent. The sole sound was from the music below and that reached him only distantly. Zulueta might just have wanted to ask him if he had seen anything on the previous night, for it was possible the boy had been afraid to identify him, recognising a dangerous man and one not to be treated defiantly. For instance, he might have reasoned, if they couldn't get enough evidence against him, Jeremy would be at liberty, free to take what revenge he liked on the boy and girl who had shopped him. 'I am a dangerous man,' Jeremy said aloud and, using what might be the boy's own language, 'no one messes with me.' But the voice he said it in was weak and small. His true feelings were expressed in what he said under his breath: I've had a rotten sort of life.

He went back into the living room, leaving the french windows open, though it was cold and a heavier rain was falling. In the bedroom he took off his wet trousers and jacket, and put on unaccustomed clothes, a sweater and jeans. It was just after midday. Time for a small gin and tonic, a little more gin than usual, one cube of ice and a sliver of lemon. He was slicing the lemon with a sharp knife when the phone began to ring, and if he didn't cut himself this was because when the sound struck him, his hands froze and the knife hung poised.

To answer or not? If he didn't answer they would suppose he was still out and try again. Eventually they would phone Inez and she would tell them. It would have been wiser not to have gone into the shop but too late to think of that now. At the ninth ring he lifted the receiver, said a strong, 'Hello?'

The phone was put down. That told him everything. Now they would come. If they left at once it would take them a matter of minutes, minutes in a single digit. So decide now how to manage this. Decide,

decide . . . Inez was in the shop and so was the fat fool.
Pity that Asian girl wasn't in, had left or was ill or whatever. Only one person remained and she would have to
do. He took the gun and went down the top flight of
stairs, Rachmaninov growing louder with every step.
She had increased the volume, perhaps thinking when
she heard his door close that he was going out again.
She was in for a rude shock.

He hammered on the door with his fists, knowing
she would now suppose he had come down to complain. He knocked again and kicked the bottom of the
door. The volume of the music fell to a murmur. Her
voice called in the horrible guttural accent she sometimes assumed, 'What is it?'

'Open the door, please. It's Jeremy Quick.'

She opened the door very slowly, as if she was drag-
ging her feet. He got one foot inside before showing her
the gun. One hand up to her face, she gasped, then
whimpered. She was in a pink dressing gown, a negligee
really, all frills and a big bow at the waist. Her greying
blonde hair was scooped up untidily on the top of her
head and fastened there with a clawed clip such as very
young girls wear.

'Come on,' he said. 'I want you upstairs.'

Ludmila was trembling all over, a withered leaf dan-
gling from a branch, shaken and set vibrating by the
wind. In her state and her high-heeled mules, she found
it hard to manage the stairs. Jeremy drove her ahead of
him. She stumbled and moaned but she made it, falling
over his threshold as he unlocked the flat door.

He left her on the floor, went to one of the front
windows and looked out. In the distance he could
hear a siren, but whether it was from a police car or
an ambulance he couldn't tell. Only the noise the fire
engines made was unmistakable, that awful yet

strangely musical bray that began their song, followed by warning howls. He listened. The sound of the siren died away. He turned round, once more pointing the gun at Ludmila. She had crawled away, seated herself in a chair. Now she wasn't obliged to walk and climb stairs, she looked less frightened, more in command of herself.

She said to him, 'Can I have a cigarette?'

'All right. This gun is loaded, you'd better understand that. I'll use it if I have to. My life is of no importance to me and nor is yours.'

He gave her a cigarette and lit it for her with his own seldom-used lighter. If he'd let her light her own, God knew what she might have done, set fire to his carpet, maybe. She inhaled, looked at the lighter, at him, said, 'That's that girl's lighter.'

It wasn't. He had thrown that one away. 'What girl?'

'The one that was strangled in the mews.'

He would have liked to smile but the muscles of his face refused to obey him.

'You strangled her. You're the Rottweiler!'

How he had always hated that name. He defended himself, knowing he sounded feeble. 'I never bit anyone. It's a foul libel. The newspapers will say anything.'

As he spoke he heard a car, then another, draw up outside. A car door slammed. He froze. He was stuck there, paralysed. Ludmila looked up, the ash falling off her cigarette on to his rug.

The use of his legs returning, he crossed once more to the window. Zulueta's car was on the other side of the street, on a yellow line. Two men sat in the one behind. The rear offside door opened and Crippen got out, followed by a man he thought might be called Osnabrook. Jeremy threw up the window and the sound of the sash rattling as it rose made Crippen look up.

Their eyes met. 'We're coming upstairs, Quick,' he
said. 'We've things to say and I expect you have too.'

Jeremy turned briefly to check on Ludmila, then
called down, 'I've nothing to say to you or anyone else.
And I'm not called Quick. I am Alexander Gibbons. I've
got a gun and I've got Mrs—er?'

'Perfect,' shouted Ludmila loud enough for Crippen
to hear.

'Mrs Perfect up here. You heard her voice. You want
to see her?'

He didn't wait for an answer but pulled Ludmila
out of the chair and with the gun in her back, pushed
her to the window. Crippen went into the shop and
Osnabrook after him. Keeping the gun levelled at
Ludmila, Jeremy dragged a chair over to the window
and motioned to her, waving the gun, to sit in it
where everyone in the street could see her. There were
more there to see by now, four uniformed officers
having arrived. They too had gone into the shop,
from which Freddy Perfect now came running, shouting, 'Ludo, Ludo!'

Ludmila blew him a kiss. Jeremy didn't like that. It
showed a levity and a sang-froid out of keeping with the
seriousness of her predicament. He pushed in front of
her, the gun pressed to her neck and called out, 'You tell
her to behave herself. I'll kill her if I have to. It won't
bother me.'

Once more Ludmila was shaking. He felt the quivering against his hand. 'Stop that,' he said to her. 'Control
yourself.'

Crippen and Zulueta had both come out into the
street, and with them one of the uniformed men. As
soon as he spoke, from the other side of the street and
using a loud hailer, Jeremy knew what he was. One of
those 'psychological' policemen, employing what they

thought were clever tactics to get a desperate man to give up his defiance.

'Let Mrs Perfect go, Quick. Keeping her up there and terrorising her is doing you no good. It's pretty useless in the end, isn't it? Let her go. Let her come downstairs and we'll come up and meet her. We won't attempt to get into your place, that I guarantee.'

'In that case,' said Jeremy, 'how are you going to get me?'

'When you realise you're on to a hiding to nothing you'll see sense. You are, aren't you? What you're doing leads nowhere and it'll just make things worse for you in the end.'

'The end for me is here, up here in this flat.'

'Give me the gun, Quick. Empty it and drop it out of the window.'

'You must be joking,' said Jeremy, 'and my name isn't Quick, it never was.'

The correction was ignored.'Let me see you empty the gun. You've done nothing yet, remember. Nothing's been proved. You've not been charged. Mistaken identity cases happen all the time. Drop the gun before you're tempted to do anything.'

The phone started to ring. That would be them calling from Inez's phone in the shop. He could reach it from where he stood and with a bit of stretching, still keep the gun pressed into Ludmila's spine.

'Hello?'

Not the police. The girl who had blackmailed him said, 'Up shit creek now, aren't you?' and laughed as she rang off.

He slammed the phone down so hard that the whole table shook. Then he edged round Ludmila to look down into Star Street once more. The psychologist was still there, conferring with Crippen. In spite of what they had promised, someone was coming up the stairs. If whoever this was, and there was more than one, tried to tread softly they failed. They hammered on his door.

Jeremy moved a little towards it, the gun on Ludmila. 'If anyone starts to break this door down, she dies,' he said, gratified to see Ludmila once more trembling. 'She's shaking with fear. That's your fault, you've caused that. I hope you're proud of yourselves. Who's terrorising women now?'

He got no reply. He didn't expect one but the hammering stopped. Insofar as he could be happy about anything, he felt pleased about the toy gun. It was just as good for a gun's purposes as a real one—with one exception. It couldn't deal the death blow in the end but, he thought, he hoped, others would do that. The footsteps went back down the stairs.

'In the state of Utah,' he said to Ludmila, 'the death penalty is execution by firing squad. Did you know that?'

'They never do it,' she said.

'They *have* done it. Last time was in the seventies. They ask for volunteers and they get far more than they can use. Most of them are so useless they couldn't shoot an elephant five feet away, so they have a couple of trained marksmen among the others. That's how I'd like to die, by firing squad. How about you?'

'I don't want to die. I've just got married.'

He laughed. The phone rang again. If he didn't answer it they would only keep on and on. The gun at her neck, just under her right ear from which dangled an earring like a chandelier. 'Hello?'

'This is Detective Inspector Crippen, Quick. Or Gibbons. Whatever.'

Jeremy said nothing.

'You're not doing yourself any favours, you know. The gun wasn't a good idea. Taking Mrs Perfect hostage isn't a good idea. If you let her go and drop the gun out of the window you'll be on the right road to getting your case very favourable consideration.'

'The more you talk like that,' said Jeremy, 'the more I feel like killing her. I've got the gun right in her ear now. If I press the trigger she'll die in half a second.'

The phone went down. More conferring, no doubt. He felt Ludmila fidget away from the touch of the gun, turn her face up to look at him. 'Why you do this?' She was beginning to lose her command of English or regain her command of a Slavic accent. 'Why me? What am I doing you pick on me?'

'You were there,' he said simply.

Another car had come. Not a car, a police van. Out of the rear door came four marksmen with rifles. He smiled. 'I'll never let her go,' he shouted out of the window. 'If you kill me you'll kill her too, I'll see to that.' He wouldn't but it did no harm to let them think it.

Zulueta had come out into the street. His face was handsomer but otherwise, in Jeremy's eyes, he looked very much like the boy he had tried to garrotte the night before. They might have been brothers. The boy's black eyes were staring up at him. 'We're not going to do anything yet—er, Gibbons. There's no hurry for you or us. But there is for Mrs Perfect. She has a heart condition—did you know that?'

Jeremy didn't and nor did Ludmila. Freddy had made it up. But Ludmila wasn't going to deny it. She put on a hangdog expression and moaned a little.

'If she has a heart attack you'll be in real trouble, Quick. Why not avoid that now? Let her come down now and we'll meet her halfway up. We have a doctor here. Put her into safe hands, Quick—I mean Gibbons.'

Jeremy shouted, a harsh strangled sound. 'What do I care for her heart? I won't care for anything soon.'

Except my mother, he thought. Oh, God, my poor mother! But, 'I'm committing suicide,' he said. 'I'm like a suicide bomber, only you'll do the killing.'

That fixed them. Zulueta went quickly inside and almost immediately the phone rang. He nearly didn't answer it. What was the point? Star Street and part of Bridgnorth Street had been cordoned off. The public, who always arrived, someone always found out, were being driven away, back from the cordons, like sheep by two sheepdogs. The four marksmen had taken up their positions. Suppose it was his mother phoning? He could say goodbye . . . He picked up the receiver.

'Yes? Hello?'

'Mr Quick?'

Who on earth was this? He felt Ludmila rigid against the nozzle of the gun. 'Who is it?'

'Lara,' she said, 'the girl in Selfridges. You were in this morning. You wanted the name of a fragrance. I've got it for you. It's Libido. Would you like me to spell that?'

'Thank you,' he said. 'Thank you very much. I don't need you to spell it.'

Libido. The source of lechery, of lust. He had never had much of it himself, but the once. Once he had. He wanted to laugh, finding that out at the end of his life, but he couldn't. He thanked her again politely, for he was Alexander now, and put the receiver down. Ludmila stiffened, twisted round and seizing his wrist, shouted, 'That's not a real gun! If it was metal it'd be colder. That's plastic, I can feel it's plastic!'

She was on her feet, surprisingly strong, grabbing him anywhere her hands touched, then scraping her nails down his face. He cried out, not for the scratches or the pain but because if she got away his last hope was gone. He kicked at her shins, still holding on to the gun, slapped her face and seized her under the arms, first from the front, her furious eyes glaring at him as she struggled, then swinging her round with all his strength, held her so close to the window that she nearly toppled out. There came a howl from below. Freddy had come out of the shop and was wringing his hands in despair.

Jeremy had her now as a shield. He held her round the waist. But to be prevented from exposing himself as their target was the last thing he wanted. He could only keep his hold on her with one hand. He raised the other and pointed it at Zulueta who had come out to pull Freddy in. If Ludmila shouted out now that the gun was a fake, all would be over, his hope of death by firing squad over . . . Suddenly he understood that of course she wouldn't! She wanted him dead as much as he wanted it and as if she heard his thought, she made a final frantic effort to struggle free.

He slackened his hold on her and she dropped to her knees, rolled away from him across the floor. Libido, he thought, that was its name now, the scent that made a murderer of him against his will and against his nature. My poor mother, he said inside his head, and suddenly smiled as he turned the gun against the marksmen.

They shot him.

CHAPTER 30

Dorothy Gibbons grieved inconsolably for her son. Nothing had been proved against him, he had never come to trial and she continued for the rest of her life to believe him the victim of injustice. The first time she ventured out of her house after the funeral, she met by chance in a local shop a woman from whom she had been estranged for thirty-five years. Neither had changed out of recognition and if Dorothy had some difficulty in identifying Tess Maynard, Tess knew her at once. They resumed their friendship and, Tess also being alone, having recently been divorced from her second husband, they set up house together. The arrangement works very well.

Staying in the Pimlico flat for only six months, Zeinab and Algy put down a substantial deposit on a house in Borehamwood, which they are buying on a mortgage, Algy having got a good job with a company of estate agents. Zeinab is pregnant again. If it is a girl she intends to call the child Inez and if a boy, Morton, for it is to Morton Phibling, as she reminds Algy, that they owe the foundation of their wealth.

Zeinab has given in to pressure from Algy and they were married two weeks ago, the bride wearing the dress which was made for her wedding to Morton. The ceremony was rather a low-key affair but the reception was very grand, taking place in Orville Pereira's new hotel in north London.

Though furious at the failure of his promised bride to turn up at St Peter's, Eaton Square, Morton has got over it by now. A lot came out of it, after all, not least his glorious triumph, scarcely equalled in his boxing days, of knocking out and laying low Rowley Woodhouse, a man half his age. His new girlfriend is the same age as Zeinab claimed to be and as fond of diamonds and expensive restaurants, but otherwise quite different, being blonde, winsome and not particularly chaste. Morton is thinking of asking her to get engaged. After some heart-searching, they accepted Algy's invitation to the wedding, Morton keen to demonstrate his greatness of soul and show off his girlfriend. He had his reward when Algy, in his after-dinner speech, mentioned him as the recipient of the bride's and groom's gratitude. Morton was never sure what they were grateful for, but that hardly mattered.

Inez was also there, with the the man who bought the Chelsea china clock whom she has married as her third husband. They sold the business and the shop in Star Street, Inez disliking the idea of staying in a place where a murderer had lived and died, and bought a house in Bourton-on-the-Water where the jaguar glares out from the living room window. If Inez is not ecstatically happy, she is quite content. You can't expect to have what she had with Martin more than once in a lifetime. Her husband adores her and she likes him very much. She tells herself, in the words of the Merle Haggard song, 'It's not love but it's not bad.'

In the cause of letting bygones be bygones, Ludmila and Freddy were invited but the invitation never reached them. They are no longer together. Ludmila had nothing against her husband, but marriage had never suited her for long and she formed a liaison with a Syrian she had met in the Al Dar restaurant, who took her back to Aleppo where she has a hard time of it. Freddy has moved in with a nice motherly woman who has a job as a cloakroom attendant in quite a good hotel. They rent a room in her daughter's house in Shepherd's Bush.

Since Zeinab has forgotten Will's and Becky's existence—and she is not alone in forgetting, so quiet and narrow has their life become—they weren't included in the guest list. Will is still living with Becky in Gloucester Avenue. He gave up working for Keith Beatty and lives on the unemployment benefit and Jobseekers' Allowance. Becky goes into the office two days a week and for the rest struggles to work from home, though she is now seeing ominous signs of being told the firm will 'have to let her go'. She and Will really need a bigger place to live but she hasn't the heart for moving and she is afraid she soon won't have the money. Will is blissfully happy. He watches television all day long, demands that she cook for him twice a day when she is at home, and he is growing fat. Becky knows he will be with her and she with him until he dies or she does, whichever is the sooner.

Zeinab, Algy and Reem Sharif, gorgeous at the reception in the largest scarlet and gold *salwar-kameez* obtainable in the Edgware Road, have always avoided the police whenever possible. Orville Pereira, who gave the bride away, has a like aversion to the law. The presence of Finlay Zulueta would have dampened the celebrations. Dancing, for instance, might have been restrained and self-conscious under his dark, cold and disapproving eye. If they had invited him he would have refused. In any case, he is far too busy to go out.

He passed his exams with spectacular success and is now a Detective Inspector. He often thinks about Jeremy Quick or Alexander Gibbons and wonders what impelled him to garrotte those women (if it was really he who garrotted them), why he took those small objects off them and why he tried to strangle a boy instead of a girl. Perhaps because Zulueta is studying in his spare time for a postgraduate psychology degree, he dwells a lot on these things, motivation, compulsion, obsession. Something that disquiets him is remembering what a guilty thrill he had got out of seeing the man shot by that marksman's rifle and how astonished he was to see Jeremy's broad smile at the time of his death. These emotions, he feels, should not be felt by a mature and responsible police officer of increasingly high rank. Still, it was permissible, surely, to wonder what had caused that smile, as if the man had wanted to die.

ALSO BY RUTH RENDELL

THE BABES IN THE WOOD
AN INSPECTOR WEXFORD MYSTERY

"I've just heard a crazy thing, thought it might amuse you. You look as though you need cheering up." Burden seated himself on the corner of the desk, a favourite perch. "Woman phoned to say she and her husband went to Paris for the weekend, leaving their children with a—well, teen-sitter, I suppose—got back last night to find the lot gone and naturally she assumes they've all drowned."

"That's amusing?"

"It's pretty bizarre, isn't it? The teenagers are fifteen and thirteen, the sitter's in her thirties, they can all swim and the house is miles above the floods."

There hadn't been anything like this kind of rain in living memory. The River Brede had burst its banks, and not a single house in the valley had escaped flooding. The Subaqua Task Force could find no trace of Giles and Sophie Dade, let alone the woman who was keeping them company, Joanna Troy. But Mrs Dade was still convinced her children were dead.

This was an investigation that would call into question many of Wexford's assumptions about the way people behaved, including his own family. . . .

SEAL BOOKS / ISBN: 0-7704-2922-X